MAULEVER HALL

She was set down from the coach at a lonely,
moorland cross-road. She was bewildered,
confused and only too grateful to find shelter
at Maulever Hall.

But soon terror was upon her once again – and
strange happenings sent her hurrying from the
dark house and its autocratic master.

Too late she discovered that wherever she went,
whatever she did, the forbidding influence of
Maulever Hall reached out after her.

Maulever Hall

Jane Aiken
Hodge

CORONET BOOKS
Hodder and Stoughton

Printed and bound in Great Britain for
Hodder and Stoughton Paperbacks, a
division of Hodder and Stoughton Ltd.,
Mill Road, Dunton Green, Sevenoaks, Kent
(Editorial Office: 47 Bedford Square,
London, WC1 3DP) by
Hunt Barnard Printing Ltd.,
Aylesbury, Bucks.

Maulever Hall

HER head ached. The movement of the coach made her feel sick. What coach? She opened her eyes and found herself staring at a fat woman in red satin.

"Where am I?" she asked.

"That's better, dearie," the woman in red leaned forward to pat her knee. "Give us quite a turn you did, going off like that. And for only a little bit of a bump, too, nothing to what I had the day the Brighton coach overturned—but that was *The Age* of course, a real flyer. Every time I come this way I vow I'll travel post another time, my husband wouldn't hear of it today. 'No, Bessie,' he says to me, 'travelling post about the countryside by yourself with the Reform Bill rioters out—not to mention the rick-burners, and all that riff-raff—is what I will not allow. The public coach may be slow, but it's safe,' he says. Of course, he didn't reckon for it's being overturned in a ditch by some drunken dolt of a coachman. But are you really feeling better, dearie?"

"Yes, much better, thank you, ma'am. But," she asked again, where am I? I—I can't remember." Her voice trembled on the words. While the woman in red had been talking she had had time to recognize the full horror of her plight. "I—I seem to remember nothing."

"Nothing?" The woman leaned towards her, avid curiosity written across her broad red face. "Not boarding the coach at Exton, dearie, and the fuss the guard made because you hadn't a ticket? And wanting to charge full fare for the child, too, the poor little dear, till we made him see reason."

"Child?" She had been aware of restless movement beside her and now defied her throbbing head to turn in that direction. He was curled up against her, peacefully sucking his thumb and gazing, half asleep, into vacancy. A very small child : a year, two years, she had no idea. I don't know much about children, she told herself in sudden panic. Not mine, surely not mine?

"You're not having us on are you?" said the woman in red,

7

her bright eyes suddenly sharp with suspicion. "You mean you really don't remember?"

"Nothing," she said. "I—I don't know my own name." Raw panic in her voice now. "And—I'm afraid. . . ."

"Of course you are," a man leaned forward from the far corner of the coach, "but don't worry yourself, miss, it'll pass off soon enough and you'll remember. It's just the shock of the blow. You caught yourself a nasty whack on the side of the coach when she went over. Just sit back and take it easy and it'll all come back to you soon enough."

"That's all very well," said the woman in red, "and very good advice, I'm sure, but if I'm not very much out of my reckoning the young lady's due to be set down pretty soon, and then what's to do?"

"Why, then her friends will meet her," he said bracingly. "The best thing that can happen. They'll take care of you, miss, even if your memory doesn't come back, which ten to one it will any minute now. But don't try and force it, let it come easy. I warrant it will soon enough."

"I'm sure I hope so," interposed a tall woman from the far side of the child, "but I've heard of cases where there's been a blow to the head and the victim's never been the same again."

"Yes," said the woman in red, "or walked around, bright as you please for a few hours, and then gone over sudden-like, dead as a doornail. But don't you fret yourself, dearie, for your colour's getting better every minute. White as a sheet you were, half an hour ago. . . . And as to your name," she leaned forward with a great gust of scent and inadequate washing, "it's on your brooch, plain for all to see: 'Marianne,' and a very pretty name too."

"Marianne," she said wonderingly. "Am I? How can I not know? It seems—yes, it might be right. But—Marianne What? Who am I?" It came out too loud. "And where am I going?"

"Why, to Pennington Cross," said the woman. "I heard you ask the guard to put you down there myself. And not best pleased, he wasn't either, it not being a regular stopping place, but you looked at him so pitiful and desperate with those big eyes of yours that he said he'd make an exception this once. Do you really not remember?"

"Nothing," said Marianne. Was she Marianne? And—what was she afraid of? Yes, probably she was. One would hardly wear someone else's name. It was a large, old-fashioned brooch: surely she should remember something about it? Once again, she racked her memory, but again without result.

"Don't force it," said the man in the far corner again. "It'll never come that way. Your friends will tell you all you need to know, when you meet them."

"Friends?" Doubtfully. She did not feel as if she had friends. That was all part of the terror that lay, somewhere, behind her forgetting.

The child at her side pulled at her skirts again. "Mam," he said fretfully, "Mam. . . ." And then a flood of child's nonsense.

"He calls you mam," said the woman in red helpfully. "I don't know what he intends by it." A meaning glance fell on Marianne's gloved left hand and, instinctively, she clasped her hands together in a nervous gesture which allowed her to feel her ring finger. There was nothing there. A little shudder of relief ran through her. Of course she was not married, nor the child hers. She looked down at her plain brown merino dress, under the heavy woollen shawl, at the coarse hand-knit gloves. For some reason the clothes surprised her. . . .Why? Once again she searched, baffled, for a memory that would not come.

The woman in red had followed her movements. "No ring?" she said. "No, I thought not. You don't behave like his mother, either, not yet like a married lady. And his clothes are better than yours, too. That plaid frock and trousers cost a pretty penny, I can tell you. Most like you're his nursemaid, or his governess, I'd think, if he weren't young for it." She sounded puzzled.

"Why do you call me a lady?" Marianne spoke with the directness of desperation.

The woman in red looked at her approvingly. "You're quick, ain't you? Nothing wrong with your mind when it chooses to work. To tell truth, I was asking myself that very question. My kitchenmaid wouldn't say thank you for the clothes you've got on. But a young lady is what you are, just the same. It's your voice, I reckon, or the way you carry yourself—I dunno. . . . Fallen on hard times, no doubt." She

9

looked round the coach for confirmation, which came, unexpectedly from the woman in the far corner.

"Of course she's a young lady. But what's that to the purpose? As for the child," she leaned forward to address Marianne directly, "if it's any help to you, his name's Thomas. I heard you say 'Oh, Thomas,' when he spilt the sauce down himself at the inn at Exton. And don't be tormenting yourself that you're his mother either," she went on robustly, "because anyone that knows anything can see you're not. Hullo, what are we stopping for?"

"Pennington Cross, I reckon," said the woman in red with the satisfaction of one achieving the last word.

She was right. The guard put his head in at the door a moment later to say: "Now then, where's the young lady as wanted Pennington Cross? Look sharp there, miss, we can't wait all day! We're two hours late already."

"And whose fault's that," said the woman in red. "We didn't ask to be dumped in the ditch and left for hours while you rode for a relief coach. As for the young lady, she's not well."

"Can't help that," said the guard. "Pennington Cross she asked for, and Pennington Cross this is, and not a regular stop either." He held out his hand to help Marianne down from the coach.

"Don't forget the child." The woman in red was helpful to the last.

She almost had. She turned and picked him up. His arms went warmly round her neck and he snuggled against her. "Mam," he said contentedly, "Mam."

There was a chorus of "good-bye" and "good luck" from the other passengers as the guard helped her out. She turned to smile tremulously up at them. They were her friends, the only friends she had.

"There you are, miss." The guard turned back to the coach. "Your box will be at the Three Feathers as arranged."

"Oh . . . my box. . . ." But he had jumped back on to the coach. The coachman whipped up his horses; the woman in red leaned out of the window to shout something, but her words were carried away on the wind and Marianne caught only the one word, "friends."

She looked around her. "Your friends will meet you." But

there was not a soul in sight; no sign, even, of a house. The name, Pennington Cross, had conjured up in her imagination a picture of a busy town centre—a market cross, people . . . help. Now she realized her mistake. This was not one of the coach's regular stopping places, but a lonely cross roads, high up on the rolling, winter-brown moor. In each direction, a road wound away, up and around the hills and so out of sight. A cold little wind blew her curls about her face and, beside her, the child whimpered from fatigue. No use standing here. Her friends had not met her. Surely she must have friends? She must seek them out, down one of these roads. But which? Two of them she dismissed at once. Since she had insisted on being set down here, she must have intended to take, not the main road, with its modern macadamized surface, but one branch or other of the little country lane. She was about to cross the road and study a weatherbeaten signpost when a sound made her start. So far, she had been mainly conscious of a vast silence. Now, just as the rumbling of the coach's wheels had merged itself in the low murmur of the wind, there was, far off, the sound of a horse's hooves. Someone was riding, fast, along the road by which she had come.

And at once, illogical and all the worse for that, terror was on her. She was no longer the reasoning person who stood there, debating which road to take, but a hunted creature, in fear of its life. Any minute now, the horseman must come over the edge of the far hill and see her standing there, exposed . . . helpless. No time to wonder why she was so afraid, time only for action. . . . She looked around her, no hedge, no ditch on these remote heights; no trees, even; only close moorland grass, where here and there sheep cropped among the patches of gorse and heather. But action had outrun thought. Already, she was running towards the nearest large patch of gorse. Why, when she remembered nothing else, did she know so well the kind of path that sheep made through these thickets? The child was pulling back on her hand, muttering one of his maddening, unintelligible phrases. "Hide and seek," she spoke as calmly as she could, picked him up and hurried towards the thicket. Did he understand? "There," they had reached the first bushes now, and she put the child down and urged him gently ahead of her. The path was just his size and he ran on ahead of her, while she had to bend double to

11

follow him, feeling, as she did so, the sharp vines of the gorse catching at her bonnet and tangling themselves in her full skirts.

At last, she stopped and put her finger on her lips as the child turned back towards her. "Hush," she whispered. And, as he solemnly imitated her gesture, she was able, over her own panting breath, to hear the horse's hooves, very near now. They were slowing down, coming to a standstill. . . . The rider must be at the cross-roads. Bent double as she was among the thick stems of the gorse, she could see nothing and yet had no idea of whether she could, herself, be seen. Time drew out, interminable with terror; the child began to stir restlessly beside her. Once again she put finger to lips, and murmured noiselessly: "Hush." Once more, it worked. The child beamed back at her and put his own finger to his lips. Smiling at him, she heard the horse's hooves again. She could tell, from the change in their rhythm, that the rider was urging his mount as quickly as possible into a gallop. How strange it was to know so much—and yet remember nothing. The child was pulling at her hand, tired of the game they had been playing. "Mam," he said plaintively, "Mam." She hesitated a moment, listening. The horse sounded far away now, but could she be sure? Suppose she should crawl out from her lair only to find the enemy waiting for her. What enemy? Suddenly her fear of fear itself swelled into panic. In a moment, she must lose control: scream, faint perhaps. "Absurd," she spoke to herself aloud and the sound of her own voice was oddly cheering. A young lady's voice, the woman in red had called it. Well, a young lady did not give way to these ridiculous terrors. "Come, Thomas," she took the child's hand once more. "Time to be going."

Just the same, she paused for a long moment, looking cautiously about her, before she emerged from the prickly protection of the gorse patch. There was nothing to be seen. The moor was silent and grey-brown as ever, sheep cropped steadily at grass which here and there was taking on a greener tint that spoke of spring on the way. But the air held a new chill now, and there was a hint of dusk over the further hills. At all costs, she must be thinking of shelter for the night. She emerged from the sheltering gorse and walked determinedly towards the cross-roads and the signpost.

It message was simple and unsatisfactory enough. One arm, pointing back the way she had come, read "Exton," and, in the opposite direction, "Plymouth." One was broken off and the fourth had been so battered by the wind that its message was barely distinguishable. It might—or might not—have read "Pennington." She looked one way and the other along the little country lane. There seemed nothing to choose between its two directions. But again the fear of fear was upon her. She dared not stand there hesitating; it would be too easy to plunge into despair. She took the child's hand once more in her own and started to walk briskly along the road that might, or might not, lead to Pennington, where she might, or might not, be expected.

A new and chilling thought struck her. At the pace he was going, the horseman must soon catch up with the coach. No doubt he would be told that she had left it at Pennington Cross; he would turn back after her. Clasping Thomas's hand more tightly, she quickened her pace, and, when he protested, wordlessly, at this, stooped to pick him up. Of course he was tired; it was very likely almost his bedtime, and she had no idea when they had eaten last. . . . As for her, she was not just tired, she was exhausted. Best not think about that. She clasped the child more tightly to her and hurried on along the rough road that might lead anywhere.

Several miles further along the main road, the lonely horseman had indeed caught up with the coach. Ruthlessly exorting a last burst of speed from his weary horse, he passed it, and stopped clear across the road. The coachman drew up swearing. He had had enough of delays for the day and was in no mood to be cross-examined. Asked if he had set down a passenger at Pennington Cross, he denied it angrily. "It's not a stop, there, see. I never drops people but at the appointed stopping places." He was by now convinced that the stranger was a company spy, sent to report on his conduct of the coach.

"But you had a passenger for the cross-roads," the stranger insisted. "A young lady."

"Young lady? Not me." Once committed to his lie, the coachman saw no alternative but to stick to it. "George," he appealed to the guard. "Have we had a young lady aboard since Exton?"

13

"Not us," said George. "I only wish we had. I ain't taken but sixpence in tips the livelong day. And now, if you please, sir, we're three hours late already."

A vast woman in a red satin dress leaned out of the window : "What on earth is the matter now? "she asked. "Haven't we been delayed enough already that you must be chattering here with your friends instead of trying to get us to Plymouth before it is quite dark?"

"No friend of mine, ma'am," said the coachman quickly. "It's a gentleman as wants to know if we set anyone down at Pennington Cross. Course I told him it was against the company rules."

"Of course you did," said the woman in red. And then, to the stranger : "You can take it from me, sir, we ain't set no one down since Exton. You must a' followed the wrong coach." And then, as the stranger reluctantly gave way for the coach to proceed : "And about time too."

The road Marianne had chosen ran steeply upwards, and she was soon breathless with the climb, and the weight of little Thomas in her arms. But at all costs she must be out of sight before her pursuer (if he was indeed following her) should return to the cross-roads. There must be no stopping till she was safe round the bend in the road. At last she reached it, almost sobbing for breath, and saw, before her, just such another prospect as she was leaving : rolling moor, the road winding around the side of yet another hill, a few sheep peacefully grazing. And, ahead of her, a black cloud cast a deeper shadow in the hills. A storm was blowing up the valley; the air was getting colder; soon night would fall. The child shivered in her arms. However exhausted she must not linger here. A backward glance, however, was reassuring. At least she was out of sight of the cross-roads. If the unknown rider did come back there, he would have no way of knowing which road she had taken. Or would he? An extra chill ran through her as she realized that, unlike her, he might know where she was going.

But there would be time, later, for terror; for the moment she must concentrate on finding food and shelter for the night. No use tormenting herself with questions. She had got her breath back now, and a few first drops of rain spattered

14

against her face. She shifted Thomas into a more comfortable position in her arms and started doggedly forwards. How long would she be able to keep on walking . . . ? That was no way to be thinking. The next hill she climbed must bring a view of human dwellings. And now some instinct told her that she was, indeed, nearing a village. The road was no wider, but there was a little grassy path beside it; not just a sheep track, but a path made by human feet. Odd how she kept discovering things about herself. She was, she was sure now, country bred. She knew about paths, and the tracks that sheep make through the gorse, and the feeling a village gives to the countryside, even when it is out of sight.

Or was she merely deluding herself with false hopes? The road had begun to climb again and the stiffness in her legs was an agony. She put Thomas down and tried to persuade him to walk a little, but his progress was so slow, and the now driving rain so harsh against her face, that she soon picked him up again.

Soon it would be dark. Where, among this wilderness of gorse and heather, could she and little Thomas pass the night? He was very tired now, drooping, half asleep in her arms, and once again she found herself on the fringe of terror. How far had they come today, and from where? The coach that had had the accident had apparently only started from Exton, but she had learned from her fellow passengers that it connected there with the night mail down from London. None of them had come on the mail, so there was no way of telling whether she and Thomas had done so. But why come here? Or could she just have been fleeing blindly from the terror those galloping hooves had represented? It was a chilling thought that she might merely have picked Pennington Cross as a spot remote enough for safety.

She stopped in her tracks. The road had turned decidedly downwards and below her lay a tiny village, snug in a corner of the hills. She could see a handful of cottages, a church and, beside it, one larger house that must be the vicarage. At least the smallness of the village narrowed her field of choice. Her fellow passengers had unanimously voted her a young lady, and she agreed with them. However strange her plight, she was not, she told herself, one of the screamers and yielders. "There's nothing like blood," someone had said. Of course, it was the great Duke, Wellington himself. Oh, it was infuriating. Why did she know about the Duke of Wellington, and nothing of herself? But the line of thought, combined with the prospect of food and shelter ahead, was oddly comforting. Surely, the more she remembered, the better. Very well then—she shifted the now sleeping Thomas on to the other shoulder. Wellington . . . Waterloo, of course, but that was a long time ago. More recently he had been First Minister. Now he was in opposition and Lord Grey was trying to force through the Reform Bill which many people thought would bring chaos and anarchy to the country. Many people . . . but who? She was back where she started from : Who am I?

Best not think of it. Be practical. So . . . how about money? She shifted Thomas to her left shoulder and put her hand into the deep pocket of her dress where, she seemed to know, her purse should be. She pulled out a handkerchief, a child's much bitten toy dog—and nothing else. She put Thomas down and felt wildly at her waist, the other side of her skirt . . . nothing. It was impossible. She could not have come so far without money. Even if, by some unlucky chance, she had spent it all, she would still have the purse. Indeed, she had been sure it was in her pocket. This was one of the memories, like that of the Duke of Wellington, that came through the curtain of forgetfulness. Or was it? Had she been deluded by the feeling of the child's toy against her thigh? No, even in the panic of this discovery, she found herself still reasoning. She had known herself, now, only for a couple of hours or so, but she did not think herself a fool. Whatever this wild journey of hers might mean, she would not have come on it without money. There was only one answer. One of her fellow passengers must have stolen it while she was unconscious.

The conclusion was ugly and irresistible, and she found herself wondering which one of them had seemed most eager for her to leave the coach at Pennington Cross. But what was the use of that? They were very likely in Plymouth by now, as safe from her pursuit as if they were in the moon. The question was, what to do now? And the answer was obvious. There was nothing to do but go on to the village and pray God she found friends when she got there.

That first glimpse from the top of the hill had been deceptive, and it was another hour of dogged plodding before she found herself among the first straggle of cottages. There were lights flickering in windows here and there, and no sign of life stirred in the street. People in country places, she knew, ended their day with the coming of darkness. In a way it was a relief to be spared the curious glances her appearance must draw. She had no idea—how strange it was—what she looked like normally, but now, she knew well enough, that mad flight through the gorse had left its marks all over her. Her cheek was scratched, and her hair dishevelled. Her bonnet must have suffered from the prickly gorse before it was sodden to her head by the driving rain. For she was soaked to the skin, and grateful to the darkness for hiding the way her heavy worsted dress clung to her figure. Another, random memory mocked her : Lady Caroline Lamb used to damp her muslins to make them cling more closely to her figure. Lady Caroline Lamb was dead . . . she shivered convulsively. What was the use of memories like that?

The church was dark, but a welcome light shone in the windows of the vicarage. As she drew nearer, she saw that a carriage stood at the double gate that served both vicarage and churchyard. A wild unreasonable hope surged up in her. Perhaps it belonged to her friends. But why should they be waiting for her here? At any rate, she now saw that it was empty, its only guardian was a small boy, doubtless bribed by the coachman to mind the horses while he retreated to the comfort of the vicarage kitchen. Automatically, she gave the horses a quick, professional glance. She knew about horses, and these were good ones.

She turned in at the vicarage gate, fought down a craven tendency to linger on the flagged path, found a door knocker in the half darkness and beat a rather timid tattoo on the door. Nothing happened. The wind blew keenly round the corner of the vicarage. It was even colder standing than it had been walking. Thomas stirred and whimpered in her arms. Time passed. . . . Her knock had not been heard. It did not seem as if anyone was expected here. . . . She knocked again, so much louder as to disconcert herself, and, this time, heard movement within. A shuffling footstep approached, and the heavy door swung slowly open to reveal an elderly maid of all work. The candle she held flickered in the draught from the door, throwing odd shadows about a gloomy hall.

"Yes?" the woman stood uncompromisingly in her way.

"May I come in?" Marianne shivered in spite of herself. "I have business with your master."

"Business? With Mr. Emsworth? At this hour of the night?" Each staccato question sounded more suspicious than the last.

"Yes." Marianne moved firmly forward into the comparative warmth of the hall, and the servant gave way before her for a moment, then stiffened as she got her first full glimpse of Marianne's appearance. From her reaction, Marianne knew that it was quite as bad as she had feared. "Best shut the door," she said with a calm she was very far from feeling, "the wind is cold tonight."

The woman looked more suspicious than ever, but complied, bristling and muttering something about "folks who shoved their way in unasked." Then, in a louder tone. "But you can't see the Master," she went on. "Mrs. Mauleverer is with him, and we never disturb him then."

Marianne recognized finality in her tone. "Very well. Is there a fire I can wait by? The child is chilled to the bone."

"Only in the dining-room." With wry amusement, Marianne realized that the woman was deep in anxious consideration about the flat silver and the candlesticks. "I don't know what to do for the best," she said at last.

"Best call your master. He will not want anyone left to shiver on a night like this. Particularly not a child."

The woman was still hesitating when a bell sounded from behind a closed door at the other end of the hall. She gave a sigh of relief. "There, he's ringing now; for coals, most like. I'll tell him you're here, miss. What name shall I say?"

Idiotic not to have been prepared for this. For a long moment, Marianne hesitated, while the woman looked at her more suspiciously than ever. Fatal to delay so. "Miss . . . Miss Lamb," she said at last, inspired by a memory of Caroline Lamb and her damp muslins.

"Miss Lamb, is it?" With abrupt discourtesy, the woman turned and walked away down the hall, the candle she carried flickering as she went. By its diminishing light Marianne looked around her for somewhere to put down Thomas, now fast asleep and heavy as lead in her tired arms. But the room was little more than a passageway, its only furnishings a vast

18

umbrella stand and a chest with a tarnished silver card rack on top. Prints hung on the walls, their subjects indistinguishable in the half light that now filtered out of the door the servant had opened. Marianne could hear the murmur of voices, and wondered how she was being described. Then a man's voice came, louder and, she thought, impatient. "Oh, very well, I'll see her. You will excuse me for a moment, Mrs. Mauleverer? Bring the light, Rose."

So she was to be interviewed here in the hall like the merest vagrant. Well, she told herself, no wonder. She took a firmer grip on Thomas and watched the tall figure approach, dark against the lamp the servant now carried. He stood for a moment looking her up and down while the maid put her light down on the chest, bobbed a curtsy, and vanished through a green baize door at the other end of the hall. Silence dragged out while Marianne returned Mr. Emsworth's gaze steadily. It was not, she thought, an encouraging face to which to pour out so strange a story as hers. He might be the most benevolent of clergymen, but he certainly did not look it. Scanty hair receded from a low, mean forehead, and a thin mouth made to straight a line across the pale face. He had been looking her up and down for as long as she could bear. If he did not speak soon, she would have to.

But now, having finished his leisurely survey of her bedraggled appearance, he spoke. "You wished to see me, Miss Lamb?" He must, after that long, cold-blooded scrutiny, have been aware of her drenched condition, and of the weight of the child she carried, but made no move to usher her into another room where she could sit down and warm herself.

"Yes. You are the clergyman of this parish?" Absurd question, his exquisitely neat clerical black answered it for her.

"Yes." A little impatiently now.

"I am come to beg your help." A frown creased his pallid brow and she hurried on. "I have missed the friends who were to meet me, and find myself, by some misfortune, penniless." His frown was blacker than ever. "I am come, in my trouble, to beg, of your charity, a night's shelter for myself and the child."

She was angry with herself as she spoke. This was not the way to do it, she knew, but she was too tired to do better.

"A night's shelter!" He sounded scandalized. "In my vicar-

19

age? My good young woman, I hope I know the world better than that, if you do not. But tell me who are your friends and I will do my best to have them sent for to fetch you. This has been an ill-managed business on someone's part."

"But that is the heart of my trouble." She was in for it now. "I . . . I have lost my memory. I do not know who I was coming to see." And she poured out her whole story, only leaving out the nameless terror that had sent her panicking into the gorse. It sounded, even to her own ears, a fantastic tale, and when she finally limped to a close with "and so if you and your wife would only have the goodness to give me shelter for tonight," she could read his answer in his eyes.

"A likely tale of a cock and a bull," he said. "You bring my wife finely in at the last of it, miss, as if you did not know well that she has been dead this twelve month and more, God rest her blessed soul. What is your plan, hey? To foist your bastard off on me in the morning, or merely to let in your knavish friends tonight, and murder us all in our beds?" He moved around her as if to open the front door. "The workhouse is the place for sturdy beggars, Miss Lamb." His face made the name a mockery. "But you had best make haste or you will find the gates closed."

Anger had driven out fatigue and fear. She moved between him and the door. "You are right," she said, "anything would be better than to accept charity from someone capable of so insulting a helpless petitioner. Where is this workhouse, sir, and I will trouble you no further?"

"Excellent." He had a trick of rubbing his hands together, as if washing them. "It is but five miles or so further down the road. You cannot fail to find it. Tell the beadle Mr. Emsworth sent you."

But: "Five miles!" she said. "Sir, I have not the strength to walk one. And the child is wet and exhausted. If you have no pity for me, have some for him. Surely there must be some woman in the village who would take us in on your recommendation?"

"And why, pray, should I recommend you? What do I know of you but that you have come here, forced your way into my house under a palpably assumed name and told me a lot of moonshine about losing your memory. No, no, my girl, you've picked the wrong man for your lures, and indeed," his

20

glance once more swept over her dishevelled figure, "it is not such a kind of draggle-tailed female that will catch me, I can tell you. Now, march, if you please."

She looked him up and down, then turned towards the door. "I would rather die in a ditch than stay to be so insulted."

"Stay a moment." A womans voice, mellow and musical.

Marianne paused on the threshold and looked back. An elderly lady in black had appeared in the open doorway at the end of the hall. "Mr. Emsworth, I hesitate to interfere in what is clearly your affair, she went on, advancing as she spoke with an air of command, "but I wonder if you are well advised in what you are doing. I have listened to all of this young lady's remarkable story, and I find myself inclined to believe her." She turned now, directly, to Marianne. "You ask, my dear, if there is not some good woman in the parish who will take you in. Will I do?"

"Oh, ma'am," began Marianne, and, simultaneously: "Mrs. Mauleverer, you do not know what you are doing," said the vicar. "You will be murdered in your bed—or worse."

"Do you know," said Mrs. Mauleverer blandly, "at my age I cannot think of anything worse, but I do not think Miss Lamb likely to murder me in my bed, any more than I suspect her of improper designs on you, Mr. Emsworth. I hope I can tell a lady, however bizarre her appearance. Perhaps it would be better for you if you could do likewise. But enough of that. Come, my dear, you are exhausted: it is time to be going. Good-bye, Mr. Emsworth, we will finish our business some other day." And she moved past the astonished vicar, with a stately inclination of her head, and a great rustling of heavy silk and bombazine.

Marianne followed her down the path to the vicarage gate, too dazed by this rapid turn of events to do anything but obey. A coachman and groom appeared as if by magic and she found herself being helped solicitously into a commodious if somewhat old-fashioned carriage and covered with a heavy fur rug.

"Best hold the child, I think," said her benefactress. "It is but five minutes' drive, and the roads are rough." She settled herself in the corner facing Marianne. "Well, here is something to break the monotony of a country winter," she went on with obvious satisfaction. And then: "Poor Mr. Emsworth,

21

I have been wanting to give him just such a setdown for years. It was all true, that romantic story of yours, was it not?"

"Perfectly," said Marianne, amused, despite her exhaustion at this naïve appeal. "I do not know how to thank you, ma'am——"

"Then do not try," interrupted Mrs. Mauleverer, "or at least not tonight. I can see that you are too tired to speak. You shall tell me the whole story in the morning, and we will put our heads together as to what is best for you to do. Who knows, perhaps you will have remembered by then?"

"Perhaps I shall." Marianne let herself nod off into an uneasy doze, which was soon interrupted by the coach's stopping.

"Here we are." Mrs. Mauleverer gave a series of orders to her servants and Marianne found herself helped out of the coach and up a shelving flight of stone steps, to where big doors stood invitingly open on a blaze of light. She was aware of blessed warmth, of a babble of voices, of the child's being taken from her. . . . Then she was drinking something warm and fierce . . . being helped out of her clothes and into bed. . . . It was soft, warm, delicious. . . . Somewhere, a fire was flickering. For a moment, she fought off the advancing waves of sleep. "But who am I?" she murmured, then slept.

2

THERE were dreams . . . dreams of flight, and terror, where always the unknown pursued, and, somehow, her feet could not touch the ground to run. Once she screamed, and woke herself, looked dazedly round an unfamiliar room, and slept again. Sometimes the cloud of sleep thinned, and she was dimly aware of light in the room, of voices and movement around her. She was hot . . . someone, surely, was bathing her forehead; then again she was cold, shuddering in her sleep and dreaming of flight across polar wastes.

Gradually the terror lessened, her sleep grew easier, and at last she opened her eyes on sunlight in a strange room. Even opening them had seemed an effort and she lay, for a while, unmoving, taking in what she could see from her bed. It was a large room, high ceilinged with elegantly moulded plaster-work there and around the chimney-piece. A cheerful fire in the hearth competed with the bright morning sunshine that picked out brilliant patches in the Turkey carpet. Heavy red curtains at the window, and exquisitely polished mahogany furniture contributed to the general atmosphere of prosperity and comfort. Her head moved a little, restlessly, on the pillow. "Where am I?"

She must have spoken aloud, for there was a starched rust-ling and the figure of a plump-faced elderly maid came into view. "The Lord be praised," she said, "she's awake at last." She creaked over to a bell-pull by the fireplace and gave it a firm tug. Then she returned to the bed. "Are you feeling better at last?" she asked.

"Much better, thank you." And then, "Have I been ill?"

"Bless you, yes. Doctor despaired of you, I think, but the Mistress never did. 'She's got to recover,' say she, 'to satisfy my curiosity.' Mistress mostly always gets her way, you'll find." And then, to someone at the door, "Tell Mrs. Mauleverer that the young lady is awake at last."

"Mrs. Mauleverer . . . of course." Memory came with the rush of lock gates opening, and then, just as suddenly they closed again, and the terror was back. She remembered the vicar's brutality, and, back from there, the desperate struggle through the rain . . . the kind strangers in the coach (but one of them had stolen her purse)—and beyond that, nothing. From what she did remember, a question instantly arose. "The child?" she asked. "Thomas?"

"Don't you be worriting about him, miss," said the woman cheerfully, "he's right as rain. Him and Martha—that's Mistress's maid—have taken a rare fancy to each other. Always did want children of her own, poor Martha did. No, you needn't be fretting yourself about young Thomas, miss, unless he gets into any more mischief than he has done already. Ah . . . here's Mrs. Mauleverer now." The room door had opened again and Marianne turned her head feebly on the pillow to get a better view of her rescuer.

"I am so glad to hear you are better." Marianne who remembered the formidable setdown Mrs. Mauleverer had given to the vicar, was surprised to find her a tiny, fragile-looking elderly lady in beautifully tended black. Lines of fretfulness marred a delicately pink complexion, but disappeared when she smiled or spoke. "No, no, do not try to move," she said now, as Marianne made a feeble effort to raise herself in bed. "You are very weak still and must not exert yourself."

"I . . . I do not know how to thank you," Marianne began, but was swiftly interrupted.

"Do not think of trying. Or rather, think how amply you will repay me by unravelling all this romantic history of yours. But tell me," she was close beside the bed now, looking down at Marianne, faded blue eyes asparkle with curiosity, "have you remembered?"

"Nothing more." The terror was close again.

Mrs. Mauleverer noticed the shadow on her face and hurried into speech : "We went over your clothes piece by piece, but there's not a mark on them. Even your shoes are country made . . . and the little boy the same. But his clothes are better than yours."

"Yes." Speaking was an effort. "I had noticed that too. I think I must be his nursemaid, or something of the kind . . . you should not be troubling yourself with me, ma'am; this is not the place . . . you are too kind . . . !" her voice trailed off.

The maidservant came forward anxiously. "I think she

24

should rest now, ma'am, if you will excuse my saying so. And perhaps a little broth."

"Yes, yes, of course, you are quite right, Gibbs." Impatiently. Then, more kindly: "You must rest, my dear, and get your strength back, then we will talk more of this. In the meantime, do not be troubling yourself; it will all turn out for the best, I am sure of it."

"You are so kind," tears pricked behind Marianne's eyes. Then a new thought struck her. "My box," she said, "there may be something in that."

"Your box But where is it?"

She was very tired now. "The coachman said . . . leave it . . . Three Feathers. . . ."

"Admirable." The old lady actually clapped her hands in glee. "I will have it sent for at once. Depend upon it, there will be some clue to your identity there. I was sure that my talking to you would bring something back. Oh, very well, Gibbs," impatiently, "no need to be making faces at me, I am going. Mind you rest well, my dear."

"'A very kind lady, Mrs. Mauleverer," Gibbs closed the door firmly behind her mistress. "But likes her own way. Who doesn't? It's getting it that's the trouble. Now, you rest easy, miss, like she told you, and don't worry yourself about anything, while I go and fetch you some nice broth. You've had next to nothing to eat, you know, for five days."

"Five days? Has it really been so long?" But she was almost too tired to finish the question and drifted off, once more, into sleep, dreamless, this time, and infinitely refreshing.

When she awoke, Gibbs was beside her with the broth, which she fed to her, with infinite patience, and gentleness, as if she had been a child. "You're very good to me," she said as the broth began to warm her.

"It's a pleasure, miss. Too little to do is our trouble in this house, as you'll see soon enough when you're up and about, as, please God, you soon will be. Well, stands to reason, when you have a full staff of servants looking after one old lady, and her, bless her, a very easy mistress—mostly. I tell you, Martha's a different creature now she's got young Thomas to look out for, and Cook's got her recipe books out, thinking up invalid dishes to tempt you, and I feel better myself for having you to nurse. It's been a long winter, miss, and a dull one, and you're as welcome as the signs of spring. The Mistress was rare down the day before she brought you home. Martha and I had been wondering whether we oughtn't to write to Mr. Mauleverer. Course, it's all different when he's here; you wouldn't think it was the same house. But he's so busy with his politics since his friend Lord Grey became First Minister that he's hardly ever home Madam misses him sadly. He didn't even get home for Christmas this year; they were at it night and day, the Mistress said—and that Reform Bill of his likely to be the ruination of the country, she claims. There——" she broke off and put the empty bowl down on a side table, "Cook will be pleased to hear you've drunk it all. Now try if you can't sleep some more. Mistress is at her dinner now but she's bound to want to come and talk to you after it. We had hard work, Martha and I, keeping her from waking you to ask you questions. She's like a child when she's got her heart set on something, and this mystery of yours is as good as a three volume novel to her."

Settling obediently down among the soft pillows, Marianne could not help a wry little smile at the idea of her adventures providing a sort of real life *Mystery of Udolpho* for her kind hostess. I have read a great deal, she told herself. Titles and and the names of authors crowded into her mind: the Waverley Novels, Miss Austen, Lord Byron's poems . . . if I am a nursery governess, how on earth did I find the time? And if I remember all of this, why can I not remember anything that matters?

But that way lay the terror. It was a relief when Mrs. Mauleverer came tapping at the door: "Are you awake, Miss Lamb? John is returned with your box and I am simply dying to have it opened. Are you strong enough, do you think, to sit up and watch while Martha unpacks it for you?" And then, without waiting for an answer. "I call you Miss Lamb, for lack of a better name, for I am sure it is not your real one."

"No, indeed," Marianne smiled. "I made it up on the spur of the moment for the vicar's benefit. I had been thinking, you see, of Lady Caroline——" And then, with a sudden change of tone: "Oh, ma'am, why is it that I can remember all these absurdities, and yet nothing to the purpose?"

"It is most provoking, I agree," said Mrs. Mauleverer, "but never fret yourself; when Dr. Barton comes tomorrow, I am

26

sure he will be able to explain it all. And in the meantime, who knows? Perhaps the sight of your things will bring back your memory."

The box was a heavy wooden one, plain, shabby, and, to Marianne's bitter disappointment, without any name or label. There was no lock, and, at Mrs. Mauleverer's command, the two footmen who had brought it untied the heavy cord around it before they withdrew.

"There," Mrs. Mauleverer turned eagerly to Martha, "now begin. Oh, very well, Gibbs, you may stay."

Martha was a thin, bright eyed, middle-ageing woman who treated her mistress, Marianne noticed, with much less respect than Gibbs did. She grumbled a good deal at being summoned away from the game she had been playing with Thomas, summing up Marianne, the while, with sharp, hostile eyes. Did she resent having to unpack for her? Or was it rather that she grudged her prior claim on Thomas!

Still grumbling, she flung open the box and revealed a top layer of child's clothes. Brightening at once: "Oh, good. I have been compelled to borrow for the poor child from the lodge keeper's little boy, and I can tell you his clothes are not at all the thing. This is much better." She shook out a white frilled shirt and a pair of nankeen trousers. "Yes, indeed, these are very much more like it. One thing is certain, ma'am, and that is that Thomas is no charity child: you can tell just to look at him that he's well born." A quick glance for Marianne suggested that the same thing could hardly be said of her. Now she lifted out a plain brown stuff dress like the one Marianne had been wearing when she arrived and laid it across a chair. It was badly crumpled, shabby and, Marianne thought, somehow pitiful. Hateful to have this strange and strangely hostile woman unpacking her things.

But Martha went on lifting more clothes out of the box: a brown woollen spencer, two severe looking flannel petticoats and two equally uncompromising night-gowns; some drab worsted stocking, three caps and a pile of handkerchiefs. "Bah, these caps!" she sneered, trying one on, then picked up a handkerchief with a suddenly puzzled expression: "The handkerchiefs are beautiful; quite out of keeping with the other things. Perhaps they were a present——"

Mrs. Mauleverer interrupted her: "For pity's sake stop

chattering, Martha, and get on with it. There must be some personal things surely?"

"Well," doubtfully. "There is this." She lifted out a shabby workbasket, and, at an eager exclamation from her, handed it to her mistress. But it proved to contain only the most basic necessities of housewifery : a few skeins of thread, needles, a pair of scissors, a heavy, old-fashioned thimble. A battered-looking leather writing-case proved equally unrewarding. And the box was nearly empty. With an expression of bored superiority Martha took out a pair of heavy buckled shoes and two pairs of soft slippers. Then came a bible with no name in it and a dilapidated volume of Shakespeare's plays, equally without a clue as to its owner.

Mrs. Mauleverer gave an impatient sigh. "Really," she said, "one might think you had gone out of your way to make sure there was no clue to your name."

"Yes." Martha gave Marianne another of her strange looks. "One really might. But have you noticed something else, ma'am? There is everything here that a nursemaid, or someone of that kind might need, but what about the child's clothes? Where are his socks? His little drawers? His night things? One would think his clothes had been snatched up in haste and pushed on to the top of the box. Did you notice how badly they were packed?" She shook out a frilled shirt as she spoke. While the other things were packed as exquisitely as if they had been silks and satins."

"Yes, yes," said Mrs. Mauleverer, "it is quite true. Now what can be deduced from that?" She looked eagerly at Marianne, as if expecting her to be inspired.

But it was Martha who answered. "It might mean that Miss there has run away with her employer's child on who knows what sudden impulse. Revenge, perhaps, for some slight? You will see, there will be a hue and cry out directly." The black eyes snapped maliciously at Marianne.

"I don't believe it." But Mrs. Mauleverer's voice lacked conviction.

"Or perhaps," Martha went on ruthlessly, "she is a member of some gang of robbers—that would account for there being no name on anything. Or maybe it's a kidnapping : the poor little boy to be held to ransom, till his sorrowing parents pay their fortune for his release."

Marianne pulled herself upright in bed. "It's not true," she said. "I'm not like that." The room whirled before her eyes. But she could not, would not let herself faint. This accusation, so dangerously like the vicar's, must be answered at once. "The idea is absurd," she went on more steadily. "If I am part of a gang, where are the rest of them? Besides, how would that account for the way the box was packed. If I had kidnapped the child, surely I would have had sense enough to do it at leisure? After all, from the evidence of the box, I was living in the same house as him. And as for your suggestion that I am a robber"—she was speaking directly to Martha now—"where, pray, is my loot?"

"Precisely." Mrs. Mauleverer sounded relieved. She was not, Marianne had already recognized, a woman of much intellectual capacity and was liable to take her cue from the strongest, maybe even the loudest arguer.

Luckily, Gibbs chose this moment to come out strongly on Marianne's side : "I've never heard such a farrago of nonsense in my life. I'd as soon believe myself capable of such wickedness as Miss Lamb. And I've nursed her night and day, and should know. She's a lady, if ever I saw one."

"Of course she is," said Mrs. Mauleverer as if that settled it. "Anyone who can see anything, can see that."

For the first time, Marianne slept deep and dreamlessly that night. Waking early, she lay for a while, listening to the first twitterings of sparrows outside and savouring a new sensation. She felt well. Yesterday's lassitude, and its terrors seemed to be gone together. She stretched luxuriously between linen sheets, giving herself up, for a moment, to the illusion of well being. Her head was clear; she felt ravenously hungry; she remembered—nothing.

The realization had her out of bed in a bound. Yesterday, she had somehow assumed that when her strength came back, her memory would come too. Today showed her mistake. Maulever Hall, she told herself, coaxing memory backwards. Mrs. Mauleverer . . . the vicarage . . .and then, the moor— and nothing. The past, then, still a blank. What of the present? Shivering a little, she moved to the window and drew back the heavy curtains. Early sunlight on a stable yard that lay quiet with nothing stirring but doves. Beyond the low range of stable buildings, a well-kept garden, and beyond that again,

29

the moor, sunlit and smiling this morning. Was it along that little winding country road that she had come, drenched and exhausted—how many nights ago?

Don't think about that. Don't think about Thomas; or the vicar's suspicions. Let it come naturally, she told herself. Marianne, she moved, now, to the big looking glass above the dressing-table. Marianne? How strange to be seeing oneself for the first time. Dark hair, curling in wild confusion around a pointed little face—too thin, surely, and the violet eyes too large over dark shadows. But how do I know that? Instinctively, she picked up the comb and began coaxing the curls into place.

"You're better, miss." Gibbs' voice startled her. "You shouldn't be up though, not before the girl lights the fire. Back into bed with you, at once." And then, as Marianne complied. "Mrs. Mauleverer sent me to see how you are. She had one of her bad nights again : been awake since goodness know when, poor lamb. She *will* be glad to hear you're better. But—have you remembered anything, miss? It's the first thing she'll ask me."

"Nothing." Marianne shivered a little in the cold bed. "Except how I do my hair, and what's the use of that?"

Dr. Barton, when he came, pronounced her perfectly well enough to get up. As for her memory, he shook his head : "I had hoped to find it restored. As it is, we can but wait and see. In the meantime, don't worry, it will do no good; may do harm."

"But how can I help worrying. Why should I stay and be a burden to Mrs. Mauleverer?"

"Burden? My dear young lady, you're not a burden, you're a crowning mercy. I'd been anxious about her—wondering whether to write to Mr. Mauleverer. Now, with you for company, she should go on swimmingly. You'll earn your keep; don't worry."

When he had gone, Gibbs insisted on helping her dress. "Anyone can see you're used to being waited on. I don't know what you were doing gallivanting about the country all on your own but for that hell-brat."

"Thomas? Is he a hell-brat?" Strange to have thought so little of him.

"Martha don't think so, but if ever there was a spoiled, neg-

30

lected, ill-conditioned little—— Here, let me button your cuffs for you."

"It's a funny thing," she held out her wrist obediently, "but these don't *feel* like my clothes. I thought the same thing yesterday when Martha was unpacking them. And yet I remember how my hair should be done. I don't understand it."

"Then don't fret about it," said Gibbs firmly. "But they're your clothes right enough, for they are every stitch the same as what you had on when Mrs. Mauleverer brought you home. And they fit you well enough, too, except that you've lost some weight, which is hardly surprising. But you'll soon pick up now, and get some colour in your cheeks. Not but what the pallor and the dark circles are becoming to you, but if you ask me, you're used to have a good high colour. Whatever else you may be, I think you country bred, not one of those lacka-daisical town misses."

"Do you? That's strange; I remember thinking the same thing myself." But this was a dangerous memory, one from the time of the terror. It was good to be interrupted by Mrs. Mauleverer who now tapped at the door to ask after the invalid and exclaim with pleasure on finding her up and dressed.

"Do you think you are strong enough to come downstairs and eat luncheon with me? I shall be so glad to have company."

"But—should I? You know nothing about me. Think," she made herself say it, "think what the vicar said."

"Mr. Emsworth? I hope I am not to be guided by his ridiculous notions. No, no, Miss Lamb, you are my guest, and must behave as such."

"But I am not even Miss Lamb."

"I am sure your real name is much prettier. Now come along downstairs, do, and stop arguing. What do you think of our grand stairway? Pitiful, is it not? I keep urging Mark to have it rehung with that striped paper you see everywhere, but he won't do it. Some nonsense about portraits—that's my father-in-law, the old tyrant——" She crossed the large down-stairs hall, "I keep begging Mark to have his likeness taken, but he won't do that either . . . it's all of a piece. One of Sir Thomas Lawrence's portraits would have been some kind of

company for me, but of course Mark was always too busy—
and now he's dead—Sir Thomas, I mean." She sounded personally affronted about it. "This way, my dear. I usually lunch
in the breakfast-room when I'm alone."

It was a sunny, comfortably shabby room, with more family
portraits round the walls. Seating herself obediently at the
small oval table, Marianne made her last protest : "But what
will Mr. Mauleverer say? May he not object to my presence
here?"

"Mark?" Mrs. Mauleverer bridled. "I hope he knows better
than to be making objections to the company I choose to keep.
Particularly when he favours me with so little of his own."

Marianne was amazed. "But, dear madam, even if you feel
you can brave his displeasure; I must be thinking of it."

"My good child have you taken leave of your senses? It is
true that Mark is of a somewhat impatient turn of character,
and indeed never could break being crossed from a child, but
I have yet to learn that a mother must be asking permission
from her son before she provides herself with a companion."

"Her son!" It was Marianne's turn to exclaim. "What an
idiot I have been! You must forgive my stupidity, ma'am, but
I quite thought Mr. Mauleverer was your husband." She stopped, horrified at what she had said, and wondering what deep
springs of grief she might not have touched.

But to her delighted amazement, Mrs. Mauleverer burst out
into her gay, almost childish laugh. "Oh, that's too rich," she
said. "Mark, my husband! No wonder you looked so shocked
when I spoke of how he neglects me. It is bad enough in a
son, but in a husband. . . . No, no, my dear, poor Mr.
Mauleverer has been dead these twenty years or more—I do not
precisely remember the date. I am afraid I found wearing
widow's weeds a dead bore and abandoned them years ago,
which, I suppose, is what misled you. But now you can see that
though I love Mark dearly I do not need to be deferring to
him on matters that concern me alone. Though as a matter of
fact I did write to him the other day to tell him all about you
and Thomas. I don't suppose he'll trouble to answer, though."
Again the faintly querulous tone. "I have not heard from his
this age. And as for Thomas," she took one of her characteristic leaps of subject, "Mark will never notice whether he's
here or not. And don't, pray, say anything more about your

looking after him. For one thing, Martha dislikes you quite enough as it is without your taking him away from her. For another, I don't want to share you with a brat like him. Tell me, do you play cards?"

"Cards? I—I believe so."

"I was sure you did. Andrew," she turned to the footman. "The card table in the library; at once."

For a moment, an expression of—what? Flickered over that marble countenance. Then, "Very good, madam," said Andrew.

Marianne was surprised to find that Mrs. Mauleverer's favourite game was bezique, delighted to find herself entirely mistress of the complicated rules of the game, and then surprised all over again to find she lost so steadily. Of course, in a sense it made no difference. Mrs. Mauleverer had suggested that they play for sixpence a thousand and had got over the difficulty of Marianne's having no money by starting off with ten shillings out of her own purse. She derived such simple pleasure from winning them back again that Marianne was reluctant to admit to herself that she was steadily, systematically and quite obviously cheating.

It was a relief when Andrew appeared and interrupted the session by drawing the curtains against the early dusk, making up the fire, and announcing with lugubrious pleasure that "that child's been at it again. Cook's in a proper passion, I can tell you."

"Well, don't," said Mrs. Mauleverer. "Tell Martha; it's her business. Miss Lamb and I are busy. No, no, don't move, Miss Lamb; you must have your revenge."

"But should I not see what Thomas has done?"

"Why? Not still harping on what the vicar said, I hope. Anyone can see he's no child of yours. Doesn't care a straw for you; nor you for him. I'm a mother; I should know. How surprised Mark will be when he hears about you! It would be just like him, after leaving me lonely all winter, to come down now to make sure you're fit company for me. He's a terrible stickler, is Mark. But no need to look so bothered, my dear, he can't help but approve of you."

Marianne wished she were so sure. Everything his adoring mother said about Mark Mauleverer made him sound more autocratic, bad-tempered, selfish and unreasonable. She awaited his letter with dread, but found herself, just the same, settling down with amazing ease into the peaceful monotony of life at Maulever Hall. Days slid past placidly, variegated only by Mrs. Mauleverer's choice of bezique, piquet or two handed whist to beat her at. The high point of each was the ceremonial arrival of the mail bag, but every day, as Mrs. Mauleverer unlocked it, Marianne's fear of an angry letter ordering her expulsion seemed more absurd. She was not, it seemed, worth writing about.

The weather was improving. She contrived to lure Mrs. Mauleverer out to walk with her down the drive to where she had found the first snowdrops and was congratulated by Gibbs on her achievement: "She's looking so much better, you'd hardy believe . . . and so are you, miss. I'd hardly know you for the waif mistress brought home that night."

A waif. It was all she was: homeless, rootless, and still, sometimes, in terror. She pushed the thought aside, and ran downstairs to find Mrs. Mauleverer unlocking the mailbag, which had just arrived from the village.

"Look!" She greeted Marianne eagerly. "It's come at last. Now let's see what he has to say about you." She opened the letter, exclaiming, "A double one, too; there's a compliment for you." And then, on quite a different note. "Oh, how dreadful, Oh, my poor Mark, what a disaster! And the poor child too! Oh, dear, I'll never look forward to a letter again —and he says nothing about you, my dear, after all—well, no wonder. What a terrible thing: we must have the chimneys swept at once. Oh, the poor dear little baby—and he says he must start north at once, so there go my hopes of a visit. Well, maybe that's just as well; we'd never agree about it. I know he thinks it a terrible misfortune, but I confess for my part if it were not for the disastrous way it had happened, I should be inclined quite to like it. After all, a title is a title. Of course it's true, as Mark always says, that there have been Mauleverers at Maulever Hall since Doomsday Book, while some of our peers—well, you know as well as I do that they get made for the oddest reasons. But just the same, if he did not mind so terribly, I should quite like the idea of Mark's being Lord Heverdon. But ring the bell, will you? I must give orders at once about the chimneys."

Marianne rose obediently from her chair, but hesitated for

for a moment. "My dear madam, I must beg that you will explain yourself. I am quite devoured with curiosity."

Incorrigibly, Mrs. Mauleverer's eyes now sparkled with delight. Gifted with an insatiable passion for gossip, it was not often that she had such a story to tell. "Why," she picked up the letter again and her face sobered as she looked at it. "Mark's ward, poor little Lord Heverdon has been burned in his bed—and all along of a neglected flue, my dear, which is why we must have our swept without delay. And poor Mark is Lord Heverdon and cross as two sticks as a result."

"But, dear madam, why?"

"Oh, dear," with a complacent sigh. "What a scatterbrain I am, to be sure, telling my story so back-to-foremost. Though I should have thought that you, so clever as you are, would have found it out for yourself. Mark has longed, all his life, to sit in the House of Commons, but he is so high-minded (quite impossibly so, if you ask me, but of course no one ever has) that he will not accept any seat that has the slightest whiff of patronage about it. Well, of course, you can imagine what the result has been; he has never found a seat, and has had to content himself with working for his friend Lord Grey in what I have always thought an almost menial capacity. But all his hopes have been set on the new parliament that will come in after his precious Reform Bill has been passed. And now look what has happened. He must sit, poor Mark, in the Lords. It is no wonder that he is so angry. And he's executor, too, for that hussy, Lady Heverdon, and must go north at once, he says, to Haverdon, to arrange for the funeral. From all I've heard of her, balls are more in her line than funerals though it's true she buried Lord Heverdon fast enough." She sighed theatrically. "So much for my hopes. I really quite thought Mark would want to see my romantic protegée and might, for once, pay me a visit in the Easter Recess. Oh, well," here a sigh of resignation, "he would probably be in a terrible passion anyway, and thank goodness, I have you, my dear. Now, ring the bell and let us make arrangements about those chimneys." She cast an anxious glance at the huge fire that roared in the hearth. "I am sure I have no wish to be burned in my bed."

3

THE spring evenings drew out; snowdrops gave way to daffodils in the park and village children came begging at the back door with draggled little bunches of primroses, but no further word came from Mrs. Mauleverer's son. Since he was her favourite topic of conversation, Marianne knew a great deal about him by now—more indeed than she cared to. So far as she could see, this new instance of negligence on his part was all of a piece with the rest of his behaviour to his adoring mother. Even as a delicate child, when she had wanted to keep him at home with a tutor, he had insisted—"yes, absolutely insisted, my dear"—on going to Eton like his father.

And after that, when she had hoped he would stay at home, keep her company and learn to manage the estate, he had taken himself ruthlessly to the university, only to leave it again, despite her tears and prayers, on the escape of the monster, Bonaparte, from Elba. "He was only a child, but he would go, and though I do not like to say it, Lord Heverdon connived it, I am sure, from the most interested of motives. If Mark had been killed the estate would have reverted to him, and what would have happened to me, I tremble to think. There is not even a dower house here, and I should have been reduced to living on my jointure."

For once, Marianne found herself on the verge of sympathy with the absent Mark Mauleverer, whose mother thought of his death in such frankly financial terms. "You mean that this house belongs to Mr. Mauleverer?"

"Of course it does. To whom else? You do not think, do you, that I would be living here, boring myself to distraction, winter after winter, if I could help it? If it had been mine, I should have sold it years ago, and moved to London, or maybe Bath—the season there is mighty pleasant—but as it is I am condemned to drag out the rest of my life here. You never saw such a wicked will: my husband left everything he could to Mark and I am dependent on him practically for the bread I eat."

36

"You mean, he pays for everything? For me, too, and Thomas?" This was a new and disconcerting idea.

"Of course he does. And I hope he knows the respect due to his Mamma better than to grumble about it either. I must have some pleasures, since he denies me the town life I should prefer, and you, my dear, are the greatest pleasure I've had this many a long day."

"Thank you, ma'am." But no amount of kind speeches could alter the fact that she was dependent on this absent, autocratic, and, she suspected, disagreeable stranger for the bread she ate. If she could only remember. . . . But that way, she knew, lay terror and the too familiar nightmare. Best not think about it. She roused herself and suggested they take a turn in the Park. "The wilderness is a perfect festival of blossom, ma'am, and the lawns like velvet already. I do admire the way you keep your grounds."

"Oh, yes." Impatiently. "They are well enough, and so they should be when you think of the sums Mark spends on their upkeep. If I had my way we would dismiss half the gardeners, and let the wilderness *be* a wilderness. Then perhaps I should be able to afford a barouche instead of that monstrous old carriage, and a few decent riding horses for my guests. Yes, Andrew?"

"Mr. Emsworth has called, madam."

"Show him in. No, don't run away dear, you must meet him some time. Best get it over with."

"Must I?" So far, although she had shaken his unresponsive hand at the church door on Sundays; Marianne had contrived to avoid Mr. Emsworth when he visited Mrs. Mauleverer. She did not at all want to see him now, but, with Mrs. Mauleverer's persuasive hand on hers, there seemed no help for it. Courtsying to him gravely, she was comforted by his embarrassment.

"Miss Lamb!" After his usual deferential greeting to Mrs. Mauleverer he came torwards her, hand outstretched. "I have been hoping greatly for a few words with you. I owe you, I feel, an apology."

"It does not matter." Indifferently, she let him seize and wring her hand with his moist one.

"Ah, but it does, it does to me. I would not for the world be out of charity with any of my little flock, and most par-

37

ticularly not with one whom my respected friend Mrs. Mauleverer delights to honour. If I may take the liberty, ma'am," to Mrs. Mauleverer, "of calling you my friend? But as for Miss Lamb, I feel we must be friends—indeed are friends already."

"Oh?" Marianne picked up her embroidery.

"Why, yes, friends and fellow-labourers. Wherever I go in the village, to whatever house of sickness and sorrow, I find that Miss Lamb has been before me. Do not think your goodness goes unnoticed, my dear young lady. God see it all, and so, I can tell you, do I."

"I do not do it with that in mind. I do it to please myself —and because there is such need. I have never seen such poverty, such ignorance. . . ."

"Never?" He took it up with bright-eyed curiosity. "You mean that you have remembered?"

"Nothing," she said almost angrily. "About myself, that is. It is only maddening that I remember so much that does not concern me. But wherever I have lived, I am convinced I have never seen anything like the conditions of some of the cottages here. Do you know that the Martins sleep twelve in a room, with beds three deep, and only one other room?"

"I do indeed, and it is on that very subject that I am come to speak with you, ma'am," he turned to address himself ingratiatingly to Mrs. Mauleverer. "I do not like the tone of the village. Is there any hope that Mr. Mauleverer will be coming down soon? His appearance would be worth a whole detachment of troops, for the people are convinced that he is their friend. And I tell you frankly, since this Reform Bill he is so concerned with was thrown out in the Lords, there are many in the village that are neither to hold nor to bind. If the King had not dissolved Parliament, I do not know what would have happened. But of course an election is unsettling too, even in a peaceful district like this where there is no question of a contest."

"No, indeed," said Mrs. Mauleverer. "I hope the burgesses know their duty better than that. But do you mean to tell me that our dolts of villagers are beginning to concern themselves with politics?"

"They are indeed, and, between ourselves, I should feel very much safer if Mr. Mauleverer were to come down and talk some sense into them."

She shuddered. "You mean we may have riots like last year? And be burned in our beds—or worse. I will write to Mark at once. Surely he must be returned from the north by now, and, neglectful though he is, the news that his old Mother is in danger of her life must bring him home post-haste. You will excuse me, I know, Mr. Emsworth; I must catch today's post."

Thus summarily dismissed, the vicar took his leave, favouring Marianne once more with an almost tender pressure of the hand, and calling her "blessed fellow-worker."

"Do you know what"—Mrs. Mauleverer settled herself at her writing desk—"I really believe that absurd Mr. Emsworth fancies himself in love with you. 'Fellow-worker' indeed. What on earth did he mean?"

"Nothing but a lot of nonsense. You know that since you do not like the idea of my walking alone on the moors, I take my walks mostly to the village. Naturally, I have got to know many of the cottagers, and they are so terribly in need of help and advice—one must feel for them."

"So that is where the kitchen scraps have been going! Mr. Boxall was complaining only the other day that the pigs' bucket was coming out half empty. No, no, never look so guilty, child; if we can stave off a riot and revolution with our kitchen scraps, so much the better. I am no fool, and know well enough how much you have saved me since you took over the housekeeping. If you choose to invest some of the saving in village goodwill, so much the better. You must let me know if there is anything more you think we should do. I have no more wish to be burned in my bed than the next person. Oh, if only Mark would agree to our visiting Bath, or better still, London, where, I have no doubt, he means to spend the summer if Lord Grey is returned to power. And now, my dear, if you will forgive me, I must finish my letter to him."

Her letter once despatched, Mrs. Mauleverer turned herself eagerly to the business of preparing the house for her son's reception. She seemed in no doubt that he would come, and Marianne wondered in just what alarmist terms she had written. A whole range of guest bed-chambers were aired and beeswaxed, holland covers were taken off the furniture of the formal drawing-room where Mrs. Mauleverer never sat, and the lustred candelabra there and in the dining-room were polished till they shone, rainbow-bright in May sunshine.

Meanwhile, Mrs. Mauleverer, satisfied with having initiated this great spring-cleaning, turned herself to the more satisfactory task of refurbishing her wardrobe in case, as she put it, "Mark brought down a party of his elegant town-friends." Luckily, Marianne had persuaded her to subscribe to *La Belle Assemblée* and she and Martha pored over the latest number for hours. Velvet, alas, was out of fashion, and Martha who combined dressmaking with her other capacities, was soon hard at work on the carriage dress of emerald green *gros de Naples* that was recommended as all the rage. Since this involved such intricacies as a three-fold cuff, a bias-trimmed skirt and matching *pelerine*, it was as much as anyone's life was worth even to speak to her for a few days and Marianne, whose conscience often pricked her about Thomas, found her, for once, glad to have him taken off her hands.

She found him crying in the corridor one morning. Martha had boxed his hears. Gibbs had told him to "run along, do." The whole house was topsy-turvy again that day, for Mrs. Mauleverer had belatedly remembered about the chimneys. The master-sweep, summoned from Exton, had arrived when they were still at breakfast, accompanied by a little black faced, snivelling boy, whose dangerous job it was to go up the huge chimneys and sweep them clean with his scarred and scabby elbows and knees. Marianne had exclaimed in horror at the very idea of this and Mrs. Mauleverer had been quite surprised at her suggestion that the boy, who could not have been more than eight years old, might not quite like the prospect. "But it is always done so, my dear. Where can you have grown up?" And she had settled cheerfully to her day's task of helping Gibbs refurbish her feathers by dipping them in hot water.

She looked up in surprise when Marianne made her request. "Take the child for a picnic in the long meadow? Why, yes, if you really wish to." Her shrug suggested that people who wanted to picnic in May were little better than lunatics, but Marianne, who had been house-bound for a week supervising the cleaning, found her spirits rise remarkably as she collected a simple meal, a large chip hat that Mrs. Mauleverer had given her because it was "too shabby for anything," and the first volume of *Anne of Geierstein* in case Thomas left her in peace to read it.

He scampered along by her side gaily enough and she found herself troubled, as she had often been before, by the fact that she could not like him better. She knew so little about children : were they all so incorrigibly given to mischief? Martha seemed to find what she called his "little ways" endearing, but Marianne was not so sure. Did nice little boys occupy themselves with pulling the shells off carefully collected snails? Perhaps she had done wrong in abandoning him so completely to Martha, but, in face of her obvious hostility, and Mrs. Mauleverer's persuasions, there had seemed no other course open to her. She sighed and began to tell him the story of the Three Bears. But he was never a good listener and soon began to pick up stones and throw them at birds.

This occupied him until they reached the edge of the wood by the long meadow. Here Marianne stopped short. She had forgotten, and Mrs. Mauleverer had probably never known that it was down to hay this year. Last time she had taken the short cut to the village, the grass had been short enough so that it did not matter where one walked, now it was a luxurious crop, almost, in this benevolent summer, ready for the scythe. She dismissed her vision of Thomas playing happily with his hoop while she read, and settled them instead on the verge of the little wood that separated the meadow from the park. Inevitably, Thomas was hungry already, so they ate their bread and cold meat and then she saw him happily started making a kind of black pudding of mud and grass while she pulled out her book and began absorbedly to read.

She had been up late the night before, playing two-handed whist for halfpenny points with Mrs. Mauleverer and submitting, as usual, to being cheated of the money her hostess lent her to play with. It was always difficult to get Mrs. Mauleverer away from the card table, and it had been well past one o'clock when Marianne had finally contrived to persuade her that it was time for bed. Martha had been impatiently dismissed some time before, so Marianne had had to help her now querulous friend to bed. This involved various negotiations with false fronts and rouge removers that she found oddly more distasteful than the sick-nursing that she practised among the cottagers. And, at last, there had been a fretful call from Mrs. Mauleverer, now looking oddly diminished in bed : "My drops! Marianne, you have forgotten my drops."

Measuring them out grudgingly, Marianne had found herself wishing, as many times before, that she knew just what these drops were. She must ask Dr. Barton. By the time she had combed out her own irrepressibly curling hair and washed her face in the cold water that stood ready on her wash-stand, it was nearly two o'clock. The waves of bored somnolence that had overwhelmed her at the card table had given place to a tense wakefulness, and she lay for another hour or so, listening to the wind grumbling about the moor, fighting off the terror that still lay in wait for moments like this. Would she never know who she was?

As a result she had walked about all morning in the slight state of remoteness that a bad night leaves behind it, and now the small print wavered before her eyes. Sir Walter was going his usual leisurely way about starting his book: his two mysterious travellers were somewhere in Europe . . . there were descriptions . . . digressions . . . more descriptions. . . .

Thomas had grown tired of his pudding and was playing an elaborate incomprehensible game on the verge of the wood. The sun was warmer, she leaned back more comfortably against the tree trunk that supported her and let her eyes flicker shut. Her dreams continued the journey of the two travellers, but now it was the bleak moor they were crossing, not the Swiss Alps. The dream turned nightmare; the terror was upon her again with the sound of galloping hooves, an angry shout. . . . Then she was awake, shivering in the warm spring sunshine.

The angry voice was not a dream; she could hear it still, and Thomas crying. She jumped to her feet and hurried in the direction from which the sound came. Rounding a corner of the wood, she stopped, appalled. Silhouetted against the light, a tall, black-haired, dark-faced man on a big brown horse was shouting furiously at Thomas who had found himself a fine new game—making tracks in the luxuriant hay. He had even, by the look of things, been rolling in it, and had, indeed, done a remarkable amount of damage for so small a child, but nothing—she advanced angrily—nothing could justify that furious tone to so small and helpless a child. The stranger's arm was raised, now, as if to strike the child, who turned, with a little gasp of fright, saw Marianne, and ran to her.

She put a hand reassuringly in his and confronted the man,

her colour was high with anger. "If you must strike someone," she said, "let it be me. It is my fault the child has done the damage. And anyway," dream-terror forgotten in real anger, "what right have you to be here, acting the bully? This is a private path leading to Maulever Hall and I have no doubt that great horse of yours has done quite as much damage to the hay as little Thomas here."

Disconcertingly, the stranger laughed and swung round on the big horse to face her. "Trespassing, am I? And you're the dragon that guards the path?"

She stifled a little gasp. She could see his face now, one side darkly handsome, the other horribly marred by a great scar across the cheek. Shocked, she felt anger ebbing out of her. "Yes," she said again, "this is a private way. You must go back the way you have come."

"And damage the hay still more?" He was still laughing at her. 'And what will you do, my dear dragon, if I tell you I have business at Maulever Hall?"

"I shall tell you that you should have come in by the main gates. This path is used only by the family. Mrs. Mauleverer will be far from pleased when she hears of the liberty you have taken."

"Do you think so indeed? Now, it's an odd thing, but I think her reaction will be quite other. But it is not fair to tease you." He lifted the beaver hat from his thickly curling hair and made her a courteous bow. "How do you do, Miss Lamb. Will you forgive me for frightening your"—he paused for a moment—"your charge."

"Miss Lamb?" she said. "You know me? You cannot be. . . ."

"Precisely," he said. "Mauleverer, and very much at your service. But amazed, I must confess, that not one of the women over there," he gestured to where the Hall lay hidden beyond the woods, "should have told you how—unmistakable I am."

She coloured angrily. What could she answer to this? Then, collecting herself: "I apologize, sir, for greeting you so rudely, but we had no cause to expect you so soon."

"My mother been grumbling that I never write to her?" he asked carelessly. "Well, what's the use of telling her I am coming, when it merely means she will fret herself into hysterics if I am so much as five minutes late. As it is, I trust I will surprise her more pleasantly than I did you. I am sorry I frightened the child, but I thought him one of the cottagers, trespassing shamelessly."

Now she was angry again. 'Of course," she said, high-coloured, "striking a cottager's child would be nothing out of the way. What is a blow more or less to *them*!" And then, appalled at what she had let herself say, she was trying to stammer out an apology when he interrupted her:

"No, no, Miss Lamb, do not apologize. You think me a savage, and, I suppose, with cause. It is no use telling you now that I had no intention of striking the child, so I will merely say good-bye until we meet again. Have I your permission to continue my journey?"

She and Thomas were blocking his path. She muttered another scarce intelligible apology, moved aside and watched him ride on silently furious at once with herself and with him. So that was the adored Mark Mauleverer! Well, his behaviour had confirmed all the bad opinions she had had of him and she could only hope that his stay this time would be as selfishly short as usual. Of course he had been going to strike the child and she could only wonder, in passing, how on earth he came to be so popular with the villagers. But no doubt it was just because he was here so seldom.

Thomas was tired and fretful after his fright, and longing to go home, but she lingered in the wood as long as possible, putting off the awkward moment of return and confrontation. Not that *he* would find it awkward. Feeding on her anger, she entertained Thomas as best she could by helping him to collect empty snailshells, but he was soon crying with fatigue and there was nothing for it but to pick him up and head for home.

Home! She stopped for a moment; it had never been more than a temporary refuge, but seemed an even more unpromising one now that its master was come back. Oh, if only she could remember. . . .

What she did remember was that the bad tempered master of Mauleverer Hall was going to find his home in a state of chaos. The sweep had doubtless finished his work by now— always providing that his boy had not got stuck, or worse still lost in one of the poliferating chimneys of the old house. But

44

the results of his labours in dirt and confusion would be with them, she feared, for some days.

She took Thomas in through the kitchen, on the pretext of collecting some supper for him on the way. She hardly admitted even to herself that she wished to avoid meeting Maulverer again until she had had time to change her crumpled dress and tidy her dishevelled hair. To her surprise, she found the kitchen and servants' hall in a state of unwontedly cheerful bustle. A scullerymaid was plucking chickens as if her life depended on it, the cook was busy over a battery of copper saucepans, and such a polishing of glass and silver-ware was going on as if they were to entertain the whole country.

"Master's home," the cook turned from the huge stove and saw her. "We dine late. He always does. You'd best take something as well as the boy, or you'll be famished before it's ready. Not but what it will be worth the waiting for, I promise you."

"I'm sure it will," Marianne sniffed appreciatively. "But I'll not be eating with them. I'll fetch myself something on a tray when Thomas is in bed."

"Oh?" The cook shrugged. "You know best, I'm sure. Oh, drat the sauce."

Marianne took Thomas up the back stairs, got him, protesting but weary into his bed and reached the safety of her own room with a sigh of relief. A quick recourse to her glass confirmed her worst fears. Her bonnet had got tilted to one side when she was playing with Thomas, her hair was wildly untidy and there was a smudge of something on her left cheek. No wonder he had called her a dragon, though hoyden would have been nearer the mark.

Of course she would not meet him this evening, but it would have made for peace of mind if she had only had something respectable to put on, just for safety's sake. She looked gloomily in her closet where hung the two limp brown stuff dresses and the cotton that was almost exact twin to the one she had on. On so mild an evening she had no choice. It would have to be the cotton, which, at least, she had just washed, starched and ironed as exquisitely as if it had been finest India muslin. She put it on rebelliously. These were not, somehow, her kind of clothes. . . . Or was she deluding herself? Was it only in dreams that she had once worn silks and

45

gauzes? Very likely. She shrugged irritably and went to work
with a will on her rebellious hair. Her hands, working almost
without volition, were doing something different with her
curls tonight. Mrs. Mauleverer, in the enthusiasm of turning
out her wardrobe, had made her a present of various bits of
tarnished ribbon and lace. Most of them, though she had, of
course, received them with proper exclamations of delight, were
fit only for the Jew's basket, but she had kept out one length
of silver tissue as more promising than the rest, and had contrived to clean it with soft soap and honey. Now, she bound it
round a coronet of hair on the top of her head, leaving only
short curls to cluster round her face. The result, her glass told
her, was charming—but totally unsuited to her plain, high-
necked dress. She exclaimed angrily and was about to pull
down the whole elaborate erection when Mrs. Mauleverer
burst into her room. "There you are at last, my dear. I was
quite giving you up in despair." And then, in obvious surprise,
"Why, you look charmingly. What have you done to your
hair?"

"I was only playing with it," Marianne hurried to draw up
her one comfortable chair for Mrs. Maulever, who settled into
it with a little sigh of what was intended to suggest exhaustion.

"Such a bustle as we have been in," she said. "And you,
wicked girl, not there to help. But, of course, you do not know
the great news. Mark is home."

"Yes, they told me. . . ." So he had not mentioned his meeting with her. Well, that was kind of him, perhaps. Since he
could say nothing good, he had said nothing at all about her.

"Yes, rode in as cool as a cucumber just when I had finished
my luncheon, and the sweep still here, and the whole house
in dust sheets, and my poor Gibbs almost in hysterics. I really
thought I should have a spasm myself, but he has a wonderful
way of taking charge, has Mark. I wish you could have heard
what he said to that poor sweep, it would have done your heart
good, my dear, after all your sighings over the little boy—an
imp of satan if ever I saw one, by the way, and left soot-marks
all over my bedroom carpet. But he's to have baths, and Sunday school, and I don't know what not, or Mark will know the
reason why. You never saw so surprised a man as poor Mr.
Bond. Though I expect the child will be more astonished still

when he gets his first bath—if ever he does. The trouble with Mark is that he has so many irons in the fire that most of them get cold when he's not looking. But, dear me, where was I? I came to tell you something most particular, and now I have quite forgot what it was." She paused, pleating the frills that ornamented the front of her purple satin dinner dress. "Ah, I have it. Dinner, of course. We dine late, you know, when Mark is home. He has town ways and will agree to no other."

"Yes, Cook told me. But of course I shall have a tray in my room."

"Nonsense. Mark is quite longing to meet you; he said so himself. He says I look years younger," she rose to prove the satisfactory truth at the glass, "and do you know I agree with him. I must try my hair the way you have done yours. You shall do it for me tomorrow; I am sure it will be vastly becoming to me. I only wish there were time tonight; we could pass as sisters could we not? But Mark is a perfect tyrant for punctuality; we had best not risk it. What a fortunate thing you are"—she hesitated—"dressed."

It was the cue Marianne wanted. "My dear madam, you must excuse me from dining. You know perfectly well that I have nothing to wear . . . I cannot appear like this . . . it would be quite unsuitable."

"I confess I wish I had thought of it sooner. Perhaps my old grey silk? But, no, you are inches taller than me; it would merely look ridiculous. No, no, my dear, you must not refine too much upon it; you look charming, as indeed, you always do." She turned from the glass as the gong sounded below. "There, Mark will be waiting in the drawing-room. Come, my dear."

4

THE sight of Mark Mauleverer waiting for them by the huge fire in the drawing-room did nothing to make Marianne feel better about her own shabby appearance. This afternoon he had been muffled in a heavy riding-cloak. Now, his carelessly elegant evening dress did full justice to his broad shoulders and spare athletic figure. If she had wanted to, she could have found no fault with his appearance. She did want to—but, as so often she stopped at the thought—how did she know what he ought to look like?

The scarred side of his face was turned away as they approached him and she thought again what a pity it was that some wretched unnecessary duel, no doubt over the merest of drunken trifles, should have marred what could have been so handsome a face. Looking at the good side of his face, before he turned to greet them, she realized that he was younger than she had thought at their first encounter. The scarred and angry face, the air of command, had made him seem somewhere in the settled forties, now, relaxed in his evening dress and smiling a greeting for his mother, he looked barely thirty.

Mrs. Mauleverer was introducing her and once more the smile lit up his eyes and warmed one side of his face. "The mysterious Miss Lamb." He took her hand. "I have much looked forward to this meeting." Was there something mocking in his tone?

Disconcerted both by this and because he had not thought fit to refer to their previous encounter, she felt herself at a loss, acutely conscious of her shabby dress and unsuitably frivolous hairstyle. But it was her place, after all, to be silent. Mrs. Maulever could be relied on to talk enough for two, though Marianne could have found it in her heart to wish that she had chosen some other theme than her own, as her patroness put it, "romantic history."

The story of their first dramatic encounter at the vicarage lasted them through the early courses of an unusually elaborate dinner, and, as he listened to his mother's tale. Marianne was increasingly aware of an occasional sidelong, cynical glance from her host.

"So you remember nothing?" he said when his mother had paused, at last, for breath.

"Nothing." Her voice sounded too loud in her own ears. "And yet I know so much."

"What kind of things?"

"Why, about books, and politics, and world affairs. How can I know that Wellington won the battle of Waterloo, and yet not know my own name?"

"It is certainly very strange. What does Dr. Barton say about it?"

"He says," without thinking Marianne fell into a parody of Barton's richly self-important tone: "He says that 'The human brain is an unfathomable mystery'." She coloured at her own presumption, but Mauleverer was laughing.

"Bravo, Miss Lamb, you have hit him to the life. I can see you are a consummate actress."

Once again there was something odd about his tone, and it was a relief when Mrs. Mauleverer changed the subject. "But you have told us nothing of yourself, Mark." Plaintively. "And I am simply dying to know what you make of the beautiful Lady Heverdon. Is she really no better than she should be?"

The colour rose in his face, leaving the scar pale. "No." Angrily. "I believe Lady Heverdon to be a much maligned woman. I have no doubt my cousin led her a dog's life, and when she tried to improve it by seeing a few of the intellectual friends whose company she quite innocently enjoyed, he spread the most malicious slanders against her. And as for the stories about her treatment of the child, her stepson, if you had but seen how she mourned his death, you would have known them for the libels they are."

"Poor little thing," said Mrs. Mauleverer sentimentally. "Did they discover how the fire started?"

"No. The nursery wing was so completely destroyed that there was not the slightest indication. It was only a mercy that the fire did not spread to the rest of the house, but that is of stone, while the nursery was the oldest part of the house and largely built of wood. But as it was they all had to turn out in the middle of the night and I do not believe Lady Heverdon has recovered from the experience yet. Combined with her grief for the poor child it has caused such a depression of her spirits that I strongly advised her, when I left, to stay no longer than she must in a place fraught with so many painful memories. Of course she is in deepest mourning still, and a residence in London, in full season, would hardly be the thing, but I rather hope I have contrived to persuade her to pay you a visit, ma'am."

"Me?" Mrs. Mauleverer's amazement was comical to behold. "You have invited Lady Heverdon to come here!"

"Yes. Is that so surprising? You are, after all, the senior lady of the family into which she married—however unluckily. What could be more natural than that she should come to you at this time of double mourning? And I am sure that when you have met her, you cannot help but love her."

Her eyes were bright with curiosity. "She is very beautiful, they say."

"Yes, and much younger than you would think from the stories the world has told about her. You will find her, I am sure, the easiest of guests. She begs you will make no effort to entertain her; all she longs for is country peace and quietness."

"My goodness," said Mrs. Mauleverer, "she must have changed greatly since she came out. Was she not known as the gayest débutante of her season? I am afraid she will be bored to distraction here."

"No, no, all she wants is country air, some riding and the atmosphere of home. I promise you I will see to it that she is not a charge on you."

"Oh." She took this in. "You stay then, to give her the meeting?"

"It would scarcely be courteous if I did not. I have it heavily on my conscience that under her husband's will I inherit much that should by rights have been hers. I have tried in vain to persuade her to let me deed it back to her, but perhaps you will have more success."

"I wonder," Mrs. Mauleverer rose with a swish of purple skirts. "Come, Marianne, we are keeping Mark from his wine. But do not be lingering too long, dear boy. I have so little of your company that I must be greedy of you when I have the chance. As for Lady Heverdon, I shall be delighted to receive

50

her, and all the more so if it means that you are to pay me a proper long visit."

He had risen to open the door for them, and Marianne could harly help smiling at his expression on being called "dear boy." But the fact remained that there had been something almost boyish about his enthusiasm over Lady Heverdon. she was not at all surprised when Mrs. Mauleverer, after making sure that the drawing-room door was safely shut, turned to her with conspiratorial enthusiasm. "My dear, I do believe he has fallen at last! And for Lady Heverdon of all people. Oh, well!" she looked, for her, almost thoughtful for a moment, then shrugged, "I expect it is all for the best. And indeed I was getting quite into despair and beginning to think I should never have a daughter-in-law. She must be a clever woman, whatever else she is, to have made him forget that scar of his sufficiently to think of paying his addresses to her."

She was absorbed in speculation about the prospective visit that she actually did not propose their usual game of cards and they were still sitting talking by the fire when Mark Mauleverer made his appearance twenty minutes or so later. Meanwhile, the conversation had reminded Marianne that he was no longer Mr. Mauleverer, but Lord Heverdon, and she searched anxiously back through her brief talk with him to make sure that she had not wrongly addressed him at any point. To her relief, she was able to decide that she had not, since shyness had kept her from addressing him by name at all.

Now, as he moved the tea tray a little more conveniently for his mother, she thought he would make an admirable lord, quick-tempered, autocratic and proud, though kind enough, in a lordly way, when it suited him to be so. He was also, she had to admit, surprisingly tolerant of the string of new questions about Lady Heverdon which had occurred to his mother during their brief separation. Yes, she would probably be with them next week; no, she was a natural blonde; twenty-five at the most. His answers were brief and to the point and Mrs. Mauleverer's questions began to flag. She put her tea-cup down on the tray and leaned back more comfortably in her big arm-chair. "It has been a long day," she said meditatively, and her eyelids flickered shut for a moment, then opened again : "How old did you say she was?"

"Twenty-five, ma'am." He spoke low and soothingly and flashed a warning glance at Marianne. The silence lengthened. Mrs. Mauleverer's head dropped back against the dark blue velvet of her chair. She began to snore very gently.

Mauleverer, or rather, Marianne reminded herself, Lord Heverdon moved the tea tray to a safe distance and crossed the room to the comparatively obscure corner where Marianne had settled herself.

"Now, Miss Lamb, a word with you."

"Yes?" She had been correcting the false stitches in Mrs. Mauleverer's embroidery but now laid it down in her lap and looked up at him with wide inquiring eyes.

"This story of yours," he said, "is all very well for my mother, and indeed you could hardly have chosen one that was more certain to take her fancy, so sodden as she is with romantic novels. But I hope you will not expect me to be caught with the same chaff. No, do not interrupt. Let me say my say and then you shall protest to your heart's content. But do not expect to make me believe your absurd pack of lies that way: I warn you, I am come forearmed. So soon as my mother wrote me of your 'romantic arrival' I checked with the Bow Street Runners. No one of your appearance—or the child's— has been reported missing. It is absurd to suggest that either of you could have vanished without some inquiries being made. You know as well as I do that you are no servant girl, however carefully you may disguise yourself as one . . ." an expressive glance summed up her wilting cotton dress. "And the child, too, though by all reports an ill-conditioned brat, clearly has good blood in him. His absence, even more than yours, must have caused comment if this had not been a put-up job of some kind. I tell you, I came down intending to send you packing without delay, but what I have seen today has made me change my mind. I do not care what devious reasons of your own have brought you here; that shall continue your own affair. What I can see is the good you have done my mother—that is my business. So I suggest that we make a bargain, you and I. You will stay on as my mother's companion, doing for her what you have so admirably done. In exchange I shall cast no doubt on your ridiculous story. Of course, if you should wish to tell me the true one, I shall be honoured by your confidence, and give you my word it shall

52

go no further. I cannot think, now I have met you, that it is anything worse than some kind of young girl's freak. Would you not feel better for having told me the whole?"

After her first attempt to interrupt him she had listened to him in the silence of mounting fury. Now, at last, came her chance to speak. "I am sorry you do not chose to believe my story. And sorry, too, that I cannot provide you with a more palatable one. I am only amazed that under the circumstances you are prepared to let me stay with your mother. I only wish I was in a position to throw your words in your teeth and leave your house tonight, but, since my story is true—every word of it—I have nowhere to go. I shall have to continue to eat your bread, however unwillingly, but I promise you I will earn every bit of it—and of the child's too. And I promise you, too, that if ever I do regain my memory you shall not be troubled with my support for an instant longer than it takes me to find my friends. If, indeed, I have any friends." His report of the blank he had drawn with the Bow Street Runners had gone deep with her. There had always, before, been the hope that somewhere she was mourned and searched for. Now he had taken even that from her.

"I am sorry you take it thus." His face, which had warmed somewhat as he urged her to confide in him was now a chill mask. "I would have felt happier if we could have reached some better understanding, you and I, but if this is how you want it, so be it. My offer stands. As for earning your bread— I am no fool, Miss Lamb. I have seen for myself all you have done in this house—and in the village too. No one I met as I rode through but was full of your praises, indeed, I confidently expected to meet some flat-faced sister of charity, rather than a bad young girl romping in my hay."

"I was not romping!" She stopped, aware of a hopeless loss of dignity.

"Of course you were not," his voice was kind again. "Merely contentedly dozing over—if I am not much mistaken —Sir Walter Scott's latest. My mother tells me you read aloud to her in the evenings."

"Yes, it makes a change from playing cards."

"Ah, cards. . . ." It seemed as if he would have said something more, then he changed the subject. "And talking of my mother, I fear it would be too much to hope that she had

53

thought to pay you anything for all the services you render her."

Marianne coloured, "Why, no," she stammered, "but her goodness has been such. . . ."

"Quite so, and you are indeed indebted to her for believing your story—but I beg your pardon, we'll talk no more of that. The fact remains that so far as I can see you have been acting at once as companion and housekeeper, not to mention taking over many of the charitable duties in the village that she should do, and, I fear, has always neglected."

Once again her face was fiery hot. "I hope you do not think I have been taking too much upon myself, my lord," she said, "I promise you, what I have given has been merely from the household surplus."

"So I have already learned. You must be aware that you have made enemies as well as friends, Miss Lamb, and they wasted no time in complaining of you. And have done you nothing but good by so doing, I may add. But we shall arrange things better in the future. First of all, you must have a salary. I have never engaged a housekeeper companion before. Do you think £50 a year would be adequate?"

"Adequate?" she exclaimed. "I may have lost my memory, my lord, but not my senses. It is absurdly lavish."

"I do wish you will stop calling me 'my lord'," he said irritably, the scar once more white in an angrily flushed face. "Has not my mother told you that I do not mean to accept the title?"

"Not accept the title! But surely you cannot help yourself?"

"That is what I mean to find out. I have sent my disclaimer, already to the College of Arms and to the House of Lords, and must await their decision. All these years I have worked for the Reform of Parliament with the idea that then, at last, I should be able to achieve a seat in the House that I need not blush to own. And now, when victory is in sight, I am frustrated like this. That poor little boy—I never met him—but God knows I have cause enough to lament his unlucky death. Of course my mother cannot understand——"

"What is it your mother cannot understand?" came an irritable voice from the far side of the room. "What are you two whispering about over there? I hope you do not mean to insinuate that I have been asleep! I merely closed my eyes for a

54

few moments because the light hurt them. I heard every word you said, Mark, and Miss Lamb is quite right : £50 is a quite ridiculous sum to give her. Ten or fifteen would be nearer the mark. A governess, I know, would think herself lucky to get ten."

"Yes," said her son, "but Miss Lamb is not a governess. Besides, ma'am you must see as well as I do—and I am sure Miss Lamb herself as well—that if she is to go on acting as your companion she must be in a position to dress herself rather more in keeping with her position."

"Oh dear," sighed Mrs. Mauleverer fretfully, "I knew I should have given you that old grey silk, my dear, but I am afraid Martha thinks she has established a perogative to my clothes."

Crimson with mortification, Marianne found herself quite unable to say anything, but Mark Mauleverer, as, it appeared, he wished to be called, had taken up the argument. "It is not a question of outfitting her in your cast-offs, Mamma. I can imagine nothing more unsuitable. I suggest that you take the carriage tomorrow and go into Exton together. I am sure that between you you will be able to hit upon exactly what Miss Lamb needs. And I am sure, too, that it will make a pretty sizeable hole in the £50 I intend to give her as this year's wages, so we will have no more argument about that, if you please. Remember, Lady Heverdon is coming next week."

Marianne had not thought she could be angrier. She must be re-outfitted must she, so as to avoid shocking the delicate sensibilities of this unknown but already, somehow, heartily disliked beauty! But she was a helpless dependent in this house; with an heroic effort, she said nothing.

"Miss Lamb is angry with me." He was teasing her now. Why should she have to stay and bear it? For a moment, she considered rising and sweeping from the room, but instead, she smiled at him sweetly : "On the contrary, how could I be angry with someone who is prepared to put up £50 to ensure that I am respectably clad. But do you think it will be enough, my—Mr. Mauleverer?" She had been tempted to call him my lord, since this annoyed him so, but lost courage at the last moment.

He laughed. "*Touché*" and I beg your pardon, Miss Lamb. As penance, I can only say that if it is not enough I shall have to stand your banker for whatever other sums you may require. Mamma, you shall be the judge. . . ."

"I think it is all a great deal of nonsense," said Mrs. Mauleverer crossly, and rose to retire

But in the morning she found the idea of a shopping trip to Exton more attractive, even if the purchases were not to be for herself. And even Marianne, however set she might be, on principle, against the idea of accepting money from Mark Mauleverer had to enjoy the spending of it. She had, she discovered, very definite ideas in the matter of dress, and the various mantua makers and milliners whose establishments they visited were soon treating her with respect on her own account, as well as in her character of Mrs. Mauleverer's protégée. Business was slack, it seemed, in Exton, and all the things they ordered would be sent home within the week. Best of all, Mrs. Maulverer's own dressmaker, on learning the nature of the case, produced, from the back of her little fitting room, a dark green dinner dress that had been left on her hands. "It would just fit miss, I am sure, and she could have it to wear while the other things are making."

"Oh, do try it on, Marianne," said Mrs. Mauleverer, "the colour should suit you admirably, and Mark will never notice if the bills come to a little more than the £50 he promised." For Mauleverer had proved all too true a prophet. Even at country prices, the minimum necessary outfit for a young lady had already run them dangerously near to their limit.

The modiste added her persuasions to Mrs. Mauleverer's and Marianne agreed to try on the dress. It did indeed suit her admirably and fitted as if made for her.

"Five pounds," said the dressmaker. "It will hardly pay the cost of the material, but since you are a friend of my dear Mrs. Mauleverer's. . . ."

Marianne had been thinking fast. "Very well," she said, "but in that case I shall not need the blue dinner dress I ordered. This will do excellently instead and I can wear it tonight."

The woman's face fell. The blue dinner dress was to have cost well over five pounds, and she had counted on selling both to this strong-minded young woman, but Marianne was obdurate. The green dress was wrapped up and the blue one, she thought, countermanded. It was therefore a surprise, and a maddening one to her when, a few days later, her purchases were sent home to Maulever Hall and she found the blue dress among them. Angry, at first, with the dressmaker, she soon learned that she had Mrs. Mauleverer to thank for the dress. Not, that is, that her friend intended to pay for it, "But, my dear," she protested, "you know as well as I do, that even with the other dress your bills will come to only £49 and a few shillings. I never saw such an admirable manager as you: the way you kept the count as we went along was a wonder to watch. And we cannot have you appearing for dinner in the same gown every night when Lady Heverdon is here."

"I do not intend to come down to dinner," said Marianne mutinously.

"Not coming down to dinner! I never heard such nonsense in my life. You know as well as I do that Mark provided the money for your outfitting with that very idea in mind; it would be scarcely honest to refuse to oblige him with your company after that. I suppose," she sighed, "that he does not think I will be lively enough company for Lady Heverdon, who has lived, I believe, in some of the gayest of fashionable circles. Do you know, my dear, I really believe that it is a case with Mark. I wonder how I shall find Lady Heverdon as a daughter-in-law? I expect the stories about her are mere gossip really, the kind that is bound to arise when a beautiful young girl with no fortune marries a much older man with a great one."

"Was she so much younger than Lord Heverdon then?"

"Oh, yes. He was a widower, you know. It was the saddest story; he married quite young, some quite produceable girl, I do not exactly remember who she was, and they lived for years together without a sign of an heir. And then, one fine day, my lady finds herself increasing at last—and died, poor thing, when the boy was born. It was only natural, I suppose, that Lord Heverdon should look about for another wife to mother his orphaned child, though it might have been more suitable if he found someone a little nearer his own age. Poor little boy, what a terrible end. No wonder Lady Heverdon wants to get away from the scene of so much tragedy. And anyway, of course, the house is no longer hers; it belongs to Mark now. I wonder what she will do. Mark says she has been left in sadly straitened circumstances under the terms of her husband's will.

57

I know it is the way things are done, but it seems an iniquitous business to me just the same. I do not see why women should not have a few comforts too, but it is only estates and property that get thought of. Look at Mark. He has been home nearly a week now, and has not come out in the carriage with me once yet, but spends all his time riding about, surveying the property as he calls it."

Marianne murmured something sympathetic, but, in fact, could not help, just a little, sympathizing with Mark Mauleverer. The weather all week had been exquisitely fine and when she had seen him setting out, each morning, on his big brown horse, she had not been able to suppress a pang of envy. How much better to be riding freely about the countryside than sitting chained to his prosy mother's side in the family carriage. Still, of course, it was odiously inconsiderate of him.

"Perhaps you will see more of him when Lady Heverdon arrives," she suggested.

"Perhaps I will. And that reminds me that she is coming in two days. Is everything ready for her reception? It must be the best linen sheets, mind, and a full course dinner every night. I'll not have her saying that I skimp my guests at Maulever Hall."

"It is all quite ready," said Marianne soothingly and for the hundredth time. "If Lady Heverdon were to arrive this instant, we are ready for her. Indeed, I rather wish she would." And get it over with, she added, rebelliously, to herself. It irritated her to see Mrs. Mauleverer putting herself out so much for this unexpected guest, and still more did it annoy her to see how her son took it for granted that she would do so. But then, perhaps this was understandable enough, for she, like his mother, was begining to suspect that this interest in the beautiful widow was a good deal more than that of an executor and trustee. His nerves had grown more and more evidently on edge as the day of her arrival approached and, since she was now the universal confidante of the household, Marianne heard about it all. Gibbs came to her near tears because he had found fault with the crystalline sparkle of the drawing-room chandeliers : "A thing I'd never a' thought to see him notice in a thousand years, miss." The cook threatened to leave if master came making suggestions in the kitchen once more, and even Boxall the bailiff stopped Marianne in the cutting garden to ask her what had come over him.

As for his mother, she was in despair. "I have longed so long for this visit," she confided to Marianne in her dressing-room on the night before Lady Heverdon was expected. "And now, to tell the truth, I am not getting much pleasure out of it. What *is* the matter with Mark? If he has read me one lecture today, he has read me six; and all about how I am to treat Lady Heverdon. Between you and me, I am sick of the sound of her name. Anyone would think she was Queen Adelaide herself, instead of a jumped up widow with not the best of reputations."

Marianne laughed. "Dear madam, do not let Mr. Mauleverer hear you say that."

"I should rather think not. But, really, the way he goes on, you would think it was I that was for approval, not Lady Heverdon. I am not to weary her with domestic chat, because her soul is above it—and a pretty housekeeper she must be, in that case. I am not to drag her about the countryside, making her call on my old friends, since she is used to the very best society . . . and, I ask you, if I may not take her visiting with me, what am I to do with her? I promise you, if she is really used to the best society, which I take leave to doubt, she is going to find it tedious enough, in all conscience, cooped up here with no one but you and me for company. Why, I am not even to suggest a game of cards with her!"

"Not play at cards? But my dear ma'am why ever not?"

Mrs. Mauleverer coloured, "Oh, I don't know, my dear, some megrim of Mark's, I suppose. I only hope Lady Heverdon has not turned Methodist, for that, in a daughter-in-law, is more than I could bear."

"Oh, well," said Marianne with an optimism she was very far from feeling, "she is not your daughter-in-law yet. And how do you like your hair?"

Easily distracted, Mrs. Mauleverer turned to admire the coronet of real and false hair that Marianne had built up on the top of her head. "Admirable," she said, "you must do it for me every night of Lady Heverdon's stay. What a talented girl you are, to be sure. My poor Martha's nose is quite out of joint, is it not, Martha?"

It was all too evidently true. Martha had been flouncing

about the room tidying her mistress's clothes while Marianne usurped her function at the dressing-table, and now slammed out of the room with some half-heard but all too obviously saucy rejoinder. "Oh dear," sighed Mrs. Mauleverer, "that was foolish of me. I shall pay for it later. But come, my dear, I hear the second gong, and you know how Mark hates to be kept waiting."

Following her, Marianne felt almost tempted to emulate Martha's sauciness. She was tired of the way the whole household revolved around Mark Mauleverer and his crotchets. Following Mrs. Mauleverer into the drawing-room, she saw at once that he was in one of the black moods she had learned to dread. Tonight, he would drink fast and take his mother up shortly on her sillier remarks, instead of merely ignoring them, or teasing her gently as he sometimes did. It was going to be an exhausting meal, with her part—that of peacemaker—one she was very far from wanting to play.

Mrs. Mauleverer, habitually blind to anyone's feelings but her own, had not noticed her son's drawn brows, and the flush along his scar that Marianne had learned to dread. She had contrived to grumble herself into a good temper by now, and merely greeted him with the usual teasing inquiry as to what he had been doing with himself all day.

"I rode to Exton," he said shortly. "The election there is as good as over before it has even begun. I never saw such a farce. If it goes thus in the rest of the country, it's good-bye reform. The Duke will be back with a thumping majority, ready to misgovern the country till he dies. And the worst of it is," he was talking as much to himself as to his mother, "one cannot help respecting the Duke, since he only does what he considers to be his duty. I sometimes wish he had been killed at Waterloo."

"Mark!" his mother was shocked out of her habitual complacency. "How can you say such a thing? I can remember when you thought the Duke a perfect God among men."

"Fifteen years ago!" His face was blacker than ever. "Come, shall we go into dinner? I am ravenous. The crowds were too great in Exton for anything so mundane as eating: drink was all they cared for, and there'll be broken heads in plenty before the election is over. I never saw such blatant treating."

Watching, with relief, as he fell hungrily upon the lavish meal the cook had sent up, Marianne did her best to turn the conversation to less irritating channels. She had been reading *Anne of Geierstein* aloud to Mrs. Mauleverer in the evenings, and this seemed an innocuous enough topic: would Lady Heverdon care for it, she asked. He did not know. "But she is a passionate admirer of Lord Byron's poems," he contributed.

"Oh, admirable," said his mother, "then she must find you the very image of Manfred and the rest of them, and won't care a bit about . . ." her eyes on his scar, which had suddenly gone livid, she stammered to a halt.

Marianne's suspicion that this was forbidden ground was amply confirmed by his mother's confusion and his white, if silent, rage. Once again, she turned the conversation. "For myself," she managed to keep her voice light, "I confess I much prefer Mr. Wordsworth even at his most prosy, to Lord Byron's melodramas, but then I am afraid I am not a very romantic kind of person."

He laughed, his short, barking laugh: "That comes admirably from you, Miss Lamb, all wreathed in mystery as you are. Do you, perhaps, prefer Mrs. Radcliffe as a source to Lord Byron, who, after all, is blessed with a sense of humour."

"Of a particularly unpleasant kind." At all costs, even in her anger, she knew that she must keep the conversation general. "So far as humour goes, I would rather have a page of Miss Austen than several volumes of Lord Byron."

"Would you really? You surprise me, Miss Lamb. We shall be discovering next that even your first name is not truly yours, but merely borrowed from the swooning young lady in *Sense and Sensibility*."

She had had enough of these continued hints that she was merely pretending her loss of memory. "Well," she said, "you may think I give myself the airs of a romantic heroine, but who are you, Mr. Mauleverer, to twit me with it? I hope you have never seen me swoon yet, which is, I suppose, the prerogative of romantic heroines, while you carry with you, plain for all to see, the evidence, that you have fought at least one duel, like the veriest Clement Willoughby of them all." There. She had said the thing she knew most calculated to hurt him and now, appalled, awaited the explosion.

None came. He was looking at her oddly. "Do I owe you an apology, Miss Lamb? Perhaps I do. At all events, shall we cry quits and drink a glass of wine together?"

She could only stammer her own apology and gaze at him, dark eyes large with surprise over her wine glass. What an incomprehensible creature he was. But Mrs. Mauleverer, very much more predictable, was shifting uneasily in her chair. "My dear, I think it is high time we withdrew." And then, as always, gratingly maternal, "You will not stay too long over your wine, Mark?"

They were hardly safe in the drawing-room when she turned on Marianne. "Miss Lamb, how could you? Surely you must have known he got that wound at Waterloo?"

"No!" Horror-stricken, she could say no more.

"Yes," Mrs. Mauleverer went relentlessly on. "It wrecked his life, my poor darling boy. Of course, I was against his volunteering : why should he, at seventeen ! But his uncle was all for it, bought him the commission, and, I am sure, hoped that would be the last of him. There were many, you know. who thought the English army would be mere mincemeat before Bonaparte. But he survived, my poor boy, to spite his uncle, and break his mother's heart—and his own," she added a characteristic parenthesis. "Did you know that he was engaged, before Bonaparte escaped from Elba, to a most eligible young lady? I will not tell you her name—it is all ancient history now, and truly I do not blame her overmuch. He came back, looking so dreadfully—I tell you, his appearance now is nothing to what it was then—and with his sweet temper so marred with black rages. Well, what else could she do but ask to be excused from the engagement? But he has never got over it—at least, not until now. So you can see why I am so full of hope about Lady Heverdon's visit. I do not really care what she is like, if she can make Mark forget his dreadful appearance—or think that he forgets it. Of course, *we* never mention it." There was infinite reproach in her tone.

"Perhaps it would have been better if you had, ma'am." Though horrified at what she had done, Marianne's spirit had not quite deserted her. She was nerving herself for the apology she knew she must make.

She bolted into it as soon as Mauleverer joined them, crossing the room to meet him as he came in. "Mr. Mauleverer, I owe you the deepest possible apology. Will you forgive me. Your mother has been telling me. . . ."

"I am sure she has." He cut her short. "I am only surprised she had not before, but it is not a subject we are much given to discussing. As for your apologies; there is no need for them. I expect I richly deserved your rebuke. And after all, it does not much matter how I came to be so disfigured. The disagreeable fact is quite enough. I feel I ought myself constantly to be apologizing to you, or any other lady for the pain she must feel in looking at me."

"Nonsense," said Marianne.

"I beg your pardon?" He was not used to being addressed so abruptly.

"I said, 'Nonsense.' Do you really think I, or any other young lady for the matter of that, could be so missish as to be swooning-ripe for a little thing like a scar? And one gained so honourably too. You do us females less than justice, Mr. Mauleverer." And then she remembered the girl who had jilted him, and felt herself blushing furiously.

But he was looking at her with unwonted kindness. "Thank you, Miss Lamb," he said, "you give me new courage."

He was thinking, of course, of next day's meeting with Lady Heverdon. Tossing on her sleepless bed that night, Marianne wondered what the unknown beauty would really be like. That Mauleverer was oceans deep in love with her she no longer doubted for a moment, and his mother seemed to have resigned herself to the prospect of the match. But what of the gay young widow with the tarnished name? Might she not think she could do better for herself than a scarred and short-tempered politician? But then, Marianne reminded herself, Mauleverer was Lord Heverdon if he would accept the title— might find he had to, willy nilly. . . . It was none of it, somehow, conducive to sleep, and when, at last, it came, it was troubled by dreams, mounting to the familiar, recurrent nightmare of terror. . . . Only this time her pursuer was no longer an unknown figure, but, catching her at last, revealed himself as Mauleverer, now hideously scarred on both sides of his face.

5

THE whole house shone. The footmen were in dress livery and powdered wigs, Mrs. Mauleverer was resplendent in a morning dress of purple *gros de Naples*, and Marianne was wearing one of her new dresses, a simple figured muslin that the mild June weather made highly suitable. She had seen to it that the whole house was fragrant with flowers from the cutting garden and had herself arranged the huge flat bowl of pansies that perfumed the state guest-chamber where once the unlucky Duke of Monmouth had slept.

Lady Heverdon had been visiting in the district, and had told Mauleverer that she would be with them early in the day, but the slow, warm hours passed without any sign of her. The sacred hour of six o'clock dinner was drawing near; surely Lady Heverdon would not be late for that? Soothing the cook's anxieties as best she might, Marianne suggested various means by which the elaborate meal might be retarded, if this became necessary, without undue disaster, but cook's lowering brow warned her of crisis to come, and she returned, with a sigh, to the front of the house. Mrs. Mauleverer was hovering in the main hall from which all the principal rooms opened. "What shall I do, my dear?" she asked. "It is high time to be changing for dinner, but if I go up, Lady Heverdon is sure to arrive, and I shall not be there to greet her. But you know how long I take to dress."

Marianne did, and knew too how it flustered her to have to hurry. She urged her to go and dress. "I will wait here," she said, "and act as your deputy if it is necessary."

Mark Mauleverer, appearing from his study, seconded her. "I cannot think what can have detained Lady Heverdon," he said, "but do you go upstairs, Mamma. Miss Lamb and I will form an amply sufficient reception committee, and you know it takes me no time at all to change. Nor Miss Lamb either, I suspect."

If true, this was not exactly flattering to Marianne, who received it with a faintly mocking half curtsy and pointed out that Lady Heverdon, too, would doubtless wish to change her dress before she dined, and they would therefore have plenty of time.

Thus reassured, Mrs. Mauleverer at last withdrew. Her son took an anxious turn about the hall. "I cannot think what keeps Lady Heverdon. I hope she has not met with an accident. I wonder if I should ride out to meet her."

"If you do," said Marianne reasonably, "she is bound to come another way; you will miss her and there will be no one here to greet her."

"What a sensible girl you are, Miss Lamb. You have the answer to everything. I cannot think how we got on without you!"

Once again, ironically curtsying for the compliment, she found it an unwelcome one. How tiresome it was to be so sensible. But Mauleverer was looking more and more anxious and she did her best to comfort him. "After all," she said, still reasonably," Lady Heverdon will hardly be travelling alone. Even if she should have met with an accident, there would be someone she could send."

"Of course there would. I am tormenting myself quite needlessly, I am sure. No doubt she has encountered friends on the way."

"Or found herself late in starting. It is often difficult to get away from one's hosts." The hall clock struck a quarter to six. "I think, if you will excuse me, I had best go and commune with the cook; there is disaster brewing, I am afraid, in the kitchen."

But he had turned away from her to listen to the front door. "Yes," he said, "it is a carriage. She must be coming at last." He stood in the doorway, evening sunshine bringing out auburn lights in his dark hair and striking ruthlessly across the scarred cheek, but, for once, Marianne thought, he had forgotten himself in the excitement of the meeting. As for her, she hovered more modestly near the main stairway. Her part would be to come forward when the first greetings were over, and act housekeeper in guiding Lady Heverdon to her rooms.

An elegant plum coloured travelling carriage came rattling along the drive and drew up at last in front of the house, and while Marianne noticed that the four horses showed no signs of hard driving, Mauleverer hurried forward to anticipate the servants in opening the carriage door and helping his guest to alight.

Watching from the shadowed hall, Marianne saw a smart-looking maid alight first, to Mauleverer's evident disappointment, and then turn and join him in helping her lady out. At last, Lady Heverdon herself appeared in the carriage doorway and paused there for a moment looking down at Mauleverer as he greeted her. The stories of her beauty had been no exaggeration, but no one had told Marianne how exquisitely tiny she was. Now, watching as Mauleverer took her both hands and swung her lightly to the ground, Marianne thought she looked as rare, and as artificial as some piece of priceless china. The golden curls, the exquisite complexion set off by a travelling dress of palest blue-grey were worthy of Meissen or Dresden at least. She was talking eagerly to Mauleverer as he led her towards the house, and Marianne thought that there was something touching and childlike about the way she leaned on his arm and looked up at him. She looked, surely, more like a girl coming home from school than a widow with a reputation.

But it was time to come forward and greet her, and, doing so, Marianne was able to hear what the clear little voice was saying: "Quite shockingly late, my dear Mauleverer, but my darling countess just would not let me go, and James never will hurry his precious horses. I know you will forgive me, because you are so good, but you must intercede for me with your dear mother, who I quite love already." She was in the hall now, blinking a little after the dazzle of sunshine outside, and moved towards Marianne with hands outstretched: "My dearest madam, a thousand apologies—oh!" she dropped her hands as she realized her mistake.

Mauleverer moved forward between them. "It is my mother who makes her apologies," he said, "for not being here to greet you. She begs you will forgive her, and here, in her place, is our Miss Lamb to show you to your room."

"Oh, yes. Of course. How stupid of me. How do you do, Miss Lamb." No warmth in her voice now, and she did not offer her hand, but stood, instead, silent for a moment, still apparently dazed by the change from sunlight to the cool shadows of the hall.

"You are tired," Mauleverer was all solicitude. "You look pale. Driving so far, and in this heat, has been too much for you. Miss Lamb will take you to your room directly."

"Thank you," mechanically. And then, warmly, with eyes for him alone: "I am a little tired, it's true. How quick you always are to notice. So like you. Yes, it has been a long day, and besides, I am ashamed to be so monstrously behind your dinner hour, but I promise you will be amazed how soon I am ready." She smiled up at him, the confiding child once more, then turned and followed Marianne up the wide stairway.

Arrived at the doorway of the blue bed-chamber, she dismissed Marianne with a cool nod of thanks. "Good night, Miss Lamb."

Ridiculous to let the bland assumption that she would not be dining with them annoy her so, and yet Marianne, changing rapidly into her green dinner dress, found herself seething with unreasonable rage. But after all, she told herself, running the comb savagely through her curls, what right had she to complain? She was an object of charity, no more, no less: it was merely her good fortune that Mrs. Mauleverer and her son treated her so well. No, she pulled her hair on to the top of her head and twisted a ribbon through it, she would not hold herself so cheap. She earned her good treatment in this house. . . . And, besides, Mauleverer himself had insisted that she join them for meals. If he did not choose to treat her as a servant, what right had his guest to do so?

It was, however, with a becomingly high colour that she hurried along, a few minutes later, to Mrs. Mauleverer's room, to be greeted with a volley of exclamation and question: "There you are at last, my dear! Tell me, is she a beauty? What is she like? How old is she? Come, quick, love, tell me all about her before I go down and face her."

"She's beautiful. And much younger looking than I expected. She might be a girl—almost."

"Is she very elegant? Does she paint, do you think? What will she think of us?"

"She cannot help but think you handsome, ma'am. Yes, she is extremely elegant, and her colour quite her own. You can see it come and go. She is a little tired tonight, she says."

"And why, pray, was she so late?"

"I am really not sure—the countess kept her, she says, but

67

she is full of apologies and promises to make the greatest haste in changing her dress."

"Good, then let us go downstairs. Will dinner be quite spoiled, do you think?"

"I hope not, but Cook will be furious and will give in her notice tomorrow, and I shall have to spend all morning telling her that her sauces are worthy of Wattier or Ude himself before she condescends to stay."

Mrs. Mauleverer laughed. "What should we do without you, my love! But come, Mark will be ready and waiting already, If I know him. I wish I could persuade that boy to pay proper attention to his appearance. Half the time he does not even bother to have his man assist him, but throws on his evening dress himself. I do not know what his dear father would say to him. I have known *him* spoil a dozen cravats before he was satisfied, and as for his coats, why, it was physically impossible for him to put then on unaided."

She seemed to think this was a great virtue in a husband, but Marianne, following her dutifully downstairs, told herself that she personally preferred Mauleverer's less elaborate style of dressing. Better a gentleman than a dandy any day.

This once, however, Mauleverer was not awaiting them in the drawing-room, and when he did appear, five minutes later, Marianne was amused to notice the signs that he had, for once, taken a good deal of trouble over his appearance. The plain set of studs he had so far worn night after night had been replaced by enamelled ones, his cravat was, for him, elaborate, and his dark blue coat, she very much suspected, new for the occasion.

Conversation limped. Mauleverer's thoughts were obviously upstairs, while both his mother's and Marianne's were in the kitchen with the irate cook. The big grandfather clock in the hall struck half past six, then quarter to seven . . . there was a rustling on the stairs and Mauleverer, hurrying to the door, led in Lady Heverdon, a shimmering vision in cascades of demure lavender-coloured ruffles.

"My dear Mrs. Mauleverer, what must you think of me!" She was the well-behaved little girl again. "My idiot of a maid is all thumbs tonight. I thought I should never be ready. And nothing would satisfy her but that I should make a full toilette : she is a sad bully, I am afraid—she was my mother's before me and thinks me a child still. I told her you would rather have me in my dirt and keep your cook—who is I have no doubt in a perfect tearer in the kitchen—but she would have it that this was an Occasion and I must be properly dressed for it." A rueful but basically self-satisfied glance swept down from her bare shoulders to the rustling gown which was, indeed, more suited to a London ball than a quiet country dinner.

She had clasped Mrs. Mauleverer's hands in her own as she spoke, in a pretty, impulsive gesture that Marianne, sardonic in the background, suspected of having been carefully rehearsed. Now she pressed them warmly and let them go. "You will forgive me, will you not? Your son has, I know, but that is nothing; it is you that I care about." She had contrived, during all this flood of talk, absolutely not to see Marianne, who found herself in the curious position of being not only invisible but, she suspected, inaudible. There was no need, however, for the moment, to put this to proof, since Mrs. Mauleverer and her son were both busy assuring their guest that she looked ravishing, which was true, and that her lateness had put the household to no inconvenience whatever, which was not.

Now Mauleverer was taking Lady Heverdon's arm to lead her in to dinner. "Oh, no," she coloured in pretty confusion, "I cannot walk before your mama. You promised you would treat me quite like one of the family if I came to you, and is this how you begin?"

"Very well then," he smiled down at her, much pleased. "An arm of each; thus."

And Marianne, meekly following, thought how lucky it was that the two ladies were small inside their sweeping skirts of silk and satin, and the doorways wide.

The dinner went off rather better than she had expected. The cook, under her inspiration, had performed perfect prodigies of preservation and adaptation. The capons that should have been fresh roast had been allowed to cool and then served up in a delectable sauce. The leg of lamb, it was true, was dark brown and not so tender as it might have been, but the side dishes made up for any deficiency by their number and variety, while Lady Heverdon praised everything with indiscriminate enthusiasm. The food was delicious; the dining-room just exactly the size she best liked; the flower arrangement in the centre of the table beyond anything. "And then the flowers in my room! Pansies—so original. I cannot tell you how sick I get of mere, expensive meaningless hot-house flowers. You are quite an original in your ideas, ma'am, I can see."

"Oh, no," Mrs. Mauleverer smilingly disclaimed the suggestion that she might ever do anything so like work as arranging flowers. "It is Miss Lamb that we have to thank for our decorations."

"Of course: Miss Lamb. I should have known. Then, thank you, Miss Lamb, for my delicious pansies." She contrived, while addressing Marianne, still not quite to see her, as if she was talking, perhaps, to some inanimate object, and Marianne, in her turn, merely bowed her thanks for the compliment—if such it could be called.

Mauleverer broke an awkward little silence by asking Lady Heverdon how she enjoyed her visit to the Countess of Lashton.

"Oh, immensely," the pretty little face lit up with enthusiasm, "I have never been so entertained. Picnics, riding parties, dancing in the evening . . . I declare I am quite worn out with it all. But you look grave, Mr. Mauleverer. You are thinking, I know, of the poor little boy, and so do I, every moment of the day, but I put a brave face on it, for my friends' sake. The Countess read me quite a lecture when I first arrived at her house: 'If grieving would bring him back,' she said, 'or depressing your friends with unrelieved black, I would be the first to urge it, but life must go on, my dear; we owe a duty to others.' Of course, I took the hint and put my blacks away, though I confess it went hard with me to give them up even for half mourning like this——" A loving hand stroked her lavender coloured ruffles as she turned from Mauleverer to his mother. "I cannot tell you, dear madam, what a relief it is to me to have come here to live quietly like one of your family. I do hope you have arranged no entertainment for me."

"Indeed I have not," said Mrs. Mauleverer, "and to tell the truth, my dear, I would be hard put to it to do so, so quietly do we live here among our country neighbours."

"That is excellent," said Lady Heverdon enthusiastically. "That is just what I shall like. We will read and embroider together, and perhaps visit the deserving poor in your village —or further afield, if it will be of assistance to Mr. Mauleverer in this election he is so concerned over. But I have not asked you yet, Mr. Mauleverer. Pray do tell me how it goes. They were sadly unpolitical at Lashton House and I am completely in the dark as to the news of the day."

"I am afraid you will waste your philanthropic activities so far as this district is concerned," said Mauleverer dryly, "for our election in Exton is as good as lost already, but I believe that it is a very different story elsewhere : the Reform Party are sweeping the country. It is all the more shameful that we should do so poorly here."

"But how can you help yourself?" said Lady Heverdon. "The seat is entirely in Lord Exton's gift, is it not? Surely you have long been resigned to waiting until your bill is passed before you can go to Parliament as Member for Exton. I only wish you would take what is rightfully yours and go at once to the Lords as Heverdon."

"I may have no alternative!" Marianne, eagerly listening, told herself this was a subject that they had discussed many times before. "I have had a most unpromising answer from the College of Arms, and even Lord Grey begins to be urgent that I go to the Lords." The tone of his voice suggested to Marianne that this, even more than the Exton election, must be the reason for his black mood of the last few days.

"Don't be angry with me," Lady Heverdon looked up at him with enormous blue eyes, "if I say how much I wish you would. Surely your bill needs defending in the Lords too— more than in the Commons, I am sure you have told me. I know how much you think of being Mauleverer of Maulever Hall—and that you have been here since the Conquest—and all that—but we Heverdons have our distinction too. Let your second son be Mauleverer . . ." she coloured prettily. "And as for me, I cannot tell you how gladly I will put on my dowager's turban and become Miranda, Lady Heverdon."

"You a dowager!" It was, Marianne thought, the inevitable response. "I can as readily imagine myself a lord. Though it is true what you say the battle there; they are the bill's inveterate enemies; even the bishops vote against it, and I think Lord Grey will end by having to make lords enough to carry it, but you know well that my heart is in another place."

"Your heart," she made great kitten eyes at him, "you know perfectly well you have no such thing, but merely a thinking machine that serves you in its stead."

"It does not serve *me* at all." His emphasis on the word "me" made it a pretty compliment. "What, Mother are you leaving me so soon? Well, I promise I will not be long behind you."

"I am sure you will not," said his mother dryly as she rose to lead the way from the room. She was not used to sitting so long silent at her own table.

Lady Heverdon had noted her tone and, pausing only for one long-lashed glance upward at Mauleverer, who was holding the door for them, she hurried to take her hostess's arm. "My dear madam, I have bored you with my talk of politics— but your son makes them so fascinating." Her raised voice ensured that he heard her. And then, as he shut the door behind Marianne: "Really, with him for my teacher, I feel that I might even end by understanding the difference between a Whig and a Tory, which, I can tell you, is something I have never been able to fathom yet, though I would not dare say it in any other company but yours, and beg you will be sure to keep my guilty secret. But now we are alone (and for all the notice she took of Marianne they might well have been) I will make bold to ask—what I have been dying to do all evening—how, deep in the country as you are, you contrive to keep so devastatingly in the mode. Why, that dress could dine out in St. James's tomorrow."

Thus shamelessly flattered, Mrs. Mauleverer relaxed and expanded in talk of leg-of-mutton sleeves, *mousseline de soie* and *La Belle Assemblée*. Marianne, silent and, she suspected, as good as invisible in her corner, thought that the old lady would soon be as completely under her visitor's spell as her son. As for him, he had seemed so much her slave, during dinner, that Marianne had found herself wondering whether they might not be already engaged. After all, Lady Heverdon's mourning, however lightly she might carry it, must prohibit any official engagement for some time to come. But his manner, when he joined them, which he did almost at once, convinced her that they were not even privately engaged yet. His eager attentions were those of a hopeful, but not an accepted lover.

The evening seemed interminable. Lady Heverdon sang a succession of Scotch ballads in a pretty, well-trained little voice and contrived to suggest that she was doing Marianne a great honour in allowing her to accompany her. Then, at Mauleverer's unexpected request, Marianne played for them. "I have heard you many times," he said, "when you thought no one was listening."

She had indeed found she could play, and acquiesced now without fuss or protest. After all, she was comfortably certain no one was listening. Mrs. Mauleverer was nodding in her chair, while her son was seated close beside Lady Heverdon, talking to her in what was very nearly a whisper. Once, pausing to turn the page, Marianne heard him say, "Miranda . . . she who ought to be admired," and skipped several bars to burst into a violent rondo and drown the rest of it.

Next day was the beginning of the Exton election, and Mauleverer had apologized to his guest in advance for the fact that he must spend the day there. Marianne rather suspected that Lady Heverdon would have liked to be invited to accompany him, but, if so, she was disappointed, for he rode off before anyone but Marianne was up. She was superintending the early morning activities in kitchen and dairy when he came in to her, dressed for the road. "Give my apologies to Lady Heverdon," he said. "And may I count on you, Miss Lamb, to help my mother entertain her? I am afraid she will find life here somewhat dull after Lashton."

How could he be so stupid? Help to entertain Lady Heverdon, when the beauty hardly admitted that she existed? But he was looming impatiently over her, waiting for her answer. "I will do my best," she said dryly. And then, with relief, "But it is my day to take the bible class in the village."

"Invite her to go with you. She has told me," dark colour suddenly flooded his face, "how much she is interested in our village arrangements. She had so little time at Heverdon that she had not properly got into the way of things there. . . ."

"I will certainly ask her to come." Marianne's tone suggested, despite herself, that the answer was a foregone conclusion, but if he noticed this, he did not show it.

"Do, Miss Lamb. I knew I could count on you." He was gone.

Sleeves rolled to the elbow, Marianne had been helping the dairy-maid make butter and now the girl recalled her to herself : "Miss Lamb—you will spoil it." "And indeed," she said afterwards to her special friend the between-maid, "if looks could curdle, we'd not have a drop of fresh cream in the house today. And the butter rancid, too, I should think."

The cook had planned a demonstration for that morning. It should have been a long and satisfying scene, beginning with her handing in her resignation, and ending, as such scenes always did, in Marianne blandishing her into staying. But today, nothing went according to plan. Marianne listened, almost absent mindedly to her recital of grievance, and then, when it wound to its expected climax of notice given, said carelessly : "Oh, very well, if that is the way you feel. You will work your month out, of course." No persuasion : no blandishment. The poor cook guns effectively spiked, had to go to work and talk herself out of her predicament—"And she hardly listened to me then either," she told her friend the butler.

"I don't expect she did. Mark my words, Mrs. Manning, this Lady Heverdon will have us all at sixes and sevens before we are done with her."

Marianne had taken her bad temper out into the garden and had contrived to soothe herself by her favourite daily occupation of doing the flowers before Lady Heverdon made her appearance. Like Mrs. Mauleverer, she had had her breakfast in bed and now appeared in the full glory of a daringly fitted plum covered riding habit. Marianne, entering the little saloon with her arms full of roses, found Mrs. Mauleverer in full tide of apology. Lady Heverdon, it seemed, had been ordered by her doctor to ride every day for her health. She had brought her own saddle-horse—but today there was no one to accompany her. "It is too tiresome of dear Mark to be gone out today," said his mother. "But you must forgive him, Lady Heverdon, for you know, I am sure, how much his politics mean to him."

"Oh, yes, I know well enough," said the beauty petulantly. And then, with a quick recovery : "But he could scarcely help the elections being today." Belatedly, she noticed Marianne. "Good morning, Miss Lamb. You do not ride, I suppose?" It was hardly a question, and Marianne, surprised at being noticed at all, contrived, among her roses, to answer the greeting without the question. She did ride, she was sure of it, but had neither horse nor habit.

74

"Oh, well," Lady Heverdon shrugged beautifully tailored shoulders, "I shall have to make shift with the groom, I suppose. I will not be gone long, dear ma'am," she was talking to Mrs. Mauleverer now, "and then I shall be entirely at your disposal for the day."

Mrs. Mauleverer looked, Marianne thought, a shade frightened at this prospect and, indeed, Lady Heverdon's tone did suggest that a galaxy of entertainment should naturally be ready for her.

The time had come to do Mauleverer's bidding, however unwillingly.

"Mr. Mauleverer sent you his apologies before he left this morning," she bolted into it. "And suggested that you might care to accompany me to my bible class in the village this afternoon."

"Oh?" Arched eyebrows rose. "A bible class!" And then, with a sudden and surprising change of tone. "Why, thank you, Miss Lamb, I shall be delighted to accompany you. How thoughtful of Mr. Mauleverer. He knows, you see," once more, this was for Mrs. Mauleverer, "how ignorant I feel myself in country living, and has promised to set about my education while I am here. So—I will make a beginning today under Miss Lamb's admirable guidance. Is this a daily duty of yours, Miss Lamb?"

"Oh, no," said Mrs. Mauleverer, "I could not spare her so often. No, it is only on Wednesday afternoons that she walks over to the village to hear the children say their catechisms. And that reminds me, you will scarce wish to walk, Lady Heverdon. I will order the carriage for you."

But Lady Heverdon insisted that a walk in the cool of the evening was what she would like above all things. "Though that does put me in mind, dear madam, of a favour I must make bold to ask of you. Could one of your men, perhaps, take a note for me to the dear Countess? I must thank her for all her goodness to me, and then, there is another thing. They talked, when I left, of making a party and riding over here to call on me. Would you be appalled, ma'am, to be the object of such a visitation? There would not, I am sure, be more than six at the most. The Countess and her companion in the carriage, my cousin and the young ladies on horseback."

"Your cousin?"

"Yes, my cousin, Ralph Urban. Though, truly, he is more like a brother to me, since we were brought up together. And that puts me in mind that I must write a note to him, too, and have him bring me the pelisse I left behind. I do not like to be charging the Countess with my commissions, but Ralph is quite another matter. He has been running my errands for years. But the first question is, whether you care to have them come. It will be merely an afternoon's visit, since Lady Lashton never sleeps from home. No need to put yourself out for them: a cold collation, perhaps, a ramble in the garden, a game at cards . . . I am convinced you would find the Countess the easiest of guests, and as for her daughters, they are the most delightful girls in the world; to meet them is to love them."

"By all means invite them." Mrs. Mauleverer was delighted at the idea of being visited by a Countess, and an invitation for any day that suited the party was despatched before Lady Heverdon went out for her ride.

To Marianne's surprise, she returned in ample time to keep their afternoon engagement, and made her appearance dressed in a close-fitting gown of palest grey muslin that made her look something between a nun and an angel. She proved herself, too, a surprisingly pleasant companion on the walk to the village. Last night's haughty manner had entirely disappeared and she plied Marianne with friendly questions about herself: could she really remember nothing! it was the most romantic thing—and what did the doctor think? was there no hope at all?

She really seemed to want an answer to these questions, and Marianne rather reluctantly explained Dr. Barton's continued hope that something might suddenly bring memory back to her in a flood. The subject was an increasingly painful one to her, since she herself had become, as the slow weeks paused, less and less hopeful, and was now almost convinced that she was doomed for life to her present anomalous position.

"And yet," she had said something of this to Lady Heverdon, "how ungrateful it is of me to say so. After all, if I did recover my memory, it would probably be to find myself in far worse case."

"Well, yes," said Lady Heverdon. "I would rather be Mrs. Mauleverer's companion than little Thomas's nursemaid any day. A spoiled brat if ever I saw one."

"What; have you met him already? I do hope he has not been making a nuisance of himself. I will speak to Martha about it if he has."

"No, no, pray do not. It was nothing." And then breaking off: "Oh, what a love of a little village!"

She proved an admirable audience at the bible class and the children, impressed by her beauty and the elegance of her dress, behaved so well that the lesson was over more quickly than usual. Emerging from the room where it was held, they found the village street unusually full of people. Mothers who usually took not the slightest interest in their children's whereabouts had come, today, to fetch them from the class and were waiting outside in a little talkative knot. Marianne, who knew how close was the liaison between servants' hall and village, was not surprised to hear whispers indicating that the village women were well aware that Lady Heverdon was likely soon to be their landlord's wife, and from her high colour and elaborate pretence of indifference, she suspected that Lady Heverdon, too, had a pretty good idea of what was going on in the women's minds.

As they passed the vicarage, Mr. Emsworth came hurrying out of the gate and stopped to pantomime surprise at sight of them. There was nothing for it but to introduce him to Lady Heverdon and watch with dry amusement as he did his fawning best to ingratiate himself with her. Marianne's dislike of him had grown rather than diminished as her encounters with him in the village had become more numerous. These days it seemed impossible to visit a sickbed or call on the parents of one of her class without his putting in a "coincidental" appearance and, more often than not, insisting on seeing her home to the park gates. Today, however, he was too much in awe of Lady Heverdon to suggest this, merely bowing to her a great many times, very low, in the middle of the village street, and promising himself the pleasure of calling on her in the near— very near future.

"What an absurd little man," said Lady Heverdon as they turned into the footpath across the long meadow. "I take it the living is in Mr. Mauleverer's gift."

"Yes." Marianne felt bound to defend Mark Mauleverer's choice. "I believe he and Mr. Emsworth were at the University together."

"I expect he is a good sort of man enough," Carelessly. "To fill a gap at a dinner table, or make a fourth at whist. But, I forget, Mrs. Mauleverer does not play cards, does she?"

"Not play at cards? Indeed she does." Marianne stopped and coloured, wishing she had not spoken. It had not occurred to her before, but of course Mauleverer must be aware of his mother's habit of cheating at cards, and must have taken this means of preventing his beloved from finding out about it. It all proved—if more proof were needed—the extent of his devotion to her.

They had reached the stile that led into the home wood now, and Lady Heverdon changed the subject to exclaim at the loneliness of the path: "Surely you do not walk this way unaccompanied, Miss Lamb?"

"Why not? There is no one here who would hurt me."

"I am sure of it. I could see that they all love you dearly in the village, and, of course, with good cause. But what about poachers? You know as well as I do that they will stop at nothing when they are out after game. I heard some dreadful tales at Lashton about savage attacks, and even murders they have committed when surprised at their work. After all, merely to be caught means transportation, so why should they stick at murder, if they think it will save them?"

"No one in the village would hurt me," repeated Marianne stoutly.

Lady Heverdon shrugged: "I expect you are right. But just the same, I believe if I were you I would let that would-be gallant parson of yours squire you home another time. Better safe than sorry, you know."

Two notes were waiting for Lady Heverdon when they got back to the Hall. One was from the Countess announcing her intention of calling on Mrs. Mauleverer on the day after next.

"Oh, dear," exclaimed that lady when Lady Heverdon told her the news. "How could I have been so stupid as to forget that wretched election. It will still be going on, and I very much fear Mark will not be able to give them the meeting."

"Never mind," said her guest. "It will be a consolation to us in his absence. It is too provoking," she went on. "My cousin will not, after all, be able to escort the young ladies. He has been called to town on urgent business. But we shall not lack for cavaliers, since they bring Mr. Merritt and Mr.

Fenner a most gentlemanlike couple, and quite devoted to the young ladies."

Marianne woke early on the day of the visit, and was relieved to see that it was brilliantly fine, for while making lavish arrangements for the comfort and feeding of this rather formidable group of guests, she had found herself wondering how they were to be entertained. Since Mauleverer did not play, the billiard table had gone to wrack and ruin, and his mother's idea of entertaining guests was to sit mildly chatting about clothes, food and the deplorable behaviour of the lower classes. Whether this would be adequate to entertain a party of lively young society people, Marianne very gravely doubted. But at least, after luncheon, they could all walk about, exclaim at the variegated blossom of the shrubberies and lose themselves, if they so desired, in the wilderness. After that, she hoped that Mauleverer, who had promised to return as early as possible, would be there to help entertain them. As for her, she intended to keep out of the way. Her part of the day's exertions would be done when the guests had been fed.

The party arrived with admirable punctuality, and Marianne, waiting to lead the ladies upstairs, was able to observe that the Countess was a thin, proud-looking woman engaged in a losing battle to preserve the remnants of pink-and-white British beauty. Her daughters, less fortunate, had their mother's pride without her beauty. As for the two gentlemen who attended them, Marianne found herself unable, throughout the visit, to remember whether the slender pale one was Mr. Merritt and the robust red-faced one Mr. Fenner, or vice versa. Luckily, the question was quite academic, since the entire party seemed to find her just as invisible as Lady Heverdon had done on the first day of her visit. The Misses Lashton chattered away to each other, as she led them upstairs, as if they were alone, exchanging frank criticisms of everything they saw, from Mrs. Mauleverer's grey morning gown (out of style) to the dressing-room's rep curtains (shabby). Later, as she handed cold meats and glasses of wine, Marianne observed, with wry amusement, that Lady Lashton's companion, Miss Barker, received and expected exactly the same treatment, losing no time in retiring to an inconspicuous corner, where she made up by an enormous meal for what she was missing socially.

Sorry for this shapeless dumpling of a woman, Marianne

joined her in her corner as soon as everyone had been served, and attempted to engage her in conversation. But it was no use. Miss Barker replied in monosyllables, darting, as she did so, anxious glances at the gay group settled carelessly around the table. Her place, it seemed, was to be seen, if necessary, but never heard. Abandoning the attempt, Marianne settled more comfortably in the corner and watched the party. It seemed to be going well. Lady Heverdon was obviously on the best of terms with the Misses Lashton and their cavaliers, and was being regaled by a minute account of everything that had taken place at Lashton House since she left. The Countess of course had fallen to Mrs. Mauleverer and seemed to be enjoying herself very much in cross-examining her about the domestic economy of Mauleverer Hall. Listening to her questions which were frank to the point of rudeness Marianne could not help being sorry for her gentle hostess who knew so little about her own household that she was reduced to making up answers as she went along. "And soup?" came the Countess's harsh and carrying voice. "I suppose you give soup regularly to the peasants in the winter months. I have found one can make a most nourishing broth out of the leavings from the servants' hall. But then I suppose our staff at Lashton must be quite double yours here. Tell me how do you manage?"

"Why, truly, I am not quite sure." Mrs. Mauleverer had been darting pleading glances at Marianne throughout the cross-examination, but now, finding these useless, she tried a direct appeal : "Marianne, my love, how do we manage?"

Thus directly applied to, Marianne had no choice but to rise and cross the room to where Mrs. Mauleverer sat, but was relieved to have her answer fore-stalled by Lady Lashton, who rose to her feet and moved away to the window. "How very disagreeable," she exclaimed, "it's actually raining."

"Oh darling Mamma!" her daughters hurried to join her and mingle their exclamations of dismay with hers. What to do now, was the universal question, and once more Marianne was aware of Mrs. Mauleverer's appealing glance. But how could she arrange entertainment for people who did not even see her? "Why not suggest charades?" she murmured to Mrs. Mauleverer, but this idea, when put forward, was condemned as a dead bore. "Charades have been out this six months or more," said the elder and plainer Miss Lashton.

At this moment, the plump companion joined Marianne with a whispered request that she might retire for a few moments. "Riding backwards in the hot sun has done my business as usual." Grateful for the excuse to escape, Marianne settled the sufferer on her own bed, promised to call her in plenty of time before the party left, and made her way down the back stairs to the little ground floor sanctum on the wrong side of the green baize door that she had made her own. There were various things here that she needed to see to. Boxall, the bailiff, had asked her to look through his monthly accounts for him before he submitted them to his master, and recognizing this as a true compliment, she worked her way through them with the greatest care, marking, here and there, a point where Boxall's mathematics or spelling had failed him. Reading through page after page of his cramped and difficult writing, she was aware of the soft incessant patter of rain on the windows and wondered with half her mind what Mrs. Mauleverer and Lady Heverdon had found to do with their visitors. At last, conscience and curiosity together became too much for her and she put down Mr. Boxall's smudged pages, sighed and made her way through the baize door to the front of the house.

6

As Marianne entered the drawing-room from a side door, Mauleverer appeared, still in riding dress, at the other end of the room. Both paused in surprise, Marianne silently, Mauleverer with a suppressed exclamation that sounded like an oath. A large round table that usually held knick-knacks and albums had been pulled out into the centre of the room and covered with a green baize cloth, and the entire party was gathered round it, bent so eagerly over their game of cards that they did not notice the new arrivals.

Bright spots of colour burned high on Mrs. Mauleverer's cheekbones, and her hand shook as she gathered up her cards. "My point, I think," her voice trembled with the excitement Marianne knew so well.

There was an awkward little stir around the table. Lady Lashton's eyebrows were high, her daughters whispered to each other across Mr. Merritt who was exchanging a speaking glance with Mr. Fenner. Lady Heverdon alone seemed entirely composed, "Yes, your game, Mrs. Mauleverer, and we are all your debtors." And then, she looked up, saw Mauleverer, and turned white. "Why, Mr. Mauleverer! This is a pleasant surprise! We did not expect you for another hour or more."

"Yes." He advanced upon them, almost, Marianne thought, threateningly. "I came home early in honour of your guests, Lady Heverdon. I beg you will present me. But first," a hard glance swept the table with its litter of cards and counters. "If you have been playing, as it seems, for real stakes, I hope you will let me repay your losses. I told you that my mother does not play at games of hazard."

"On the contrary," said Mr. Merritt, "she plays all too successfully."

Mauleverer advanced another step and seemed to tower over him. "I do not know your name, sir, but I demand to know what you mean by that."

Merritt's round red face seemed to crumble and he shrank back in his chair under Mauleverer's furious glance. "Why—

82

I—I meant nothing at all, sir; merely that Mrs. Mauleverer has had a most remarkable run of luck which, as a charming hostess, she richly deserves."

Lady Heverdon had risen and moved round between the men. "And, truly," she said, "we are all tired of cards and grateful to be interrupted. But it rained so——" her voice was apologetic, almost pleading, and she gazed up at him with her huge blue eyes distended.

His dark gaze met hers uncompromisingly. "It has stopped raining now," he said, "and I shall be glad to show your guests about the park—such as it is."

But Lady Lashton and her daughters had risen and, among a little flutter of introductions, announced that it was very late —the moon was new—they could not risk being benighted. Marianne was watching Mrs. Mauleverer whose feeble excitement had given way to a look of almost childish terror at her son's appearance. Now she rose: "I am not well," she said. "I beg you will excuse me." And then, with almost a gulp of relief: "Miss Lamb!"

Marianne was across the room in an instant and supported her friend through brief, awkward leave takings before leading her up to her own room. She said nothing until Marianne had put her into a loose negligée, then settled on a sofa, moaning, half to herself, "Mark will be so angry. Did you see how he looked?" And then: "Send me Martha: I must have my drops, quickly! And tell them I will not come down to dinner. Make what apologies you will to Lady Heverdon. I cannot . . . cannot face him."

Martha, summoned from the nursery where she was playing with little Thomas, rose grumbling. "I said no good would come of it. Nor ever has. Yes, yes, I'll go to her." And then, with a quick, venomous glance for Marianne, "You see who she needs when she is ill."

"I am glad she has you."

When Marianne returned, reluctantly, to the drawing-room, the visitors had gone and Mauleverer and Lady Heverdon were, all too evidently, quarrelling passionately. "You should have explained," wailed Lady Heverdon as Marianne entered the room.

"I thought it enough to tell you." His brow was as black as ever and he ignored the pretty disorder of golden curls, the pouting appear of a red mouth turned up to him. "Ah, Miss Lamb. Tell me, how is my mother?"

"Very unhappy," said Marianne, "and far from well. She begs, Lady Heverdon, that you will excuse her absence from dinner." She longed to say: "And excuse mine, too," but knew that the proprieties demanded her presence. She could only hope that Mauleverer would change his mood with his costume, but one glance at his face when he joined her in the drawing-room an hour later, showed it as overcast as ever. She was glad that she had taken the precaution of coming down early and establishing herself, apparently very busy, with some work in her accustomed corner. He did not seem to see her for a moment, then came across to her, "Is my mother better?"

"No." She did not mean to spare him.

He looked taken aback at the curt monosyllable. "You think me, then, a brute, Miss Lamb?"

"Frankly," she looked up at him with wide, thoughtful eyes, "and since you ask me, Mr. Mauleverer, yes." He gave a smothered exclamation and turned away to pace the room, as she bent once more to her work to hide her face, now crimson at her own daring.

"You do not understand." He had come back to stand over her again, as he had over Merritt.

"No," she agreed calmly. "You are quite right. I do not understand. But you cannot frighten me as you do your mother —and that poor Mr. Merritt."

He laughed, a short harsh bark of a laugh. "Yes, poor man, he was almost in a jelly of terror, was he not, but, as to my mother . . . Miss Lamb, you must let me explain."

"I would not dream of troubling you so. Explain to Lady Heverdon, if you like. She is your guest?"

"And you?" He looked at her quizically.

"I am your mother's friend, if you do not think it presumptuous of me to say so. Indeed, I do not care what you think, I love your mother, and I think you treat her monstrously."

"Oh, I do, do I?" She had shocked him out of the sullens into anger. "I suppose I should let her go about the country, to Bath, to London, wherever she likes, and make a laughing-stock of herself and a nayword of me by her cheating at cards. That would be kindness, would it?"

"It might be better than to leave her cooped up on her own

here, so wretched for lack of company that she has become subject to a woman like Martha. What are those drops she takes? Have you ever thought that there might be worse things than a little innocent manipulation of the cards?"

"You mean?"

"I do not know what I mean, but I am not happy about Mrs. Mauleverer. I think you should take her to London to see a doctor—even if it does mean that she may disgrace you at the card table."

Lady Heverdon came sweeping into the room in all the confidence of a low cut and desperately becoming gown of violet silk. "Mauleverer!" She held out both hands to him. "You have forgiven me?"

"How can I help it?" His glance, as he bent over her, joined his words in tribute to her absolute beauty.

The evening was a success after all—at least, from Lady Heverdon's point of view. Mauleverer, suddenly in tearing spirits, entertained them with a vivid description of the scenes, worthy, he said, of Hogarth's pencil, that had taken place at this, the second to last day of the Exton election. Lady Heverdon hung on his words, the perfect listener, and Marianne had nothing to do but eat her dinner, enjoy his turn of vivid description, and wonder how Mrs. Mauleverer would be in the morning.

It was, disconcertingly, Marianne's part to rise, when dessert was finished, and lead the way back to the drawing-room, but Lady Heverdon, pausing only to give Mauleverer her best smile and urge him not to be long behind them, took her arm as amicably as if, she thought, she had been one of the proud Miss Lashtons.

"Lord, what an exhausting day," sighed the beauty, dropping on to a sofa with a great swish of silk. "The Lashtons are well enough, in their way, but those two hangers-on of theirs are mere nothings. Heavens, I thought I should never keep from laughing outright when Mauleverer gave poor little Merritt that set down. I have never seen a man so frightened in my life : he really thought it would be pistols at dawn. And so did I, for a moment. What a temper Mark Mauleverer has! But I confess I like it in a man—except when it is directed at me. I believe he was really angry with me for a moment. Well, he did tell me some long story about his mother and cards, but, I ask you, my dear creature, what else could I do, with the rain pouring down and those two Lashton girls far too stupid for charades? But it is all over now, and we are better friends than ever for the quarrel. Do not they say that quarrelling is the beginning of. . . ." She paused, coloured prettily and was silent for a moment, then, since Marianne said nothing, went on: "But who would have thought that a sweet old lady like Mrs. Mauleverer should be such a shameless cheat. You never saw anything like it: the Miss Lashtons getting more frigid every minute, and Merritt and Fenner exchanging glances and the old Countess sitting there with her eyes practically starting out of her head—she is much too rich to like losing money. It would have been comic if it had not been so embarrassing. But what could I do? I was never more grateful for anything than when you and Mauleverer appeared. If I were he I should consider seriously having the old lady put away where she will be free from temptation. I am sure there are very good sort of homes for people like her. Nothing like a madhouse, you understand, but some comfortable country house where they would have an eye to her. Do you not think it would be the best plan? As things are, he can never have a quiet moment when he is away, wondering what she may not do next to disgrace him."

"But she is so happy as she is." Marianne could not bear the idea of her old friend being shuffled out of sight into some genteel form of prison. "After all, it is merely to keep her from playing cards."

"By the simple expedient of never being able to play oneself! It would not suit me, I can tell you, but maybe she would do well enough here." Lady Heverdon was talking half to herself, and Marianne realized with an odd little pang that she was already planning her married life with Mauleverer.

"Mrs. Mauleverer has been kindness itself to me." She began what she herself felt to be a fruitless plea for her patroness.

"Of course she has, and I have no doubt her son breathed a hearty sigh of relief when he heard of your arrival. Or did he, do you think? Tell me, does that memory of yours show any sign of returning? I have been absolutely drowned in questions from the Lashtons all day about your mystery and found myself hard put to it to know what to answer. The

Countess was not best pleased to meet you, I am afraid. She has an idea about you—but no, I am ashamed even to remember it."

"An idea about me? Who I might be, you mean?"

"Why, yes, but you would not like it, and indeed I myself do not for a moment believe it. It is all very well for the Countess, she has not had the pleasure of knowing you, as I have. But it is true that it would explain one point that I have found puzzling in your story—and you too, I have no doubt."

"What's that?" Marianne's voice was sharp with interest.

"Why, the question of where you were going in that coach. Why had you asked to be set down at Pennington Crossroads? Nobody knows anything about you in the village, and this is the only house of any size in the district. It almost looks as if you must have been coming here."

"Yes, I have thought that very thing myself."

"Well, then, why?"

"I cannot imagine. If you have any idea, or the Countess either, I beg you will tell it me. I would rather anything than this total blank."

"Is it still total?" Lady Heverdon's voice was oddly insistent.

"Yes. I dream, sometimes, of terror, but when I wake it is all vague, all confused. . . . If only I had some clue—something to start from—I sometimes feel that it might all come back. Lady Heverdon, I beg you will tell me what the Countess said."

"Very well then, but remember it comes from her, not me. For my part I do not believe a word of it. It is perfectly obvious that the child is nothing to you."

"The child?" Marianne had had terrors of her own along these lines.

"Why, yes, Lady Lashton is a worldly old person you know, and thinks the worst of everyone. She says the only reason she can think of why a young lady, which, by the by, she concedes that you are, should be wandering about the countryside with a child—is, well, the worst one."

"You mean she thinks the child is mine?"

"Of course, and Mauleverer the father. Why else were you coming here? That is what she says, of course. For my own part, I do not believe a word of it, and nor, I am sure, will you, but I think it the part of a friend to tell you what the world is apt to say." And then, putting out a hand to take Marianne's: "My dear Miss Lamb, you must not take it so hard; it is only the slander of a gossiping old woman. But you can see, on the surface, how patly it all fits together. Your arrival—and Mauleverer's calm acceptance both of you and of the child, which, frankly, does not seem to me at all in character. What a stroke of luck for him if it is true to have you so conveniently deprived of all memory of his offence. But of course," she said again, "I do not for a moment believe it."

"Thank you." Marianne could hardly speak. In her most fevered and desperate imaginings, she had never thought of anything so appalling as this, though she had often wondered why she had been on her way to so remote a spot. There was a horrible logic about the explanation—and yet, by instinct, she rejected it utterly. "No," she said at last, "I do not believe it. But thank you, Lady Heverdon, for warning me. Forewarned, I hope, will be forearmed against such a slander." She spoke more boldly than she felt. It could not be true . . . and yet it explained everything. There was a sound of stirring in the hall. Mauleverer must be coming to join them. She rose hurriedly to her feet. "Lady Heverdon, will you make my excuses to . . . to . . ." she could not even manage to name. "I am sorry to desert you, but, truly, I *cannot* stay tonight."

"Of course not," said Lady Heverdon kindly. "I understand just how you feel and am only sorry I chose so unfortunate a moment to speak, but truly, I thought you should know."

"Yes, thank you. . . ." Marianne hardly knew what she said as she made her escape through the side door. It was only afterwards, when she lay, her tears sobbed out, on her bed, that she found herself thinking that the result of Lady Heverdon's illtimed confidence had been that she had achieved an evening alone with Mauleverer. No doubt in the morning they would announce their engagement.

The terror was back that night, worse than ever, and she woke in the small hours of the morning, and lay, staring at the ceiling as it gradually whitened, and asking herself what she should do. Of course there was no truth in Lady Lashton's slanderous suggestion. Her knowledge of herself—and of Mauleverer—convinced her of this. They were not that kind of people. But—how to protect herself, and him? To remember, was the only way. She lay torturing herself with vain attempts until the sounds of movement on the floor above told her that the servants were stirring, and she heard the maids giggling their way down the back stairs. Soon it would be time for her to get up, and suddenly she knew what she must do. She must have had a reason for coming to this district. Somewhere, surely, she must be known. It was up to her to find out where. She would set about it this very day. And, soothed by this determination, she fell asleep.

It was late when she woke and she hurried into her clothes, hoping against hope that she might be down in time to see Mauleverer before he rode off to Exton. However moody and difficult he might be in society, he seemed uniformly brisk and cheerful in his dealings with his servants, and she liked to watch him settle a handful of problems, produced by steward or butler between breakfast and the saddle. But today, hurry as she might, she was too late. Dressed at last, she heard the stir in the courtyard below, and ran to her window in time to see the well-known figure ride out of the stable yard. No use hurrying now. She lingered until she saw Mauleverer emerge from the little wood beyond the house and set his horse to the slope of the moor. It was maddening to have missed him, for she had counted on learning from his manner this morning whether he had, as expected, proposed and been accepted the night before. Besides, she needed his permission before she could put her new plan into action.

But at least she could make a beginning. She drank a quick cup of coffee in the breakfast-room where an empty place and a chair carelessly pushed back still bore witness to Mauleverer's presence, then hurried upstairs to his mother. Already, her conscience was pricking her because in her absorption with her own problems, she had forgotten her friend's indisposition of the night before. It was at once a relief and faintly disconcerting to find Mrs. Mauleverer sitting up in bed and making a hearty breakfast, apparently as cheerful as if there had been no painful scene yesterday. She certainly made no reference to it, greeting Marianne with the news that she and Martha intended to hold a root and branch inquisition into her wardrobe this morning. "After all," she said archly, "we may have an engagement to celebrate any day now, and you know what that will mean in the way of visiting and society."

"Yes." Clearly, if Mauleverer had proposed last night, his mother had not heard of it, but then, she was not likely to have, since he never, to Marianne's knowledge, visited her before he left in the morning. But this project of Mrs. Mauleverer's came most handily for her, and she made her request at once, feeling herself, infuriatingly, blushing as she did so. It was horrible to have to ask even so small a favour as this, but what else could she do, penniless as she was?

"A riding habit?" Mrs. Mauleverer exclaimed. "Why, I am sure I must have several put away somewhere, and, goodness knows, they are no use to me: my riding days are over long since. And Martha does not ride, so you are most welcome, my dear, though I am afraid they will be horribly out of style, and not the best of fits. But do you ride? I had never thought of it."

"I am sure I do. And Jim Barnes was saying only the other day that the old bay mare needs exercising. If Mr. Mauleverer would but give me permission to ride her, I could get about the countryside a little, and, who knows, someone might recognize me."

"Oh, I see. Because you must have been going somewhere." Suddenly scarlet, Marianne wondered whether Mrs. Mauleverer, too, had been treated to the Countess's theory about her. Probably not, for she was going on in her calm inconsequent way: "Yes, I have sometimes wondered if we ought not to take you about the district more, but I am afraid I have been selfish: I do not want to lose you, my dear. Still, you are quite right, and anyway, if you do ride, it will be a good thing for you. You have not seemed yourself just lately, your colour is not so good as I like to see it; Gibbs was remarking on it to me only yesterday. Yes, you must certainly take up riding, and as to my habits, I remember now, they are put away in the closet in the red room. Go and help yourself; it will be better than to trouble Martha."

Marianne quite agreed with her, although, as so often, she felt vaguely troubled at this new instance of the curious power Martha seemed to have over her mistress. Meeting her in the hall, she hurried to disarm criticism by explaining what she was doing.

"The mistress's riding habits? Yes," Martha looked merely amused, "they are in the red room all right, but you'll find them a shabby enough lot, I'm afraid." And then, with her usual near-insolence: "Going riding with Lady Heverdon, are you?"

But Marianne, hurrying away down the corridor, pretended not to have heard.

The riding habits were indeed, at first glance, a sufficiently depressing spectacle. It looked as if the closet in the red room had not been turned out for several years and the habits hung in it, limp, and dusty and smelling of age. Carrying the whole armful to her own room, Marianne once more encountered Martha who smiled derisively: "Not exactly the heights of fashion."

"No." Marianne closed her door and laid the miserable garments out on her bed. All but one, she dismissed, at once, as hopeless, and determined to get Mrs. Mauleverer's permission to take them to the village next time she went there to take her class. The poverty-stricken mothers of some of her children would be glad enough of the material. But in the meantime she turned her attention to the one possibility, a dark blue worsted habit, very much less worn than the others, presumably because there was a long jagged tear in the skirt. The first thing was to take it downstairs and out by the side door into the garden. In the privacy of the little cutting garden, she shook and brushed and brushed and shook until she had got rid of every particle of dust. Then she took it back indoors and tried it on. It was as she had suspected. The whole outfit was much too large for her that she would be able to get rid of most of the tear in the course of altering it. Dressmaking, fortunately, seemed to be another of the things she could do. She pinned her alterations firmly together, borrowed some blue sewing thread from Gibbs and returned to the garden to air the dress as she sewed it.

Lady Heverdon found her there some time later. "So that's where you are hiding yourself! I thought the house was bewitched this morning: I might have been in one of those fairy tales where you are waited upon by invisible hands. Mrs. Mauleverer is rooting about in her wardrobe with that harpy of a maid, and as for her son, I suppose it would be too much to hope for a host's attentions from him so long as his wretched election lasts. I wish, now, that I had taken his advice and postponed my visit till it was over, but I did not understand that he meant it so literally when he said he must go to Exton

every day. I must say, it is not exactly my idea of hospitality."
Her peevish tone answered the question that had rung in Marianne's head all morning. Mauleverer had not, after all, proposed. She rather wished that before he did so he could hear the tone in which his beloved spoke of his passion for politics when he was not present. It might, she thought, go far towards effecting his cure.

Perhaps the same idea had occurred to Lady Heverdon, for she changed her tone suddenly: "And here I am, grumbling to my patient Miss Lamb because I miss him so," she said. "Well, the election will be over today, and then—we shall see. But what are you so busy at?"

Marianne explained, colouring as she did so, since this new plan of hers was so clearly the result of Lady Lashton's malicious gossip.

But Lady Heverdon merely nodded sympathetically. "An excellent plan. I am surprised that you have not thought of it sooner. And of course Mauleverer will give his permission: he is the most generous of men. And think what an advantage: you will be able to ride to the village for your lessons." Why the sharp little glance as she spoke.

"Oh, no," said Marianne at once. "I like the walk to the village. And, besides, it would mean leaving the mare standing. No, I had thought of going up on the moor. There must be lonely houses there whose occupants may not even have heard the stories about me. Perhaps, somewhere, I shall be recognized."

Lady Heverdon smiled her ravishing smile: Perhaps you will. But I must be off for my own ride—what a pity you cannot accompany me, Miss Lamb.

7

LEFT alone, Marianne sewed busily for a while, enjoying the hot sun and the quietness, broken only by the buzzing of bees in her favourite yellow climbing rose and, far off, the call of a cuckoo. She finished the last seam and leaned back more comfortably. Soon she would go indoors and try on the dress, but, just for a moment, it was restful to sit there, eyes half closed, and accept the impartial blessing of the sun.

"Minerva sleeps!" She opened startled eyes to see Mr. Emsworth standing over her, a red rosebud in his hand. "For she was the Goddess of housewifery, as I am sure you know, Miss Lamb, and wise as you are, I believe that I find your domestic competence even more admirable. What order, what blessed reason you have brought to this household; what happiness to Mrs. Mauleverer, who loves you, I believe, quite like a daughter, and will, I am sure, treat you like one. And when I think of how lamentably I misjudged you at our first meeting there is nothing for it, my dear Miss Lamb, but to go down on my knees and ask your forgiveness." And absurdly, amazingly, he did so, first carefully selecting a dry paving stone for his clerical black knee. "Forgive me, Miss Lamb!" His shovel hat was under one arm, the other held out the rosebud to her.

She looked at him in amazement. "Mr. Emsworth, have you taken leave of your senses?"

"No, my dearest, my esteemed, may I not say my adored Miss Lamb, I have come to them at last. It is true that for a while wordly considerations have held me back, but what are considerations of this world compared with those of the spirit? Your conduct in the village is such as to outweigh the mystery of your past—and, besides, what right have I to cavil where my patron and patroness are satisfied? If Mr. Mauleverer and his mother choose to treat you as a member of their family, that is good enough for me. No, Miss Lamb, when you are mine you shall never hear a word of censure as to the past. It shall be my pleasure, my privilege, to protect you from the

world's slanderous tongues. I have consulted my bishop and
he is of a mind with me in this; the Mauleverers, I know, will
approve, the good people of the village will be delighted, and
what do we care for the rest of the world? Together we will
toil in the vineyard to which God has called us : I will be the
oak to which, frail and tender vine that you are, you shall
cling through storm and trouble. After all, suddenly practical,
"if you have remembered nothing so far, it is extremely unlikely that you ever will—Dr Barton agrees with me on this
point, and even if you should do so, it might be better than
one fears . . . and, if not, why, you will easily be able to forget it again. Mrs. Mauleverer has often urged me, for the sake
of my little flock, to marry again, and will be delighted, I am
sure, by our news. Who knows—they may even give you a
dower of some sort. Do you not think so?"

She had listened to him so far in helpless astonishment, but
now he paused for her answer and occupied himself by taking
a large white handkerchief from his pocket and tucking it
under his knee, shifting, as he did so, into a slightly more
comfortable position on the hard flagstone.

"Am I to understand that you are asking me to marry you?"

He looked up in surprise at the disdainful note in her voice.
"Yes, Miss Lamb, with passion, with adoration, with devotion,
I am asking you to be my wife. The unfortunate past shall be
forgotten in the future's ecstasy. The bishop will marry us, I
am sure, and in the cathedral, if you wish it. Mrs. Mauleverer
will continue your dear friend; Dr. Barton says it is the best
possible thing for you. It is only to say yes, my dear, my
exquisite Miss Lamb, and see what a prospect of happiness
opens before us." And once again he held out the rosebud to
her in his yellow hand.

"Do get up, Mr. Emsworth," she said impatiently," "you
will catch the rheumatism if you kneel there much longer."
And then, as he rose, somewhat creakily to his feet, "I can say,
with truth, that I have never been so surprised in my life.
That you—you of all people should make me such an offer,"
she paused for a moment, remembering all the bitterness of
their first encounter, then continued : "I am only sorry that
when you consulted so many other people about this project of
yours, you did not think to consult me. Mr. Emsworth, I
would not marry you if you were the last man on earth."

The rose dropped to the ground. "Miss Lamb!" He was angry now and she changed her tone suddenly. Fool that she was, she was in no position to make an enemy of this foolish man. She rose and held out her hand to him: "Forgive me, Mr. Emsworth, I spoke in haste. You have surprised me so much with this flattering proposal that I did not think what I was saying. But I am sure that if you think a little, you will be grateful for my refusal. How can I think of marrying, plunged, as you yourself have said, as I am in mystery? No, no, I will not take advantage of your goodness so, nor let you live to regret it as you must do. Suppose I was to remember? Suppose you were to find yourself married to a servant maid, or—who knows—something worse. The bishop is very kind, Dr. Barton very encouraging, but I will not so risk your happiness and my own. Just think who you might find were your parents-in-law!"

"Of course," he admitted, "I had thought of that. But, Miss Lamb, your beauty, your virtue, your many qualifications to be a clergyman's wife. . . ."

He was winding himself up for another set speech but she cut him short: "I shall never forget your goodness, Mr. Emsworth, but, believe me, it is impossible. I cannot think of it, nor can I imagine how the bishop came to give his consent."

"It is true:" Thoughtfully. "I did have some difficulty in persuading him. And you really think you might remember?"

"At any moment," she said untruthfully. "And, just think, Mr. Emsworth, I might be quite a different person when I have. I might care nothing for good works and think only of dress and amusement. Then where would you be?"

"Do you truly think so?"

"I am almost sure of it. Look what I am doing now. This is no charitable work I am busy with: I am sewing for myself. I am vain, Mr. Emsworth; I am frivolous. In my heart, I am sure of it."

He took a step backwards. "Miss Lamb, I do not know what to say."

She held out her hands to him. "Let us shake hands, then, and part friends. Mark my words; you will live to be grateful to me."

Taking her hand in his clammy one. "I believe that I am so

already. And," he looked nervous, "shall we say nothing of this?"

"Nothing."

He took his leave so hurriedly that she rather suspected he was afraid that even now, at the last moment, she might change her mind and decide to accept his rash offer. Alone, she allowed herself the luxury of laughter at the absurdity of the scene, but was interrupted, almost at once, by the appearance of Lady Heverdon.

"What, still at work! What a diligent girl you are to be sure. But I am positive you would rather be interrupted by me than by that petrified bore of a vicar. Did he tell you the news of the election, or was he too busy with his canting talks of blankets and the Holy Ghost? I cannot bear that man."

Marianne could not help laughing. "He is not exactly charming, poor Mr. Emsworth." What a blessing that Lady Heverdon had not arrived a few minutes sooner. "But what is the news of the election?"

"As bad as possible, in Exton at least. No wonder poor Mauleverer was so glum yesterday. The election—and the Reform Bill, are all in all to him, are they not?"

"He is certainly very much concerned about them." Marianne thought she knew what was in Lady Heverdon's mind. The beauty, she was sure, had decided that Mauleverer had delayed his proposal until the election was over. Well, it was very likely true, but no affair of hers. She bent assiduously to her sewing, and Lady Heverdon wandered away to pick herself a nosegay, returning, however, to complain of the heat of the sun and the tedium of the day. "I declare, it is going on for ever. I told Mauleverer last night that he would owe me the most devoted attention when this election was over, and indeed I do not mean to spare him. Heigh ho, what a dead bore politics are. But when it's over I intend to take him about the countryside on a series of visits: I am quite scandalized to find how little he is known in the district. That poor old card-sharping mother of his has been, I think, more of a liability to him than he has quite recognized." Her tone, said, more clearly than words, that when her time came she would change all this. "But he is generous to a fault," she went on, "and too good-hearted to see what all the world does. Do you not find him the most handsome of men, Miss Lamb?"

"With that scar?" Marianne bit off her thread. "Hardly."

"Oh, you are a hopeless rationalist! You need to see with the eyes of the soul, as I do, to recognize Mauleverer's real worth. Do you know what Merritt thought fit to call us yesterday?"

"No?"

" 'Beauty and the Beast.' Poor Mauleverer, he would scarcely be flattered if he knew, though truly I do not think he cares a jot about his appearance. Only look at the way he dresses. Fenner said he would be ashamed to let his groom wear one of my poor Mauleverer's coats. But I intend to get him to Weston when we go to London, and then we shall see. It is almost sinful to do so little with so elegant a figure. Truly, I think him the best built man I know, and you are at liberty to tell him I said so."

"I shall scarcely have the opportunity," said Marianne dryly.

"Why not? Don't think I am not aware of those early morning colloquies of yours, and indeed you seem made to be a confidante. I have no doubt you know everyone's secrets in this house, so quiet as you are, and so demure."

"Secrets?" Marianne laughed. "I know what Mr. Mauleverer hopes to get for his hay this season, and when he means to begin the wheat harvest."

"There you are! Indispensable Miss Lamb. I do not know how we shall manage without you." And then, conscious of having said more than she had intended, she hummed a few bars of "Dost thou remember" and moved away across the garden, bending gracefully as she went to pick here a pink and there a sprig of lavender for her bouquet. Left alone, Marianne sewed strenuously for a few minutes. The engagement must be as good as settled after all, or surely Lady Heverdon would never speak so definitely. And her doom, too, was sealed: "I do not know how we shall manage without you." Well, it was only what she expected, but this recollection did not make the certainty any less unpleasant. How happy, after all, she had been in this big, rambling ill-organized house, where she had found so much to do, and so many friendly faces. No wonder the idea of leaving it was so painful to her. But leave it she was sure she must, and she resolved that however bad Mauleverer's mood might be this evening she must steel herself to making her request about the bay mare.

Afternoon drowsed into evening. The shutters that had kept the drawing room cool all day were thrown back. The changing bell rang, and still there was no sign of Mauleverer. Conferring with the cook as to the advisability of keeping dinner back, Marianne lingered as long as she dared in the kitchen, hoping that she might see Mauleverer ride into the stable yard. But it was no use; Mrs. Manning was becoming restless and thinking of her sauces, and there was no further excuse to stay. She ran upstairs to change and she was standing at her open window, brushing her hair in the last glow of the sun when Mauleverer rode into the stable yard. Her first instinct was to draw back into the shadows, but already he had glanced up and seen her there, her hair loose about her face, the brush in her hand.

"We are beaten Miss Lamb. Horribly beaten!"

"Oh, dear, by very much?" She leaned down to hear him better.

"Deplorably! And I am equally late and shall be in blackest disgrace." He jumped down from his horse. "Make what apologies you can for me, Miss Lamb." He was gone and she returned to her mirror to pin up her hair with hands that, absurdly, trembled. Why was her colour so high, her eyes so bright? It was relief, of course, that Mauleverer was bearing defeat so well. But then, she should have known he would.

She tapped on Mrs. Mauleverer's door to deliver her son's apologies, although she very much doubted whether it was mainly for his mother that they were intended, and then went on to Lady Heverdon's room, only to find that she had already gone downstairs. Following, she found her arranging the sweet-scented bouquet she had picked that afternoon in a vase in the drawing room, scattering, as she did so, a little storm of water drops on the polished mahogany. She made a charming picture, Marianne thought, with her curls brushing the flowers as she arranged them. Now, hearing the door open, she started, coloured, turned and said, in tones of purest disappointment: "Oh, it is you, Miss Lamb?"

"Yes. Mr. Mauleverer send his apologies: he is but now returned, but will be with us directly."

"And the election?" Lady Heverdon had lost interest in her task and dropped the flowers on the table.

"Lost."

"Oh, dear," Lady Heverdon made the face of a frustrated child, then turned, suddenly wreathed in smiles as the door opened once more and Mauleverer appeared. "Oh, my poor Mauleverer," she went towards him, hands outstretched, "I hear that we are to condole with you."

"Why, yes," he took her hands and smiled down at her. "But it is not the end of the world you know. We have lost a battle, but not, I think, the war."

"And what, pray do you mean by that?"

"Why, that the news from the rest of the country is very different. Exton has merely proved, what I have always known, that it is not fit to send a member to Parliament—at least not under the present system. But the wind of change is blowing irresistibly elsewhere. We shall have, I think, an immense majority in the new House, and should carry all before us."

"Ah! how exciting!" As she looked up at him, blue eyes wide with enthusiasm, Marianne was amused to remember her heartfelt sigh that afternoon: "Heigh-ho, what a dead bore politics are." There was no doubt about it, she was a most consummate actress. No wonder if Mauleverer was fooled to the top of his bent. Anyone would have thought that the results of the election were the most important thing in the world to her. But she was spared the necessity for any further demonstration of enthusiasm by the entry of Mrs. Mauleverer, who had, Marianne now realized, lingered to the very last to avoid the possibility of a tete-à-tête with her son. Of course, they had not met since yesterday's painful scene over the card table. But it was all forgotten now in the excitement of the election news and the little flurry of walking in to dinner. When they were safely settled, with Lady Heverdon, as usual, at Mauleverer's right hand, she bent towards him with her sparkling smile. "I am to be a petitioner to you," she said, "on Miss Lamb's account."

"Miss Lamb?" A puzzled frown drew the black eyebrows together.

"Why, yes. She is too modest, I believe, to speak up for herself, but she has had her eye, this age, on that bay mare that eats her head off in your stables."

"The bay mare, Sadie?" He sounded more puzzled than ever, and darted a quick characteristically irritable glance at Marianne.

"Yes. She has decided she is a horsewoman and wishes to show us her form. I am sure you can have no objection?"

"Of course not, if Miss Lamb wishes to ride. Indeed, I cannot think why we have not thought of it sooner. But not on the bay mare, Miss Lamb," at last he was speaking to her directly. "She is no mount for a lady."

"And I am no lady." Marianne was irrationally furious at having her request thus anticipated.

He laughed. "I'll not argue that point with you, but if you will meet me in the stables tomorrow morning I will see if I cannot find something for you to ride."

"Jim Barnes says the mare needs exercising," she said mutinously.

"I daresay he does, but that does not mean you shall be allowed to risk your life on her until I have seen you on something safer." His tone was final and he turned the subject to a lively discussion with Lady Heverdon of their plans for the next day, his first, as she said, of freedom since she had been his guest. She proposed at once that they should ride over and call on her friend the Countess, but when he countered with a suggestion that he should take her for a promised ride around the boundaries of his estates, she agreed with a pretty waiving of her own plan: "We will survey every bush and every briar, pat the children on the heads and comfort all the poverty-stricken old women. Only that I am sure there is no poverty on your estates."

"I am very much afraid that there is, and indeed I am grateful to you for agreeing so readily to my plan for tomorrow, since there are, in fact, some houses my bailiff wishes me to look at. It is not only that the tenants do not pay their rent. He tells me that they live absolutely like pigs and are destroying the property, but I cannot find it in my conscience to turn them out without visiting them first myself."

"Quite right," she said approvingly, "but nor must you endure such sad tenants. Lord Heverdon was always strictness itself in questions of rent; he found it was the only way that would answer. Give those sort of people an inch, and they will take an ell, and not respect you for it either."

"Very true; and yet I rather hate to turn some of these people out. The Martins particularly have been here since time out of mind, and, what binds me to them still more, he served in my regiment at Waterloo. And a fine soldier he was; I cannot understand why he has been so unlucky since. Boxall has found him quite unemployable, and he is reduced, I believe, to breaking stones on the roads."

Marianne, who had been listening eagerly, could no longer keep silent: "Yes," she interrupted, "and for two and sixpence a week! Do you wonder if he gets something behind with his rent? And have you ever asked Boxall why he found him unemployable, Mr. Mauleverer?"

"Why, no, I do not propose to keep a bailiff, and bark myself. But what are you insinuating, Miss Lamb?"

His tone was very far from encouraging, but Marianne did not care. The Martin children were the star pupils of her little class and had shyly taken her home to the clean-scrubbed, penuriously poor little house where she had met and respected their haggard parents. It had taken some time before the full story of their misfortunes had come out, but she knew it now, and had been waiting for an opportunity to tell it to Mauleverer. This was not a good one, she knew, but she could not let them be evicted without a word. "You know very little about village affairs," she said now, "if you do not know that Martin and his wife were betrothed before he went for a soldier—at your suggestion, I believe."

"Yes." His voice was dry. "Does that make me responsible for whatever hobble he makes of his later life?"

"Well—I suppose that is a matter for your conscience. What I suspect you do not know is what happened when he finally returned—and, you know, it is not easy for a private soldier to extricate himself from the army as it is for the gentry. He did not get home for several years, having served in the Army of Occupation in Paris. He wrote, however, faithfully to his Jenny, in care of the Hall, since she was working here at the time. But she had none of his letters. And Boxall wooed her vigorously himself, suggesting that Martin must be dead, since there was no word from him. She had at last agreed to an engagement when Martin walked into the village one morning. He had been discharged at last on grounds of disability with some pitiful sum as compensation for all he had suffered for his country. Jenny proved faithful—but perhaps it would have been better for them both if she had not. She broke her engagement to Boxall and married Martin on the spot . . . and Boxall has found him 'unemployable' ever since.''

Mauleverer's face was dark with anger. "You are accusing my bailiff of dishonesty, Miss Lamb.''

"Not exactly. Or, at least, not in regard to you. I think him an admirable man at his job—and where his private feelings are not concerned. But I do not think him a sound judge in the case of the Martins, who, by the way, are my friends. Their children are the most promising in my little class. Given a chance, they might do anything, but what will happen to them if you turn their father out of his cottage? There is no other house in the village—and you know that no other village will have him, circumstanced as he is. It will mean the work-house, and the death of hope. Only give them a year's grace and I promise you the oldest boy will be earning enough to pay their rent : he has a perfect genius for figures, if only he had the time to study, but he works in the fields so long as it is daylight, and his sisters, too, when they can find work. You never saw a more hard working or a more devoted family.'' She paused, amazed at her own temerity. "I . . . I am sorry. I have talked too much. But I do beg, Mr. Mauleverer, that you will see the Martins and judge for yourself before you evict them merely on Boxall's recommendation.''

"You are a good friend, Miss Lamb, and I will certainly do so.'' His voice was kinder now, but Lady Heverdon broke in impatiently. "Only remember, Miss Lamb, that Mr. Mauleverer merely promises to judge for himself. He cannot be keeping all the rag tag and bobtail of the parish merely because they have 'promising children.' A landlord has a duty to himself, nor do I believe it a good thing, on the whole, to pamper the poor.''

"Do you call two and sixpence a week pampering?'' Marianne could not help the exclamation, but was relieved when it was lost in the little rustle caused by Mrs. Mauleverer's rising to remove to the drawing-room. Once settled in her favourite armchair, she began to cross-examine Marianne about the fate of the Martins—"I remember her well; one of the best girls I ever had in the house. Are they really so wretched?''

"I am afraid so.'' It was incredible to Marianne that her patroness should not have known, but then she had always been amazed at the little interest Mrs. Mauleverer took in village affairs. She was going on to tell her a little more about the Martins, in the hopes of getting Mrs. Martin work as a seamstress at the Hall, when Lady Heverdon broke in: "Oh, Miss Lamb, a truce to your Martins, I beg you. I hope I am as hearty a philanthropist as the next person, but really to have one draggle-tailed family providing the topic of conversation for all of dinner, and then afterwards too, is more than enough. Favour, us, instead, with some of your delicious music, I beg you."

So Marianne was firmly fixed at the piano when Mauleverer joined them and she spent the evening as she had so many others, providing background music for the running flirtation carrying on between host and guest. Mrs. Mauleverer slumbered peacefully in her chair; Marianne passed from Haydn to Beethoven to Auber, and Mauleverer and Lady Heverdon, heads close together on the sofa, talked and laughed as if they were alone in the room. It was a relief when Mrs. Mauleverer nodded at last into wakefulness, announced that she was worn out with the exertions of the day and thus gave the cue for everyone to retire.

Marianne was up betimes next morning and found, to her satisfaction, that the riding habit, now altered, aired and pressed looked better than she had dared hope. She found Mauleverer already in the breakfast-room, drinking green tea and reading the latest report of the Corn Committee. "You have a good day for your riding lesson." His smile always made one forget the disfiguring scar.

"Yes—but I do not expect it to be a lesson. I am positive that I can ride." She helped herself to scrambled eggs and took her usual place at the end of the table.

"Memory is a curious thing. You still have no clue as to who you are?"

"Not the slightest." There was comfort in this admission, on his part, that at last he accepted her loss of memory as genuine. "And yet I do remember so many things—like being able to ride, and play the piano. . . ."

"Yes—but stranger even than that is the fact than no inquiries have been made for you or the child. I know you did not wish us to advertise on your behalf—though I begin to wonder whether I did right in agreeing to the ommission— but surely your friends must be looking for you?"

"Perhaps I have no friends."

He smiled again. "It seems unlikely. But one thing did occur to me: Suppose that, all the time, you are French."

"French?"

"Why, yes. I know you speak it as well as English. And your name—Marianne—could as well be French as English. Had you not thought of that?"

"No, I confess I had not. You mean I am a refugee—a member of the families that left with Charles X last summer?"

"Exactly. It would explain much that is baffling about your position . . . particularly the irrational terror from which you say you suffer. Last year's July revolution in France was not, it is true, to be compared for frightfulness with the scenes that were enacted there at the end of the last century, but it must have carried, just the same, its burden of terror, just because of those earlier horrors. I am more and more convinced that this is the answer. How shall you like to find yourself French, Mademoiselle?"

"I do not know. . . . It is true, it seems a logical explanation . . . and equally true that I do, sometimes, find myself actually thinking in French, as if I had at least grown up talking both languages—but, no, it does not seem right somehow."

He rose. "Well, no need to look so anxious. If you have truly lost all your friends for good, at least you have found new ones and just as eager, I hope, to serve you. As for this idea of yours that if you ride about the district like a heroine in a romance, someone will rise from under a hedge, crying, 'Thrice welcome, long lost daughter,' frankly, I do not set much store by it. But I am sure the riding will do you good. We have kept you, I fear, somewhat selfishly mewed up here looking after our affairs." An angry retort to his remark about the romantic heroine had sprung to her lips, but she suppressed it with an effort. Of course he thought her ridiculous, but this was no moment to be irritating him. She preceded him, in somewhat chilly silence, to the stable yard, where, to her surprise, three horses were awaiting them, two with side-saddles. One of these was the neat little grey that Lady Heverdon had brought with her, the other the big bay mare with the dubious reputation.

Mauleverer, too, looked surprised. "What is this?" he asked the groom, "I gave no orders about the bay."

"No, sir, but Lady Heverdon sent word to say that she will ride too."

And indeed at this moment Lady Heverdon herself made her appearance, resplendent in a dark crimson habit that contrived, somehow, to suggest a hussar's uniform without any departure from feminine good taste. She hurried towards them : "Thank goodness, I am not too late. I would not have missed this for anything. Who knows, perhaps memory will come back, Miss Lamb, when once you are mounted?"

"I do not see why it should." Everything was going wrong this morning. She moved towards the big bay mare, but Lady Heverdon was ahead of her. "No, no, you must ride my gentle Zephyr. Do you not remember what Mr. Mauleverer said last night? I am not come to interfere in the lesson; merely to act as audience, and, perhaps to give the poor neglected bay some exercise."

"On the contrary," interposed Mauleverer, "you are not to ride her either. Do you think I intend to let you break your neck?"

An awkward little three-cornered discussion ended in the two ladies taking turns to trot demurely up and down the drive on Zephyr. It was maddening to Marianne, who had allowed herself visions of an invigorating canter over the moors with Mauleverer, but at least she proved to her own satisfaction, and his, that she could indeed ride. "Very well," he said at last. "I am satisfied, Miss Lamb. I only wish we could mount you at once, but I will make inquiries for a lady's horse—we should certainly have another one."

She protested, but, for the moment, fruitlessly. She had learned, by now, that a certain set to his jaw made further argument a waste of time. Besides, Lady Heverdon was reminding him of his promise to ride the bounds of the estate with her. "What a pity that Miss Lamb cannot accompany us."

Marianne watched them ride out of the yard side by side, then turned to the groom. "Well, Jim," she asked, "what do you think?"

He grinned at her. "I know what you're thinking well enough, miss," he said, "but I tell you it's as much as my job's worth to let you." The bay mare was being walked about the yard by a boy, tossing her head restlessly as she went. Marianne moved over to stroke her nose. "She's dying for it, Jim, and so am I. Just once down the drive and back; they are safe out of sight by now."

"And if you break your neck?"

"I shan't, and you know it. Why on earth should Mr. Mauleverer be getting another ladies' horse when poor old Sadie is eating her heart out for work? Come on, Jim, have a heart."

He grumbled—and yielded. After all, it had been his idea in the first place: "There's not a bit of vice in her, miss," he confided as he put her up. "It's only that she scared Mrs. Mauleverer once or twice, when, if I may say so, madam was a bit past it. She don't deserve her reputation, truly she don't, and if I've told the Master so once, I've told him a dozen times. But give a horse a bad name. . . ."

"I know." Marianne smiled down at him and was off. It was, as a matter of fact, a sufficiently exciting ride, since the mare was restive and she was out of practice, but they returned, at last, the best of friends.

"And now what?" asked Jim, as he helped her dismount.

Marianne knew exactly what he meant. It was all very well to have defied Mauleverer once, but how was she to break it to him that she had done so? "Leave it to me, Jim," she said, with a confidence she was very far from feeling.

"I should rather think I will, miss."

It had all taken a good deal longer than she had expected, and by the time she had caught up with her usual household tasks, she was a little late for her lesson in the village, and found her class of children awaiting her anxiously in their improvised schoolroom. "Us thought you was never coming, miss," the eldest Martin girl came forward to greet her. "On account of the mist."

"Mist? What do you mean, Sarah?"

"She'm coming down from the moor, miss. You'd best start home early tonight; her comes fast when she comes." And indeed as the class rose to recite their catechism Marianne noticed that the light was beginning to fail in the little room. She did not like to scamp the lesson, which was, she knew, the great treat of the week for many of these poverty-stricken children, but remembered that some of them had even further to walk home than she had. She therefore dismissed the class after half an hour, promising to make up the time next day if the fog lifted.

She hurried her farewells and started along the well-known footpath. The mist was already thick in patches, particularly along the little stream that ran through the village, but when she reached the long meadow she found it almost clear and walked briskly across it, rather enjoying the mysterious effect of the grey curtain that now completely concealed the rise of the moors. Noises were muffled too; sheep in the far meadow sounded melancholy and miles away and she had already lost any trace of the village. If the blacksmith was still at work down at the forge she could not hear him, nor yet the other village noises that usually sounded clearly to here, the barking dogs and shouts of children. The home wood, when she reached it, looked strange and almost sinister in the half light and she found herself, for a moment, oddly reluctant to climb the stile that led into it. But, pausing for a moment before she jumped down into the wood she looked back and saw that the mist seemed to be following her across the meadow. She had best not linger.

It was lucky she had taken this path so often, for it was almost dark in the wood, and she had to rely largely on her nimble feet and her memory to guide her. She hurried along, aware of the chill dampness in the air, and wondering whether Mauleverer and Lady Heverdon were returned from their ride yet. They would have but a dismal time of it, if not, and she was ashamed to find herself wondering whether Lady Heverdon might not be irritated into betraying the sharp side of her temper which, so far, she had contrived to keep hidden from her devoted host. She might be short-tempered with her maid and curt to Marianne: she was invariably all smiles for Mauleverer.

Thinking of this, Marianne forgot to watch the little path, caught her foot on a root, tripped and half fell. At the same instant, a shot rang out and something whistled above her head. She gave a cry of mixed anger and fright—for it had been a very narrow escape indeed—and stood, for a moment, recovering from the shock and listening for the sportsman's horrified apologies. Dead silence. And then, a rustling. Some-one was coming to see what had happened to her: not openly, with appalled exclamations, but quietly, secretly, nearer and nearer through the little wood. He was coming, as the shot had, from ahead of her, cutting her off from the Hall. Sud-denly, it was the terror all over again, and she reacted by

107

throwing herself off the path into the thickest of the wood. Even as she did so, she called herself absurd. She had merely disturbed a poacher who had taken advantage of the mist to try and add a rabbit or pheasant to his family's meagre diet. And yet—terror bade her be still, shivering, huddled among the thick branches of a yew tree.

She could hear nothing. Was the poacher coming along the path? Expecting, no doubt, to find her lying there injured? Or had he heard her flight! But then, surely, he would thank his lucky stars and go quietly home rather than risk being identified. The penalty for armed poaching was seven years' transportation; it would be a brave man who risked that merely to make sure she was not hurt. Ridiculous to have been so frightened. She was just going to emerge from her hiding place when, once more, she heard stealthy movement. It was very near now. Someone was moving cautiously, quietly, to and fro among the bushes. Looking for her, but not with any idea of succour. He was very close now and she buried her head in her arms in one swift silent movement so that the whiteness of her face should not betray her. Hardly breathing, she heard him go past, almost within reach. Then he was moving away again and she allowed herself a little breathless sigh of relief. He was quartering systematically through the wood on this side of the path : only the panicky impulse that had driven her deep into the prickly yew had saved her.

It was darker and very cold. She had no idea how long she had huddled in the yew tree's uncomfortable safety, but she knew that she was stiff and chilled to the bone. Her ankle hurt where she had twisted it in the fall that had saved her life. Her back was aching from the crouched position into which the unknown's approach had frozen her. How long must she stay here? Suddenly she lifted her head to listen eagerly. Yes, footsteps were approaching from the direction of the house. And this time there was nothing secret about them, they were quick, definite. She heard a dog bark and a moment later Mauleverer's favourite spaniel, Trixie, had burst into her hiding place.

She put her arms round the dog and burst into almost hysterical laughter then she heard Mauleverer's voice : "Here, Trixie, heel, you brute——" and then, "What's that? Miss Lamb?"

"Here." It was more difficult to get out of the yew tree than it had been to force her way in, and Mauleverer had found her by the time she emerged, with a last rending tear of calico skirts.

"Good God," he saw her white face by the light of the lantern he carried, then caught her in his left arm as her bad foot gave way under her, and she swayed towards him. For a moment she lay there, half conscious against him, grateful for the strength and safety of him, then felt, exquisitely, amazingly, his lips against the hair above her forehead. It was momentary, a butterfly touch, no more, but sent a thrill through her that brought astonished enlightenment. How long had she loved him? She stirred a little, then wished she had not, as he helped her, gently to stand up.

"You are hurt?" his voice was anxious, but otherwise just as usual. Could she have imagined that lightning, magic touch? "What in the world is the matter, Miss Lamb?"

She must seem lunatic, hiding here. "Someone shot at me!"

"A poacher? I heard the shot and thought I had best come to meet you, but, surely, not 'at you,' Miss Lamb." He was helping her gently back to the path as he spoke.

Already, in the safety of his arm, the terror seemed absurd, and yet—"I . . . I do not know," she said. "He only missed me because I tripped as he fired. And," she shivered, "then—he came looking for me, very quietly, in the darkness."

"To see what he had done, no doubt. Can you manage to walk, with my arm?" They were on the path now and she contrived to hobble along beside him. "I expect he wanted to see what harm he had done without being seen—none of the villagers would willingly hurt you, I am sure. But—it would mean death to have wounded you. . . ."

"I know . . . I suppose that must be it . . . and yet. . . ." Memory of the terror was all about her still, and she shivered against the warmth and comfort of his arm.

"Not much further now." He must have felt the tremor that ran through her. And then, "Lady Heverdon! You should not be out in this mist."

"I could not contain my anxiety any longer." Her figure loomed towards them. "Have you really found her." And then, "Good gracious, Miss Lamb, what can be the matter?"

She has had a close shave of it with a poacher, but is none

the worse I hope, or will not be when once we get her safely indoor and to a fire."

"A poacher! I told you it was not safe to be walking through the woods alone. But, poor Miss Lamb. Come, lean on me." And she took Marianne's other arm to help her into the house.

Once indoors, Lady Heverdon listened to Marianne's story with exclamations of horror, hardly allowing Mauleverer to fit in his brief, pertinent questions. No, Marianne answered him, she had not the slightest idea of the identity of her assailant, nor could she be absolutely certain that he had fired at her on purpose; it could easily be, as Lady Heverdon insisted, a poacher's accidental shot. "There not much we can do about it, in that case," said Mauleverer at last, "but I will at least have a few inquiries made in the village." And he left them alone to give his orders.

Lady Heverdon hung over Marianne anxiously. "You look worse and worse," she said, "and must let me help you to bed."

"I must thank Mr. Mauleverer properly."

"Be advised by me, and leave that till tomorrow, my dear. There will be time enough then, and, frankly, your appearance, though I hate to mention it, is not quite the thing for the drawing-room."

Thus reminded of her dishevelled state, Marianne submitted, though not with a very good grace to being helped upstairs. Once in her room, and suitably horrified by the white and scratched face in the mirror, she tried another protest: "But I shall be quite well enough to come down to dinner."

"Nonsense. Your ankle is swollen already; if you use it any more tonight you may well be laid up for weeks, and I know that would not suit you, so active as you are. No, no, let me be your messenger to Mauleverer tonight. I will thank him as prettily as possible on your behalf—though mind you I cannot think how he came to take so long to find you. I was getting quite anxious about both of you; he had been gone an age when I started out to meet you. I suppose he must have missed his way in the fog . . . or perhaps he had too much to think about. You are my good friend, are you not, Miss Lamb?"

"Why, yes?" She did not try to conceal surprise at the sudden question.

"I know you are, and shall therefore trust you with what

must remain a secret to the rest of the world—and even to Mrs. Mauleverer for some time longer. But I do not believe I even need to tell you; I have thought that your sharp eyes had pierced our secret this long time past, and, oh, it has been a relief not to have to act the indifferent in front of you."

Marianne's face had been white before, now it was chalky. "I do not understand you."

"Discreet Miss Lamb! I knew I could count on you. But between us it shall no longer be a secret, and, since I know how thoroughly you respect my beloved Mauleverer, I shall allow myself the luxury of talking freely to you about him. We dare not trust his mother with our secret, poor creature that she is, but you are another matter."

It must be true. And she—she must have imagined that brief, miraculous moment in the wood. Colour flooded her face. The wish, no doubt, had fathered the thought. But Lady Heverdon was gazing at her expectantly. She must say something. "But why the need for secrecy?"

"Can you ask that? And I so recently widowed, and then, so dreadfully afflicted by poor little Lord Heverdon's ghastly death? I cannot be talking of love and marriage for months yet; I am almost ashamed to be thinking of them, but how can I help myself? And, besides, Mauleverer is so masterful . . . so passionate . . . I do not know how I shall contrive to make him wait until I am out of mourning. You must help me, Miss Lamb, with your cool common sense; he has, he has told me, the greatest respect for your judgement. But what a selfish brute I am to stay prattling of my happiness when I can see you are fit for nothing but bed. Sleep well, my dear, and keep my secret for me. You are the only person in the world, besides us two, who knows it."

Marianne could eat none of the food that was brought her, and did not expect to be able to sleep either, but about nine o'clock Gibbs came tapping at her door with a mug of warm milk: "It will give you a good night's rest," she said. "Lady Heverdon thought you might need it."

It tasted strange—bitter, but Marianne drank it eagerly. She did not care what it contained, whether opium or laudanum. Lady Heverdon had been right; more than anything she needed the oblivion of sleep. In the morning, she would face her wretchedness.

8

THE drug Lady Heverdon had given Marianne was stronger than terror, stronger even than despair. She slept long and dreamlessly and woke to face harsh facts. No comfort anywhere. Mauleverer and Lady Heverdon were engaged. She had imagined everything—except her own love. There was nothing imaginary about that. Nor anything that bore thinking of. She jumped out of bed, found her ankle much better and dressed hurriedly.

Downstairs, the house was oddly quiet for so late an hour. She looked in to the morning-room and was amazed to find Mrs. Mauleverer, for whom it was not late but very early indeed.

"Ah, there you are, my dear," the old lady brightened when she saw her. "How glad I am to see you better. The house seems sadly dull and quiet, does it not, without them? They were disappointed not to see you before they left, and Mark left his particular commands that you were to take care of yourself and not be rambling about in the woods alone."

"They are gone?" Marianne controlled her voice with an effort.

"Yes, to London. Mark had letters from Lord Grey yesterday that made it essential he return at once, and Lady Heverdon decided to avail herself of his escort for the first part of her journey home. To tell you the truth, my dear, I am not altogether sorry to see her go. I am afraid it was sadly dull for her here, with Mark away so much of the time on his election business. I expect it will be easier. . . ." She let the sentence drag, but Marianne understood perfectly what she meant, and wondered whether she was right. It seemed to her most unlikely, from remarks that Lady Heverdon had let drop, that she would be any satisfaction to Mrs. Mauleverer as a daughter-in-law. Indeed, the old lady would be lucky if she contrived to avoid being put away in some asylum for the elderly. Pity for her kind friend made her almost forget her own misery and she devoted the morning to making her more cheerful, being rewarded, as they took their light luncheon together, by Mrs. Mauleverer's remark that it was "very pleasant and quite like old times."

For Marianne, in the quiet misery of that morning, it was hard to believe that anything would ever be pleasant again, but she was not one to sit down under misfortune. More than ever it was essential that she find some other shelter for herself and the child. Relieved that her ankle was so much better, she put on her riding habit after luncheon and descended on the stables.

Jim Barnes met her with a knowing look. "So he gave permission, did he, miss, before he left?"

She looked him straight in the eye. "I am here, am I not? Saddle her up for me, Jim."

"Shan't I ride with you, miss?"

"Good gracious no; you have other things to do than that."

"But what about the poachers?"

So the story was all about; she might have known it. She shrugged, "Lightning never strikes twice in the same place you know!" She hoped she was right, "Besides, you can tell everyone, Jim, that I have not the slightest idea who shot at me, so I am a danger to no one."

"You're a brave girl, miss, if you'll excuse my saying so."

Absurdly, she rode out of the stable yard with her eyes full of tears.

It was a hot still day with nothing stirring on the moor save sheep, and, above her, skylarks, but she noticed neither sunlight nor birdsong. She was free, at last, to give rein to the misery that had lain, all morning, heavy and cold about her heart. If Lady Heverdon's confidences last night had left my room for doubt as to the engagement, Mauleverer's joining her for the journey to London would have settled the question. Of course they were engaged, had been for the entire duration of her visit. Absurd not to have realized this sooner, and as for that moment of delusion in the wood last night . . . she coloured crimson merely at the recollection, her only consolation the thought that there was no way in which Mauleverer should have guessed at her shameful mistake.

It was unlucky for her that she should have reached this nadir of misery and let herself slump, self-condemned in the saddle, at the moment when an adder reared up in the path in front of Sadie. So far, the bay mare had borne her rider's in-attentiveness tolerably enough, but she had always been ter-rified of snakes. Now she started, shied, and bolted.

Jerked suddenly into wakefulness, Marianne hung on, but that was about all she could do. For a mad twenty minutes or so she forgot misery, terror, everything in her determination not to be thrown. It was, in a curious way, exhilerating to have suddenly simplified into this wild struggle for survival and when at last Sadie slowed from her mad gallop to a weary canter and then, at last, to a walk, Marianne's first feeling was almost one of disappointment. For a while, back there, in her terror of death, she had really been alive. . . .

She bent to pat the terrified and sweating horse and murmur soothing endearments to her. Then she looked around. It had been impossible, during their wild flight through the heather, to do more than realize that, mercifully, Sadie was keeping to one moorland path after another. Now she was completely lost. The moor rolled away on all sides; the sheep grazed, the larks sang. She had not the slightest idea which way to turn for home. Nor had she much inkling as to how far they had come in that wild rush, but it seemed unlikely that either of them would have the strength to get home without resting first. If Sadie was sweating and trembling, so was she.

They had reached a place where the grassy track forked in two, and she pulled Sadie to a halt for a moment to consider whether to go on or back. She had seen no sign of human habitation since they had left Mauleverer Hall. Surely, fairly soon now, there must be something—a village, a shepherd's hut, somewhere she could rest for a while and get advice about the shortest way home. She chose the slightly more marked of the two tracks and turned Sadie along it, congratulating herself, as she did so, on the fact that Sadie had not lamed herself. Then she would really have been in trouble. . . . Besides, it would be bad enough if it became necessary to confess to Mauleverer that she had taken the mare without permission and been run away with, without having to own to damaging her. But probably it would never come to that. The election was over; Lady Heverdon was in London; what reason was there for Mauleverer to return to the Hall?

She felt, suddenly, exhausted and it was with a sense of almost frantic relief that she saw, as Sadie laboured her way over a curve of the hill, a little wood below her, with chimneys sticking out of it, and a stream running down into a secluded valley. Twenty minutes of Sadie's dejected amble down the hill brought them into the little wood which turned out to be a tangle of neglected undergrowth, with long brambles trailing across the path and dead branches here and there, over which Sadie picked her way fastidiously. Marianne's heart sank. No smoke had been coming from the chimneys she had seen: could the house be deserted?

A few minutes later she sighed with relief and pulled Sadie to a standstill. They had pushed their way through the green fringes of the wood into a little clearing. Facing them stood a low, grey stone house, weather-beaten and moss-grown, but just the same unmistakably lived in. Windows stood open on to the sunshine; a faded green curtain had blown out of one of them and caught on the yellow rambler rose that climbed all over one end of the cottage—for it was little more. And, if further confirmation was needed that this remote clearing was actually inhabited, it was provided by a well-tended vegetable garden that lay between Marianne and the house. Neat rows of peas and beans ran with military precision towards the house; beyond them was a square bed netted for strawberries, and beyond that again a tangle of neglected herbaceous border with the tallest hollyhocks Marianne had ever seen.

It was very quiet in the clearing and Marianne suddenly had the feeling that she had moved out of the real world into some fantastic fairy tale where spellbound princesses were waited on by invisible hands. A cuckoo called somewhere in the wood, and a jay screeched farther off, but there were none of the little human noises that Marianne associated with life at Maulever Hall. No pail clinked, no dog barked, no quick, suppressed giggle spoke of the full life of the servants' hall. Sadie moved uneasily with a sudden clinking of harness and at the same moment Marianne became aware of a dark figure crouched under the strawberry netting and, apparently, quite unaware of their arrival. She jumped down, tied Sadie's reins to a tree and moved along beside the bean rows to the strawberry bed.

Now that she could see the crouching figure more clearly, its appearance chimed in remarkably with her fairy tale fantasy. Only this was not the princess but the witch, an old woman in rusty black who muttered to herself as she reached here and there among the leaves and dropped the rich red berries into the silver bowl she carried. Silver? Marianne rather thought it was; it certainly shone like silver, in contrast to the old woman's straggling hair and shabby, old-fashioned dress. The hands that worked among the strawberry leaves were brown and tough as a village woman's; the face was turned away from Marianne.

"Excuse me, ma'am." Marianne's voice sounded odd to her.

The old woman took no notice and Marianne tried again, louder: "I beg your pardon, ma'am——"

The old woman straightened up, as far as she could under the strawberry netting, turned round and saw Marianne standing a few feet away from her. "Dear me." She emerged from the strawberry nets and stood for a moment considering Marianne out of faded blue eyes that looked remarkably bright and intelligent in the tanned face. "Am I supposed to be expecting you?"

Marianne had been too much surprised by her voice to speak sooner. She had taken it for granted that this shabby looking old creature with the wild white hair and tattered black shawl would speak in the broadest Devon, but her clipped consonants and drawled vowels were pure Mayfair. Her face, too, was a surprise. Weatherbeaten to the quality of old leather and marked with the calm of age, it nevertheless had a quality quite absent from the old faces Marianne was used to in the village. There were lines of humour round the eyes, and of command round the mouth; this was not just an old woman; it was a person. And she was still looking inquiringly at Marianne.

"I . . . I beg your pardon, ma'am, for intruding on you like this, but I have lost my way on the moors," she said.

"You will have to speak louder than that, child, if I am to hear you," said the old woman calmly. "I have been deaf these fifteen years and more."

"I . . . I am so sorry." Marianne repeated her explanation, pitching her voice on the high note she had found answered with the deaf old women in the village.

"Good," the voice held approval. "Lost your way have you? Horse bolted with you by the look of things? Not hurt are you? Or the horse?"

"No, but tired—and so is Sadie."

"Bring her round the front then. She can eat the lawn for me, while I find something better for you. Begin with a strawberry?" She held out the bowl.

"Thank you." It was silver, and antique, curiously chased silver at that.

"Think me crazy, do you? But why? It's unbreakable, which is more than you can say for my pudding basins. No joke getting replacements out here, I can tell you. But you look exhausted, bring your horse and come." She hitched up her black skirts to reveal a pair of military-looking Hessian boots and led the way around the edge of the vegetable garden, past the riotous herbaceous border to the front of the house. Here a neglected lawn, rather like a hayfield, stretched from the little stream right up to the front of the house. To Marianne's relief, she saw that a well-beaten path crossed the lawn and lost itself in the tangled wood beside the stream. This was clearly the way back to civilization.

For the moment she let Sadie loose in the rich grass of the lawn and followed her ancient guide to the front door that stood hospitably open among more climbing roses. Inside, the house bore a curious resemblance to its owner. Here, too, were odd contrasts and strange contradictions. A Persian carpet lay on the brick floor; a rough wheelbacked chair was drawn up to a delicate lady's writing desk; a charming little book-case, full of leather volumes, stood on top of a plain deal chest. The odd and charming effect of the whole was accentuated by the silver vases that stood everywhere, all of them full of buxom sweet-scented country roses.

"Sit down," the old woman gestured Marianne to a delicate little sofa whose upholstery had faded to a strange silver grey. Then she raised her voice to an eldritch screech: "Mary, Mary, where have you got to now? We have a visitor."

A door to the back of the house popped open and another old woman put her head round it. "A visitor?" This voice was rich cockney. Compared with her mistress, this old woman might almost pass as young; her face was unlined and her figure robust in the striped cotton gown and voluminous apron. "A visitor?" she said again, "well bless us and keep us all and where did she spring from?"

"From the moor. And that will be enough talk, Mary. We will have a luncheon at once. Our guest is exhausted."

117

"A luncheon? Dinner more like at this hour and there's nought in the house but cold meat, my lady."

"Then off with you and bring it, and don't 'my lady' me," said her mistress. Then, turning to Marianne. "I know you will not want to stay for anything more elaborate, since your parents must already be anxious about you. Now, tell me about yourself. Where do you come from? Who are you? And what are your family thinking of to let you be riding about the moor, alone on a bolting horse."

Marianne smiled at the brisk, imperative string of questions, but set herself to answer them as simply as she could. "My name is Marianne Lamb," she began, "I am companion to Mrs. Mauleverer of Maulever Hall. And it was my fault, not Sadie's. I was not thinking what I was doing, and an adder startled her."

"You must be a good rider. Companion eh? I've heard of Mrs. Mauleverer. Plays cards, don't she? Has a son who never got over being scarred at Waterloo. But good enough sort of people; none of your jumped up second generation gentry. You might have done worse for yourself. Lamb, you said? Marianne? Mother reading French books? Or just Jane Austen? Well, one thing, it won't take you much more than an hour to reach Maulever Hall by road—that is if that mare of yours can still go. Ought to have a rub down really, but there's only me and Mary. Mary's scared silly of horses, and I'd rather talk to you. Pretty girls don't drop into my garden every day, and it's pleasant to talk to someone I can hear. Ah! food; thank you, Mary, that will do. Don't want to hurry you, my dear, but best eat fast and be on your way or they'll have the search parties out from Maulever Hall. Come back another day and tell me what you're doing tied to Mrs. Mauleverer's apron strings."

"I'd like to." Marianne found herself enormously drawn to this ugly old woman, with her sharp eyes and her oddly mannish way of talking. "If you're sure I won't be a nuisance."

"Nuisance! I should think not. Came down here for solitude; that's true enough; but that was twenty years ago, and I had a broken heart for company. Forgotten what it felt like now, but occupying, I remember, very occupying. I missed it for a while. . . . Quiet in the country. Mary said, why not go back to town, but I ask you, why? Can't leave the garden for

118

one thing—always something to do there—have some strawberries? No? Well then, best be going, if you've the strength, and you look to have. Not a town girl either, are you? Knew it at once. Yes, do come again, my dear, I'd like it."

Slightly dazed, Marianne listened to her curt but lucid directions as to the best way back to Maulever Hall and then rose to take her leave. "I do not know how to thank you, Lady ..." she paused expectantly.

"Lady Fiddlesticks! I thought I'd got Mary trained out of it at last, but she's obstinate as they come. I ask you : Lady Gardener of Mud Hall? Or Lady Boots and Barrows?" She had, in fact, kicked off her Hessian boots on entering the house, but now put them on again to see Marianne to the road. "Call me Mrs. Bundy. It will do. I suppose you can mount the brute unaided?"

"If you've a garden bench I can use."

"There's an old tree trunk I sit on between chores."

Safely in the saddle, Marianne bent once more to thank her hostess, whose real name she did not seem likely to learn. But, "Come again," said Mrs. Bundy.

Riding slowly homeward, Marianne was amazed to find that for a little while she had forgotten her wretchedness. Mrs. Bundy had had a broken heart once—twenty years ago—and had forgotten what it felt like. Hard to imagine. But, I must visit her again, she thought.

She was very late for dinner and found Mrs. Mauleverer hovering somewhere between anxiety and irritation; the anxiety genuine, if querulous, the irritation carefully fomented, Marianne suspected, by her patient enemy, Martha. She kept her explanation as brief as possible and did not mention the fact that Sadie had run away with her, merely saying that she had lost her way on the moors and stopped for directions. For some reason that she did not, herself, quite understand, she made no mention of her odd, engaging hostess, letting Mrs. Mauleverer think that she had merely stopped at some remote moorland farm.

It was nearly a week before Marianne found time to pay another visit to the cottage in the valley where she was received like an old and welcome friend by both Mary and her mistress. The strawberries were finished, but as she helped her new friend gather raspberries she found herself talking more freely than she had expected to about her own circumstances. Mrs. Bundy was a good listener and if she deduced a good deal from Marianne's few and guarded references to Mauleverer and Lady Heverdon she did not show it, concentrating her questions on the point of Marianne's identity. "So you are riding about the countryside hoping someone will recognize you? Optimistic, don't you think? There's been no hue and cry that I've heard of, and, recluse that I am, I hear most things. It's odd—very odd. But you're well enough where you are, hey?"

"Oh yes." Marianne knew she did not sound quite convinced.

"If not; come here. Always welcome. Plenty to do in the garden. You'd be bored, of course, but there are worse fates. No, no, don't make a song and dance about it; just come, any day, if you want to. Mary likes you too; so no problem there; said so only the other day. There, that's enough of those and my back's breaking. Not so young as I was, you know: can't stoop, can't carry, can't sleep—deuced boring, old age, if you ask me. Let's go and have lunch."

After that, Marianne rode over to the cottage at least once a week. There was always a warm welcome for her, and plenty of satisfactory talk. Mrs. Bundy might call herself a recluse, but she kept very much in touch with the world beyond her valley. All the latest books and papers found their way to the little house and Marianne enjoyed listening to her acute comments on the latest article in the *Edinburgh* or the *Quarterly Reviews*. She was keenly interested in politics too, and amazed Marianne by her brilliant thumbnail sketches of such leading political figures as Grey, or Wellington, or Althorp. She spoke with authority, and Marianne was all the more delighted by an occasional flattering reference to Mauleverer's backstage work for the Reform Bill. She must, Marianne realized, have many and faithful correspondents in London to be so thoroughly *au courant* with affairs there, and she was often tempted to ask Mary who she really was, but refrained. If her kind hostess wished to remain Mrs. Bundy, she must be allowed to do so.

Meanwhile, summer was drawing towards autumn. Corn was stacked in the fields and the first of September had brought the neighbouring gentry out with their guns. Mrs. Mauleverer hoped daily that her son would come down for a few days' shooting. But his Reform Bill was still being discussed in committee of the House of Commons. Marianne did not expect him. What she was waiting for was the mysteriously still-deferred announcement of his engagement to Lady Heverdon. Even if her state of mourning precluded its public anouncement, surely it was time he told his mother about it. There had been, in fact, only one brief note from him since he had returned to London and that had been mainly concerned with the things he had left behind him in his sudden departure from the Hall. Of course, it had fallen to Marianne to make up a parcel of several cambric shirts, two velvet waistcoats and a file of papers about the Exton election. If she dropped two angry tears into the parcel before sealing it up, that was her own affair.

Lady Heverdon, on the other hand, had written Mrs. Mauleverer a long double letter, lavishly crossed in a hand so delicate and spidery that Mrs. Mauleverer had thrown it to Marianne ordering her to read it aloud: "If you can make it out, that is."

It seemed to consist largely of a chronicle of the vicissitudes of her journey back to London, with the word "we" very much to the fore, and left Marianne with just the picture she had expected of sociable nights spent with Mauleverer by the roaring fires of country inns. There was no actual mention of Mauleverer, but when Lady Heverdon said that "we found it impossible to make ourselves hurry," it was obvious enough what she meant. Every day, when the mail came, Marianne steeled herself for the inevitable announcement of the engagement, and every day suffered the pangs of exquisite disappointment.

Meanwhile, her own suitor had not been idle. She had thought she had given poor Mr. Emsworth such a set-down, that day in the cutting garden, that he would never trouble her again, but she had, it seemed, very much mistaken her man. He had kept away from her for a week or so after her refusal, but then the old encounters began again. She could not object to his visiting her bible class, since it was conducted under his auspices, but she hated the way he insisted on seeing her home after it, with jocose remarks about poachers and his anxiety on her behalf. Worse still, he had visited Maulever Hall when she was out riding one day and had contrived to enlist Mrs.

Mauleverer on his side. The old lady dearly loved a romance, whether in three volumes or in real life, and refused to believe that Marianne was entirely unmoved by her suitor's devotion. It would be, she hinted, the most satisfactory possible conclusion to Marianne's adventures. "Of course, I would miss you grievously, my dear, but, after all, it is not as if you would be going far. And the vicarage is a very good sort of house indeed. It has four reception rooms, if you count that tiny front room, and I am not sure how many bedrooms, but enough for the kind of family a clergyman can afford. Mr. Emsworth has no expectations, it is true, but the living is his for life—truly, child, you could do much worse."

It is always disconcerting to find oneself less indispensable than one had thought, and Marianne found Mrs. Mauleverer's persistent urging of Emsworth's suit increasingly trying. The last straw came one windy morning when they were busy putting the summer's crop of dried lavender into bags—a ladylike occupation which Mrs. Mauleverer particularly enjoyed. "I have written Mark about you know what, my dear." Mrs. Mauleverer tied a neat bow of purple satin ribbon round a bag and put it on one side. "I am sure he will agree that it is the very best thing you can do. I told him how much I should miss you: I really think I should have to have a little excursion—to Cheltenham or maybe even Bath to recover the tone of my spirits. If you were to be married at Michaelmas I could make an autumn tour of it, before the roads get too bad. I am sure Mark will think that best: I explained to him that you were hanging off merely for my sake and that such a plan, if he were to propose it, would leave you free to follow the dictates of your heart."

Marianne could hardly believe her ears: "You told him that?"

"What a pretty blush! If Mr. Emsworth could only see you now . . . he would renew his suit at once. But there is no need to be in such a fidget, my dear. After all, Mark is in some sort in the position of your guardian, strangely circumstanced as you are. And you may be sure I gave you every credit for propriety of behaviour. Naturally you were quite right to refuse Mr. Emsworth when he came to you so unprepared, but the case will be quite other when he comes to you with my sanction and Mark's, which I daily expect. Of course, best of all, as I told Mark, would be for him to come down and play a father's part in seeing Mr. Emsworth on your behalf. Not of course, that you are in a position to demand much in the way of settlements, but what is reasonable I am sure Mark would get for you."

"My dear madam," Marianne could not contain herself no longer, "I do beg you will write Mr. Mauleverer again and tell him there is not the slightest necessity for him to be putting himself out on my behalf. I am only sorry that you have so misled him. I have told you, surely, often enough, that this is no question of maidenly coyness on my part. Can you honestly remember how Mr. Emsworth treated me at our first meeting, and still imagine that I could, for a moment, consider marrying him? I told him when he spoke to me that I would not marry him if he was the last man on earth, and I mean it."

"Tut, tut," said Mrs. Mauleverer. "Methinks the lady doth protest to much. Poor Mr. Emsworth, how long, I wonder, will it take him to live down that deplorable mistake of his— and that reminds me of another point that Mark might be instrumental in settling for you: there is the question of the child. I do not quite know how Martha would bear to part with him, and, truly, Mr. Emsworth has never seemed particularly eager to take charge of him. . . . But Mark will know what is best to do; he always does. If only he would come, that is, but frankly, I have no great hopes of it, what with that miserable bill, and Lady Heverdon still in London when one would have thought she would have been visiting some of her fine friends, like those discourteous Lashtons. Do you not think it monstrous that the Countess has never invited me to visit her?"

Marianne thought it entirely understandable, considering the awkward circumstances attendant upon the Countess's visit to Maulever Hall, but this minor irritation was lost in her major annoyance over Mrs. Mauleverer's totally misleading letter to her son. She was almost enraged to the point of sitting down and writing him, herself, to explain how matters really stood, but how could she? If he came down, she would have to explain herself in person, but, as Mrs. Mauleverer had said, it seemed most unlikely that he would do so or, indeed, that he would take any notice of what must, she told herself, seem to him a trivial matter and no concern of his.

In the meanwhile, she did her best to disabuse Mrs. Maulerer of her *idée fixe* by being curt to the point of rudeness to Mr. Emsworth when he called next morning on a transparent pretext connected with his tithing day. The result of this was very far from being what she had hoped or intended. Having finished the business that brought him, Mr. Emsworth turned suddenly to Mrs. Mauleverer: "My dear madam, I have a request—a humble petition to make to you. My dear— may I say adored Miss Lamb is angry with me, and, I fear, with cause. I have been waiting, on your hint, for some word of sanction—of approval from Mr. Mauleverer, whose word must, of course, be law with me. Indeed, were I to think that the alliance I am contemplating might be unpleasing to him, I would stifle the passion that beats here," he laid a yellow hand on his waistcoat, "I would tear it from my heart rather than displease my esteemed, my revered patron. Mr. Mauleverer's behaviour to Miss Lamb—so distinguishing always, so, if I may say so, almost brotherly—why, it was one of the first things, I believe, that opened my eyes to the virtue, the excellence, the solid worth that lay so ready to my hand. No, no, I cannot think that Mr. Mauleverer would be adverse to my suit, but, madam, passion cannot be denied forever, nor do I blame Miss Lamb for being angry with me for what must have seemed to her a deplorable delay. Young ladies, I know, make a practice of saying 'No' the first time, but that does not mean that they are not awaiting a repetition of the offer, sanctioned by their friends. I know I was too sudden at first, but I have done my best, for these last few weeks, to make amends for that by the assiduous delicacy of my attentions. Indeed, these have been such, I think I can say, that the whole village is in momentary expectation of a happy announcement. I fear I may have laid my esteemed, my adored Miss Lamb open to some breath of scandal. No wonder she is angry with me. I must—I owe it to myself and to her to make amends. Mrs. Mauleverer, may I have your permission to address a few not I hope ill-chosen words to your interesting young friend alone?"

At some points in this oration, Marianne had been hard put to it to refrain from laughing, but now, as Mrs. Mauleverer got to her feet, dropping skeins of embroidery silk in all directions, she felt very far from laughter. "Dear madam, do not go. Mr. Emsworth can have nothing to say to me that I would not much rather hear in your company, and I certainly have nothing to say to him that you cannot hear."

"Come, come child," Mrs. Mauleverer shook out her skirts preparatory to leaving the room. "That is drawing it a thought too high. Mr. Emsworth has spoken very properly, very properly indeed. He is entitled to an interview and, let me warn you, my dear," this is an undertone which Mr. Emsworth was supposed not to hear, "gentlemen like a little coyness well enough, but best not carry it too far. I am sorry we have not heard from Mark, but you may trust me to see you well enough through the whole business." And with these would-be reassuring words, she got herself fairly out of the room.

Mr. Emsworth had been standing by the window, pretending not to hear what Mrs. Mauleverer said, now he crossed the room and took Marianne's reluctant hand. "At last we are alone." His voice throbbed with spurious emotion.

"Yes, Mr. Emsworth?" She must go through with it now.

"Miss Lamb! My dear—my esteemed—may I not say my beloved Miss Lamb? I am come back to you, you see, and with the approval of your honourable patroness. I hope, during these last weeks, I have contrived, by the assiduous delicacy of my attentions to convince you of the depth of my regard, the sincerity of my passion. You have noticed, I am sure, how punctiliously I have escorted you home, with what burning yet genteel ardour I have awaited you at the church door on Sundays, what pretexts I have contrived to visit you here. I can tell you that my attentions have not gone unobserved elsewhere : the whole village is talking of your good fortune, Miss Lamb. We will have a school, I think, instead of a mere bible class—your education, I am sure, is quite sufficient for the rudiments that are all these poor children need. The Bishop gave me a hint only the other day that something of the kind might prove beneficial in these disturbed times. 'An unmarried vicar,' he said to me, 'is almost an insult to the Almighty.' And he left me in no doubt that his wife, Lady Fanwell herself will call upon you. 'Of course,' as he said, 'it would be pleasant to know that the girl's family are not such as to disgrace her in her new position,' but I assured him that I had it on Dr. Barton's authority that there was little chance of your remembering anything now. So we will just forget the past and go forward into the future, hand in hand, confident in the knowledge of God's blessing—and the Bishop's."

At last he paused. Marianne had learned that it was no use trying to interrupt him when he got launched on one of his orations, but now her chance had come. "Mr. Emsworth, you are forgetting something."

"No, no," he interrupted her, "be assured I am not. I have thought of everything. Mrs. Mauleverer will act as mother of the bride—it will be a most genteel ceremony, for Mr. Mauleverer, I am sure will give you away; the wedding breakfast is to be held here, at the Hall—we will not invite many guests, but a sprinkling of my good friends will come, I know, and wish me joy. And if it is of settlements you are thinking, be assured that I am generosity itself : you shall not suffer for dubiety of your antecedents, nor yet for your lack of dower. Though of course if Mr. Mauleverer were to decide to give you some small token in recognition of your services—well it would not be unwelcome—we would not say 'no,' would we, my love?"

"Mr. Emsworth, I am saying 'no' now. I told you, plainly, when you came to me before, that I would not have you, and I do not see what reason you have to imagine that I might have changed my mind." She had heard, as she was speaking, a bustle in the house that suggested the arrival of visitors. At all costs she must put an end to this painful and ridiculous scene. "I am sorry if the courtesy I owe to your cloth has deluded you about my feelings, Mr. Emsworth, but believe me when I say, once and for all, that I will not marry you. And now, with your permission, I will leave you."

But he had her hand again. "I know how it is," he said with the falsely benevolent grin she had grown to loathe, "you think me too calm, too rational, too collected. The ladies, I am told, like a little show of passion; they must feel their power —and ours. They must be carried off their feet by the demonstration of our love. It is not, perhaps, quite in the usual run of clerical behaviour, but for your sake, Miss Lamb— Marianne—what would I not do?" The hot hand pulled her to him, the blubbery lips closed on hers. He was stronger than she would have thought and her struggles were unavailing for a breathless, intolerable moment. He tasted of Dr. James's powders, and smelled of camphor. Then, suddenly, he had let her go and stood over her, gasping a little, like a fish.

"I am sorry if I intrude," said a cool voice behind her, and she turned to face Mauleverer. "My mother sent me to give you my blessing, Miss Lamb, but I wonder if that is exactly what you want. Are you"—he paused—"welcoming Mr. Emsworth's attentions?"

"Thank God you are come. I do not seem able to convince Mr. Emsworth that I do not intend to marry him. Will you stand my friend and do it for me?"

"Willingly, if that is what you really want. He is not a bad match, you know." He spoke as coolly as if Emsworth were a thousand miles away. "The vicarage is his for life as, I have no doubt, he has told you. My mother thinks it an admirable match for you."

"I know she does," Marianne gave way at last to her anger. "I know that, circumstanced as I am, I should be grateful to anyone who will take the risk of having me, but I'll not make a Smithfield bargain of myself for all that. As for you, Mr. Emsworth I would be grateful for your proposal if your behaviour had not put gratitude out of the question."

"Yes," said Mauleverer, "I have yet to learn, Emsworth, that it is the part of a gentleman to force his attentions on so visibly reluctant a young lady."

"Reluctant fiddlesticks," Emsworth had regained his composure. "Miss Lamb chooses to play it coy with me, no doubt for reasons of her own, but we shall come to an understanding yet. As you yourself have observed, my dear Miss Lamb, you cannot carry your goods to every market."

"That will do." Marianne had known, if Emsworth did not, that Mauleverer was holding fury on a tight rein; now he let go. "Leave us, sir, before I say something your cloth—if nothing else—will make me regret. And I warn you, If I hear of you troubling Miss Lamb again, by even so much as one of your insinuations, I will give you the horsewhipping you deserve, cloth or no cloth." He walked over to the door and held it open. "Good day, Mr. Emsworth." And then, closing it behind him. "Miss Lamb, I wish I could have spared you that."

"Thank you," she said mechanically. "It does not matter."

"Not matter! Of course it does; that you should have been exposed to such insult, in my house—but I think he will not trouble you again."

She could laugh now. "I am sure he will not. You arrived most opportunely. I do not know how to thank you. . . ."

"Then do not trouble yourself with trying. I consider it my fault that you have been so ill-used. To tell you the truth, I thought I saw how the wind was blowing before I left here last time, but—forgive me—I thought—I imagined—I had reason to believe—that you were not averse to Emsworth's suit. There seemed no need for interference, since I look on you as a young lady who is amply able to look after herself. It was only when my mother wrote me of your obstinacy in in refusing our esteemed vicar, and of her own enthusiasm for the match, that I thought I had best come and see you had— well, fair play. I am glad I did."

"You mean you are come all this way on my account. It is too good of you."

"Not at all. I consider myself responsible for your well-being, Miss Lamb, until you find yourself a family, which, I take it, you are no nearer doing."

She shook her head. "I have almost give up hope."

"Never do that; it would not be like you. And now, I think we must go and break it to my mother that she is to be foiled of her romance. It is really very inconsiderate of you, Miss Lamb. She had it all planned, even down to the decorations in the church and the dishes for the wedding breakfast."

Marianne could not help laughing. "I am sorry to disappoint her."

"Never mind, perhaps we shall have another romance to offer her. She certainly seems convinced of it. And that reminds me; Lady Heverdon sends her kindest regards."

9

MRS. MAULEVERER'S delight at her son's unexpected visit quite outweighed her disappointment at the failure of Mr. Emsworth's suit. "I think you foolish, my love, and so I told Mark, but he seems convinced that you mean what you say, and I have promised that Mr. Emsworth shall trouble you no more. At all events, it is delightful that I shall not be losing your company. But only think of Mark coming all this way merely to arrange your affairs for you! Frankly, I had no idea that he would come. There have been times when I have written and urged him to visit me—and on matters of far greater moment too—and not had so much as an answer for my pains. But I think I know how it is; your business is merely his pretext; he has news, I am sure, about the course of his suit to Lady Heverdon."

And over luncheon she teased him unmercifully with questions designed to elicit some declaration of how matters stood between him and the beautiful widow. He answered them readily enough: yes, indeed he had seen Lady Heverdon frequently; she had taken an elegant set of lodgings not far from his own rooms in Mount Street. No, he did not think she had yet decided where she was to live; he was still settling her late husband's estate, which had been left in considerable confusion. No, she had no house of her own, but was thinking of buying one in London when the estate was settled; in the meanwhile she seemed to amuse herself well enough, despite the emptiness of town. "And, of course, it is not so dead as it usually is at this time of year, owing to the excitement over the Reform Bill. I had the honour to escort Lady Heverdon, one day last week, to listen to the debate in the House."

"Did she enjoy it?" Marianne could not help asking.

He laughed. "She said it reminded her of the Black Hole of Calcutta, and could not imagine how our legislators survived being cooped up for hours on end in such an atmosphere. I think she enjoyed the visit we paid, next night, to the play a good deal more."

Mrs. Mauleverer, who had drooped at the mention of politics brightened up at once. "Oh, the play: I am sure Lady Heverdon is an admirable critic of the drama."

"Yes, indeed. She has even, she tells me, tried her hand at writing a play herself, and promises to let me see the result. Is she not a talented young lady? Mrs. Norton will have to be looking to her laurels."

Marianne looked up at him quickly. This was surely an odd comparison for a lover to make. Mrs. Norton was brilliant enough, by all reports. She had had a play produced, published two books of poems, and now ran almost a *salon* at her house at Storey's Gate, but though gentlemen flocked around her, the better sort of ladies tended to look at her just a little askance, particularly since her name had been linked, in the gossip columns, with that of the Home Secretary, Lord Melbourne. No, it was an odd comparison for a man's beloved.

But Mrs. Mauleverer noticed nothing. She had drunk three glasses of her favourite sweet sherry to celebrate her son's arrival, and her words flowed freely. "Beautiful, brilliant, accomplished," she said. "Yes, she is all that, and more. But what I want to know, Mark, is when I am to welcome her as a daughter-in-law. I know she is in mourning still, but she carried it, I thought, lightly enough."

"Yes," said her son, "she does not wish to burden the world with her woes."

Once again, Marianne gave him a quick glance. She had often heard Lady Heverdon use this very phrase. Had Mauleverer really reached the point of parrotting his beloved's words, almost regardless of their sense? Or had she detected the very faintest trace of irony in his tone? No, she was deluding herself.

His next words confirmed this. "You are ready, then, ma'am, to be relegated to dowagerdom? I am glad to hear it, for I do not believe Lady Heverdon, beautiful and brilliant as she is, would take kindly to sharing a house with her mamma-in-law. From various remarks she has let drop, I rather think her view is that the elderly should keep themselves to themselves. Will you like retiring—with a companion, of course," he sketched a bow in Marianne's direction, "to genteel seclusion at Bath or Cheltenham?"

Her eyes shone. "You know I should like it of all things. I

do not know what Lady Heverdon intends—if you have given her the right to be thinking thus—but I am sure I do not wish to be the kind of old lady who advises the housekeeper and dotes on her grandchildren. Bath will suit me very well."

"Yes," he said thoughtfully, "but I am not quite sure that it was precisely Bath that Lady Heverdon had in mind."

"Oh, well," said the old lady. "Cheltenham will do well enough."

Marianne was watching Mauleverer's sardonic, almost harsh expression. Could Lady Heverdon have told him of her plan about the asylum for the elderly, and he, already, have agreed to it? If so, he was far gone indeed.

But Mrs. Mauleverer had returned to the attack. "I can see that it is all settled between you," she said, "and I do not understand why you insist on maintaining this pretence of secrecy. If she is planning my retirement to Bath, of course she must have engaged herself to you."

"One would think so." He was still looking at her with that strange, sardonic expression. "What would you say then, ma'am, if I told you that she also has plans for this house? That will show you how deeply she is concerned over all that affects me. Heverdon Hall, she tells me, has such painful associations for her that she would as lief not live there—and truly it was a gloomy old barrack of a place, even before the fire. But Maulever Hall—this house she thinks quite unworthy of my dignity. It needs a whole new front; Gothic towers at each corner; a ruin in the shrubbery—oh, and I quite forgot, the kitchen wing to be redesigned to resemble an abbey."

"Good gracious," said Marianne. "With those little pointed windows? How on earth will the servants see to do their work?"

So far he had addressed his remarks exclusively to his mother, now he turned almost as if he had forgotten Marianne: "Miss Lamb, you prove yourself a sordid soul. What are mere considerations of the servants' convenience compared with the poetry of a Gothic elevation?"

She had never found him so irritating. "I am sorry if I strike you as sordid, but I cannot help thinking you will have a great many spoiled dinners. And as for the Gothic frontage, I think it a horrible idea. Maulever Hall has no great architectural distinction, it is true, but it looks what it is, a gentleman's house, with all the marks on it of a family's life. I know that one wing does not balance the other, but I like to think that is because the Mauleverer who built the first one died fighting for his king against Cromwell and so diminished the family fortunes by his loyalty that the other wing had to be botched up as best the architects could. There is all of history in the appearance of your house as it now stands : give it a Gothic front and you will merely be making yourself ridiculous. And now, ma'am, I beg you will excuse me. I have a visit to make."

Mauleverer rose to open the door for her and favoured her with one of his baffling smiles. "Tactful Miss Lamb. You leave me, then, to discuss my prospects of happiness with my mamma? I should, I suppose, apologize to you for discussing family matters so freely in your presence, but I look on you quite as one of us. . . ."

"Why, thank you." She could not keep the irony out of her tone, and swept him a faintly mocking curtsy as she spoke. Then instantly, she reproached herself and went on : "And thank you again for your goodness this morning."

His smile was suddenly warm. "It was a pleasure, Miss Lamb."

Marianne had promised to visit the cottage in the valley this afternoon and though the events of the morning had made her later than she liked she did not feel she could disappoint her friends. Saddling Sadie for her, old Jim looked doubtfully at the sky. "There'll be a storm later, miss, don't ride too far. Sadie don't like storms." And then, with a glance across the yard to where a boy was rubbing down Zephyr, "It's lucky you've got the Master's permission to ride her, ain't it, miss?"

Should she confess that she had not? No, if she did, he would refuse to let her go, and she had been anxious about her friends since the last time she had visited the cottage. Mary had not been well; she must get there today and make sure she was better, or, if not, prevail upon Mrs. Bundy to allow her to find them some other assistance. Besides, she wanted passionately to get away from the house and, if possible, even from memory of the day's galling events. It would have been better, she told herself, if Mauleverer had not come back so soon. If only she had had time to forget him, to teach herself to think of him as engaged to Lady Heverdon . . . but instead there had been a moment this morning as he dealt ruthlessly with Mr. Emsworth when incorrigible hope had raised its head. Absurd, of course. She had known at the time, and the conversation over luncheon had amply confirmed that knowledge, but hope is a hard-dying plant. She wrestled with it still as she rode over the moors towards Mrs. Bundy's lonely house. Even at lunch there had been something, surely, a little odd about Mauleverer's tone as he spoke of Lady Heverdon?

"Stop it!" She spoke aloud and Sadie pricked up her ears. It was time for the burying of hope, time too to be thinking of finding herself a new home. That, doubtless, was the reason for something she had felt as strange in Mauleverer's tone. He was trying to tell her that among the other improvements Lady Heverdon planned for Mauleverer Hall was her own banishment. She would be well advised to burn her bridges today and ask Mrs. Bundy whether she might come and live with her. She knew she would be welcome. . . . And yet, she did not want to leave Mauleverer Hall . . . and the less she wanted to, she told herself, the more essential it was that she do so. No use deluding herself that it was affection for Mrs. Mauleverer that kept her there.

She was hardly half way to Mrs. Bundy's when the air grew dark around her. Jim had been right; one of the moorland's quick, violent storms was blowing in from the sea. She looked around her. No hope of shelter on these bleak uplands. Whatever she did, she was in for a drenching—but she must not burden Mrs. Bundy by arriving in such a condition. She turned Sadie's head towards home and reproached herself as she did so for the sudden joy she felt that, after all, she need not arrange her own exile today. Tomorrow would be time enough. . . .

Thunder growled far off, there was a flicker of lightning on the horizon and Sadie started nervously. "Sadie don't like storms," Jim had said, and Marianne remembered the episode of the snake and wondered if she had been wise to come. But she had had to get away. Wise from experience, she took Sadie along at a steady pace, talking to her soothingly as she went. Big drops of rain began to fall; the next flash of lightning was nearer, and closely followed by its roar of thunder. Sadie shivered, but kept steadily on as the isolated drops thickened into a downpour. Then lightning forked down the sky and one tremendous crash of thunder deafened Marianne for a moment. Her first instinct was to take a firmer grip on the reins for fear Sadie should bolt, but instead, the horse gave one convulsive start of terror and stood stock still, shivering all over. Nothing would move her, neither persuasions, threats, blandishments. She stood there, a shivering effigy of a horse, while water trickled from Marianne's hair down the back of her neck. There was nothing for it, at last, but to dismount and try to lead her home, inwardly cursing Jim as she did so for his far too casual warning: "Don't like storms" indeed. It was going to be a long walk home. At each lightning flash and thunder peal Sadie stopped again and had, once more to be coaxed and blandished forward.

They were not even in sight of the Hall when Marianne heard the sound of a horse being ridden hard towards her. Illogically, absurdly, she knew at once that it was Mauleverer, come to look for her, and the knowledge was its own misery. He would be furious, of course, because she had been riding Sadie against his orders; he would think her ridiculous not to be able to coerce the brute into obedience, and, worst perhaps of all, he would see her in her present hatless, drowned and dishevelled state. Her habit was clinging to her now, like Caroline Lamb's muslins and, at thought of Mauleverer, she was hotly aware of every emphasized curve.

There he was now, slowing Zephyr to a canter as they came over the hill and he saw the draggle-tailed procession she and Sadie constituted. Well, there was nothing for it but to set her teeth and go steadily on to meet him. Or at least, there would have been, if the closest flash and peal had not rent the sky just above her. Even she admitted terror this time: it seemed as if the lightning had struck the earth just beside her and, for a moment, stockstill like Sadie, she was shudderingly expecting to find herself hurt. But, no, the moment passed, she was merely cold, wet and wretched. As for Sadie, she seemed beyond movement now, her head down in such a posture of terror and despair that Marianne forgot her own wretchedness in feeling, simply, sorry for her. Besides, as she whispered consolation and endearment into the velvety ear, she could pretend not to see Mauleverer, not to hear the infuriatingly regular beat of Zephyr's hooves. When had she listened to a horse's hooves before . . . ?

He was beside her now, pulling Zephyr up and looking down at her. "Miss Lamb, I thought I told you Sadie was not safe for you to ride." She had expected scorn, but this was fury; his face was white, the scar livid across it; he seemed not to notice the rain that streamed from the brim of his hat and down his cheek; his whole attention, like his angry eyes, was fixed upon her.

She would not lose her head. "You seem to have been right."

"Of course I was right. Jim Barnes shall lose his position for this."

"No, no; you cannot do that. I let him think you had given me permission."

"I might have known it. Efficient, devious Miss Lamb! You did not exactly tell him, you merely let him think you had my permission. No wonder he looked so amazed, and so frightened, when the horse I had ordered for you arrived today."

"Ordered for me?"

"You think me, I can see, totally neglectful. Did we not agree some time ago, that riding exercise would do you good? Did I not say I must find you a horse? Well, it took me a little longer than I had expected to find just what I wanted . . . and, in the meanwhile, you have been risking your life on Sadie."

"No, truly, it was not as bad at that. She minds me well enough as a general thing."

"Yes." The old sardonic expression was back and it was a relief to her to see it. "I can see she does. That is why you are drenched to the skin and reduced to leading her. But I suppose I should be grateful it is no worse. She might have bolted with you."

"Oh," how safe she felt now he was here, "she did that long ago."

"And you went right on riding her! I hope you do not expect me to admire your courage, Miss Lamb."

"Of course not. I know precisely what you think of me."

So far he had been leaning down from the saddle to throw his words at her, but now he leaped lightly to the ground beside her. "Do you so? And how, pray, do I think of you?"

"Why, as a burdensome dependant who must be sent packing on your marriage."

"I see. When I marry Lady Heverdon, you mean?"

"Exactly."

"You think you will accompany my mother to the Home for Distressed Gentlefolks Lady Heverdon has picked out for her. I believe you delude yourself, Miss Lamb. I doubt if my beloved would consent to making my funds available for both of you. We will have our dignity to consider, remember: naturally I must take up my title; we could hardly be announced, at a ball, as Lady Heverdon and Mr. Mauleverer. There will be no need, even to change the monogram on the bridal sheets, so in some ways it will be economical enough; but I do not think we shall be able to keep you, Miss Lamb, able-bodied as you are. No, I believe you must be thinking of packing up and moving on."

"And so I have been."

"Admirable. And who, pray, is to be the lucky man, if not Mr. Emsworth?"

"You seem to think there is no other career for a female but matrimony."

"Well, is there? I grant you a few Phoenixes—a Miss Mitford or a Miss Austen may do well enough. Do you propose to commence author—and spinster all at once, Miss Lamb?"

"I am convinced I have not the slightest talent that way, Mr. Mauleverer. Anyway, for the moment my one thought is to get home and into some dry clothes. I will think about my future some other time."

"Practical Miss Lamb! But I am not sure that even I can persuade Sadie to move on while the storm still rages so. We will shiver here a few moments longer, I think, before we make the attempt, and you shall pass the time by telling me what you think of my bride-to-be."

"What I think of Lady Heverdon! I hope I know my place better than that."

"You speak like a kitchen maid! Your place indeed! Sometimes, Miss Lamb, I think you have a perfect genius for making me angry—indeed, I suspect you of doing it on purpose. I am sick to death of this mystery of yours."

"Not half so sick as I am."

"I expect not. You were not meant to be a patient companion, a humble dependant. . . . I have seen the flash in your eyes often enough, the ironic twist of your lip when you thought

136

no one was noticing you, humble and quiet-seeming in your corner. Why are you not afraid of me, Miss Lamb?"

"Afraid of you? Why should I be?"

"Because I have the devil's own temper—everyone knows that: servants tremble at my frown, my mother knows better than to rouse me—even my Lady Heverdon—but you have made it clear you do not wish to discuss her. And here are you, dependent on me for the bread of charity, and without so much proper respect as will prevent you from taking my horse without permission—in direct contradiction of my orders —and risking laming her—or worse—in your mad gallops about the moors."

She could not help laughing. "Hardly a mad gallop today."

"There, I said so: you are not in the least afraid. Where are your tremors, Miss Lamb?"

"I am sorry to disappoint you—and, indeed, I was afraid, when I first heard you coming—only, you see, I was so very glad to see you."

"Mauleverer to the rescue—eh? But do not delude yourself: I am no parfit gentil knight, Miss Lamb. I am a bad tempered, ugly, frustrated man. They've thrown out my bill again, you know, and Grey says I must go to the Lords, like it or not, and fight for it there."

"Oh—I'm sorry." Forgetting rain and cold she turned to him impulsively. "I'm so sorry."

And now, amazingly, he was smiling. "You really care, don't you, Miss Lamb?"

"About your politics? Of course I do."

"To the devil with my politics. You care about me, Miss Lamb. The curling lip, the flashing eyes were for my folly, but there have been tears, too, for my sorrows, laughter for my joys. Did you think me totally blind?"

"Not blind so much as besotted." It was out before she could stop herself.

He laughed his harsh laugh. "As well you might. And indeed, it is true that Lady Heverdon had me enthralled for a while. I am not even ashamed to confess it to you. It is pleasant for an ugly brute like me to find himself so publicly adored, and by such a beauty. You thought she had me fooled to the top of my bent, did you not, observant Miss Lamb, sitting at your piano night after night and wasting your

Beethoven on her dull ears? Well, perhaps I was, at first. She is surpassingly beautiful, you must admit—far more lovely than you, even when you colour up with anger, and your eyes sparkle as they are doing now. And she is a lady of family, of title, of accomplishments—there is no mystery about her. Am I not mad, Miss Lamb, to prefer a waif, a beggar who does not even know her own name?"

His long speech had given her time to collect herself. "Quite mad," she said composedly. "Nor do I believe that you do. You are mocking me, sir, and I cannot think what I have done to deserve it."

"Can you not? You do not remember, then, sitting night after night, looking so quiet and so cynical? You do not plead guilty to thinking me a doting fool, and showing it?"

"If I showed it, I apologize."

"That's better. You thought it impossible, did you not, that any female could be so enamoured as Lady Heverdon seemed of such a bad-tempered botched up creature as I."

"I certainly thought you bad-tempered. I still do. Look at you now."

His scowl changed to a reluctant smile. "Exactly. No woman in her senses would marry me. Miranda Heverdon's finances must be deplorable indeed for her to have considered it for a moment. Well, I have looked into them, and it is true, they are. She is oceans deep in debt; has been, I suspect, since before she married my cousin, and his will has left her no chance of recovering herself. Oh, yes, she needs to marry badly enough to be grateful for so easy a mark as I must have seemed. She told me, you know, that you had engaged yourself to Mr. Emsworth."

"Oh." Marianne was beginning to see. "She told me that she was engaged to you."

"She lied. I have been a fool, but not such a fool as that. Flirtation is a game that two can play at; she gave me my cue; I followed it; she has no grounds for complaint."

"Poor Lady Heverdon."

"Yes, poor Lady Heverdon, if you like, and now, enough of her. We have established that I am ugly and impossible. I am, however, rich; I look like finding myself a Marquis *malgré moi;* I have a passably entertaining career ahead of me, and a foolish old mother who cannot help cheating at cards. I have a house in the valley over there on to which I do not intend to build a Gothic front, and another house in Yorkshire in which I do not intend to live. I shall always be bad-tempered, but I hope I should be good to my wife, so long as I respected her, and she me. . . ."

"I hope you would too, but I do not see what it has to do with me."

"It has everything to do with you, and you know it. Come, Miss Lamb, the time for coyness is past. You are the only woman I know with whom I can imagine living a reasonable life. You are not afraid of me; you do not cower when I scowl; you are damnably intelligent and know what I mean when I talk politics—you will make, by and by, an admirable politician's wife. Can you not imagine yourself running a *salon* in London?"

"Yes, very much more easily than I can imagine myself married to you. And now, Mr. Mauleverer, I am cold and wet, and the thunder has slackened. Let us go home."

"Is that all your answer?"

"What else should I say? You do not want a wife, Mr. Mauleverer, you want a housekeeper with political interests."

He ground his teeth. "Damnation. I have done it all wrong; I knew I would. But how can I imagine that you might love a thing like me—what right have I to appeal to you on sentimental grounds? My time for romance was over sixteen years ago."

"So your mother told me. Oh, no need to growl at me; I know you think yourself disfigured beyond repair. I tell you, Mr. Mauleverer, if you are sick to death of my mystery, I am equally so of your appearance."

"I am sorry if I bore you."

"No need to be. You will never do that."

"And what, pray, am I to understand by that?"

"What you will."

"Marianne! What a fool I am!"

She smiled up at him. "I think so."

He looped Zephyr's reins more firmly round his arm. "Miss Lamb, I have loved you, despite myself, I think from the first moment of seeing you. I will be honest with you and confess I fought the feeling—I tried to remain, as I thought, faithful to Lady Heverdon. It was impossible. Marianne, I adore you.

139

If you will not marry me. I have no hope of happiness left. I hope I shall not actually destroy myself, but I shall most certainly degenerate into a bad tempered, wretched, old bachelor."

"Worse tempered than ever? Impossible." But her eyes gave him a different answer.

"Marianne! Is it possible? Can you really love me?"

She smiled up at him. "How can I help it?" And was in his arms. The rain poured down, the thunder still rumbled in the distance and occasional lightning flashes lit up the hills around them. They took no notice. The two horses, quietly cropping here and there at the close grass of the path occasionally twitched on the reins so carelessly held. At last, he raised his head to look down at her : "My darling, you are soaked to the skin."

"So are you. Does it matter?"

"Nothing matters. This is happiness, my love. I thought I had lost all chance of it; I pretended to myself that I might have some respectable substitute with Lady Heverdon . . . and now, now I have you. Tell me you'll love me always."

"Always. And you'll not mind if we discover I'm a pauper?"

"Why should I, so long as you are mine? Marianne, marry me soon. I have known so much unhappiness, I shall not believe in my good fortune until I have you safely tied to me for life."

Safe in his arms, she smiled again. "Should I be coy, do you think, and ask for time? Mr. Emsworth says young ladies always refuse offers of matrimony the first time."

"Damn Emsworth. Shall we make him marry us?"

"No, that would be too unkind—not that he ever cared a rap for me, but imagine the affront to the poor man's pride."

"Very well, let it be the bishop then, so long as it is soon. Next week, Marianne?"

"The week after. I must have a wedding dress, I suppose, and other things suitable for your wife. I shall be a sad charge on you, my darling."

"Terrible." He bent to kiss her again. "I do not know how I shall bear it. But, come, the worst of the storm is over, and you are shivering. We must go home."

"Yes, home. And I thought it could never be that. Oh, Mark, if I am shivering, it is with happiness."

"If you look at me like that, we shall never get home. Come, up you go. Sadie will come quietly enough now, I think. And that reminds me to give you a terrible scold all the way home for disobeying me."

"Yes? Shall we start straight in quarrelling like a properly married couple?"

"Do you know, I think I loved you first because you would not be afraid of me. Do you remember how you stood up to me about the Martins? And you were right about them, by the way."

She laughed. "Naturally I was right."

"Do you intend to be so always?"

"I intend to adore you, always and for ever. Always provided we neither of us catch pneumonia in the meantime."

THE rain was still falling steadily when they rode into the stable yard twenty minutes later, but they were too warm with happiness to notice it. "What you need," Marianne was slightly in the lead and leaned back to speak to him over her shoulder, "is a shrew of a wife, to keep that temper of yours in order."

"And you will be my shrew?"

"I mean to tame you."

"How?"

"Why, by cruelty of course, as Petruchio did. I shall wear you away with my moods and exhaust you with my tempers." Her laugh belied her words. "But, look, there is poor Jim Barnes with the hangdog air of a man condemned. Tell him he is not dismissed."

"Your first command?"

"My first petition, my darling."

He jumped from his horse and turned to hand her down, then called to Jim Barnes who was being very busy with his back to them in a corner of the yard "You—Jim—here a moment."

"Yes, sir?" He came forward reluctantly and Marianne suspected she could detect the traces of tears on his weather-beaten face.

"You have served me how long?" Mauleverer had kept Marianne's hand in his and now pulled her gently to his side. She saw the head groom's faded blue eyes flicker with sudden comprehension before he answered : "Twenty years, sir, and your father thirty years before that."

"Too long to be learning new tricks, eh? Well, Miss Lamb here says it was all her fault and I must forgive you. Indeed, I do not see how I can help it, since she has merely had her way with you, as she does with the rest of us. If I cannot resist her persuasion, why should I expect you to? So—it is all to be forgotten—but if I ever catch you letting her risk her life again, I'll not dismiss you; I'll break every bone in your body."

"Yes, sir," said Jim Barnes, "and I'm sure I wish you very happy, sir."

Mauleverer laughed and turned Marianne to guide her towards the house. "I seem to be very transparent," he said.

"Happiness is transparent." She smiled up at him. "That is its virtue." And then. "Do you know, Mark, you look quite different when you laugh like that."

"Like what?"

"Why—happily, without the bitterness. Was she very beautiful?"

"Who?"

"The girl you were engaged to."

His arm went round her waist in an embrace that was very nearly a shaking. "Surpassingly! The Cleopatra of her time. Men shot themselves daily for her love; I do not know how I managed to survive her faithlessness." And then, laughing "And you, my dear, are merely a hussy to remind me of her. I have remembered her, it is true, with bitterness, but it is all over now. You are my happiness, my life . . . Marianne, if you should fail me. . . ."

"I shall stick like a burr—Oh. . . ." They had climbed the stairs still arm in arm and now paused, confronting Martha who stood at the far end of the long upstairs corridor. Her black eyes seemed to snap at them, then she curtsied respectfully to Mauleverer and turned to disappear into Mrs. Mauleverer's room.

He smiled down at her ruefully. "It is fortunate that we do not intend to make any mystery of our happiness, my love. Now, hurry and change your wet clothes before we give rise to any more scandal—and before you catch a chill, which I care much more about, while I go and interrupt Martha in breaking the good news to my mother. But first, even if the whole household should be watching, one kiss."

"I do not care if the whole world is watching." She raised her face to his.

At last he let her go. "We will be married next week," he said, his voice shaking slightly on the words. "For the time being, I am master, and that is my decree. Yield in this, and afterwards you shall rule me with reins of gossamer."

She smiled at him tremulously, shaken, herself, by the passion that had roused in her to meet his. "I am glad you are

143

master." And then, with a recovery of her lighter touch. "And as to the reins of gossamer; I will believe in them when I feel them tried."

"Infidel! Unbeliever! I intend to be the mildest of husbands."

"Naturally. Always provided that you get your own way in everything."

"You shall pay for that, little shrew," he reached to pull her to him again, but this time she escaped him, still laughing, closed the door of her room behind her, and stood for a moment, leaning against it, savouring the strange rich taste of happiness.

It continued all evening. Mrs. Mauleverer was first amazed, then, characteristically, lachrymose, and finally, delighted, and they dined in an atmosphere of enthusiastic planning. From time to time, she would look from her son to Marianne and murmur all over again: "Never been so surprised. I was perfectly certain it was to be Lady Heverdon." And Mauleverer would catch Marianne's eye with one of the familiar, sardonic smiles, she had grown to love and say, once more: "Disappointed, ma'am?"

"No, no." Dinner was over and they were sitting on, talking in the flickering light of the candles, low now in their sockets. "To tell truth, Mark, lovely though she is, I was always a little afraid of Lady Heverdon."

"I think you were right to be." He caught Marianne's eye and said no more.

When his mother rose to move to the drawing-room, he accompanied them: "Will you play to me, Miss Lamb?"

"With all my heart." She was grateful for his quick instinct that avoided an apparent repetition of those tête à tête evenings with Lady Heverdon, and grateful, too, for the chance to let her hands find their way through his favourite Beethoven sonata while her freed mind went on roaming about the fringe of unfamiliar happiness.

Mrs. Mauleverer was soon nodding over her embroidery, and Marianne too felt herself exhausted with all that the day had held. Was it really only this morning that Mr. Emsworth had proposed to her? She finished her sonata and sat for a moment, slightly drooping at the piano."

"You are tired." Mauleverer crossed the room to take her

hand. "Best go to bed. There will be time to be happy in the morning."

"A lifetime to be happy."

"Happy?" Mrs. Mauleverer woke with a jerk. "Yes, my dear children, most happy, but wonderfully sleepy too. Come, Marianne, it is time for bed. We must think about your trousseau in the morning." And she chattered gaily about silks and gauzes as he escorted them upstairs, and hovered enthusiastically close as he bent to kiss Marianne's hand. "A lifetime of happiness," he repeated her words. "Sleep well, my love."

She wanted to lie for a while, and continue the exquisite tasting of good fortune, but fatigue had its way with her, and it seemed no time before she was roused by a quick tapping at her door.

"What is it." She sat up in bed and looked around her. It must be very early still; the room was full of shadows.

"May I come in, Miss Lamb?" Martha's voice. Why?

"Yes?" Her voice questioning, she sat up in bed and pulled a shawl around her.

Martha was fully dressed. "There is someone who says he must see you, Miss Lamb. At once. Alone."

"Who? Where?" She was still dizzily rousing from sleep.

"A man—a stranger. I never saw him before. I was out with the child—there's no keeping him in bed these mornings. He awaits you in the wilderness. Must see you, he says, on a matter of urgency—and secretly. 'Ask her,' he said, 'if she wants to know who she is'."

"Who I am?" Marianne was out of bed in a flash. "Thank you, Martha. I will go as soon as I can dress."

"Let me help you." They had spoken throughout in whispers.

Marianne's hands trembled so much that she was grateful for Martha's surprising offer of assistance. "Why the secrecy?" she asked.

Martha looked up from the buttons of her dress. "He did not say: No doubt he will explain."

"Yes . . . what kind of a man?"

The sharp black eyes met hers for a moment. "A gentleman. There. You are ready. Best lose no time. The servants will be stirring soon."

"Yes. Thank you, Martha." She ran downstairs, her heart

high with anticipation. She would be able to tell Mark her true name, to marry him without the shadow of a doubt hanging over her. And yet—why the secrecy? Her spirits dimmed a little as she let herself silently out at a side door and hurried across the dew drenched grass of the cutting garden and through the gate into the wilderness.

Closing is behind her, she looked around. Ornamental trees and bushes grew thickly on this side of the wall in well-ordered simulation of a wilderness. Scarlet berries hung thick on the berberis, and here and there leaves were beginning to turn. Birds, interrupted by her coming, were taking up their morning song all around her. There was no one in sight. Could this be some strange practical joke on Martha's part? Doubtfully, she started down the winding path that led to the centre of the wilderness, then stopped at sight of the man who was sitting on the bench there. His back was towards her, and he was oddly muffled, considering the mildness of the autumn morning, in a capacious black travelling cloak. A twig cracked under her soft shoe and he rose and turned to meet her, his cloak still held protectively around his face. . . . Then, at sight of her, he let it drop and came forward, arms outstretched in greeting.

"Marianne; my love, it is really you."

She stepped back, eluding his grasp, and gazed at him with dilated eyes. Surely she had never seen that sallow face, nor heard the curiously lisping voice before? Or—had she? Suddenly, horribly, she was not sure. Was there, after all, something familiar about the shrewd eyes under colourless brows? Was this, perhaps, and, somehow, horribly, the beginning of memory?

His hands had dropped to his sides. "You mean—you still do not remember? I had hoped that the sight of me, the sound of my voice would bring memory back to you. Marianne, you *cannot* have forgotten it all."

"Forgotten what, sir?" Her voice shook a little and she took another step backwards, away from those white, pleading hands.

"I could not have believed it. Do you remember nothing—nothing, Marianne?"

She looked at him steadily. "I am sure that I never saw you before in my life.', But it was not true. More and more, she was tormented by near-memory. She had heard, and, surely,

146

hated that melodious, lisping voice before. But when? Where? Well—he was telling her. She fought down terror, and listened.

"Oh, my God. To have to tell you." His voice shook with emotion. "Try, think, listen to me. The little church on the hill, Marianne, and the rector who took snuff during the ceremony? Surely you must remember how we laughed about it afterwards? Oh, that day I had such hopes, such happiness . . . Marianne, how could you forget?"

Her hands, cold as ice, clasped each other for comfort. "What ceremony, sir?"

"Our marriage, my love, what else?"

"Our——?" she swayed where she stood and he moved to steady her, but she sprang away from him and leaned, hard, against the back of the bench. "I do not believe it." The feel of the rough wood under her hands gave her confidence, and she faced him more resolutely. "It is true that I have lost my memory, but I could not have forgotten that."

He looked at her ruefully. 'That is what I thought. You do not remember walking down the hill together after the ceremony? It was spring, and the hawthorns were in full bloom. You leaned on my arm, which now you will not touch, and spoke, so sweetly, so simply of your happiness, your gratitude. . . . And then, later, do you not remember the nightingale that sang under our window? You lay in my arms, Marianne, and smiled up at me : 'It is my heart singing,' you said."

Her hands clutched the back of the bench to tightly that the rough wood bruised them. "I don't believe it."

"They warned me I might not be able to make you remember." Slowly, almost regretfully his hand went to an inside pocket and he brought out a paper. "You left this behind, that terrible night. Look, Marianne, your marriage lines." He held them close, so that she could read the crabbed writing. Her name leapt out at her : "Marianne—Loudon?" she whispered.

"Yes. Odd, was it not, that when, as I suppose, you found yourself compelled to choose yourself a name, you should pick one with the right first letters."

She was still staring with huge eyes at the document which recorded the marriage of "Marianne Loudon, spinster, of this parish," and "Paul Rossand." She looked at him inquiringly. "Paul Rossand?"

"Your humble servant. Your husband, Marianne."

"I don't believe it." But now she was trying to convince herself.

"My poor darling." He put the paper away. "I had so much hoped, when I learned where you were, that I would be able to make you remember. And yet—I do not wonder, cannot blame you for wanting to forget. Oh, Marianne, if only I did not have to tell you, but how else can I save you?"

"What do you mean, sir?"

"Oh, do not call me sir." It seemed a cry from the heart. "You who have lain in my arms. Call me Paul, my love, and forgive me for what I have to tell you."

"Forgive you? Why?" she paused, wrestling with unbearable belief. Then a new thought struck her. "The child?" she asked. "Thomas?" He must be lying. If he claimed that the child was hers, she would be sure of it.

He was shaking his head. "If only he were ours. But that is the heart of the matter, my poor love. They told me you were cured, or at least that marriage would complete your cure, but then, when you failed to conceive the child you longed for, I began to see the dreadful symptoms return. You began to forget things, Marianne, and to imagine them, and I saw that strange, wild look in your eyes again. And then, one night —I shall never forget it—I woke and found you gone. And next day there was worse still; the vicar's adored little grandson was gone too. I kept quiet for your sake, covering your absence as best I might, but in my heart I knew what must have happened. I have been searching for you ever since. Thank God I have found you at last, and, I hope, before it is too late. If we return the child unharmed, I am hopeful that they may let me keep you with me. You must fetch him, Marianne, and come away with me, quickly. We have lost too much time already talking here." And then, on a new note of urgency. "Hurry, Marianne, I cannot risk the madhouse for you."

"The madhouse?"

"Of course—you do not remember. And it was only for a few weeks, before I persuaded them to release you to my care. Only trust me, Marianne, and all will be well. I cured you once; I am sure I can do it again. But, hurry . . . and tell no one at the house. We cannot afford to be questioned You

148

must fetch the child and come away with me now, before anyone is stirring. If your story once becomes talked of, it will be impossible to keep you out of the madhouse. Do not trouble to bring any clothes—your own await you at home. Just run, fetch the child and return to me here. The carriage awaits us beyond the park. I dared not come openly to fetch you, for your host's sake as well as your own. Only think what it must do to his career if it were to become known that he had been harbouring a married woman—a kidnapper. For everyone's sake, you must leave as mysteriously as you came. Your disappearance will be a nine days' wonder, no doubt, but no more so than your arrival."

Almost, against her will, against her heart convinced, she stood for a moment gazing at him. "Married?" she said at last. "Your wife?"

"Yes, yes," he said impatiently. "How can I convince you?"

His hand went out to touch the light shawl she had thrown over her shoulders. "You have a mole, here," he touched a point just below her shoulder-blade. "How often, when we were still happy, I have kissed it, and called it your beauty spot. Surely you remember that, my dearest?"

She did not remember, but now, at last, in anguish, she was convinced. "Very well," she said. "I will fetch the child."

"Good. But make haste, Marianne, for your own sake."

She turned and ran back through the shrubbery, through the gate in the wall and across the cutting garden. Her skirts were heavy with dew now, and her thin shoes soaking, but what did it matter? "Married!" She stopped at the entrance of the cutting garden and gazed for a moment at the house. It seemed a bitter lifetime since she had run hopefully out into the morning, but closed shutters and drawn curtains along the front of the house told her that it was still very early. Last night, this had been her home, her happiness. . . . Today. . . . She shivered and drew her shawl more closely round her shoulders as if its light warmth could help the chill about her heart.

A cock crowed over at the home farm. "Hurry," he had said, "hurry. . . ." Her husband. White, soft hands and that unmistakable voice. . . . How could she have forgotten? Or—had she wanted to forget? Did that explain everything? For now, reluctantly, bitterly, she was convinced that those stirrings of memory she had felt while they talked had been real.

149

She did remember this man, the sallow face, the grey unfathomable eyes, but not with love, not as a wife should.

Hurry . . . hurry. All the time her eyes were on the second floor window of Mauleverer's room. He must be still asleep there, behind closed red curtains, dreaming, perhaps, of her and of happiness. How could she tell him? What would this new blow do to him? Ever since the first shock of discovery, her mind, below the surface, had been frenziedly hunting expedients, trying this and that way out. But there was none: she had really known it all the time. Married . . . shadowed with madness . . . a kidnapper. It was true, what Rossand had said. Rossand—her husband! But he was right. Even to have sheltered her might mean the end of Mauleverer's career. What if it should be known that he had engaged himself to her! Her hands were busy tearing her handkerchief into tiny pieces. Merciful that it had gone no further.

"Hurry." The lisping voice echoed in her brain. What was she doing, standing here gazing at closed red curtains? She must indeed be gone before the house stirred. Now her mind was busy with phrases from the letter she must write Mauleverer. She would be gone when he read it. It was the only way. "Good-bye, my darling." She turned and hurried towards the house.

Martha was waiting in her room. She should have expected it. "Well?" Black eyes agleam with curiosity. "Good news, I hope?"

"No. Martha, I have to leave, at once, and take the child."

"Thomas? Impossible. I won't allow it. What right have you?"

This too she should have expected. And suddenly her whirling thoughts fell into place, a decision was taken almost it seemed unconsciously. I am not mad, she told herself. I remember that I do not trust him. I was running away from him—from my husband. And I am not going back to him. "Martha, will you do something for me?"

"Not if it concerns Thomas."

"No, no, I think you are right. I must go, but Thomas is best here. You will look after him. Let me think." She pressed her hands to her brows. "What time is it?"

"Nearly six o'clock."

Hurry . . . hurry. "I must write a letter—two letters." Her

mind was racing ahead again. Mrs. Bundy; impossible to take any clothes; a clean break and be done with it. It was the kindest way; the only way. She wrote rapidly: "Sir—You have convinced me that I am fit only for retirement from the world. But not with you. I am going to a friend who will, I am sure, give me asylum. Do not try to follow me: no one at the Hall knows where I am going." Nothing about the child. Let him assume that she had taken him with her. She reread the note. Would it protect Mauleverer? She thought so. More and more she found herself suspecting her husband's motives. If his story had all been true, surely he would have claimed her openly. Why did he muffle his face in his cloak? He is afraid. . . . He must have ill-treated me. . . . Oh, if only I could remember.

"Six o'clock," said Martha as the stable clock began to strike.

"Yes." Once again she wrote: "My darling—I can never call you that again. I am married. I have just learned it. I think my heart is breaking. Do not try to follow me. What is the use? I am going to friends, who will be good to me. God bless you. I shall always love you." A tear fell on the paper as she signed her name.

But there was no time for tears. The servants were stirring now. It was lucky for her that old Jim lived with his wife in one of the lodge cottages across the park. After yesterday's scene he would never let her take Sadie, but the stable boy would be another matter. Best not risk the time it would take to change. "Will you give that to the man in the orchard?" She handed the first note to Martha. "But not yet. Wait till you see me ride up over the hill."

"You are really going?" Martha took the note.

"I must."

"And your clothes?"

"I will send for them. If I can." She knew that she never would.

"You have money for the journey?" It was not solicitude on Martha's part, she was sure, but, more likely, the wish to be well rid of her.

"Enough." The word journey had given her an idea. "I shall catch the coach at Pennington Cross and send Sadie back from there. She'll find her way home right enough. Now, I must go." She had been moving about as she spoke, gathering a few necessities into a tiny bundle that she could attach to Sadie's saddle. Impossible to take more. "Good-bye, Martha."

"I suppose you know what you are doing."

"I wish I did not." At least Martha made no move to stop her, nor pretence of regret at her going, but merely stood and watched with enigmatic black eyes as she picked up her note for Mauleverer and ran down to leave it in his study. Putting it down in the centre of his desk, she stopped for a moment, her hand caressing the back of his chair where he would sit while he read it. If she let herself hesitate, she would be lost. She turned and ran from the room and out by the back way to the stable yard.

The stable boy looked frightened when she told him to saddle Sadie for her, but complied readily enough. After all, she and Mauleverer had made no secret, last night, of their happiness. He must think she would soon be his mistress.

The thought released the tears that were all the time, so dangerously near, and she had to turn away for a minute to hide them. There would be time for tears—presently.

"You are riding at once?" The boy was looking at her dress.

"Yes." Haughtiness was the only answer.

He helped her to mount with obvious reluctance and she felt suddenly sorry for him. She should have asked Mauleverer not to be angry with him. Too late now. On impulse, she took off the brooch she always wore and handed it to him. "Give Mr. Mauleverer this, will you—and my love." She urged Sadie forward. It was the best she could do to protect the boy from the first surge of Mauleverer's anger. At the thought, tears blinded her, and she let the reins lie loose on Sadie's neck as the mare set forward on the familiar track up the hillside. Her own misery was bad enough, but the thought of Mauleverer's was almost more than she could bear. "But what could I do?" she whispered to herself, turning to look downwards and back, with blurring eyes, to where the Hall stood quiet in morning sunlight. "What else could I do?"

For a moment, the urge to turn and ride back was almost irresistible. Surely it would be better for Mauleverer if they faced their tragedy together? At least there would be no chance of his feeling rejected as he had been once before, by that other girl. The temptation was so strong that she pulled

152

Sadie to a standstill. She would see him once more; feel his arms around her for the last time, say good-bye. "Yes," she told herself, "and wreck his career." And then: "Good God, I am talking to myself. Perhaps I am mad, perhaps it was all true."

She urged Sadie forward. All the more reason for making a clean break of it. She had taken her decision and must abide by it. By now Martha would be giving the stranger—stranger! Ironic word for one's husband—would be giving Mr. Rossand her note. Suppose he tried to follow her—he had a carriage, he had said. He might well, guided by Martha, drive round to Pennington Cross and try to intercept her there. Well, he would not find her, but the sooner she was safely hidden in Mrs. Bundy's secluded valley, and Sadie running free over the moor, the better. "Hurry," she whispered to herself. It had been, somehow, the key word all morning. If only there had been more time—time to think, to disentangle unbearable truth from suspected falsehood in the stranger's story, but always there had been the feeling of hurry, and worst of all, when she had got back to her room, the pressure of Martha's presence. "But I was right," she told herself finally, setting Sadie to a canter, "there was nothing else I could have done."

She was exhausted with misery when at last she turned Sadie down into the quiet valley, but at least she had seen no one in her desolate ride. There would be no witnesses to carry news of her whereabouts back to Maulever Hall. She had meant the break to be complete, and had succeeded. Oceans of desolation lay in the thought. But it was done now. She jumped down, untied her bundle from the saddle, looped up Sadie's reins securely and turned her loose. "Home," she whispered through the tears that would keep coming. "Home, Sadie." The mare twitched an ear and began peacefully grazing on the luxuriant grass of what had once been Mrs. Bundy's lawn. Suddenly desperate, Marianne used the reins as an improvised whip to urge the mare away, but Sadie only looked round at her reproachfully and went on with her meal. Almost frantic now, Marianne was looking round for a stick when Mrs. Bundy's voice stopped her: "Leave her, child. She'll go when she's fed." And then. "I suppose you know what you're doing." She was leaning out of the low window of her bedroom, wearing a man's velvet shooting jacket over

153

her nightgown and an embroidered cap over her straggling grey locks. "Come to stay, have you? Not much luggage."

"If you'll have me." Marianne dropped the stick she had found and instead of beating her, bent to give Sadie a last caress. Soon, Mauleverer would be touching her. Tears started again. She made herself answer Mrs. Bundy's last remark. "It's all I have."

"Very desperate," said the old woman. "I'll come down. Quietly, as you come in. Mary's ill. Very glad to see you, to tell truth. Glad anyway, of course; always welcome, but now —well, could call it an answer to prayer. Not that I go in for praying—much." She vanished from the window and met Marianne, finger on lips, in the doorway of the house. "Come in," she whispered. "She's asleep. Sit down; rest; something to eat; tell me about it later."

"Thank you." Marianne stumbled to the little sofa, and sat for a moment, head in hands, willing her whirling thoughts to settle. Mrs. Bundy returned from the kitchen. "Drink this," she handed a glass. "My own cordial. Can't beat it. Never tried. You'll feel better presently. Stands to reason. You couldn't feel worse."

Grateful for the instant comprehension, Marianne swallowed the fiercely bitter brew and felt it burn its way down her throat.

"Dandelions," explained Mrs. Bundy. "Nothing like them. There, now you feel better."

It was true. Marianne raised her head and looked about her, noting at once a sad change in the room she had grown to love. Withered michaelmas daisies drooped in tarnished silver vases. On the little writing desk, a drift of browning petals marked where a few late roses must have stood. Books and papers lay everywhere, on the floor, on tables and even beside her on the sofa. And, over everything lay the faint smear of neglect. Furniture that Marianne was used to seeing mirror-bright with beeswax was now dull to match the tarnished, blackening silver.

"Never was much of a polisher." Mrs. Bundy had followed the direction of her eyes. "Other things more interesting. But I don't like it." She picked up the dried rose petals and sniffed at them. *"Pot pourri,* I suppose, at a pinch." She dropped them out of an open window. "Now," she moved towards the kitchen door. "Breakfast. Half your trouble is that you're hungry."

Once again, it was true. But, "I wish it was the whole of it," said Marianne.

"That's better." Mrs. Bundy's voice approved her return of spirit. "No use giving way to it. Never was; never will be. Fight it. It's the only way. It's taken me twenty years, but I've learned. I think. Ham and eggs."

She might not be a polisher, but she was a remarkably good cook. "Don't talk. Eat." She put the platter of frizzled ham and delicately fried eggs on the kitchen table, poured herself an enormous tankard of coffee and watched with approval as Marianne ate. The bread was stale. "Mary's last baking," she explained, cutting a slice.

"What's the matter with her?"

"Old age mostly. You can't avoid it, and she's lived hard. My fault; I blame myself. I knew she was carrying too much weight. Should have slowed her down sooner, but she knew how things ought to be done. Very difficult to change, that. She's been a whole staff of servants to me for twenty years. How do you stop? I don't know. Now we'll have to look after her. Not an easy invalid. You are coming to live here, aren't you?"

"If you'll have me."

"Have you! It's enough to make one believe in miracles. I was wondering whether to send for you. Didn't like to, though. After all, you've got your own life."

"Not now," said Marianne.

"Oh?"

"It's all over."

"At—what? Twenty? Seems a bit premature. But we'll talk about it later. It's time poor Mary had her breakfast. Lord, she'll be glad to see you. Hates like poison to have me waiting on her, poor thing. Habit's the devil. Water gruel and hot milk."

11

MARY'S faded eyes lit up at sight of Marianne. "You will look after milady?" Her voice came feebly from one side of her face.

"Yes, if you will eat your gruel." Marianne had to feed her like a child, but when, at last, she settled back against the pillow there was a little more colour in her cheek. She caught Marianne's hand with her good one—for the other lay limp and useless on the bedspread. "You will stay?"

"Yes."

Mrs. Bundy was in the tiny kitchen boiling up a noxious-smelling brew of herbs. "She is better today, I think." She poured the concoction into a jug. "She must have this with her lunch."

"Should you not call a doctor?"

"And have him bleed her? She's as weak as a cat already. No, I have seen this kind of case before; the worst is over now; she will get stronger gradually, though I fear she may never regain the use of her arm. You are really come most happily, my dear. Your horse has gone, by the way."

"Oh." Marianne put down the tray she had been holding and moved towards the window. It was high morning now and autumn sunshine picked out the colours of late hollyhocks and Mrs. Bundy's favourite dahlias. But she looked at the quiet garden through a veil of tears. The last link was broken. Sadie was on her way back over the hills where she must never go again. At the Hall, the search would be out for her. It seemed impossible that she would never know how Mauleverer bore it.

"Come into the other room." Mrs. Bundy's voice was unusually gentle. "You can cry in comfort there. Will it help, do you think, to talk of it?"

"If only I was sure I did right. . . ." It was a relief to pour it all out to so understanding a listener.

"Yes, I see," said Mrs. Bundy at last. And then, "I suppose he really is your husband? Ever seen a marriage certificate before? That you remember, I mean."

"No. I thought of that. It's quite true; I have no way of being sure it was genuine—though it looked it. But—there were things he knew." She had omitted Rossand's reference to the mole on her shoulder and now coloured crimson at recollection of what he had said.

"I see. Poor child. But as to the document—I will have inquiries made. Best to know the worst, I always think: Marianne Loudon, you say, and Paul Rossand?"

"Yes."

"Very well." She made a note of the names. "You believe him, then, about the marriage. But not the rest of the story?"

"No. Do you think me mad, ma'am?"

"No. Very level-headed young woman, I've always thought. Aside from loss of memory, which could happen to anyone. You think you were running away from him?"

"I'm sure of it."

"And the child?"

This was a sore point. Increasingly, Marianne's conscience had been troubling her about little Thomas. "I . . . I do not know what to think."

"Then best not trouble your head about him," said Mrs. Bundy robustly. "Sounds a tedious brat enough, if you ask me. Just as glad you didn't bring him. What was Rossand's story? You'd stolen him from the vicarage? Should be easy enough to check. He didn't say where, or who, I suppose?"

"No." Looking back, Marianne realized that Rossand's story had been oddly free from proper names. "The church was on a hill, he said."

Mrs. Bundy laughed. "Like a few other English churches. Still, the child's disappearance should have caused a stir. There's no harm in a few inquiries."

"You think his story was true then?"

"Not for a moment, but you'll feel better if I prove it false. But you're not mad. Had it not occurred to you that a shock like this morning's would have sent you over the edge at once? I think Mr. Rossand disproved his whole case by the way he approached you."

"Oh. I had not thought of that."

"You had no time to think of anything. One might almost think he had planned it that way. I suppose you were right to come away."

The doubt in her voice found its echo in Marianne's heart, but she answered firmly enough: "I am sure I was, ma'am. I love Mark Mauleverer too well to let him involve himself in my disgrace."

"Quite so. But he might feel differently about it. Never did believe in sacrifice much, myself. Too selfish, I suppose. But don't look so wretched, my dear. You know more of the state of the case than I do, and anyway, it's done now. Waste of time to fret. We'd better air your room."

She kept Marianne occupied with practical matters for the rest of the day. Delicate old linen sheets had to be aired in the sun and then made up on the cot bed of an attic bedchamber whose dormer window looked up to the hills over which Marianne had come. Then, laughing and apologizing for her own poor housewifery, Mrs. Bundy set Marianne to work on cleaning and polishing the living-room back to its usual state of shining comfort. Meanwhile, she was busy among the trunks she kept in yet another attic and emerged at last with an armful of clothes to be altered for Marianne. "You don't mean to send for your box, I take it?"

"How can I? It would spoil everything. Do you think there is any chance of their learning that I am here?"

"Not the slightest. All my connections are with Exeter, quite the other way from Maulever Hall. I know of them, of course, but I am positive no one there has the slightest idea that there is even a house here."

This confirmed Marianne's own impression. She had never heard anyone at the Hall speak of this lonely house of its strange owner, and some instinct had prevented her from speaking of it herself.

"Three coaches at least stop at Pennington Cross in the early morning," said Mrs. Bundy. "They will certainly think you have taken one of them."

"Yes." She had intended the break to be complete, and yet could not help a wild hope that somehow Mauleverer would find out where she was. If only she should look out the window and see him riding down the path. She had cried too much already. She jumped to her feet: "Let me clean the kitchen now," she said.

Mrs. Bundy let her wear herself out with housework and sent her to bed at last so exhausted that she slept in spite of herself. "Things will look better in the morning," were her farewell words.

At least they looked no worse. How could they? The sun shone; there was a great deal to do; Mary was a little better. Avoiding thought, Marianne scoured and polished till the little house smelt throughout of Bath-brick and beeswax. It was interesting to discover that she knew how to cook, and gratifying to have Mary drink up the broth she made her. Mrs. Bundy congratulated her on her housewifery: "Though I fear that it casts the gravest doubts on your antecedents, my dear. Where can you have learned to manage a kitchen range and bake such good bread?"

Marianne sighed. "I wish I knew. But I have given up hope, now, of remembering. If meeting my own husband did not bring back my memory, what will?"

"It is certainly hard to imagine." Mrs. Bundy had retired to her writing desk while Marianne was busy in the kitchen and written a long letter to her man of business in London. In the afternoon, a boy from the farm at the bottom of the valley paid them his daily visit, bringing provisions and the two-days-old London papers, and took the letter which, Mrs. Bundy explained, would not get into the post until next day. "But time, it seems to me, is the one thing you have, my dear."

"Do you think so?" Marianne was haunted by anxiety for Mauleverer. Measuring his passion by her own, and keenly aware of the desperate streak in his character, she was tormented by visions, each one grimmer than the last, of the excesses into which despair might plunge him. There was no one at the Hall to whom he would turn for comfort. He would not think of making his mother his confidante, and Marianne could not blame him. Her exclamatory sympathy would be merely a last straw. What, then would he do? He might do anything. It did not bear thinking of, nor did she dare let herself remember his words, up on the moor that day: "You are my happiness, my life . . . if you should fail me." She must not think of it, for—it all came back to this—what else could she have done?

Daily budgets of bad news from the farm-boy, George, merely intensified her anxiety. The rejection of the Reform Bill had touched off riots all over the country. But at least Lord Grey had not resigned on the defeat of his bill. Parliament had merely been prorogued until December and a committee was already at work in drafting a new bill. No doubt Mauleverer would be engaged in this work. Marianne had found that constant activity was her best comfort and could only hope that the same would be true of him.

It was the uncertainty that was such anguish. Night after night, tossing on her pillow, she beat her brain for ways of getting news of the Hall—and found none. Her own misery, she told herself over and over again, would be bearable if only she could be sure that Mauleverer was making head against his. And yet, when she did, at last, learn that this seemed to be just what he was doing, it proved the coldest of comfort.

It was a bright afternoon when late October was playing at August although the first frost had already picked out, here and there, a leaf in gold, and laid blighting fingers on Mrs. Bundy's dahlias and climbing nasturtium vines. She and Mariannne were out in the garden, lifting the dahlias, while Mary sat on a bench in the sun and grumbled because she could not help.

George came whistling down the lane and handed Mrs. Bundy a fat bundle of papers and letters. "Terrible goings on in Bristol." He loved to be the bearer of bad news. "They've burned the Bishop's Palace, and sacked the Mansion House and I don't know how many private houses besides. Father says there'll be bloody revolution if they don't pass this Reform Bill soon. There's wild talk in Exeter already; I've heard it myself. Riot and rick burning and I don't know what all is what we'll be having; and how you dare stay here, three women alone, is more than I can imagine."

Mrs. Bundy laughed. "Who would hurt us? Indeed, who, but you and your father, knows we are here? And, really," she looked down at her mudstained black skirts and the inevitable hessian boots, "you could hardly say that I looked like a typical bloated aristocrat. Do I grind your face, George?"

He looked puzzled. "Grind my face, ma'am? I should think not indeed."

"Or make you eat cake? But it's not fair to tease you. Take him indoors, Marianne, and give him his cyder." And she picked up her bundle of mail and papers and went to join Mary on her bench.

Always talkative, George excelled himself that day, and

160

when Marianne finally got back to the garden Mrs. Bundy had finished her letters and was deep in the papers. She smiled over them at Marianne: "Has that ancient mariner left at last? Not that he's got a long grey beard, but he talks enough. How he does love a disaster! But it seems to have been largely mismanagement at Bristol. Imagine allowing Sir Charles Wetherell to go in procession there after his attacks on the bill in Parliament. He was lucky to escape with his life, if you ask me And over the roofs of the Mansion House too! But there's good news in the papers for you, Marianne. At least, I think it good. I know you have been worrying yourself to death over Mark Mauleverer. It seems you need not have been. He has been behaving, by all accounts, as sensibly as you could wish."

"Oh?" Why did the words strike so chill?

"Yes; look." Mrs. Bundy's earthy finger pointed out a paragraph of London gossip, which described a great Whig ball at Devonshire House. Among the celebrities listed as present was, "the new Lord Heverdon, who took his seat in the Lords, our readers will remember, in order to vote for the Reform Bill. Last night, he was consoling himself, we thought, pretty well for its failure at the side of the beautiful Lady Heverdon, who is not, we should point out, his wife—yet."

Marianne let the paper fall. It was impossible. It must be true. It was unbearable. She had to bear it. But how *could* he? She would never know. "We have not finished digging up the dahlias," she said, and went strenuously back to work. Mrs. Bundy left her alone, and for that small mercy she was grateful.

From then on, political and social notes alike kept Marianne informed that Mauleverer was still in town. His name was constantly mentioned in connection with the committee that was redrafting the Reform Bill. This would have been all very well, but it appeared, too, in the notes of an unusually brilliant winter season—and always coupled with that of Lady Heverdon. A kind woman, Mrs. Bundy forebore to comment, but then, no comment was needed. He had forgotten her already. Marianne set herself, resolutely, to forget him.

It was easier determined on, than done. At last she came to the conclusion that it was partly anxiety for Mrs. Mauleverer and little Thomas that kept her so sleepless and so drawn. Since Mauleverer was still in London, and had by all the

161

evidence entirely forgotten her, was there any reason why she should not pay just one visit to the Hall and find out how things went there? She put this, one wet October evening, to Mrs. Bundy.

"How would you get there?" Mrs. Bundy could be relied on to be practical.

"There is a farm cart, George tells me, that goes most of the way, on Thursdays. It is but to walk the last two miles or so."

"You have it all worked out, I can see. Well, I can't say that I blame you. But wait, at least, until I have my answer from London. Suppose you find that you are not married after all?"

"It would be rather late in the day," said Marianne bitterly.

And yet, she could not help hoping, had indeed decided long since that hope was her worst enemy. When the long awaited letter arrived, at last, from London, she knew that she had been right. Mrs. Bundy read it through quickly. "Yes," she said at last, "Marianne Loudon to Paul Rossand, April 14th, 1829. You were married some time, my dear." And then : "Wretched man, why does he never carry out my instructions in their entirety! He has not sent me a copy of the licence : we still do not know where the marriage took place, and I should like to know where your church on the hill was situated. After all, someone must know something about you there. I will write again."

"Thank you." Marianne tried to sound as if she cared. It was all over, all totally, hopelessly over. How right Mauleverer had been to embark, at once, on a new life. Now, she must make herself do likewise. But, first, she would pay her visit to Maulever Hall and free herself of her anxiety on account of her friend there, and of Thomas. If she might also learn a little more news of Mauleverer himself, well, that was not the main purpose of the visit.

"You really think it wise?" asked Mrs. Bundy.

"I do not see how I can bear not to."

"Very well then."

There seemed to be about six Wednesdays in that week, but Marianne woke at last to the excitement of Thursday morning —and the sound of rain on the roof. "You will never go in this," said Mrs. Bundy, over home baked rolls and coffee.

"I must. If I wait, Mark Mauleverer may return to the Hall, and then, of course, it would be impossible."

"True," said the old lady thoughtfully, "but surely, with the excitement over the bill so intense, he will not be returning now?"

"Probably not," Marianne admitted. "But—oh, please understand . . . I feel I must go."

Mrs. Bundy laughed. "If it will make you better company than you have been all week, you had best go and get it over with. But I am afraid you will have a sad wet time of it in the farm cart. Here," she reached into a cupboard and brought out a man's military cloak. "This will keep you dry if anything can; it saw much service in the Peninsula." Her hands were gentle as she shook it out of its folds. "I never thought I'd lend it to anyone. You see, child, broken hearts do mend—at last."

Twenty years ago. Marianne gave a little shiver as she wrapped the cloak around her. Thirty days of absence from Mauleverer had been hard enough to bear. Impulsively, she turned and kissed the old lady. "You are very good to me, ma'am."

"I thought I should never love anyone again," said Mrs. Bundy. "But since I find I do, you will have the goodness to take care of yourself. To lose you, would be too much."

"Never fear," Marianne laughed ruefully. "I think you have me on your hands for good."

"Selfishly, I hope so. Well, if you must go, you had best make haste. Farmer Thorne never waits; not even for me."

And indeed when Marianne had picked her way down the muddy lane to the farm she found the cart about to start. "So you've come." Thorne moved over to make room for her on the hard seat beside him. "I thought you'd have more sense." He spoke in the broad Devon Marianne found so difficult to understand, but she knew him for a blessedly taciturn man, and merely said, "Yes, I've come," climbed up and settled herself beside him.

That was the sum total of their conversation. From time to time Farmer Thorne addressed a remark of encouragement or warning to his steadily plodding horse. Otherwise he sat in stolid silence while the rain poured in little rivers from the brim of his hat, and Marianne's cloak became slowly saturated

163

with it. At last he halted the horse. "Here you are. I can't take you any nearer, without I go out of my way."

It was almost an apology and she took it in the spirit in which it was meant: "Of course not."

"You walk through there," he indicated a footpath with his whip. "It won't take more than an hour or so. You'll get wet."

Marianne laughed. "I am wet. Thank you, Mr. Thorne." Her spirits were rising mercurially just at the nearness of the Hall.

He detained her for a minute. "But how'll you get back?"

"Oh, they'll send me, I expect."

"Pity they didn't send *for* you in that case." He spoke to his reluctant horse and they moved slowly forward down the lane.

Marianne climbed lightly over the stile and started off along the little path. She was stiff with cold, though still comparatively dry inside the heavy cloak, but the exercise soon warmed her and she walked swiftly on, her hopes soaring still faster ahead of her. In vain she tried to steady her racing imagination. She had come simply because Mauleverer was not here. There was not the slightest hope of seeing him. But at least, answered hope, she would have news of him, know at last how he had taken her disappearance, understand, perhaps, what lay behind his renewed association with Lady Heverdon.

Hope was incorrigible, and for a while she let herself dream of impossible happiness. The few miles of her walk seemed nothing and she was amazed when she emerged, quite suddenly, on the carriage drive a little below the house. She stopped. Hope had painted in other colours. When she had dreamed of the Hall, it had lain as she had so often seen it, in sunshine, the grey stone softened and the red roofs mellowed by the play of cloud shadow from above. But today the house looked blind . . . dead. In a moment, she realized why. The shutters were closed over the windows of all the principal apartments. What could be the matter? Was Mrs. Mauleverer ill? Or even dead? No smoke rose from the family's end of the house; only, from the kitchen quarters, a thin grey column spoke of life continuing. She hurried forward, angry with herself because the idea of Mrs. Mauleverer's illness had instantly suggested the possibility that her son might have come to bear her company.

She had never knocked on this door before. The sound echoed hollowly, mockingly through the house and for a moment she wished passionately that she had taken Mrs. Bundy's delicately implied advice and stayed away. This was no longer her place. She should not be here.

The door opened slowly. James, the under footman, stood there in his shirtsleeves and stared as at a ghost. "Miss Lamb," he said at last, "'well, I'll be jiggered."

"Good day, James." She stepped past him into the hall, noting as she did so the dust sheets that covered everything. The big chandelier that hung above the stairwell was hidden in a cotton bag; the red turkey carpet on the stairs was covered by a piece of drugget. This was not how she had imagined her home-coming. Home? Bitter word. She turned to face the man, who was still muttering his amazement to himself. "Where is your Mistress, James? I am come to see her."

"Then you've had your journey for your pains, miss. The Mistress is in London with," he hesitated for a moment, an intolerably knowing look on his face, "with Mr. Mauleverer."

"In London!"

"Yes, miss." His face was wooden now. "Reckon Martha can tell you the rights of it, best of anyone. *Miss* Martha I should say, since she was left in charge here." His tone was scornful as he turned away. "I'll tell her you're here, miss."

Marianne had meant to ask him to take her wet cloak and get it dried for her, but surprise at what he had told her had combined with something oddly repellant in his manner to make her forget. He had never been a favourite of hers, but had certainly never before treated her with such scant courtesy. Aware of chill, she took an impatient turn about the hall, glancing as she went into the open doors of the familiar rooms, all strange and forbidding now, in their shroud of dust sheets. Mauleverer had taken his mother to London with him, and, stranger still, had left Martha behind. What could it mean? She had stopped at the foot of the stairs and was gazing with misty eyes in at the doorway of Mauleverer's study when a peal of childish laughter made her look up. As she did so, something cold, damp and repulsive fell on her face, blinding her for a moment. At first, imagining horrors, she thought she would be sick, then she saw that it was only a floorcloth, damp and filthy from some housemaid's bucket. Another peal of laughter, this time from further down the upstairs hall, told her—if she had not known it already—that she had Thomas to thank for the foul welcome. Horrible child. She shuddered and angrily told her conscience that she had been right to leave him behind. Imagine such carryings-on at Mrs. Bundy's.

Martha came rustling down the front stairs, something she would never have done in the past. And—she was a Martha transformed by black bombazine and a jingling bunch of household keys. No wonder she was known as "Miss Martha" now. She greeted Marianne coolly, as an equal and without either surprise or pleasure. "Mrs. Mauleverer will be sorry to have missed you."

"I am sorry not to find her here. How long is she to be in London?"

"So far as I know, for good. There was no talk of a return when they left. Mr. Mauleverer has much to keep him in town." Her tone made it clear that she was not speaking only of politics.

"And his mother stays with him?"

"Yes, they have taken a house." She volunteered no further explanation, and Marianne could not bring herself to question her. Impossible to ask this hostile woman the thousand questions she had intended to put to Mrs. Mauleverer. She faced the bitter truth that her journey had been for nothing. Even if she could bring herself to ask, Martha would never tell her the things she really wanted to know—how Mauleverer had taken her disappearance, how he had seemed, what he had said. . . .

Martha was looking at her with faintly insolent inquiry: "You are come for your things? Mr. Mauleverer had them packed up for you and said you must have them if you should come."

Could that have been all he had said? Impossible to ask. And out of the question, of course, to take them. In her bitter disappointment at Mrs. Mauleverer's absence, she was only now recognizing another problem with which it faced her. She had taken it for granted that she would be sent back in the carriage, at least so far as she would take it; now she would have to make her own way. "No," she said, "I came merely for news of the family. I will send for my things another time." They were still standing in the cold hall, since Martha had made no move to ask her in, or even suggest she take off her wet things. For a moment, she thought, angrily, of insisting on some semblance of civility, but what was the use? Much better to take her leave at once and face her wretchedness alone.

Martha's thoughts must have been moving along similar lines. "I am sorry not to seem more hospitable," she said, "The fact of the matter is that I am up to my eyes in business, since the whole task of tidying and cleaning the house has been left to me, and, between ourselves, we expect a happy announcement daily. I must have everything in apple-pie order. But you are cold and wet," she pretended to notice it for the first time. "There is a good fire in the servants' hall, I am sure. You had best go there and dry yourself and I will have them give you a cup of tea." She reached grandly for a bell pull, but Marianne intervened.

"No, thank you," she said coldly. "I have come a long way, and must not linger. Only, when you write Mrs. Mauleverer, tell her I was sorry not to find her."

"Of course." The bright black eyes said, more clearly than words, that she would do no such thing.

Routed, Marianne turned and made for the big front door. Martha made no move to summon a footman to see her out, but merely stood, at the foot of the stairs, gazing at her, with the same faintly supercilious smile that had played over her face throughout the interview.

"Good-bye, Martha," with an effort she kept her voice cool and courteous as she pulled the heavy door open.

"Good-bye, Miss Lamb." The emphasis on her name mocked her as she pulled the door to behind her.

It was raining harder than ever and she stood for a moment in the shelter of the portico, wondering what to do next, Almost, for a moment, she wished she had swallowed her pride and accepted Martha's offer of shelter, even in the servants' hall. Her friend the cook would have made her welcome, she knew, and, more important still, might have given her some of the information she yearned for. But the tone of Martha's offer had made acceptance impossible. Martha had not intended her to stay. Why had she never realized before how completely the woman was her enemy? But this was no time to be standing dreaming. She was miles from home and seemed to have no means of getting there. Her eyes wandered drearily across the rain-drenched park and lit on the lodge cottage at the far end of the drive. Jim Barnes, the groom, lived there; his wife had always been a friend of hers. She moved out into the rain and walked slowly down the drive. Shelter first, misery could wait.

"Miss Lamb!" The warmth of Mrs. Barnes's greeting brought sudden tears to Marianne's eyes. "Well, this is a surprise—but you're drowned. Come in by the fire this instant and let me get those wet things off you before anything else. Have you been to the Hall?"

"Yes, I am just come from there."

"And got but a chilly welcome, I'll be bound. Jim says that Martha's neither to hold nor to bind now she's mistress there. He'll be right glad to see you, Jim will. We've often worried about you, he and I, since you went off that day. Lord, miss, how I do chatter, but it's so good to see you." She had been busy helping Marianne out of the drenched cloak as she talked, and now stooped to feel her skirts. "Soaking too! Miss, it's a terrible liberty, but let me fetch you something of mine. You'll catch your death else. Jim won't be back for his tea for hours; you can get dried out by the fire and changed again before he comes."

Marianne accepted the offer gratefully and was soon settled in front of the roaring fire, while her clothes steamed nearby and Mrs. Barnes plied her with cups of tea and questions. She had meant to say nothing of where she was living, even to Mrs. Mauleverer, but Mrs. Barnes's interest was so obviously sympathetic that she felt bound to tell her, in general terms, about her new life.

"Well, I'm glad you're happy," said the old woman at last, but with a doubtful look that belied her words, "but it was a great blow to us, miss, just the same, your going off like that. I suppose you acted for the best, but I never want to see the Master look like that again, I can tell you. He was over here, you know, before we'd finished breakfast, to ask if Jim knew where you were . . . and his face; there was death in it, miss. You might have left him some word, something to soften the blow. . . . For a blow it was, and to the heart, if you ask me. We'd all thought, if you'll excuse me saying so, that you'd be the new mistress, and dearly welcome you'd have been. And then to go off like that, without a word—well, I suppose you knew what you were doing."

"Without a word?" Marianne had listened in amazement. "What can you mean? I left a note for Mr. Mauleverer, explaining everything."

"He never had it, miss. He was like a madman all morning, questioning everyone, but of course no one knew anything, except the stable boy. Jim said when he gave the Master your brooch, and the message—just your love, like that, he thought he'd faint clean away. He's never spoken of you since, miss, not to anyone, so far as I know."

Jim, when he came home for his tea, confirmed this. "No, he didn't exactly give orders that you wasn't to be spoke of, miss, but he might just as well have." And then, in answer to her eager questions: "Martha? I never heard that she'd said anything about your having a visitor that morning. I heard her talking about your going often enough in the servants' hall, when she thought fit to honour us with her presence there. Her idea always was that you'd remembered who you were, all of a sudden, not liked it much, and gone off for very shame. Cook always argued with her, and so did Gibbs and I, but the rest of them . . . well, you know how it is, miss: things were a lot easier in the servants' hall before you took over the housekeeping. Many's the quarter of tea or sugar that I've seen slipped out unbeknownst. They'd got to think they had the right to it, see, so of course they didn't like your meddling overmuch. And when we all thought you were to be the mistress—well, there were some that were pleased, and some, if you'll excuse it, that weren't."

"Martha!" Marianne had been half listening to what he said, while her thoughts raced ahead of him. "Of course. She saw me write the note; she must have guessed where I would put it, and destroyed it. No wonder she was not pleased to see me."

Jim Barnes laughed. "I'll warrant she wasn't. She's in her glory now, running things here. You must be the last person she wants to see. And that was a funny business too," he added thoughtfully. "I'd never have thought to see the day Mistress would part with her—all in all she used to be to her before you came. But the night before they left for London there was a great carry-on up at the Hall, Cook told me, with the Master raging and the Mistress in tears, and Martha packing her things one moment and unpacking them again the next . . . and the long and short of it was that Gibbs went to town with the Mistress and Martha stayed here to make life a misery to the staff at the Hall. But what it was all about, miss, I haven't the faintest, and nor has Cook, nor any of the others, save Martha herself, and she's always been one to keep her own council. You'll be writing the Master now, won't you, miss, and making it all right with him?"

Marianne shook her head. "I don't know. I don't know what to do." It was all inconceivably worse than she had imagined it could be. She rose, suddenly longing to be home discussing it all with Mrs. Bundy. "Jim, I have a favour to ask of you. I thought Mrs. Mauleverer would send me home in the carriage; I cannot possibly walk it; will you lend me Sadie, ride part of the way with me, and bring her back?"

He rose at once. "With all the pleasure in life. We've missed you, Sadie and I. But'—he paused unhappily and then went on in a rush—"will you mind, miss, if I bring the horses round to the park gates? I'd as lief that cat Martha didn't know what I was doing."

"Of course. Indeed, I would prefer it, Jim."

"Then I'll go and fetch them. But—won't you ride the other—the one Mr. Mauleverer bought for you? She's a honey, and you've never even been up on her."

"No, no." The idea was somehow unbearable. "I thought she would have been sold long since."

Again he looked uncomfortable. "The talk in the Hall is that she's being saved for Lady Heverdon." And then, impulsively. "Oh, miss, write to the Master, do, and explain."

"I will if I can think what to say." She never would.

12

IT was dark when Marianne reached the valley at last, and one look at her face made Mrs. Bundy stifle her own and Mary's anxious questions and urge her brusquely into bed. The bad news, for it was clearly that, could wait till morning.

Exhaustion proved a good friend. Marianne slept heavily and woke late. Mrs. Bundy had urged her to spend the day in bed, but she soon found she could not bear to lie there, alone with her thoughts, and crept shivering downstairs to huddle over the fire in the living-room and tell her friend all about it.

"Might have known it," was that lady's summing up. "Perfectly obvious that that Martha's no better than she should be. You don't think she was in your husband's pay?"

Marianne thought for a moment. "No," she said at last. "I think she just wanted to be rid of me, once and for all, and took her chance. What a fool I was that day."

"You were under pressure."

"It's no excuse. Oh, if only I had it to do again."

"What would you do?"

It was a good question. Marianne shook her head. "I don't know. More to the point: what shall I do now?"

"Nothing," said Mrs. Bundy. "What else can you do?"

It was true. All the wretched way home, Marianne had tried at different versions of a letter to Mauleverer, and none of them would do. She had stepped out of his life—what purpose was to be served, except a selfish one, by trying to re-enter it?

As the days dragged by Mrs. Bundy began to be afraid that this new misery was going to be too much for her young guest. Marianne attended punctiliously to the domestic duties she had taken over from Mary and did her best to seem cheerful and composed as she went about the house. She and Mrs. Bundy still had a nightly game of chess, but now Mrs. Bundy always won. Marianne tried to eat, and pretended that she slept, but the house was too small for the pretence to be successful. Mrs. Bundy wrote another letter to London and did her best to help Marianne in the gallant pretence that everything was all right.

The news provided an ample distraction. The riots touched off by the Lords' rejection of the Reform Bill had not died down, as optimists had said they would, but had rather increased in violence. The usual bonfire night celebrations of November 5th had turned into a demonstration for Reform, with mitred figures of the Lords Bishops who had voted against the bill burning, instead of Guy Fawkes, all over the countryside. George was in daily seventh heaven of premonitory disaster. "They've burned down Gisburne Park in Yorkshire," he would announce one day, and "stoned Lord Tankerville's coach," another—"and nearly killed the lady who was with him." When a riotous mob set light to a pease rick near Devizes and gave three cheers for the conflagration as they watched it burn, he brought his presages of disaster nearer home. "It is not safe for you ladies, here alone." He was sitting in the kitchen drinking his cyder and indulging in the daily chat that was part of his reward.

"Oh, nonsense," sleeves rolled up, Marianne was busy at their weekly baking. "Who should hurt us?"

"It's all very well to laugh." George put down his mug and came over to whisper portentously in her ear. "But there's a man in the village—been staying at the 'Bird and Bush' several days now—and talks of nothing but blood and vengeance. 'Down with the aristocrats,' is his cry, and there's a plenty that drink the ale he's so free with and listen to him."

"But what's that to do with us?" Marianne turned her dough out on to the floured board and began to knead it with swift, confident movements. "You could hardly call us aristocrats, could you, George?"

"That's just it, miss." He sent a conspiratorial glance beyond the open door to the little front sitting-room where Mrs. Bundy was busy at her desk. "He says she's the worst of the lot."

"Mrs. Bundy?"

"Herself. According to him, she's not Mrs. Bundy at all, but a real live Duchess," awe crept into his voice despite himself. "Duchess of Lundy, not Mrs. Bundy at all. What do you think of that now?"

"Well, even if she is, what is that to the purpose? She hardly lives like an aristocrat, does she? And, being a woman, could not have voted against the bill, even if she had wanted to."

"You don't understand, miss." Despite herself, Marianne was impressed by his earnestness. "This man is saying that her being down here is all part of a plot—don't ask me what—but something to do with spying out the weaknesses of the workers, or something."

"You know that's nonsense, George. Mrs. Bundy's been here for twenty years and more."

"Oh, yes, I know it's nonsense, but that's not the point. It's what the others think that matters. I wish you'd persuade her to go away, miss, till the worst of it is past; I truly do."

There was something uncomfortably convincing in his tone, and when he had gone and Marianne had set her loaves to rise, she washed her hands, took off her apron and joined Mrs. Bundy in the other room.

"George at it again?" the old lady had a disconcerting habit of anticipating one's thoughts.

"Yes. I don't quite like the sound of what he told me today. There's some man in the village who says you're the Duchess of Lundy."

Mrs. Bundy shrugged as she sanded and sealed a letter. "And what's so remarkable about that? It's never been more than half a secret anyway." She looked around her. "'Hardly the setting for strawberry leaves, what? And if you start calling me Your Grace, I'll shoot you. I can, too." She had whisked a businesslike little gun out of her desk as she spoke. "I'm not quite the helpless, unprotected old lady they think me. Shall I give you a demonstration? I used to be able to hit a wafer across the room."

"Pray don't; it would frighten poor Mary quite out of her wits."

"Very well then," she stroked the gun tenderly before putting it away. "He gave it to me," she said, "before he went off to the Peninsula. Didn't like me being alone in the country— we had riots then, you know, and survived them. And mutiny, too, in the fleet. George would have loved it. I suppose he wants us to pack up and go back to London."

"Yes—or at least, away."

"Flight, eh? Never was my long suit—except from myself, and what's the good of that? Oh, I take the gun to bed at nights, by the way. And now, what's for lunch?"

173

To Marianne's relief, George reported next day that the stranger had left the "Bird and Bush." "Tried to get a mob down here last night, miss—I warned you he would—but father and I were there, see, and we soon persuaded 'em you was harmless."

Marianne could not help laughing. Harmless was not at all the word she would have used to describe Mrs. Bundy. "So you think it's safe for us to stay after all, George?"

"I reckon so, for the time being anyway. The talk in the village is all of the cholera now. They've got it bad in Sunderland, they say. D'you think it'll spread here, miss?"

"I devoutly hope not." The dread disease has been reported for some time as spreading across Europe, but, at the moment Marianne could hardly help feeling grateful that it had distracted the volatile minds of the villagers.

"So we can sleep quietly tonight, can we," was Mrs. Bundy's reaction. "Good. All a lot of nonsense, anyway."

It had been a crisp December day and Mrs. Bundy and Marianne had taken advantage of the fine clear weather to work hard in breaking up and fetching a supply of twigs for the fires. Marianne, working doggedly on till her back felt like breaking, had told herself that surely this should earn her a proper night's sleep. And indeed, she found herself almost nodding off over her evening game of chess with Mrs. Bundy, who beat her in two short games running, scolded her for not putting up a better fight and ordered her off to bed : "You're asleep where you sit already."

But, as always, as soon as Marianne was settled in bed, the ghosts she managed to keep at bay during the day time came out to haunt her. Could she have written Mauleverer another letter? Could she still? What would she say? It was very late before she fell asleep at last, and even then she was tormented by maddening, inconclusive dreams. Gradually they worked up into the old, familiar nightmare of unknown terror and galloping hooves. Then, sweating with fear, she was awake, to lie, as always after this dream, fighting her way back to calmness and the real world.

She was lying very still, deliberately trying to relax her way back into sleep, when an odd crackling sound startled her awake. What could it be? And now, surely, she smelled smoke. She was out of bed in an instant and, running to her

174

window looked out to see smoke and flames pouring out of the kitchen wing at the back of the house.

Mrs. Bundy woke at once. "Fire?" She was out of bed on the word and wrapping herself in the big military cloak she had once lent Marianne. Then she took the little gun from under her pillow, picked up the box that always stood by her bed, and hurried downstairs after Marianne. Here, an appalling sight greeted them. The kitchen was already an inferno of flame, and the little porch over the front door was also burning fiercely. Ten minutes more and the stairway would have gone.

"Lucky you woke." Mrs. Bundy opened the door of Mary's downstairs bedroom, which, fortunately, opened not off the kitchen but from the tiny dining room. "We'll go out this way."

Mary was slow to rouse, and by the time they had got her wrapped in a heavy shawl the sitting-room was in a blaze. "This window's big enough," Mrs. Bundy threw it open. "Out you go. No arguing; you'll have to catch Mary."

Landing soft in a flower bed Marianne turned back to help the incoherent maid. Then, Mrs. Bundy handed her the box, wound her cloak more closely around her, and followed. "And just in time, too," she summed it up as they looked back to the blazing house. "Arson, of course. It would never have started on two sides at once. I trust he's gone." Her hand, Marianne saw, was on the pocket where she had put the gun.

"He?" Marianne asked.

"The stranger from the village, I should think. Well, not much use dallying here to warm ourselves by our fire, as Mr. Garrick would say. Best get down the lane to the farm." She looked back, for a moment, at the blazing house: "I was happy here. I never expected to be. Life's full of surprises."

It seemed to take a very long time to get the now hysterical Mary down the lane to the farm. "Lucky there's a moon," remarked Mrs. Bundy as they turned the last corner to where the big farmhouse stood silent and dark against the sky. And then, "We're going to be unpopular." But she proceeded to beat a resounding tattoo on the seldom used front door of the house.

At last an angry voice hailed them from an upstairs window. "What the devil's to do there?" It was Farmer Thorne himself, his nightcap oddly illuminated by the flickering candle he held.

Mrs. Bundy explained their plight in her usual swift, laconic style, and his angry tone changed to amazement and horror before he hurried down to let them in.

By the time he was able to send some of his men up to the cottage, it was past saving.

"No news to me," said Mrs. Bundy when this was broken to her. "I never thought there was a chance. There wasn't meant to be." She laughed. "Poor man. What a lot of trouble. No doubt he thinks we're all dead in our beds by now. It's thanks to you that we're not, my dear." She and Marianne were sitting huddled over the blazing fire that had been kindled for them. Mary had been put, grumbling, to bed, but Mrs. Bundy had refused to go. "Shouldn't sleep; what's the use?" Now she turned to Farmer Thorne. "You think it won't spread?"

He shook his head. "Too damp for that; it'll burn itself out in the course of the day."

"Good. Then can you spare one of your men to do an errand for me?"

"Willingly, ma'am."

"Thank you. Then send him, if you please, to Exeter, to hire me the best travelling carriage he can find—at once. And horses, of course; four of them; good ones. For the Duchess of Lundy. Send someone you can trust. We'll start as soon as it gets here." She was speaking, now, to Marianne.

"Start?"

"For London. Where else? I should like to get there before the news of my death—and yours. Don't look so puzzled child. Has it really not struck you that there may be more in this fire than Reform Bill madness? As for me, I strongly suspect that we have your husband to thank for tonight's work. If he *is* your husband, which, to tell truth, tonight's work tends, to my mind, to confirm. Do you not find it a most matrimonial bit of behaviour?"

"You mean——" Marianne could hardly believe her ears. "You mean you have lost your house—everything, simply because you sheltered me?"

"But not my life—thanks to you. Never look so distressed; I've been thinking, for some time, that I was tired of this

176

country vegetable existence. Now, thanks to you, it's all over. I look forward to stirring times in town. I wonder if we shall get there first?"

"First?"

"Ahead of Mr. Rossand. I hardly think he will have lingered here. And neither shall we, just in case he should come back to make sure of success and try and finish you off by some other genteel method of murder. You must be a great inconvenience to him, my dear. I wonder why." She rose briskly. "And now I think we should take advantage of Mrs. Thorne's kind offer of beds and rest for a while. We start as soon as the carriage comes. You sleep so little anyway, I am sure you will not object to travelling night and day. I have a mind to get to London first."

"But poor Mary——"

"Mary stays here. I have already arranged it with Mrs. Thorne."

There were a thousand questions Marianne would have liked to ask, but Mrs. Bundy's manner made them all equally impossible. One, however, seemed essential. "I must call you Your Grace?"

Mrs. Bundy swore a good round military oath. "You'll call me ma'am. It's good enough for the Queen; I'll bear it. And now, rest, child. We shall be busy in London."

To her own surprise, Marianne fell asleep almost at once, and woke, much refreshed, to broad daylight and the manifold sounds of the farm. She found Mrs. Bundy, or rather, as she was trying to make herself style her, the Duchess already downstairs talking to Mr. Thorne.

"Good," she smiled at Marianne. "I was about to wake you. The carriage is here; we start at once; Mrs. Thorne has provided food; we will eat and sleep on the way." She picked up the box she had rescued the night before, hitched up the brown stuff gown Mrs. Thorne had lent her, wrapped her military cloak firmly around her, and held out her hand to Mr. Thorne. "I am much in your debt."

"It is a pleasure. We'll take care of Mary, never fear."

"Thank you. I know you will. You've been a good friend, all these years. Come Marianne."

The hired carriage was ancient and battered-looking. Mrs. Bundy inspected it gloomily, paying particular attention to its wheels, then turned to cross-examine its driver and give an approving glance to the four horses. "Your team's all right, at least. Can you drive 'em?"

He had been gaping in astonishment at her bizarre appearance, but reacted with instant respect to her voice. "Yes, ma'am—I should say Your Grace. I used to drive for Sir John Lade."

"Oh, you did, did you? And what made you leave him?"

"Marriage, ma'am, the curse of the working-classes. Don't you fret yourself, I'll get you to London, all right and tight. The horses is good, and the carriage ain't so bad as it looks."

She laughed. "It could hardly be. Very well, you're to decide when to change the horses; I'll leave all to you; and there's ten pounds extra if we get to town tomorrow morning."

"Tomorrow morning!" And then. "Ten pounds! In with you, ma'am. Why are we loitering here!"

"A good man, I think." The Duchess settled with a sigh on the lumpy horsehair seat. "We are going to be monstrous uncomfortable. What's that strange smell, do you think?"

"Fish, I believe."

"Delectable! I shall go to sleep." And she put her booted feet up on the opposite seat, leaned back as comfortably as possible, and closed her eyes.

Marianne was left to dreary contemplation of the desolate past and unpromising future. "Who am I?" creaked the carriage wheels. "Who am I? Who am I? Who am I?" For, against all the evidence, she could still not quite make herself believe in Marianne Rossand. And yet—if he was not her husband, why had Rossand tried to kill her? And there, she thought bitterly to herself, is a fine comment on matrimony. Inevitably, this brought her thoughts circling back to Mauleverer. She was going to London. Would she see him? What would they say? And, "down," she whispered to the hopes that would, incorrigibly, try to spring up. There was no room for hope; of that, at least, she was certain.

The Duchess gave a little grunt at last and woke up. "It's cold," she said. "Colder still tonight. Remind me to buy some blankets when we next stop.

"You really mean to travel through the night?"

"Said so, didn't I? Afraid I'll collapse on your hands, eh?

Don't worry; I'm as tough as I look—and a good bit younger. Think I'm in my dotage, don't you? Well, I'm not. Aged ten years overnight when James was killed. Or so they said. We'd only been married six months. Oh, well; it's a long time ago now." Surprisingly, she laughed. "I can see the questions boiling inside you. And time I talked about it, I suppose. Besides, if you're going to live with the Mad Duchess, you'd better know something about me."

"Is that what they call you?"

"So I'm told. I've never been back, you know. Couldn't face it at first, couldn't be bothered later. Don't look so anxious: I find I'm looking forward to it now. Think of the changes! Regent Street and all poor Prinney's other buildings; gas lighting; Sir Robert Peel's policemen. And how about you? Know anything about London?"

"No, I don't think so."

"Where do you remember?" The question was intentionally sharp, as if to startle an answer out of her.

"Country," Marianne answered at once. "Cliffs, the sea: I can swim and sail a boat, I'm sure."

"Odd in a young lady. Nothing else? It would be—convenient if you were to begin remembering."

"I know—but it's no use. I've tried and tried."

"Then don't." The Duchess had heard the quiver in her voice. "Ask me some more of your questions instead."

"Well, where are we going, ma'am?"

"Why to London, of course."

"I know, but where will we stay? We are hardly dressed for an hotel." Marianne looked down at her drab dress, a gift from Mrs. Thorne's eldest daughter.

"No, we'd hardly be welcome at Mivart's." The Duchess stretched out a booted foot and looked at it reflectively. "How I am going to hate dressing. But to where we're going: Lundy House, of course. Never heard of it? Oh well—it's not as big as Apsley House, nor so splendid as Lord Hertford's, but it's on Park Lane, and quite comfortable, so far as I remember. I expect my nephew will find house room for us easily enough."

"Your nephew?"

"The Duke, God bless him. He's bound to be home, on account of the carryings on in Parliament. Very conscientious, poor John is; always has been from a child. Didn't like to take the house at first, but I was in no mood for Dowager-Duchessing it in Park Lane. Don't suppose I'll enjoy it much now, but never mind." She took pity on Marianne's perplexity. "James left the house to me, you see. And everything else he could, too, poor darling. Not much comfort at the time, I can tell you, but, you know, there's a lot to be said for money. I can afford my pleasures—such as they are. You're to be one of them, and no argument. Boring for me to dress like a Duchess, but I'll enjoy dressing you as my ward."

"Your ward? But, my dear ma'am——"

"Why not. Can't go round calling yourself Miss Amnesia—don't want to call yourself Mrs. Rossand; I can quite see that. Besides, I'm not convinced of that yet, and nor, I think, are you. No: my ward: Miss Lamb, if you like; anything else, if you'd rather. No history; no questions answered; no trouble at all. There are advantages, I find, about being the Mad Duchess. I took James's horsewhip once to someone who asked impertinent questions. Richly deserved—made quite an impression in town—all the gossip columns—I didn't care, why should I? John was a bit bothered, poor boy. That's when he gave in and agreed to take over the house so I could come down here and have some peace. But wouldn't have it as a gift; still in my name; said he was my steward; nonsense of course; but it comes in handy now."

"You mean we are going to stay, without any warning, at Lundy House with your nephew. But, surely, his wife. . . ."

"No wife, worse luck. Can't think why not. Certainly not for lack of trying—on their part. Very eligible duke, John is; not quite in the same category as Devonshire, perhaps—no Chatsworth, for one thing—but marriageable, you know. Must drive the London Mammas wild to have two of them still uncaught. One on each side of the fence, you might say. Should warn you, I suppose, that John is an arrant Tory. Wait till you hear him in the Reform Bill. I hope they haven't broken all his windows, but I expect they have. Still; couldn't be colder than this." And she ended the conversation by wrapping her cloak more closely around her and falling asleep again.

13

IT was early in the morning, and bitterly cold, when the coach rattled, at last, on to the first paving stones of London. The Duchess opened one eye sleepily at the change in the motion of the vehicle, then closed it again: "Wake me when we get there."

Marianne had no watch, but the emptiness of the streets, and the glum grey sky combined to convince her that their driver had earned his extra money. "But ma'am," she ventured, "hardly anyone is stirring. Surely you will not arrive, unannounced, at this hour?"

"What else?" The Duchess roused herself to look out of the carriage window. "I've no mind to go on freezing any longer than is necessary, I can tell you. Besides, I propose to be a great trouble to poor John, and 'begin as you mean to go on,' is my motto: always has been. Anyway, I bet you we find he's been up all night at the House; very likely to catch him just before he retires. Waste of time to try and consider other people; always get it wrong; just more trouble for everyone. Now you've waked me up." She sat up straight in her corner and ran ruthless fingers through her straggling white hair. "Still don't quite believe I'm not in my dotage, do you?" What an uncomfortable gift she had for reading one's thoughts. "I went white when James died. How they talked. God, how tedious it was. All over now. Poor James; the forgetting was the worst, in a way. I used to cry because I couldn't cry. Understand?"

"I think so." Impossible, in fact, to imagine forgetting Mauleverer.

"No, you don't." As usual the Duchess read her thoughts. "But you'll find out—if it comes to that, which I hope it won't. Good God, how town has changed. This was all open country when I was a girl. I can remember primrosing here. Ah well, march of progress, I suppose. Never could understand why it was assumed we *did* progress, but never mind; it sounds better. Nervous?"

"A little."

"No need to be. John's almost too mild. Terrified of me, too, poor boy. Well, not a boy exactly; in his forties I suppose by now; an old man to you, eh? But a good nephew to me, I'll say that for him. You'll be all right in his house. Don't know why I didn't think of it sooner. Bring things to a head, see? Someone, surely, will recognize you. No need to look so frightened; I've confidence in you, if you haven't in yourself. You've done nothing to be ashamed of, and the sooner we prove it, the better. Besides, I've a score to settle with your Mr. Rossand. I liked that house."

"If it really was he," put in Marianne.

"Of course it was he: tried to persuade the villagers; failed; did it himself. Stands to reason. The only thing I want to know is where he went next. Is he hiding in the country somewhere? Does he know we escaped? Lots of questions. Anyway bound to learn you are alive sooner or later, and bound, I take it, to do something about you. I wonder why you're such a threat to him. By rights, John should have some more information about that marriage licence by now—it's taken him long enough, but I suppose he's been busy over this bill like everyone else."

Marianne was appalled. "You mean it is the Duke who has been making inquiries on my behalf?"

"Who else? He's always handled my affairs—and very capably too. Hardly a commission one would entrust to a stranger. No need to look so distressed. John doesn't mind; not enough to do, half the time, but be a Duke. Good for him to have an interest. Good God, look at the Duke's house! Did you ever see anything so pitiful as all those boarded windows. I'd seen them damned before I made such a concession to the mob, and so I'll tell him—and John, too, if he's done it to my house. But of course it stands further back. That was Apsley House," she explained belatedly, "this is Park Lane—the Green Park over there, though it hardly looks it now, and— Ah, here we are at last. Hmmm—the railings aren't a bad idea, and I suppose the gates lock." The carriage had turned through the gates in a high ornamental railed fence as she was speaking, and now came to a halt in front of what seemed to Marianne a perfectly enormous grey stone house.

More than ever aware of their tatterdemalion appearance,

182

Marianne wished she had the courage to point out that the Duchess's borrowed bonnet was askew over wildly straggling white hair. Surreptitiously patting her own ringlets into some kind of order, she felt the Duchess's sardonic eye upon her: "Past praying for, if you ask me. I wouldn't worry." Their driver had opened the carriage door and let down the steps by now, and with these far from encouraging words, the Duchess climbed lightly out, instructing the man, as she did so, to, "Knock me a good peal on that door."

The man looked frightened, but obeyed, while Marianne joined the Duchess in the arched portico.

"I shall be glad of some breakfast. Ah, at last——" The Duchess broke off as the big door swung slowly open to reveal a sleepy-looking footman half in, half out of his livery jacket. "My good man," she went on, "that is no way to receive guests. Is the Duke at home?"

"His Grace? At home to company at eight o'clock in the morning? And to a couple of gypsies too, by the look of it." The man yawned insolently. "Best be off with you, before I send for the Peelers."

"You mistake the matter a trifle." Unruffled. "And I have no wish to lose you your position. I have no doubt that those of your fellow servants who are somewhat older—and wiser—than you have told you of the Mad Duchess. Well, here I am. If my nephew is not at home, you will bring me the house-keeper. She will make arrangements for my reception, and that of my ward."

There was something in her tone that did not encourage discussion. Reluctantly, the man stood aside to let her and Marianne enter the spacious entrance hall, "No need to look so alarmed," the Duchess told him kindly. "I really am the Dowager Duchess. Now, fetch Melton, if you please."

The man seemed to find his wits and his tongue at once. "But the Duke is here," he said. "He is but now returned from the House. He is eating his breakfast—supper—what you will. I do not like to disturb him."

"I am glad to hear he is so formidable a master. In the study, no doubt? Come, Marianne." And the Duchess tramped down the tessellated hall in her cavalry boots, threw open a door at the far end, and said, with obvious pleasure, "Ah, John, the very thing we need: breakfast. Oh, and tell your man I really am the Mad Duchess; he is in perfect fits for fear of having done the wrong thing."

The tall man who had been sitting with a cup of coffee beside a blazing fire came forward, hands outstretched. "My dear Aunt, this is a most unexpected pleasure." And then: "Breakfast? Of course. James, two more breakfasts. Quick."

He was not at all what Marianne expected. His aunt's affectionate but faintly disparaging remarks about him had made her imagine a frail, elderly, cypher of a man, but this was a fair-haired giant who was now taking her hand in acknowledgement of his aunt's introduction of "My ward, Miss Lamb," Taller than Mauleverer—her inevitable standard of comparison—he was also much broader in the shoulder and gave an impression of rugged outdoors health, even in his present costume of a fur-lined banyan, or dressing-gown. His smile, as he greeted her, was reassuringly warm. "My aunt has written me about you, Miss Lamb. You are most welcome to Lundy House."

Stammering her thanks, Marianne thought him the most perfect gentleman she had ever met. Nothing in his behaviour gave the slightest hint at their unexpected arrival and bizarre appearance. He was urging the Duchess, now, to the chair by the fire that he had vacated and bringing up another for Marianne. "You must be perished with the cold." He seated her. "And are come direct from Devon?" The question was for his aunt.

"Non-stop." She smiled up at him with evident affection. "We found ourselves in need of a protector, and are come, of course, to you."

"I am delighted to hear it." He smiled back at her. "Not that I believe it for a moment. When you need a protector, Aunt, chaos is come again."

"Thank you." She stretched out her booted feet to the fire. "But just the same, we have a great many problems, Miss Lamb and I. We need clothes, to begin with. My house burned down, night before last." She threw it in casually.

"Your house! The rioters? Impossible!"

"Yes, quite impossible. Not rioters. Miss Lamb's husband, we think, if he is her husband."

"I notice you call her Miss Lamb—excuse me," he turned to Marianne. "This must be a painful topic to you."

There was something warming about his smile. "Please don't apologize," she said, "I am used to it. And, your Grace, I must thank you——"

"Oh, come," the Duchess interrupted her. "Are you my ward, Marianne, or aren't you? If you start calling John 'your Grace,' we'll all be exchanging formalities here till doomsday. And as for thanking him; why not thank me. I made him do it."

The Duke laughed. "You see," he said, "she bullies us all. But, no thanks, Miss Lamb, I am only happy to think that I may have been of some service to you. And—I hope I have better news. Have you ever been to Romney Marsh?"

"Not that I know of—but of course that does not mean much."

"Quite so. But did not this man, Rossand, who pretended to be your husband, talk of marrying you at a little church on a hill?"

"Yes?"

"Well, there you have it. Paul Rossand married Marianne Loudon at Dymchurch, in Kent. I cannot, off-hand, think of a flatter bit of England. You could no more talk of walking down the hill from church—if it had been Rye or Winchelsea, it would have been something else again, but Dymchurch—I can only assume that his memory betrayed him when he was inventing corroborative detail for your benefit."

"You mean—he's not my husband?"

"It seems to me most unlikely. I think it far more probable that he searched the records until he found a marriage that fitted in with his story and contrived to obtain a copy of the certificate."

"So his name is not Rossand, and mine has never been Loudon?"

"Precisely." He looked pleased, as with an apt pupil "So that in a way you are no further on than before—but at least you are not married."

"At least!" Oh, what a gullible fool she had been to accept the *soi-disant* Rossand's story so easily—and yet, he had known so much about her. She coloured at the memory.

"I take it," went on the Duke in his measured tones, "that he produced sufficient evidence to convince you—at the time—that you had been married to him."

185

"Yes." He seemed to share his aunt's gift for reading one's thoughts.

"The trouble is," he said thoughtfully, "that you are in such an exposed position, undefended by memory. After all, he may have known you—but not as a husband. I think you were entirely right to come to London, Aunt."

She twinkled at him. "I am delighted to have your approval. Yes, I think Marianne's public appearance, in our protection, should precipitate something. Clearly impossible to go on as she is. Ah, is that breakfast? Good to see you, Mrs. Melton. Come to make sure it's really me?"

The black-garbed housekeeper rustled forward: "Yes, breakfast is ready in the small breakfast room, your Grace. And may I say you're a sight for sore eyes, ma'am. I never thought I'd live to see you back where you belonged."

"No tears, now." The Duchess rose to her feet. "The time for them is past. Besides, I want my breakfast. You've worn well, Melton." And then, with one of her swift changes of tone: "Shouldn't you be in bed, John? Up all night in that stuffy chamber. Don't wait on us; Melton will manage."

"No, no," he opened the door for her. "This is much too exciting an occasion for anything so tame as sleep. Besides, I want to hear your plan of campaign, Aunt. I have no doubt you have it all mapped out—and still less that I am to play a part. Best break it to me now."

She laughed and helped herself to scrambled eggs. "You're right, of course. Nothing wrong with your wits, John, I'll say that for you. I thought a ball—a welcome home for the Mad Duchess—appropriate, surely?"

He laughed. "The least I can do. When?"

"The sooner the better. I want Marianne to surprise the world when I launch her; no time for gossip first. Two weeks from today?"

"I don't see why not. But do you mean to keep Miss Lamb mewed up here in the meantime?"

"Impossible. I wish I could, but she and I have clothes to buy. I'll need my diamonds, John; all of them. As for Miss Lamb: no introductions; policy of mysterious silence; get them all agog; introduce her at the ball and see what happens."

"But, ma'am," Marianne could not keep silent no longer. "You cannot mean to give a ball for me!"

"I don't. Told you it was John's ball—and my welcome home. But the ideal opportunity for you to make your début."

"But, consider! I may be nobody—worse."

"I'll chance it." She shrugged and drank coffee. "Known as mad already; what's the difference? Besides, I don't believe it. What megrim have you in your head now? Decided you're someone's by-blow and least said soonest mended? Well, I've thought of it myself, but what's the odds? We'll ask the Duke of Munster and all the other FitzClarences. Anyway, I don't believe it. Wouldn't explain Mr. Rossand—or whatever his name is, for one thing." She turned back to her nephew. "Very well, two weeks from today. We'll make the arrangements; I know you're busy. Weippert's music still the best?"

"I believe so. You will have the bills sent to me, of course."

"'I shall do nothing of the kind. My house, isn't it? My ball? My idea? Very well then."

He did not argue the point further, but Marianne noted, with amusement, a tiny glint of determination in his eye. It would be interesting to see who won. But she had her own protest to make. "I cannot let you do it," she said. "And, besides, I have no clothes. . . ."

"Just what I said. We are going to be busy, you and I. Are you up on the latest fashions, John?"

He laughed. "I'm afraid not."

"Wretched boy. Well, do you know if Madame Breguet is still making?"

"Yes. I heard two ladies complaining of her bills only the other day."

"Good. Send a message to her for me, John. I will see her at five o'clock. And now, to bed with you; you're out on your feet. And, to tell truth, we're not much better. Do you think the admirable Melton will have our rooms ready yet?"

"I'm sure of it."

Marianne was still trying to protest as the housekeeper led them upstairs, but the Duchess made short work of her. "Haven't paid you any wages, have I, all the time you've been with me? Doing the work of an entire staff, too. What do you pay your servants, John? All of them? No, no, never mind, no need to work it out. Marianne takes my point. She's not stupid. Besides," a brown hand rested, for a moment, lightly on Marianne's, "I shall enjoy it. Never had daughters . . . never had children, come to that. It's a lot to miss. Let me dress you, my dear."

This was unanswerable, but Marianne addressed a last protest to the Duke. "But the ball . . . sir, you cannot wish to be involved in such a proceeding. As your aunt says, I may be anything. . . ."

He smiled down at her very kindly. "Why so you may, and you surely cannot be so brutal as to deprive me of the pleasure of finding the answer to your mystery. I am sure my aunt is right; this is the way to do it. Besides, you know as well as I do that she always gets what she wants. My only stipulation is that you save me the first dance at your ball."

It was too much. Marianne fought down tears and retired hastily into the bedroom that had been allotted to her, only to be overwhelmed all over again by its luxury. Strange to think of the Duchess leaving all this for the cottage in the valley. Or —not so strange. Velvet curtains, linen sheets, down pillows— she settled luxuriously on the bed—what was the use of them after all? The Duchess was kind, her nephew was wonderfully so, but what good was that? Mauleverer would be asked to the ball, no doubt—and dance all evening with Lady Heverdon. But she was too exhausted to be kept awake, even by tears.

Madame Breguet welcomed the Duchess with tears in her eyes. "The belle of her day," she explained to Marianne in her strongly accented English: "Ah, the costumes we have designed together, Her Grace and I. And now, we begin again, is it not?" The black eyes flashed knowingly. "A ball dress for a *jeune fille* who makes her first appearance? Silver tissue over white satin, *sans doute*? Caught up, here and there, with white roses. Or will there be jewels, perhaps?" The black eyes were asking the Duchess a question.

"No, no," she sounded amused, "no jewels, Madame Breguet. Just a young girl at her first ball. How I detest these puffed sleeves, but they will suit you, Marianne. And a white rose for the headdress, too. It is Isidore, these days, Madame Breguet, or Nardin?"

"You have not lost touch, I see, your Grace! Either is excellent. Myself, I prefer the effects M. Isidore achieves; especially for a very young lady like miss here."

"Very well, Isidore it shall be. Remind me, Marianne, to

make the arrangements. And as for me, I shall be the complete dowager in black velvet—and diamonds."

The two weeks that followed were strange ones for Marianne. At Lundy House, preparations for the ball went on apace, and the Duchess entertained herself and her visitor with the daily roll call of acceptances. "Of course, it's curiosity in the main," she said. "They've all heard about me; I expect they want to see if I wear Hessian boots to dance in. Not that I shall dance, of course. I shall leave that department to you, my dear. Which reminds me : can you dance?"

Marianne laughed. "I think so."

"I hope so." And she took advantage of the Duke's early return, that night, from the House of Lords, to make him lead Marianne through the steps of a few of the most popular dances. "Yes," she nodded approval at last, "you can dance. But you do not remember London?"

"Not in the slightest."

"It's very strange. I cannot understand how a well brought up girl like you should have missed coming here. But you don't know the people either." She had tried firing off the names of her prospective guests suddenly at Marianne, in the hope of getting a reaction, but without the slightest sucess. Some names of course, Marianne knew. She was frightened to think that the Duke of Wellington was coming—"no need to put yourself in a pucker about him, my dear; he's an old friend of mine. But you don't remember Melbourne, or D'Orsay, or Alvanley?"

"I'm afraid not."

"It's very strange. But depend upon it, someone will remember you. In the meantime, we'll go nowhere. I wish you to come as a complete surprise."

"But, poor Miss Lamb," intervened the Duke. "You cannot, surely, intend to keep her mewed up in the house here for two weeks?"

"Oh, no. I've no objection to her going out, so long as she does not go into society. It's hardly the weather for riding in the park, though. I do not see why Miss Lamb should want to go out."

"No reason to go out? With all of London to be explored? You do Miss Lamb less than justice, Aunt. Now, I was considering inviting her to come and see the new printing presses,

189

Mr. Barnes has put in at *The Times* newspaper. And then there's the Mint, and the Tower of London and the new London Bridge and all kinds of things that I am sure she would like to see. I do not suggest the Houses of Parliament, though I suspect it is what she would like best, because there, unlike other places I have named, we might perhaps meet someone in society."

The Duchess laughed. "You might indeed. But, for the rest of it, if it will amuse you, my dear, I have no objection. And if you should meet anyone, John, you must just suffer from a temporary lapse of good manners and fail to introduce Marianne. Pretend you have forgotten her name—anything."

He laughed. "I could hardly forget what I have never known. Very well then, we start tomorrow, Miss Lamb. What shall it be? *The Times* or the Tower?"

"But, surely, you must have so much to do——"

"Nonsense." She had already learned that he could be quite as dictatorial as his aunt. "I have nothing to do that I shall enjoy half as much as this. And, besides, who could wish to stay in this house, in the state of chaos to which you ladies have reduced it."

The Duchess rapped his knuckles sharply with her paper knife: "You are an ill-conditioned, ill-mannererd boy, John. When did you hear of a ball being given without a little preliminary chaos? You should be grateful that we do not leave the organizing of it to you."

"I am, Aunt, believe me. I'd rather organize a General Election than a ball."

"And so you may be doing any day soon, by the sound of things. Thank goodness, Parliament will be in recess by the night of the ball—and I hope without rioting this time. I find the town quieter than I expected."

"It's the news of the cholera, I think. It's not good, you know. And, that reminds me, I do not wish to interfere in your arrangements, Aunt, but I do suggest that you do not serve either fruit or water ices."

"As bad as that, is it?" She looked at him sharply, "Very well. It will be a saving, at all events."

"A drop of frugality in your ocean of extravagance?"

She threw her snuff box at him. "And to think I told Marianne here that you were a mild and biddable man. Why didn't I know how you'd come one? I should have been back here long since."

He had caught the box neatly and now opened in and took a pinch, saying reprovingly: "A deplorably outmoded habit my dear Aunt. I am glad you thought me mild and biddable—once."

He was still the easiest and most courteous of cavaliers, and Marianne was amazed at how much she enjoyed her series of sight-seeing excursions with him. Indeed, it seemed almost ungrateful that all the time her eyes were at a stretch, wilfully turning one stranger after another into the familiar figure of Mauleverer. If only they could have gone to the House of Lords; but she had to admit the sense of the Duchess's prohibition. The old lady had also dealt ruthlessly with Marianne's timid suggestion that she would like to call on Mrs. Mauleverer. "No, no. You are not here. Practically speaking, you do not exist until the day of the ball. I'll not have you spoiling everything with your sentimental pilgrimages. Mrs. Mauleverer and her son have accepted my invitation—and so, by the by, has Lady Heverdon. You must just wait till then to see them. After all, you are not too desperately bored in the meanwhile, are you?"

"Far from it. The Duke has been wonderfully kind."

"He is kind. I told you that long since. Afraid you're taking advantage of him, eh? I wouldn't worry, if I were you. Not many girls would, anyway, but I like it in you. Pining all the time after that bad-tempered Whig of yours, aren't you? Never mind; won't hurt John if he does break his heart a little; good practice, if you ask me. Get over it, find another girl; you wait and see. And in the mean time, just don't worry: it's a bad habit."

Marianne laughed. "Of course you are right, as always, ma'am, but I wish it were as easily done, as said."

"And you're thinking I'm a fine one to talk of getting over broken hearts, aren't you? But, remember, I was married to my James. Quite another matter. Besides, you might change your mind yourself. I'm sure John would think the chance worth taking; if he thought about it at all, which I'm sure he doesn't. No need to frown like that; you may surprise yourself yet. Look at the way he's carrying on with Lady Heverdon."

191

All too clearly this last "he" referred to Mauleverer, or rather to the new Lord Heverdon. Unluckily for Marianne's peace of mind, his behaviour in first refusing and then taking his title for political reasons had caught the public's fancy, and there were almost daily paragraphs about him in the newspapers. The ones reporting his speeches in the Lords gave her much pleasure. He was losing no time in making a name for himself. But the others—and there were many more of them —were a misery. Hardly a day passed without his being reported as appearing at this ball or that rout in attendance on "his cousin, the beautiful Lady Heverdon." To add piquancy to the situation—for the gossip columnists—all the world, apparently, knew that Lady Heverdon had another devoted slave in her cousin, Ralph Urban, and the chances of the two suitors were discussed in terms reminiscent of the race track or the stables.

These mentions of Ralph Urban gave Marianne some hope, for she remembered the affectionate terms in which Lady Heverdon had spoken of him long ago at Mauleverer Hall. But a visit to Covent Garden plunged her once more into despair. She had persuaded the Duchess to let her and the Duke make a surreptitious visit to the pit, where no one was likely to know them, in order to see *Fra Diavolo,* but her evening was ruined by the spectacle of Lady Heverdon flirting outrageously with Mauleverer in a stage box. And—he showed every sign of enjoying the languishing glances so lavishly bestowed upon him by those huge blue eyes. To see him for the first time, after all this misery, and to see him thus! It was almost more than Marianne could bear. She pleaded headache and they went home before the farce.

Meanwhile Lord John Russell had introduced a revised version of the Reform Bill in the House of Commons and it had been triumphantly carried by a two-to-one majority very early on a Sunday morning in mid-December. "Thank goodness for that," said the Duchess. "Now they are in recess at last we can be sure of our guests." Even the Duke, deploring it, considered the bill as good as carried, and his aunt teased him unmercifully about the failure of his party to hold back the tide of progress. She liked to quote Sydney Smith's Taunton speech about Dame Partington and her broom at him, and Marianne was constantly amazed at how sweetly he bore it. Imagine teasing Mauleverer when the word was going against him.

"Anyway," said the Duchess, "town should be quiet for a while and we need not fear that our guests will be pelted with mud, or paving stones, when they arrive tomorrow. What shall we worry about instead? The hothouse flowers being killed by frost? The musicians getting drunk? Or a case of cholera among the guests?"

Marianne shuddered. "Do not joke about it, ma'am, I beg you."

"Or if you insist upon worrying," suggested the Duke, "Why not choose some really probable subject, as for instance my going mad in white linen at the confusion of the house. When I met my steward in the study this morning, we found ourselves forced to confer between a potted palm tree and a half erected bandstand. I go in hourly terror of finding that my bedroom has been converted into a retiring room for the ladies."

"An excellent idea," said his aunt. "Why did we not think of that, Marianne?"

In fact, she was an admirable organizer, and the evening of the ball arrived without any worse disaster than the discovery that the moth had got into the red carpeting for the front entry. And that, as the Duchess lost no time in pointing out, merely proved that her nephew had been grossly remiss in the discharge of his social duties. "As if it needed proving. I am convinced our enormous number of acceptances are as much out of curiosity about you as about me, John. I am sure a misanthropic Duke is quite as much of a phenomenon as a mere Mad Duchess. It is going to be a terrible crush I am afraid."

"Yes, I am certainly misanthrope enough to wish it were well over. We shall be lucky if we do not have several faints and a case or two of the vapours. Which do you propose to indulge in, Miss Lamb?"

"I shall wait and see," said Marianne.

14

THE Duchess refused to let Marianne take any part in the final preparations for the ball, but sent her firmly to bed for the afternoon: "I want you in looks tonight. You are not to get up until Isidore arrives to do your hair. Here; this just arrived." She handed Marianne the latest volume of Sir Walter Scott's *Tales of My Landlord.* "That should keep you quiet."

The whole house smelled of hot house flowers and echoed with the manifold noises of last minute preparations. Someone was hammering in the room below Marianne's; further away, a violinist was trying out a few bars of his music; the caterer's men were bringing chairs and tables for the supper, and, apparently, dropping most of them. And, above, in the servants' quarters, there was a constant scurrying of feet as they, too, made their last minute preparations. The very idea of sleep was an absurdity; Marianne lay down on her bed and opened her book.

She was waked by Fanny, the maid the Duchess had insisted on engaging for her. It was dark already, and the girl's candle made flickering shadows on the ceiling.

"Good gracious, Fanny. Is it very late?"

"No, no. Just time to eat this." Fanny put down the tray she was carrying, removed the candle to a place of safety, and crossed the room to draw the heavy blue velvet curtains. "It's a fine bright night," she said. "There won't half be a squeeze. Everyone'll come. I should think. You should hear the questions they ask one about Her Grace—and about you, too, miss. Ain't you excited?"

"Yes, I rather think I am." She made herself eat some of the cake and drink the milk the Duchess had ordered for her. "Is Isidore here yet?"

"Yes, he's with Her Grace." Fanny took the silver and white ball dress out of the closet and shook out its folds before laying it lovingly along the full length of a small sofa, where it looked, Marianne thought, almost complete in itself.

"Isidore will want to see it," the girl explained. "We'd best be getting you into your under-dress now, miss, if you're ready."

Since Isidore and Fanny were both perfectionists, it was a long and exhausting time before the last tiny silver button was fastened and Marianne was pronounced ready.

"You'll be the belle of the ball, miss, and no mistake." Fanny handed Marianne her long white gloves and stood back to survey her handiwork. "Oh, miss, do you think he'll pop tonight?"

"Pop?"

"The question, miss. The betting's even in the servants' hall. I don't see as how he'll be able to help it, the way you look tonight. Oh! Your Grace!"

The Duchess stood in the doorway and looked Marianne over: "Excellent," she said at last. "Just what I intended." And then, with a laugh, "And what do you think of me? Will they think they're getting their money's worth of Mad Duchess?"

"They must think you superb, ma'am." And indeed Marianne was amazed at the transformation that Isidore, dark brown velvet and diamonds had made in her friend's appearance.

"I think they will treat me with respect, which is what I intend. A great bore, but worth it for once. Come down and let's see what John thinks of his reformed aunt. Not that he'll have eyes for me. Time we were down anyway. I asked the Duke to come early."

"The Duke?"

"*The* Duke. Wellington, of course. Wellesley, when I knew him and no higher in rank than my James. A long time ago, but not one to forget his friends. Said he'd be early; he'll be early. With two dukes to support you, I should think you'd do. There, John"—he was awaiting them at the bottom of the sweeping stairs—"What do you think of us?"

"Magnificent," he took her hand, and, "Enchanting," he took Marianne's, and held it for a moment before turning back to his aunt. "I'm afraid you are going to be a great disappointment to the people who expect to find you wearing cavalry boots, ma'am."

"I intend to be. Is everything ready?"

"Down to the last bon-bon dish. And here, I rather think, is the first guest. To your places, ladies; the battle begins. Remember my dances, Miss Lamb. A host must have some privileges, and I think I shall have earned them."

From then on it was a whirl of introductions, curtsies and compliments. At first, Marianne tried to remember the names that were shouted, in stentorian tones, down the great entrance hall, then she gave that up and concentrated on remembering faces, and, still more, on watching for a flash of recognition in one of the pairs of eyes that met hers with admiration, or curiosity, depending on the sex of their owner. It never came. Her programme was scrawled full of the initials of her intended partners, but she knew none of them, and, it seemed, none of them knew her. The rooms were full, now, though not yet crowded, and it was almost time for the dancing to begin. If she was not careful, her programme would be quite full, and still Mauleverer had not come. If he did not, the evening was dust and ashes.

The musicians were striking up in the long hall. "Good," said the Duchess, "you two children must go and lead the set. I'll stay on duty here a while. Did I see D'Orsay asking you for a dance, my dear?"

Marianne consulted her programme. "Yes, I believe so."

"Then your social worries are over. Though why that French dandy should have such influence is more than I can imagine. Tell him I said so, if you wish. No, perhaps best not."

The Duke took her arm to guide her through the crowd. "How does it feel to be a success, Cinderella?"

Dust and ashes were bitter in her mouth, but she managed a smile. "Unreal."

The Duke was to take out the Princess de Lieven for the first dance and his aunt had told the Duke of Devonshire that he was to partner Marianne. Now, with the musicians striking up their first notes, and the couples forming below them down the long hall, Marianne found herself grateful for the choice. The Duke was kindness itself, but once the music began his slight deafness made conversation impossible. She was free to spend all the attention she could spare from the half-forgotten intricacies of the quadrille in searching the room for Mauleverer. By the end of the first dance, she was sure he was not on the floor, and was glad to take the Duke's arm for a stroll about the rooms before the next set was formed.

196

Still there was no sign of Mauleverer, though she half thought she had caught a glimpse of Lady Heverdon in one of the further rooms. But they were so crowded that it was difficult to be sure. The Duke was complimenting her in his diffident, pleasant way on the crowds who had come to do her honour. The music was striking up again, the loud preliminary chords proclaiming that the next dance was to be a waltz. Her own Duke—absurd to think of him like that—the Duke of Lundy was approaching to claim her hand.

As she took his arm, she was aware, for an instant, through a gap in the crowd, of a tall figure making an unusually purposeful way towards them. Could it be? She was almost sure it was Mauleverer. But a huge dowager in a saffron-coloured turban bore down on them, effectively cutting off her view. Trying in vain to look past her, Marianne submitted to an introduction. The Dowager, it seemed, was some kind of cousin of the Duke's. Her voice said everything that was polite, her hostile eyes summed Marianne up from top to toe. This was the other side of the picture. On the surface, perhaps, society was welcoming her enthusiastically, but what of the currents below?

The Duke gave her arm a little, encouraging shake. "You mustn't mind Cousin Hester. I'm afraid she has let herself be a trifle embittered by a family of five plain daughters."

"Oh dear!" Laughing, grateful to him, Marianne could not resist turning for one last eager glance towards where she thought she had seen Mauleverer.

Once more, the Duke seemed to read her thoughts. "I do not believe he is here yet."

"I thought I saw him." She did not pretend not to understand.

"Do not——" He swung her into his arms without finishing the words of—what? advice? warning? that he had intended. How kind he was—and how well he waltzed. Impossible, now, to be looking about the room, and yet, as she surrendered herself to the intoxication of the dance, Marianne could not help wishing that it was other arms that held her. To waltz with the Duke was pleasure, with Mauleverer it would be ecstasy. Angry with herself for the ingratitude of the thought, she bent backwards to smile up at her partner, and, as she did so, saw Mauleverer standing on the stair that led up

197

to the musicians' gallery. Just time to take in the white, set face, then the swoop of the dance had taken her clear across to the other side of the room. When she next looked, he was gone. But, surely, he had seen her and would approach her at the end of the dance?

It seemed as if it would go on for ever. At each climax of the music she thought, now—now it will be over, now I shall see him . . . and each time the musicians slowed, swooped and went on again. Distracted, she missed the beat and would have stumbled if the Duke's firm arm had not held her up.

"You are tired? Would you like to go and see who my incorrigible aunt is bullying now?"

"A little. Yes, do let us." Might not Mauleverer have gone to demand an explanation from the Duchess?

But when they found her, surrounded by an admiring group of elderly men who had once been her husband's fellow officers, there was no sign of Mauleverer.

The evening began to seem endless, and Marianne went through the motions of pleasure with a smiling face and a heart of lead. It was almost a relief when, dancing the third quadrille with an enthusiastic young cavalry officer, she heard an ominous tearing of material as he trod heavily on one of her silver flounces. Excusing herself, she made her way to a small downstairs saloon that had been turned into a ladies' retiring room. It seemed heavenly dark and quiet and, for a moment, she thought it was empty and that at last she could give way, if only for a moment, to the misery in which she felt herself drowning. Then, as she moved forward, she was aware of movement in a corner. Someone was before her in wretchedness. Her dark figure was bent almost double on a little sofa shaking with tears. Forgetting her misery, her flounce, her waiting partner, Marianne hurried across the room. "My dear madam, what is the matter? What can I do for you?"

"Marianne!" At her voice, the woman raised her head. It was Mrs. Mauleverer, but Mrs. Mauleverer appallingly changed. She seemed to have aged ten years since Marianne had last seen her. Her cheeks had fallen in and her eyes were shadowed with enormous dark circles. She held out a trembling hand. "Oh, Marianne, why did you leave us?"

Marianne took and held it gently, feeling it icy cold. "I had to, ma'am. But—you are ill. You should not be here. Let me have your carriage sent for." No time now—and yet how could she help it—to be thinking of Mark.

"No, no." The hand in hers shook more convulsively than ever. "I am not ill. Do not say so. They will send me away; I know it. Lady Heverdon has it all planned: to an asylum for aged persons. Marianne, why did you leave me? Oh, if only I had my drops!"

"Your drops?" Marianne thought she was beginning to understand.

"Yes. Mark made Martha stay behind in the country. I cannot manage without my drops; I don't care what they say. Is it better to be like this?" She raised her ravaged face to Marianne's. "Perhaps I had got to depend on them, but surely it is better to be able to sleep . . . to enjoy life . . . than to be like this. Oh, Marianne, what shall I do?"

"Come up to my room, to begin with. You cannot possibly appear as you are. Fanny—my maid will look after you." She was helping her, as she spoke, to the second doorway, which communicated directly with the back stairs. "But how could Mr. Mauleverer let you come like this?"

"He did not know. He notices nothing these days. Oh, Marianne, how could you do it? I am afraid he will marry her, and we shall all be wretched." She was sobbing hard, and shaking so much that Marianne had difficulty in getting her up the stairs. She settled her at last on her own bed, rang for Fanny and gave her orders. "She must stay the night, of course." She let Fanny pin the flounce and run a comb through her curls. "Arrange about a room, Fanny. No, I do not think a doctor will be necessary. At least it can wait till the morning. There, thank you, that will do admirably. I must not stay longer from the ball."

"No indeed, miss. Your partners will be missing you sadly, such looks as you are in. Oh, miss, has he——"

"I must go," Marianne cut short the question. "Take good care of Mrs. Mauleverer for me."

Hurrying downstairs, she found the Duke looking for her. "My dance," he said. "I began to fear you had played me false, Miss Lamb." He took her hand to lead her out on to the floor, but she held back for a moment.

"Will you do me a great kindness?"

199

"You have only to name it."

"I must speak to Mr. Mauleverer—Lord Heverdon—alone."
She felt her colour rise as she spoke and hurried to explain.
"His mother is ill; I have taken her upstairs; I must speak to
him about her."

"Of course." He spoke as if it was the most natural thing
in the world and she could have kissed him for it. "I will find
him at once; but where shall I bring him?" He looked about
the crowded room. "I know—the little office; it is stacked full
of furniture, but you will not mind that. Go there, and I will
bring him to you."

"Oh, thank you."

The little office was indeed full of the furniture that had
been moved out of the other rooms, but Marianne managed to
find the corner of a chair to sit on, and rested for a moment,
tormenting herself with how to begin her interview with
Mauleverer. She need not have troubled herself. He began it.
Shutting the door behind him with the carefully controlled
gestures of whitehot rage, he loomed over her, taller, surely,
and gaunter than she remembered him.

"Well, Miss Lamb, so you condescend at last, to see me.
Are you sure you can spare the time? With your ducal messenger waiting outside, too! Have you been contriving at ways
to insult me still further than you already have, that you make
him, of all people, your messenger?"

This was worse than she could possibly have imagined.
"Insult you? What can you mean?"

"You thought it a compliment then, to accept my suit, and
then vanish in the night when you discovered a better prospect? I grant you, Mauleverer of Maulever Hall is but a poor
catch compared with the Duke of Lundy; what I cannot understand is why you troubled to play me at all. Was is merely for
the entertainment of the thing? Or, perhaps, to keep your
hand in? You must have been deathly bored in our country
solitudes. I cannot imagine how you stood it so long, with
nothing but a crazy old woman for your companion."

This brought anger to her assistance. "The crazy old woman
you speak of is your mother, sir, and it is about her that I
wish to speak to you. Oh, it is true that I had had some idea
of explaining that disappearance of mine. I had meant to tell
you about the letter I wrote you, and the tears that fell on it,

but what is the use? You have condemned me unheard. To explain would merely be wasting my time, and yours, for which, I understand, you have found better occupation. I will not keep you long from Lady Heverdon, but there is something I must say to you. It is my fault, I think, that you discovered the hold Martha had over your mother. I should have known that you would act with your usual rashness. Have you no affection for Mrs. Mauleverer? Do you not understand that such an addiction as hers must be handled gently? To cut her off, so brutally, from the drops on which she relied for the comfort and companionship you have so signally failed to give her—it is surprising she is only ill, and not mad indeed. And as if that was not bad enough, you have let Lady Heverdon threaten her with being put away in some prison of an asylum for the aged—I did not think you could be so cruel."

"Oh, now I am cruel, am I? It does not occur to you, I take it, that the beginning of her present affliction—and I grant you that she is very far from well—but have you stopped to think when it was that she became ill? It was the day you left us, Miss Lamb, without word, without a sign. Do you at all remember how happy we thought we were, the three of us, that night? And, in the morning, we woke to find you gone. We will not speak of what I felt, since I am sure of it cannot interest you, but my mother had become devoted to you. I think she would have minded less if it had been I who had vanished. If you could not bring yourself to explain to me, you might at least have left some word for her."

"Oh, my God." This was turning the tables indeed. "I never thought of that. But you must believe me when I tell you that I did write the fullest explanation I could to you. I can only imagine that Martha destroyed it, in the hopes of making still more trouble."

He laughed, the wild sardonic laugh that she remembered and feared. "She certainly succeeded. But tell me, pray, what was this explanation of yours? You were my affianced bride, remember? It is hard to believe now, is it not? We were to be married within a week. Can you imagine it? My mother's first words when she came downstairs that morning were of wedding favours. Then—I had to tell her. And you blame me that she is ill."

"You must let me explain."

"I am eager to do so." But his face remained closed and hard as ever.

"You see—I had learned that I was married—or so I thought."

"Married! Not, I take it, to His Grace, the Duke of Lundy?" His fierce, sardonic glance swept over her figure in its flounces of silver gauze. "I must say that for a married lady, you give a very good imitation of a débutante. If I did not know better, I might fall in love with you myself, so innocent you look in that dress. I wish you the best of luck, Miss Lamb, but spare me, I beg your explanations."

She was fighting back tears. "Mark, try to understand. A man came—a stranger—and told me he was my husband; proved it to me, as I thought. And—there was worse than that. It must have meant a scandal ruinous to your career."

"Should not I have been the best judge of that? If you had loved me as I loved you, you would have at least given me the chance. Oh, don't cry, Miss Lamb; it is too late for that. And you will ruin your ball gown." Angrily, he held out his handkerchief.

His use of the past tense had been too much for her self command. "As if I cared for that. Oh, Mark——" But the door behind him had opened, to reveal Lady Heverdon and, behind her, anxiously hovering, the Duke.

"Thank God I have found you," Lady Heverdon swept forward with a swish of crimson draperies. "Your mother has vanished, Mark. I have looked for her everywhere. I hardly dare think what new mischief she may have got herself into. Oh, I beg your pardon, Miss Lamb. I declare I quite failed to recognize you in that dress. I hope I see you well." Her curtsy, as she spoke, was the most delicate of mockeries.

Returning it, Marianne spoke to Mark. "Your mother is upstairs, in my room. My maid is looking after her. I think it will be best if she spends the night here."

"You are very kind," he said formally. "If it is not too much trouble."

"Of course it is no trouble. I love Mrs. Mauleverer."

"I am relieved to think her in such good hands." Lady Heverdon's voice was mocking. "At what time shall we send the carriage for her tomorrow?"

"No need to do so?" The Duke had come forward to

Marianne's side. "I am sure Miss Lamb would enjoy a longer visit from her friend. . . ."

"Oh, thank you," Marianne turned to him impulsively, grateful for his support.

"I must thank you, too." But Mauleverer's brow was darker, his expression more savage than ever.

"Only best not let her play at cards." Lady Heverdon laid her hand lightly on Mauleverer's arm. "They are striking up for the cotillion, Mark; I would not miss it for anything." There was no mistaking the proprietory gesture with which she led him away.

The door closed with a little sigh behind them. Marianne found she was still twisting Mauleverer's handkerchief between her hands. She raised her tear-drowned eyes to the Duke. "Thank you," she said again.

"I am sorry——" he broke off. "No, I'll not pretend to be sorry. He is a fool—and a mannerless one at that. How could he——" Again he broke off, moved a little nearer to her and began again: "Miss Lamb—Marianne—I know I should wait longer, but I cannot bear to see you like this. I do not hope for anything; I do not expect anything, but let me just give myself the happiness of telling you how much I love you. I know it can seem merely an ill-timed intrusion on your sorrow, but—remember me, will you?"

"Oh!" And then, after a little pause: "I'm sorry——" and the tears came in a flood at last.

"Don't be sorry, Marianne." How did she come to be in his arms? "Loving is worth it. I know you can only think of me, now, as a refuge—a support on your trouble. I am only too happy if you *will* think of me as that. And, perhaps, some day. . . ."

"No," she raised her drenched face to his. "It would not be fair. I love him too much. I can never get over it."

He dried her face gently with his own handkerchief. "Never is a long day, Marianne. Only remember. I shall always be here." He raised her hands that still held Mauleverer's handkerchief, kissed first one and then the other, and let her go. "And now, if you do not want a perfectly devastating scold from my aunt, we had best go back to our guests. Can you face them?"

"Of course I can. Duke, you have given me back my

courage." And she let him take her arm and lead her back to the ballroom.

It was still comparatively early and there were hours of evening to be got through, now without the stimulus of hope. Marianne danced her way dutifully through her list of partners, smiled, sat out, ate chicken and drank champagne at the Duke's side, and wondered if the ball would ever end. And all the time, wherever she turned, she seemed to see Mauleverer, assiduous at Lady Heverdon's side. Even the Duchess commented on it in her dry dispassionate way. "She's left that cousin of hers at home tonight," she said, "and makes the new lord dance attendance instead." Her wise old eyes preached endurance to Marianne. And then, "Do you realize that you are a mad success, my dear? We shall have paragraphs in all the papers tomorrow."

"But no one has recognized me."

"Or if they have," said the Duchess. "They have kept very quiet about it. I wonder. . . ." She did not say what she wondered. Instead, "John tells me Mrs. Mauleverer stays the night."

"Yes; she is not well. I do hope you do not think it forward of me to invite her."

"Fiddle," said the Duchess. "Are we really on such terms, you and I? Besides, John tells me he invited her. Poor John." Her voice said that she knew everything. And then, "Marianne, if you cry here, I will shake you, *coram publico*. Duke" —this time it was the Duke of Wellington she summoned— "come and talk some sense into this ward of mine. She actually thinks Mrs. Jordan a better actress than Mrs. Siddons."

The hours dragged by. Candles winked and sputtered in their sockets; the new gas chandeliers were heating up alarmingly; the rooms were emptying at last when the weary musicians struck up for one last quadrille, and the Duke came to claim Marianne's hand. "It is really the very last," he led her out to the top of the set. "And I know you wish to end as gallantly as you have carried on."

"Thank you." But, despite herself, her eyes had travelled down the room to where Mauleverer stood facing Lady Heverdon. "You have been very kind."

"I have been very selfish."

"I don't think you know how to be selfish. Oh, I wish. . . ."

"So do I." But the dance had begun. Only once, as she moved through it, did she have to encounter Mauleverer. His hand, when he touched hers, was cold as ice, his eyes seemed not to see her; the music changed and he passed on down the room.

From the doorway came the footmen's stentorian cries as one by one carriages drew up to collect the exhausted guests. "Lady Heverdon's carriage stops the way," was the cry now, and Marianne saw Mauleverer leave the set to escort her home. It is all over, she told herself. Finished.

"There," the Duke seemed to echo her thought. "It is finished. And you are exhausted. Do not wait for the last guests to go; that is my part. Try and get some sleep." He smiled. "For, indeed, it is morning already. The morning always comes, Miss Lamb."

"You mean: it is always darkest, before the dawn." But she smiled back at him, grateful for the attempt at comfort, before she turned away to climb slowly up the great stair.

15

THE aftermath of a ball is always depressing. When Marianne woke, late and jaded to inevitable grey December weather, the great house was still being tidied up. Fanny, bringing her chocolate and rolls in bed, strongly urged the desirability of her staying there. "It's nothing but confusion belowstairs, miss, and you look a trifle peaked, if you don't mind my saying so. Nor there's nothing in the world to get up for. His Grace has gone out of town on business—up first thing, he was, and gave his orders. And the Duchess, she's writing letters and says she's in a devil of a bad temper—excusing me, miss, but them's her words—and not to be disturbed. And as for the old lady; she's sleeping like a baby in the room next door; I borrowed a draught for her from Her Grace's maid and she looks to be making up several weeks' sleep. Why don't you try and do so too, miss? You could do with it."

But Marianne could not rest. She was up and dressed in a warm walking dress of dark red merino when Fanny reappeared with a note for her. "The callers have started already," she announced, "but they're being sent away fast enough. You should hear the lies: 'Her Grace is slightly indisposed.' I wish they could hear what she said. Oh," she handed over the note, "this came for you. No answer, he said."

From Mauleverer? Marianne opened it with a hand that would shake; and read:

"I must see you. There is something you need to know. Tell no one, for your own sake and that of those you love. Perhaps you were right not to trust me before. This time you must. I shall await you at the entrance to the park." And the signature, in the unknown, precise handwriting: "Paul R."

"The entrance to the park." She moved to the window and looked up across Park Lane. Despite the cold, the usual little group of idlers was gathered there. A pedlar was selling hot chestnuts, muffled to the eyes in rags; a woman called her wares in a voice so hoarse as to be incomprehensible. The place was admirably chosen for a secret meeting. "Tell no one." She did not want to meet Paul Rossand once more alone. And yet, if she took a companion, he would be bound to see and would simply disappear once more. Besides, who could she take? If only the Duke had been at home, she might have consulted him. The Duchess? No, she was in "a devil of a bad temper." Best see Rossand first. After all, there was no possible chance of her coming to harm in so public a place. It would be time enough to tell the Duchess about it when she returned.

It had taken her hardly any time to make up her mind. "I am going out for a turn in the park," she told Fanny, "fetch me my warmest pelisse." How odd it was to have, actually, a choice of clothes to wear and how convenient that Fanny was much too much in awe of her to do more than look her protest at a young lady's venturing out unaccompanied.

It was good to be out and good, too, to be alone for once. She dodged her way through the carriages on Park Lane and walked briskly along the other side. The woman pedlar had disappeared, but the chestnut seller was still there, surrounded by an eager crowd of boys. Pausing for a moment to watch them, Marianne took the chance to look about her. No sign of Rossand. She shrugged, and entered the park. Perhaps it was all a hoax. She took a brisk turn along a path that crackled with frost under her feet. Back to the entrance, then once more out among the leafless trees. If he did not appear before she got back to the entrance, she would wait no longer. She lingered for a moment at the point where she had turned before, admiring frost patterns on the shady side of a silver birch tree. Her feet were cold in their thin shoes. Now, she would go home.

"Miss Lamb." He was so near her that she started despite herself. "I am glad to see that you have come alone."

"Yes, but I do not intend to stay. So, tell me quickly what it is that you have to say to me." As on the last time, he was closely wrapped in a heavy travelling cloak, but she would have known that sallow face and lisping voice anywhere. Only, this time, more experienced in society, she recognized that the cloak almost certainly hid the elegant garb of a young man of fashion. Young? Impossible to be sure, but certainly not old. And, more than ever she was sure of this, not to be trusted.

But, "I wish you would understand that I am your friend," he said.

"Why should I? You lied to me before."

"Yes." He admitted it at once. "But for your own sake. Now I am come to tell you the truth. You may wish I had gone on lying."

"What can you mean?"

"Let us walk," he would have taken her arm, but she moved a little away from him. "It is too cold for you to be standing. Besides, for your own sake, and that of others, you will not wish us to be overheard. You really are alone?"

"Yes. I hope you do not think I am afraid of you."

"Of course not." He seemed amused at the idea. "An adventurous young lady like you. You did not believe me, before?"

"No."

"Quite right." He said it, almost with approval. "I am sorry to have to admit that we have never been married, you and I. But, at the time, I could think of no other story so likely to get you safe away from the predicament in which I found you. And, at all events, the story did serve its turn. You left, though not, to my sorrow, with me. And—you have survived."

"Survived? What are you talking about?"

"About attempts on your life. Were you not shot at, once, in the woods? And did not the house where you sought asylum burn down, mysteriously, in the middle of the night."

"Yes. I thought——"

Now he laughed outright. "Of course. You thought I did it. Oh, poor Miss Lamb. Almost, for your sake, I could wish I had. But it was not I you met just after the shooting, was it? I did not give you permission to ride a dangerous horse. Nor was I in the district when the house you were staying in burned down, though it is true that I had been there shortly before, posing as an agitator, and had learned, as I thought, that you had found a safe asylum. Miss Lamb, I know it will go against the grain with you, but, for your own sake, you must realize who your enemy is."

"My enemy? You cannot mean Mr. Mauleverer?"

"Yes, Miss Lamb, or rather, Lord Heverdon—so long as you do not regain your memory."

"I do not know what you mean."

"You never did fathom it, then? I wonder that an intelligent girl like you should not have done so, but I suppose you were blinded by your infatuation for him. It was all so absurdly obvious. Little Lord Heverdon burns to death in his nursery in the north of England—completely, mark you, so that not a trace remains. And three days later you turn up with a child on your way to Mauleyer Hall, where the heir to Heverdon lives. I do not know what good you originally thought you would do by going there, but your dangerousness, so far as Mauleverer was concerned, was negatived by your loss of memory. Comic, isn't it, Miss Lamb, to think that you found shelter in the house of the man from whom you were fleeing. Do you wonder I think you the luckiest girl in the world to have survived?"

Still she would not believe it. "You mean that little Thomas——"

"Is Lord Heverdon. It was an ingenious idea, of Mauleverer's, was it not, to make a parade of not wanting to be a peer . . . and then be forced 'for political reasons' to take his seat in the Lords. Who, knowing all that, would dream of suspecting how foully, in fact, he played for his title? And will do so again, if you do nothing to prevent him. You—and the child—are become too much of a threat to him, Miss Lamb, now that you have found such powerful protectors. I suppose he fears some London doctor may restore your memory—at all events, he leaves for Mauleverer Hall tonight. I would not give much for the child's chances when he gets there."

"I don't believe it." And then, admitting doubt. "But how do you know?"

"I have made it my business to do so. It was madness, Miss Lamb, to leave the child at Mauleverer Hall, exposed to such danger. I cannot think how he has survived so long, except, I suppose that Mauleverer thought there was no danger of his identity being discovered. But now—with you in London, and so powerfully protected—it is no wonder that he hurries down there as soon as his committee breaks up this afternoon. I cannot go myself. Besides, I have no authority. But surely you could make up some story to satisfy the servants and remove the child to a place of safety. Best of all, you could bring him to London; there must be some one in town who can identify him as Lord Heverdon."

"Surely, Lady Heverdon. . . . Oh!" Marianne paused, horrified.

"You have seen it at last. Of course, she is in the plot too. You must know what a blow her husband's will was to her. Once the child is out of the way, she will marry Mauleverer—or Lord Heverdon, to give him the title he covets so—and enjoy the entire estate."

"Good God." Appallingly, now, everything fell into place. Something strange about Lady Heverdon's behaviour when they first met. That cold greeting had not been pride, but shock. She had pretended to be tired, turned pale—no wonder. And, later, she had known a surprising amount about Thomas —again, no wonder. "She knew me all the time?"

"Of course. You were the nursemaid at Heverdon House. Mauleverer, I believe, had never met either you or the child—I expect he preferred to carry on his villainy from a distance, but Lady Heverdon could not help but recognize you. I tell you again, it is a miracle that you survived."

"But you—what is your part in this?"

"I am not permitted to tell you."

She rallied. "That is absurd. You came to me, before, with a tale you now admit to have been a fabrication from start to finish. You cannot expect me to believe you, now, unless you can give me some proof of your bona fides."

"But can I trust you?"

"The question is, can I trust you!"

"Very well then, but I put my career in your hands. I am one of Sir Robert Peel's new policemen."

"You. . . ? A member of the police force? I don't believe it."

He shrugged. "Have it your own way. I cannot offer you proof, since it is exactly part of my assignment that I should appear other than what I am."

"But if you are," once again she was hesitating, "why cannot you act to protect the child?"

"How can I? So far, they have been too clever for me; I have suspicion enough to convince me, but no proof that I could take to court—or even to my superiors. I must be able to prove that a crime has been committed before I can take

210

action. That is what has hamstrung me all along; that is why I came to you before with what you so justly condemn as a story of a cock and a bull. But, at least, you must confess, I saved your life. I doubt if you would be quibbling with me here if you had stayed much longer at Maulever Hall. Wait, if you like, until the child's sudden, and doubtless quite 'accidental' death proves me right, but I would not want to have your conscience afterwards.''

Horribly, his story held together. Against every instinct, and every wish, she felt herself begin to believe him. And yet—no, it was impossible. "Surely there must be someone who can vouch for you, without endangering your task?''

"I can hardly send you to Sir Robert Peel. But—stay, you could, I suppose, go to our Bow Street office and ask whether they have an officer of my name. I do not see that that can do any harm. Will that satisfy you?''

"I suppose so. But what is your name? Not, I am sure, Paul Rossand.''

He laughed. "I can see you will never forgive me that first deception. But what else could I do? As it is, I fear I have gravely exceeded my commission for your sake. Telling you my name is merely the last of a series of offences for which I might easily be dismissed. I must ask you to word your query discreetly.''

"Of course.''

"Very well then.'' He looked carefully around to make sure that no one was in earshot, then leaned close to her, to whisper: "Ask them at Bow Street if John Barnaby is not one of their best men. But lose not time, I beg you. Mauleverer's committee may break up any minute and then, I have it on the best authority, he leaves for Devon at once, And, one other thing. For his sake, as well as mine, tell no one where you are going, or why. So far, as I have told you, I have no proof against him. If he can be prevented from the crime he now contemplates; if little Lord Heverdon can be saved; who knows, it may be possible to restore the child to his rank without any undue scandal.'' She was uncomfortably aware of his sharp eyes, studying her face. "If you wish, perhaps you can save him. He has been influenced throughout by Lady Heverdon about whose past career I could tell you things—but that is not my business, now. My aim it to save the child, and, if

211

possible, to avoid a scandal which must play the very deuce with the Reform Bill. Just imagine what a handle it would be for the Tories! That is why I have such unusual latitude in handling this case. My instructions come from the top, Miss Lamb, from the very top. Lord Grey"—once again he looked carefully around to make sure they were alone—"Lord Grey," he whispered, "cannot afford to have Mauleverer discredited. There is your chance, Miss Lamb, if you care to try and save him. Remove the child; bring him back to London; claim, if you like, that you have recovered your memory, that you remember running away with the child in a fit of pique over Lady Heverdon's injustice—she was a deplorable mistress, as I am sure you can imagine. Do that, and though there will be a nine days' wonder, and you must fall under a certain amount of censure, that will be the end of it. You have powerful friends; they will bring you off. And—if you care for it—you will have saved Mauleverer."

"'You mean—nothing will be done?"

"Nothing. You have my word for it. But, you have not much time." As if to underline his warning, London's golden-voiced churches began to chime the hour. "May I escort you to Bow Street? I cannot, of course, come in with you, but I do not like to think of you going there alone."

It was the clincher. If he was so certain, he must, indeed, be what he claimed. "No need," she said. "I believe you. God help me."

"At last. You will not regret it, Miss Lamb. But, remember, not a word to anyone, if he is to be saved." He drew his cloak still more closely round his face, ready to leave her.

"But where can I get in touch with you?"

"I hope there will be no need. The less hint of collusion between us, the better. But, if it is absolutely vital, a note to Bow Street will always find me."

This assurance laid to rest her final doubts, or, rather, her last glimmering of hope. He must indeed be what he claimed. But there was no time, now, for anguish, for the horrible laying together of one tiny fact with another that must prove Mauleverer a villain. If she was to save him from the results of his crime, she must act at once. And save him, of course, she must. There was no question about that. Hurrying back across the frozen park, she looked at herself almost with horror. Mauleverer was a proved villain, had even tried to kill her—and she still loved him, was still prepared to risk anything to save him from the consequences of his crime. Crossing Park Lane, Oh, the poor Duke, she thought.

She re-entered Lundy House, as she had left it, by a side door and got safely to her room without meeting anyone. She must be alone to achieve some order in her frantic thoughts. Mauleverer was a villain. It was not possible. And yet—how little, in fact, she knew of him. That he was fiercely ambitious, she had always been aware. Could it be that love had blinded her to the true direction of that ambition? That was the rub; that was what weakened her passionate, instinctive defence of him. She loved him so. How could she trust her judgement of him? And yet, Paul Rossand, or rather, Mr. Barnaby had given her no cause to trust him either. Why should she believe him against Mauleverer?

Absurd to have let him convince her so easily. She picked up her pelisse and fur muff and hurried downstairs. She had never taken a hackney carriage before, but found one easily enough in Park Lane and told the man to drive her to Bow Street police station. He gave a little whistle of surprise at the instruction, but whipped up his horse, readily enough, while she sank back in the musty interior and went on wrestling with her chaotic thoughts.

At Bow Street, she made her inquiry bluntly and without preamble. "Mr. Barnaby? Course he's one of ours, miss, but you can't see him now. He ain't here."

"I don't want to see him. But there is such a man?"

He laughed. "Course there is. Jim," to a colleague who was lounging against the wall trimming his nails with a penknife. "Here's a young lady wants to know if John Barnaby is real!"

"Real. I should rather think he is, and so do a plenty of burglars and other such, I can tell you. Just be grateful you ain't ever likely to run into him in the way of business, miss, that's all."

She thanked him and left. What to do now? Driving back to Lundy House she tried to think, to plan. . . . Impossible, still, to trust her own judgement: she must defy John Barnaby's instructions at least to the extent of consulting the Duchess. *She* would not be blinded by her feelings: she would advise her.

She found Fanny in her room mending the silver flounce that had been torn last night. It seemed a lifetime ago.

"Mrs. Mauleverer is awake and asking for you, miss." Fanny bit off her thread and admired the set of the flounce.

"I will go to her presently, but first I must see the Duchess. Ask her maid if she is well enough to see me for a few minutes, will you?"

"Of course she'll see *you*, miss." But Fanny returned almost at once with the news that the Duchess had gone out. "A gentleman came to see her, miss, and wouldn't be denied. She saw him at last, it seems, then asked for you, found you were out and sent for her carriage and is gone off with him. Goodness knows where."

"Did you happen to learn his name?"

"Yes, miss. Barnaby, it was, John Barnaby. He wouldn't say at first, but when he sent up his name, the Duchess saw him at once."

That settled it. Hope drooped and died. "You don't know where they went?"

"No. But they're to be gone some time. The Duchess has taken her maid."

What new development could have made John Barnaby change his plans? He had been so urgent that she tell no one and now had himself taken the Duchess into his confidence. Surely this was flying in the face of his instructions from Lord Grey? It was the political argument, she knew, that had convinced her. It made appalling sense that Lord Grey might stretch many a point to save the character of a man who was so identified in the public mind with his Reform Bill. So— what was she doing sitting here? Perhaps Barnaby had decided to sell out to the Tories. . . . There were all kinds of possibilities, none of them pleasant. The only certainty was that she must act without further delay.

"Fanny, I must have a travelling carriage. At once."

"A carriage, miss?" Fanny's tone underlined incredulity.

"Yes, I must leave for Devon as soon as possible. Give the orders, will you. There is no time for talk."

"But, miss——"

"Don't argue, Fanny. Give the orders and then pack me a cloak bag—merely the barest necessities. I shall return directly."

Fanny looked more and more puzzled. "But you will take me with you, surely?"

"No." Her tone made argument impossible, but as Fanny went reluctantly off to order the coach, she admitted a qualm to herself. Impossible to take garrulous Fanny, but—to make so long a journey unaccompanied? The Duchess would not like it—she did not much like it herself.

There was a timid knock at the door of her room, and Mrs. Mauleverer put her head round it. "Oh, there you are at last, my dear." She looked much better this morning. "I have been longing to see and thank you. I cannot imagine what possessed me to make such a spectacle of myself last night. I am afraid this London life does not suit me so well as I thought it would."

Here was the answer. Who better than Mauleverer's own mother to accompany her on this chancy journey? She kissed the old lady and went straight to the point. "Do you really feel that? And are you strong enough for a journey?"

"I'd go anywhere with you. And indeed I feel a different creature this morning. But what do you mean?"

"I have to go down to Maulever Hall at once. I cannot take my maid, but do not like to go alone. Will you come with me?"

"With all the pleasure in life, my dear. But do you really mean to start at once? I do not see how I could be ready so soon."

"I must," said Marianne. "I will lend you what you need for the journey, and, surely, you must have left clothes at home."

"Oh, yes," she was brightening up every minute. "And Martha will be there. Do you know, I shall be glad to see Martha. But I must write a note to Mark and explain."

Here was a new difficulty. Marianne tackled it at once. "My journey must be secret, for reasons I hope to be able to explain presently. Could you not merely write Mr. Mauleverer that you intend to spend a few days with me?"

"I suppose so. I am sure he will never miss me." Her voice held such bitterness that Marianne found herself once more reluctantly forced towards believing in the villainous Mauleverer of Barnaby's description. And yet, as always, there was an argument for the defence. What, after all, had his mother ever done for him?

While Mrs. Mauleverer wrote her note to her son, Marianne, with very much greater difficulty, composed one to the Duchess. Whatever John Barnaby had said, she found that she could not simply go off without any explanation. Very likely there was no need—she might even find the Duchess and John Barnaby at Mauleverer Hall before her. And yet—why should she? Nothing was safe, nothing was certain. Nor was it safe to say much in her note. Suppose some prying servant should open and read the letter. She wrote, therefore, briefly, and to the point : "I have received news that makes me anxious about the child, and am gone to fetch him. Mrs. Mauleverer accompanies me." She signed, simply, "Marianne," the only part of her name that was certainly hers. Not even Barnaby knew who she was. All he had told her was that she had been the nursemaid at Heverdon Hall. He had not even told her her name. Perhaps he had never known it. Why should one know a nursemaid's name?

16

THE journey, made in an old barouche of the Duke's that was generally used for servants and baggage, was far from luxurious, but Marianne's only concern was for speed, and this, fortunately, she was able to pay for, since the Duchess had insisted on making her a lavish allowance. She began by bribing the coachman, who had not been best pleased at the prospect of setting off so far from London, "and with Christmas just coming too." But his sullen expression changed to a beaming smile when Marianne handed him a handsome pre-Christmas tip, and promised him as much again if he could beat the time she had made when she came up from Devon with the Duchess.

He was sure he could do it. The barouche might be old, but had been well built in the first place. Its springs were still good, and, like all the Duke's possessions, it had been kept in admirable order. "Not much fear of busting an axle or a splinter bar and being held up that way," he promised her. "If we're half lucky in the cattle we find on the way—some of them post horses is nobbut dirt, and fit for waggons if that—but if so be as we has a bit of luck; I hope I can get you there tomorrow evening. It'll be a rough night for the old lady, I reckon?"

"Better than freezing on the road for two days or so. Besides, we are in a hurry."

He grinned at her. "So I reckoned."

For a while, Mrs. Mauleverer chattered away cheerfully enough about last night's ball, questioning Marianne over and over again about her various partners, and Marianne, keeping anxiety at bay, answered patiently that, yes, the Duke of Devonshire did have £140,000 a year, she believed; Lord Grey had been there, but had not danced. "And the Duke of Lundy?" Mrs. Mauleverer sounded sleepy now. "Such a handsome man. Tell me, my dear——"

"Ah," Marianne interrupted her as the coach slowed and stopped. "We change horses here. Shall I settle you for the night, ma'am?" She wrapped the old lady snugly as she could in the furs she had brought.

"Really," said Mrs. Mauleverer with a rare flash of humour. "Anyone would think we were retreating from Moscow. Oh, dear, I wish the night were over."

So did Marianne. Her companion soon nodded off to sleep, but she found herself feverishly awake, listening to the rain that beat fitfully against the carriage windows and tormenting herself with questions. Would they be in time—And—in time for what? What would they find at Maulever Hall?

Maulever Hall . . . Maulever Hall, groaned the carriage wheels. The wind was rising. It was going to be a wild night. She spared a thought for the coachman and groom, outside in the wind and weather. They must be well paid tomorrow. Tomorrow : would it never come? And, when it did, what would it bring? A last, restlessly, she slept and dreamed the old dream of danger and a horseman pursuing. It was reassuring to wake as the carriage lurched over a pothole in the road and hear nothing but its familiar noises and, close to her, Mrs. Mauleverer's little, bubbling snore. They were driving fast. The coachman intended to earn his reward. Get there in time, said the coach wheels now, get there in time, get there in time . . . and at last, dreamlessly, she slept.

When she woke, grey light was filtering into the carriage. The rain had stopped, but when she looked out of the window she saw a thin dusting of snow on the ground. They were passing through a village where nothing seemed awake but cocks and hens. It must be very early.

Mrs. Mauleverer woke with a grunt. "Where are we?"

"I've no idea."

"I haven't slept a wink all night." she looked pinched with cold and fatigue. "Can't we stop for a while and rest?"

"I dare not." Impossible to explain. "Look, the sun is rising."

But Mrs. Mauleverer would not be distracted by the sight of glowing light over snow-covered fields. "I wish I hadn't come," she wailed.

So did Marianne. It seemed madness, now, to have brought her. Relenting, she promised that when next they stopped to change horses, they would at least take time to drink some hot coffee. "The men will need it anyway. They must be perished with cold."

"Not half so much as I am." But she cheered up somewhat over coffee and hot rolls, and Marianne, too, was cheered by the coachman's telling her that they had made admirable time so far, and, if the snow only held off, should reach Maulever Hall by dinner time—"late dinner." He grinned at her, pleased with himself after his night's exertions.

A feeble mid-winter sun had already thawed the night's sprinkling of snow from the roads and the carriage lumbered steadily on while Marianne and Mrs. Mauleverer dozed in their respective corners, too tired, by now, for talk. It was dark by the time they reached Exton, where both of them were jerked awake as the coach rattled on to cobblestones. "Not much longer now," said Marianne.

"No, thank goodness. I hope I never have to make such a journey again. I am all of an ache from head to foot."

So was Marianne, but she listened patiently to Mrs. Mauleverer's catalogue of complaints. "And they won't expect us, either," she wound up, "most likely there'll be nothing fit to eat in the house, and the beds not aired, and no fires—oh dear, I do wish I had stayed in town, I don't know what I was thinking of to let you persuade me to join you on this mad jaunt."

Marianne was busy with a problem of her own. John Barnaby had urged her to waste no time in removing little Thomas —or rather, she reminded herself, Lord Heverdon—out of danger's way. But it was no use thinking of taking him away tonight. She knew herself to be too exhausted for a further journey, and, besides, she could not possibly ask her exhausted coachmen to start out again, and there was, she knew, no carriage now at Maulever Hall. Besides—she was wrestling with the old doubts again—would it not be better to stay and see if Mauleverer really did arrive? Surely her mere presence, and his mother's, would be enough to foil any design he might have on the child. And, I don't believe it, she told herself. She would stay and prove Barnaby wrong.

Mrs. Mauleverer cheered up a little when they turned at last into the driveway that led to Maulever Hall, but their first sight of the house was discouraging. No lights burned in any of the front rooms, so that it was nothing but a blacker shape against the starless blackness of the night.

The groom jumped down and beat a resounding tattoo on

the front door. It was raining again and Marianne and Mrs. Mauleverer waited inside the coach. The delay seemed interminable and even Marianne was growing impatient when, at last, they saw a little flicker of candlelight behind the glass at each side of the big door. It opened a crack and Marianne, peering impatiently through the darkness, could see someone apparently questioning the groom. Then, at last, it swung wide as he hurried back to the coach.

"Strange goings-on," he said, as he opened the door and let down the step. "Seems all the servants are away to Exton on some Christmas junketing or other. Master's orders, the housekeeper says. Very glad to see us she is, too, now she's certain we aren't a pack of housebreakers."

"Queer sort of housebreakers, arriving by coach." Marianne jumped lightly out and turned to help her grumbling companion.

"Is it really you, miss?" Martha awaited them in the doorway, screening a candle against the wind. "Lord, but I'm glad to see you. I never thought I'd see the day——" And then, in amazement: "Mrs. Mauleverer!"

The old lady pushed past her into the hall: "Her corpse, more likely. I'm perished with cold. What's this I hear about the servants being away? I never heard of such an ill-managed business."

Marianne turned to tell the men to take the carriage round to the stables. "Can you find your way? I'm afraid everything seems to be at sixes and sevens here."

Her apologetic tone mollified the men: "Lord bless you, miss," said the coachman, "we're old campaigners, Bert and me; we'll be all right. Do you look to the old lady; she must be starved with the cold."

Marianne found Mrs. Mauleverer and Martha still talking in the front hall. "For tonight only," Martha was saying. "It'll be so cold in your apartments."

"Did you ever hear of such a thing?" Mrs. Mauleverer turned her disgust on Marianne. "There's not a servant in the place, except Martha and the under nursery-maid. No fires, no food, nothing! What can Mark have been thinking of to send them all off like this?"

"I cannot imagine." But Marianne's voice shook a little. Her imagination was running a grisly riot round the idea that he had purposely cleared the house of witnesses to the crime he planned. "And Thomas?" she asked.

"Oh, he's here, right enough, but not a bit well," said Martha. "That's why I'm so glad you've come, miss. I've been near distracted all day, with no one to send for the doctor. If he's no better in the morning, do you think your coachman could go for him?" There was new respect in her voice. Mrs. Mauleverer must have told her whose coach it was. She turned, now, to lead the way upstairs. "I've made so bold as to suggest to Mrs. Mauleverer that you and she should sleep in my wing," she said. "There haven't been fires in the rest of the house all winter. You'd freeze there. And to tell truth, I'll be glad to have you; it's lonesome in this great house all empty. I don't half like it." She looked nervously over her shoulder as she spoke, and the candle flickered in the draught of her movement.

Mrs. Mauleverer shuddered in sympathy. "I don't like it either. Very well, Martha, just for tonight you may have fires lit for us in your wing." They had reached Martha's room by now and she sighed with relief at sight of the roaring fire on the hearth and settled luxuriously in the chair that was pulled up close to it. "What's that?" she started nervously as a door banged somewhere in the house. "I thought you said there was nobody here, Martha?"

"Doubtless it's our driver and the groom," said Marianne quickly, aware of panic in the air. "I told them to settle themselves as best they might." And then, bending to light a taper at the fire, "What we need is more light." And she began to light the candles that stood in brass holders on the chimney-piece.

"I'm glad to see you, miss, I really am," once more Martha admitted surprise. "I've been properly blue-devilled, sitting here all on my own, and the child ill and all."

"Oh, yes, Thomas: what is the matter with him?" Fears jostled together in Marianne's head.

But Martha's answer was reassuring: "Nothing but one of his feverish chills. A couple of days in bed should set him to rights—I hope."

So much for her idea of taking the child away tomorrow. But had she not already abandoned it? Only she must face the fact that Mauleverer's sending away of the servants had a sinister look. Impossible to be sure of anything: "Well now," she was intentionally brisk, as much to reassure herself as the others, "what we need is food. Martha, do you look after Mrs. Mauleverer and have this girl of yours light the fires in the next room for us—we will sleep together, I think—and I will go down to the kitchen, make sure the men have found what they need, and bring back a supper for us. You have had yours, I suppose?"

"Yes indeed," Martha shivered dramatically. "We ate before the light went. I didn't fancy venturing all that way down in the dark. I don't like this house, miss, not empty like this."

"Don't be absurd." But Marianne had to admit to herself that she did not particularly enjoy the walk down the long, draughty corridor; her candle flickering in her hand; doors, on each side of her shut on rooms she hoped were empty. The house was full of noises, creakings and whisperings, like a ship at sea. The wind was getting up; cold little draughts whispered around her feet and the candle's leaping flame made odd shadows on the walls. The corridor seemed endless, but she reached the back stairs at last and saw light shining from under a baize door. Opening it, she found herself in a different world. Lit by a big hanging lamp over the table, and a huge fire on the hearth, the big kitchen was warm and smelled comfortably of food. The coachman and groom were sitting at the table, food spread around them, tankards in their hands. The old campaigners had indeed made themselves at home.

They jumped to their feet at sight of her, and assured her, in answer to her questions, that all was right and tight with them—"But it's a rum go, just the same, miss, finding the house empty like this."

Heartily agreeing with them, Marianne had to conceal a sharp pang of disappointment when she learned that they had found themselves quarters in the grooms' apartments above the stables. Just for tonight, she would have preferred to have them nearer, but pride forbade her suggesting it. Besides, they would naturally wish to be near the horses.

The big larder was well stocked, providing evidence, if more had been needed, that the servants' excursion to Exton had been sudden and unexpected. Marianne collected a tray full of what she thought Mrs. Mauleverer would like best, put the candle on it, and sighed with relief when the coachman, volunteered to accompany her back upstairs: "To open the doors for you, miss." Thus escorted, she found that the journey lost all its terrors, and laughed at herself for the imagination that had set all kinds of horrors stirring behind the closed doors along the upstairs corridor. Just the same, she told the coachman that she would come down, after supper, to lock up behind him and the groom when they adjourned to their sleeping quarters. She would feel very much safer, in this echoing, empty house, if she was certain all the doors were double locked and bolted.

It was late by now. Mrs. Mauleverer nodded over her meal of cold meats and rather stale bread; little Thomas was sleeping peacefully in his room next to Martha's, and Jane had gone shivering off with her candle up the steep second flight of stairs to her tiny garret-room. The fire was burning low. Mrs. Mauleverer yawned and rose: "Well, I'm for bed," she said. "Martha?"

There was an odd little moment of tension in the room, before Martha, who had been busy with some sewing in the corner away from the fire, got slowly to her feet and came forward: "Yes, Mrs. Mauleverer?"

"I am worn out, Martha. Help me to bed."

The housekeeper's keys jingled at Martha's waist as she came forward another step. "Yes, Mrs. Mauleverer."

Marianne, reluctantly piling plates on the tray before return-it to the kitchen and locking up, was aware of a quick, word-less interchange between the two other women. Martha had Mrs. Mauleverer's arm and was supporting her as she rose shakily to her feet. "You *are* tired," now her voice was warm with sympathy, "you have come too far and too fast today."

"Yes." With a reproachful glance for Marianne. "I cannot imagine why we hurried so. And all to find an empty house at the end of it. What are you doing now, Marianne?" Her voice was sharp.

"I must take down the tray and lock up after the men." She had already explained this.

"And then wake me from my first sleep when you choose to come to bed? I thank you, no. Martha shall sleep with me. You will, won't you, Martha?"

"If you wish it." Again there was unwonted warmth in Martha's voice.

Marianne had intended to ask for her company on the bleak walk down to the kitchen, but how could she now? "Very well," she picked up the tray, "I will sleep on the sofa in here." Nothing would induce her to sleep in Martha's room. And yet—she opened the door and plunged once more into the dark and draughty corridor—had she misjudged Martha all the time? All her behaviour tonight seemed to point to a genuine affection for Mrs. Mauleverer. Had she not, perhaps, allowed herself to be misled by old Gibb's jealousy of Martha into totally unjustified doubts about her? And had she in her turn misled Mark Mauleverer? Certainly, Mrs. Mauleverer, deprived of her drops, had been an infinitely more pitiful figure than she had ever presented when she had them.

She found the coachman and groom still sitting at their ease over the dying fire, but they professed themselves ready to go to bed. "It's been a long day, miss."

It certainly had. She thanked them once more, then saw them out and shot the heavy bolts behind them. Then, pausing for a moment in the firelight glow of the kitchen, she faced the question that had been haunting her since they arrived : Had it all been for nothing? A wild goose chase? She shivered and moved closer to the fire. Probably it had. And—what was she going to do tomorrow? It had been all very well, in London, to plan to remove little Thomas from Maulever Hall and so away from any possibility of danger. But what about Martha? She would undoubtedly refuse to part with him, particularly since it would be impossible to explain his removal. She sank in the cook's rocking chair and stared into the dying fire, chin in hands. She had been a fool to come bolting down here. Her eyes, gravelly with fatigue, flickered shut, then opened again reluctantly. At least one good thing had come of the journey—the reunion of Mrs. Mauleverer and Martha. And what would Mauleverer himself think of that? He must have taken his mother to London to get her away from Martha's influence. He would hardly be delighted to have had her brought back so suddenly. Inevitably, her tired brain conjured up his angry face, as she had seen it last at the ball. How brutal he had been to her, that night, and yet—she could hardly blame him. If only she could have explained. . . . But the time for explanations was past. Perhaps, at the ball, if Lady Heverdon had not interrupted them, she might have managed to make him understand, but now there was nothing for it but to try to teach herself to forget him.

Forget him? She never would. Marry the Duke and catch herself pretending that he was Mauleverer? She liked him far too well for that, but what had that to do with loving? And —he had loved her too. Impossible, here in the house where she had known him, not to believe this. So—he could not have tried to kill her. Lies—had it all been lies then? And yet? why had he sent the servants away? What was the threat that hung in the air of this dark, silent house? Idiot—she was dreaming. She jumped up from the chair, picked up her candle and was about to start the long walk back to the housekeeper's wing when she stopped, head up, listening. Surely there was a new noise mingling with the roaring of the wind on the moors. No —she strained her ears—yes, a carriage was coming up the drive.

Her hand shook so much that she put the candle down on the kitchen table. Mauleverer? Was it all true, then? And, if so, what should she do? It was coming very fast. Four horses, certainly, driven hard. Whoever it was, she would have to let them in, since no amount of knocking was likely to wake Mrs. Mauleverer and Martha, now, doubtless, fast asleep in their remote wing. Now she heard the knocking, fast and impatient, on the big front door. It sounded like Mauleverer. Suppose she pretended not to hear. Rain beating against the kitchen windows gave her her answer. She could not leave anyone out of doors on such a night. Besides, it might not be Mauleverer. Perhaps it was the Duke, come in search of her. It would be like him to have come.

Whoever it was, he did not mean to be left outside. The knocking came again loud enough to wake the dead, she told herself, and shivered uncontrollably as she picked up her candle. At all events, she must go and see; there was a little window beside the front door through which one could reconnoitre visitors unobserved. Or at least, she soon realized, one could in the daytime. As she approached down the hall the impatient knocking stopped suddenly. Of course, whoever was outside had seen the light of her candle. She hesitated a moment, then went to the little window just the same; it would be madness to open without making sure who it was.

An impatient voice from outside gave her her answer: "Open up in there; it is I, Mauleverer."

Of course it was he. She had known it all the time. She put down the candle on a chest and began, with shaking hands, to pull back the heavy bolts.

"And about time, too." He was across the threshold in one angry stride, then stopped, looking at her, with—could it be? —horror? "You?"

"Yes." At the idea of explanation, a great tide of fatigue washed over her.

"True then." He seemed to be speaking to himself. Then, ignoring her, he turned to shout an order to his man outside. And yet, I don't believe it." He closed the big door behind him and stood for a moment with his back to it, looking down at her. The candle cast a strange sideways shadows on his face, revealing it as haggard with fatigue. "Well," he took off his soaking beaver hat and threw it down on a chair. "At last I am in time, it seems."

"In time?"

"To prevent this new folly of yours." He swung off his huge greatcoat, which was also, she saw, soaking wet, and dropped it, too, on a chair. "I come far and fast on your account, Miss Lamb."

"In your curricle! The significance of his drenched condition struck her.

"How else? It is my fastest carriage. But no matter for that. A little wetting won't hurt me. So long as I am really in time."

"In time for what?" she asked again.

"You look exhausted." He ignored her question. "I suppose you thought it safe enough to wait till morning. Well, it is too late now. The child stays here."

Horribly, it proved the truth of everything John Barnaby had told her. "Never!" she exclaimed. "Mr. Mauleverer, I beg you, think again. Let me take him away—anywhere—I promise you will never hear of either of us again."

Now, fantastically, he was looking at her with pity. "So it was all true," he said. "Madness is the only explanation." And then, in a gentle tone that contrasted oddly with his grim appearance, "I promise you, Miss Lamb, you shall come to no harm. You have my word for it; Mauleverer's word."

She was sickened by this attempt to secure her complicity in what he was planning. "Mauleverer's word! The word of a murderer!" There: it was out. She took a step backwards at the change of his expression.

"A murderer? But this is raving lunacy. Who, pray, am I supposed to have murdered?"

"Why no one—yet. Only let me take little Thomas, and go. I swear we will be no trouble to you. No one need ever know."

With an impatient gesture he turned away from her and began systematically lighting candles that stood ready along high chests on each side of the hall. Shadows receded; light glimmered on the arms that hung high on the walls, catching here a shining sword-blade and there a polished hilt. "There," he returned to face her. "Now we can see each other. It is time we come to an understanding, Miss Lamb. First: the child. It is true, then? He is Lord Heverdon?"

"I believe so." Did she? Face to face with Mauleverer, all her doubts of John Barnaby's story returned a thousand-fold.

"And you meant to run off with him again." This time it was not a question. "Could you not have trusted me, Miss Lamb? Surely there has been that between us which might convince you that I would see you safe out of your troubles? I suppose I am a bad tempered brute—and I admit that I said more, the other night, than perhaps I should have—but you must know that, always, at a pinch, I shall be ready to serve you. It can all be hushed up, never fear."

"Hushed up! Are you mad?"

"No, but I begin to be convinced that you are. Or"—his haggard face darkened—"is there something worse than abduction? If so, you had best tell me at once."

"Abduction? What do you mean?"

"Do you call it by some prettier name? It is not like you, Miss Lamb. I thought at least that you were one who could face facts; I see I was mistaken in this, as in everything. But, very well, if we must mince words, let us call it the child's removal from his friends' custody. Whatever you choose to call it, I can see that it might sound oddly to your new patrons. I do not altogether blame you for wishing to cast a veil over the past, but surely a new abduction is hardly the way to go about it."

227

She passed her hand wearily over her forehead. "Do you know, I cannot understand a word you are saying."

"No? you were not wont to be stupid, Miss Lamb, I can only assume that you do not wish to understand me. God knows, I have spoken plainly enough : what more do you want? I have promised to see you safely through the scandal that must attend the discovery of the child's identity. I will do more. If your new friends do abandon you as a result of these disclosures, you may be sure of an income from me."

"As a bribe for what? I would rather die. Do you really know me so little as to think I will connive at the child's"— she hesitated at the word—"at his disappearance?"

"God give me patience! How can I impress it upon you that the whole purpose of my coming here is to prevent you from disappearing with the child. Tomorrow, I shall take him to London and take the steps that are necessary to establish his identity. And, as I have said over and over again, I will do everything in my power to protect you from the consequences of this revelation."

The ground seemed to rock under her feet, and she put out a hand to the wall to steady herself. What a fool I have been. You will take him to London? Tomorrow? You promise?"

"Why should I promise? And to you, of all people. But I shall most certainly take him, if that will satisfy you; though why it should is more than I can understand."

But she was hardly listening to him. "You mean, you do not mind his succeeding to the title?"

"What, as Lord Heverdon? Miss Lamb, what is the matter with you? You must know that always, my ambition has been to be a Commons man. Do you really think that the chance of acquiring a miserable two-generation title would send my bonnet over the windmill?" He was silent for a moment, black thoughts chasing each other across his face. "I believe that at last I am beginning to understand. I was right to think you mad, Miss Lamb. There is certainly no other excuse. You have been thinking that I would try to prevent the child's identification? That I was so delighted with my new honour and my place in the Lords as to be ready to commit—what? Miss Lamb, to keep them. You called me a murderer a while ago and I thought you merely hysterical. Did I do you more than justice? Do you honestly believe that I would conspire against the child? I can see that you do. You were going to carry him off, safe away from my machinations! I thank you, Miss Lamb, for your confidence in me!"

She swayed on her feet. "What am I to believe?"

"Why, nothing to my credit, it seems."

"But the servants. Why, then, did you send them away?"

"Send away all the servants? What do you mean?"

"They are all gone to Exton—on your orders."

"Nonsense." There was something wonderfully reassuring about his tone. "Why in the name of all that's ridiculous should I send the servants to Exton?" And then: "Oh, I see, to clear the way for my deed of darkness. You imagine me, then, a sort of Richard Crookback! Was I intending to smother my nephew, Miss Lamb, and what, pray, did I mean to do with the body?"

She shook her head. "I suppose I was mad. But——" Something had been stirring at the back of her mind. "Lady Heverdon?" She thought for a moment: "How did you find out the child was Lord Heverdon?"

"I was told—by Lady Heverdon's cousin, as a matter of fact, Ralph Urban. She never saw the child when she was here."

"Nonsense." It was her turn now. "If you can believe that, you can believe anything. She saw him—and disliked him. I remember being puzzled by it at the time, but I see now that it was no wonder. Mr. Mauleverer, I have been a fool: I admit it, and do not expect you to forgive me, but you have not been very brilliant either. Of course she must have known the child, if, as I am beginning to doubt, he is indeed Lord Heverdon."

"Oh yes, he's Lord Heverdon, never doubt of that." Both of them turned in surprise at this new voice from behind them. A man was standing half way up the main stairway, a lantern in his left hand, his right negligently in his coat pocket. Now he came a few more steps towards them, so that the light from the branches of candles along the side of the hall caught his face.

"Mr. Barnaby!" said Marianne.

"Urban!" said Mauleverer.

17

"AT your service." His eyes were on Mauleverer as he put down the lantern in an embrasure of the stairs. "And yours," he turned, still standing above them on the stairs, and sketched a bow to Marianne.

"You are Lady Heverdon's cousin?" she said. "Ralph Urban. Not John Barnaby at all!"

"No more than I was Paul Rossand. I am afraid you are a very gullible young lady after all, Miss Lamb. Or shall I call you——" He shrugged. "No, I believe not. We have not quite played out our comedy of errors yet. Or—tragedy, perhaps?"

Mauleverer took a step forward. "What are you doing here?"

"An unpleasant duty. I am really sorry it has had to come to this." And then, his voice hard: "You will stay where you are. Both of you." His right hand was out of his pocket now, and the gun it held was pointed steadily at Mauleverer. "I am a good shot." Almost apologetically. "And this is one of Mr. Collier's new pistols. I can fire several shots without reloading."

"Are you mad?" But Mauleverer stayed where he was.

"Not in the least. It is Miss Lamb here, I am afraid, who will be found to be insane. Only think of her killing both you and the child! I am afraid it will take more than your friend the Duchess to extricate you from the consequences of that double crime, Miss Lamb."

"The child! What do you mean?" In her cold bewilderment she began a step forward, but a warning movement of the gun halted her.

"Please do not move, Miss Lamb. It would not suit me at all to have to shoot you. I need you—alive. It was—obliging of you both to come so quickly. I was afraid I might have to spend another day in those damned draughty bedrooms up-stairs."

"You were here all the time?" Instinct told Marianne to keep him talking.

"Of course. Waiting for my honoured"—he paused—
"guests." And then, "I do beg, Mr. Mauleverer, that you will
keep still. Of course, it will not make much difference in the
long run, but the angle is not quite right for Miss Lamb to
have shot you from here." And he took another slow, careful
step down the stairs towards them.

"You must be mad," Mauleverer said again.

"Do you think so? Now I consider myself remarkably sane.
It has taken, you know, a great deal of planning to arrive at
this satisfactory conclusion. With you and the child dead, my
cousin—my dear cousin will inherit, at last, the estates she
should have had all the time." There was something very
strange about his tone as he spoke of Lady Heverdon.

"She is not your cousin at all." Mauleverer's voice was
harsh.

"Of course not. You are there at last." He made a little,
mocking bow of congratulations as he stood above them on
the the the stairs, the gun steady in his hand.

But, he is vain, Marianne told herself. Keep him talking
about how clever he has been. "Then you will marry her?" she
managed to keep her tone one of simple amazement.

"Precisely, Miss Lamb. As I have always meant to do. Once
widowed—twice widowed—what's the difference? But it will
be quicker this way." He came another step down the stairs
and lifted the gun a little. "I am a very quick shot, Miss Lamb.
I do not recommend your attempting anything. Should I tie
you up first? Stun you perhaps?" He seemed to consider for a
moment. "No, I do not believe it will be necessary. Besides, I
shall need you to lead me to the child's room."

He meant every word of it. In a moment, he was going to
shoot Mauleverer before her eyes. If that happened; nothing
mattered. But—he had come very near her now, doubtless with
the idea of turning on her as Mauleverer fell. She turned her
head suddenly upwards to the head of the stairs behind him:
"Martha!" she exclaimed, and then, as he turned almost involuntarily to look behind him, jumped for the hand that
held the gun.

It went off with a roar as they struggled for it, and, in the
same instant he had thrown her backwards. She was aware, as
she fell, of the gun, flying out of his hand, and of Mauleverer,
leaping sideways to snatch something down from the wall,

then her head struck the corner of a chest and the world exploded.

She came to herself a few moments later, her thoughts a catherine-wheel of terror. Then the dizzy kaleidoscope settled, past and present coalesced: she remembered everything. She was lying in the recessed corner at the foot of the stairs in Maulever Hall. Her head ached villainously, but through the pain she was aware of a strange shuffling sound punctuated by tortured breathing and the clash of metal on metal. With an effort, she opened her eyes. Mauleverer was backed against the big front door, defending himself with the sword he had snatched from the wall. She could see his face, white with strain and drawn with fatigue. Between her and him was the dark shadow of his attacker, pressing in relentlessly as is confident of victory.

Mauleverer parried a blow, and spoke, panting: "This is all very well, my dear Urban." Again a lunge and a parry. "But if you should be so fortunate as to kill me—which"—a pause and a quick stroke—"I do not at all expect, you may have a little difficulty in explaining how Miss Lamb there came to do such a thing."

"Never fear, I shall think of something." But for a moment his guard had dropped and Mauleverer seized the chance for for a quick stroke that seemed to flash along Urban's sleeve.

"Your sword is blunt." But now Urban's calm was obviously a matter of fierce effort.

"Not too blunt, you will find." Thrust, parry; thrust, parry. Mauleverer was pressing the attack now, and then, suddenly: "Miss Lamb, I hope I see you better."

It worked. Once more, for a vital instant, Urban's attention was distracted, and in that moment, Mauleverer's sword had caught his and sent is flying across the room.

"Now, Mr. Urban," his voice grated with fatigue, but the hand that held the sword at his opponent's breast was steady as a rock. "It is your turn to stand very still. Do not think I shall have the slightest hesitation in killing you." And then, still concentrating on his antagonist: "Marianne, the gun."

Swaying on her feet, she contrived to get across the room to where it lay, and pick it up. "I have it." She knew that he had not taken his eyes off Ralp Urban.

"Good. Can you use it?"

How strange it was to remember. "Yes. My father taught me"

"Then do so, if he moves. I do not recommend it, Urban. You cannot see her, I know, but Miss Lamb means business as much as I do."

"Not Miss Lamb." Leaning against the wall to steady herself, she held the gun pointed at Urban's back. "Miss Urban."

"He is *your* cousin?" Very slowly, still keeping his sword at the ready, Mauleverer was manœuvring his way around his defeated adversary to join her. "You have remembered?" He was at her side now.

"Yes—everything." She let him take the gun. "What are we going to do with him?" From their tone, Urban might already have ceased to exist.

"For the moment, tie him up. Urban, I have the gun now. Your hands behind your back, if you please. Hurry! I should be delighted to have a reason for killing you."

"You will pay for this!" But, slowly, reluctantly, his hands crept to join themselves behind his back.

"Do you know, I rather think that it is you who will. What we have to determine is, how. Marianne, the cords from the curtains, I think."

Silently, she fetched the heavy golden cords that looped back the curtains from the front windows. The candles were burning low in their sockets. One of them guttered and went out, leaving a strong smell of tallow.

"Thank you." Mauleverer took the cord with his left hand, then passed her the gun. "Your cousin has the gun now, Urban. I am going to tie you up. Do not delude yourself that I shall come between you and it."

"God damn you both." But Urban stood still while Mauleverer tied his hands and then allowed himself to be drawn backwards into one of the big wooden arm-chairs that stood on each side of the hall.

"There." Mauleverer tied him to it securely. "I am sorry if I hurt you. He did not sound to mean it. "You are bleeding?"

"A scratch!"

He carried himself well in defeat, this cousin of hers about whom she could remember little else that was good. For the memories were sorting themselves out now, into a pattern of villainy that she still found it hard, in spite of all the evidence, quite to believe.

"'He really is your cousin?'" Mauleverer's question tied in with her thoughts.

"Oh, yes. We grew up together, he and I. It is no wonder, when he came to me and told me we were married, that I was deluded by a feeling of familiarity. No wonder he knew so much about me either. But what a chance you took——" For the first time she spoke to the man who sat so still in the chair. "Were you not afraid I might remember you?"

He shrugged. 'I have taken chances at every step in this game. It's half the fun of it, my dear cousin. But, tell me, now I have played and lost, what do you intend to do w'th me?''

"I wish I knew." It was Mauleverer who answered. "If we go by intentions, hanging is too good for you, but in actual fact you have not contrived to do much harm after all—except to yourself and, I suppose, Lady Heverdon."

He spoke the name so calmly that Marianne flashed him a quick, surprised look. Could he really be so unmoved by the discovery of Lady Heverdon's treachery? Or had he not, perhaps, realized the full implications of what Urban had said.

His next words showed that he had. "For some curious reason," he said, "I continue to have a certain regard for Lady Heverdon's feelings. Besides, she bears my family's title. For her sake, I should be sorry for an open scandal. But I am not to be the judge in the matter." He turned to Marianne. "It is for you to decide. But, before you do, I must confess I should be glad to understand what has been going on."

"I am only now beginning to understand it myself," she spoke slowly, ordering her thoughts as she went along. "To begin with—how odd it seems—I am—may be something of an heiress." She hated herself for colouring as she spoke. But it was impossible not to remember that Mauleverer had lost a fortune by the discovery that little Thomas was Lord Heverdon. And she had, perhaps, found one. She knew him well enough to be horribly certain that this was the end of any faint hope there might have been of a reconciliation between them. She hurried on, afraid that he might misinterpret her pause. "My uncle—and Ralph Urban's—is lord of one of the Channel Islands—quite a small one, Barsley, perhaps you may not have heard of it. He is an old man, and childless. I am his younger brother's child, and Ralph the youngest's. We were both orphaned as children and my uncle brought us up. He always said that Ralph should be his heir, rightly, I think. They're a rough lot, the islanders, and, besides, Barsley is the nearest of the islands to France. Its lord needs to be a fighter —certainly did in Bonaparte's time. My own mother was a refugee from France."

"Of course," Mauleverer said. "Your name; your perfect French. Why did we never think of the Channel Islands? But what happened to change your uncle's mind. Is he still alive, by the way?"

"I—I suppose so. He was, when I left home. He—he was angry with Ralph and said I would prove the better man of the two. He wanted me to come to England and earn my keep for a year—to prove myself a man, he said, without help from him. If I did that, he would make a new will in my favour. But I thought he would have forgiven Ralph long before that. Truly, I did, Ralph," her voice had an odd note of appeal in it. 'I never wanted to be Dame of Barsley. Oh, it's a beautiful island, if you care for wild scenery, but there's no one to talk to in the length and breadth of it. I was glad to come away. My cousin Ralph helped me to find a position with his friend, Lady Heverdon. He said we had best not tell her about being cousins. Were you planning all this already, Ralph?"

"Of course I was. What an obliging fool you were, to be sure! I never enjoyed anything so much in my life as to see the future Dame of Barsley, with all her airs and graces, meekly acting the part of a nursemaid." His face darkened. "It should all have been so easy. With you and that wretched little boy burned in your beds, I'd have been heir to Barsley, and Lady Heverdon"—his voice softened on the name—"We thought she would be free at last to enjoy the fortune she had earned by marrying that worthless cousin of yours." This, angrily, to Mauleverer. "The lawyers had not thought fit to tell her how he had tied up his estate against her."

"I begin to suspect that he had his reasons," said Mauleverer.

"What did he expect? A dirty, decrepit old man marrying a young beauty like her? He should have been grateful for the patience she showed him. But we've had the devil's own luck, she and I. Tell me," he turned his head to glare angrily at Marianne who had sunk down in the chair across the hall from his. 'How did you and the child come to escape that night when I set fire to your wing?"

She looked at him, almost with pity. "Do you remember that Lady Heverdon pleaded the headache as an excuse to send Thomas and me away early? I felt sorry for her—she was kind to me, you know, in her way. When I had got Thomas to bed, I came back to her rooms to ask if I should try and massage the pain away. Her door was not shut fast. I heard you talking as I came down the hall—and what I heard made me stay to listen. I don't think I quite believed my ears at first, but then, do you remember, you laughed and told her not to worry. 'You'll be in mourning tomorrow.' That was enough. I went back to our wing and packed my box. It was early still. I knew you would not dare act till all the servants were in bed. I told one of the footmen I was running away to join my lover. He took my box to the coaching inn for me—I suppose he did not dare speak up in the morning. I took good care that he had no idea I was going to take the child with me; that's why I dared pack so few of his clothes. I waited till the house was quiet, woke little Thomas—goodness, how cross he was—put bundles of clothes in our beds and stole away with him to the coaching inn.

"I was coming to you, of course," she turned to Mauleverer. "I knew you were the child's guardian. What a journey it was! And terror all the way. I had no means of knowing whether our escape had been discovered or whether we were thought dead in the fire. Every time a horseman caught up with the coach, my heart was in my mouth for fear it was my cousin. If he had caught me, I should not have had a leg to stand on. I could prove nothing against him—and, so far as the world could see, I was an absconding nursemaid who had abducted her charge. But we reached London safely and, to my relief, found that a coach was starting almost at once for Exton. I hardly remember how I got across London to the inn it started from, but at least by then poor Thomas was so worn out that he slept for a great part of the next journey, and, indeed, so did I. By the time we had changed coaches at Exton I began to think our flight could not have been discovered, for anyone travelling post would have caught us long before. I drowsed off, I remember, and was waked by screams, the coach tipping over, then blackness. How odd it is," she went on thoughtfully, "to remember both lives now—and what a miracle that I did, in fact, reach Maulever Hall at last, and find shelter there. But, tell me"—oddly, she found herself slipping into the old tone of irritated affection when she addressed her cousin— "was it you who came after the coach at Pennington Cross?"

He had been lying carelessly back in his chair, simulating ease, but now straightened up to stare at her blackly: "God damn you, yes. Do you mean to tell me you were there all the time?"

"Yes, hiding in the gorse."

He swore a worse oath. "And I believed that rascally coachman! He told me he had let no one down since Exton—the passengers all confirmed it; there was a fat woman in a red dress, I remember, who was particularly positive."

She could not help smiling at him. "Poor Ralph. I expect they did not like your manner overmuch. But what did you do then?"

"Went to Maulever Hall, of course, with some tale of a cock and a bull and losing my way. There was no sign of you there and I decided I had been on a wild goose chase all the time. I thought you both burned in your beds, you see, only Miranda heard some rumour about a woman and a child who boarded the midnight coach on the night of the fire and insisted I investigate. Well—that once—she was right."

Marianne shivered. "You must have got to Maulever Hall before me." She remembered the long, bleak walk across the moors, with the child heavy in her arms, and terror behind her. "I was—lucky."

"You had the luck of the very devil, then and later. Why did I miss you, that time in the wood? It makes me mad merely to remember it. Over and over again, I should have had you, and always, like a sleep-walker, you escaped without even realizing you had been in danger." He was upright in the chair, his eyes very bright, his smile mocking. "But tell me, dear cousin, what are you going to do with me now?"

"Did you always hate me?"

"Hate you?" He sounded genuinely surprised. "Of course not. I believe I love you a little. But you should not have taken Barsley from me. Oh, yes," his voice was mocking again, "I quite forgot to tell you. Our uncle died a little while ago. May I salute you, Dame of Barsley!"

"He left it to me?"

"All of it : every acre, every penny. And, for me, a moralizing instruction to mend my ways—no more gambling, no more horse-racing, and, perhaps, if my reformation deserved it, in the end, you, of your great generosity, would make me your steward. Steward! I, who love every inch of the island! You do not even want to live there! I know every rabbit track on the cliffs; every one of the smugglers' landing places; each tenant's property to an inch. So, perhaps, says my uncle, I might, one day, be worthy to be your steward! Do you wonder if I have been a little mad?"

"But when did this happen?"

"Soon after Lady Heverdon came here on a visit and nearly fainted at sight of you. I cannot think how our uncle's lawyers have been so long about tracing you, though the helpful suggestions I made to them may have had something to do with it Oh, well," he shrugged, "I have played my game, and lost. It is your turn now."

"It is not fair." Marianne was surprised to find herself so indignant. "You were brought up to be lord of the island. I am sure Uncle Urban did not intend such a will to stand. Poor uncle—so he is dead at last after all his alarms and ailments, and I cannot even cry for him. It was impossible to love him," she turned, almost in apology, to Mauleverer, "and yet he was good to us in his way."

"'In his way!" exclaimed Urban. "The way of a bad-tempered, malingering old miser. You may play the hypocrite about him if you like, but I shall not. He made me what I am, and then punished me for it."

Mauleverer had been leaning wearily against the arm of a chair, his face in shadow, but his posture showing how intently he was listening to what they said. Now he straightened up. "This is all very well," he said, "'but it scarcely helps us now. You confess to attempting murder, not once but many times, Mr. Urban. What do you expect us to do with you?"

"What you please. I really do not care—now. It will make a magnificent scandal, will it not? Do not delude yourselves that I will spare anyone if I am brought to my trial. You will look a pretty fool, Mauleverer, and my cousin here little better than a madwoman."

"Oh, don't——" Marianne knew he was going the worst

way to goad Mauleverer into acting against him. "Remember Lady Heverdon. If you stand trial, she must be implicated. After all, she came here, saw me, saw the child—it cannot help but come out that she was equally involved with you. Surely you don't want that?"

Cousin, you are more intelligent than I thought you. No, you are quite right. She has had trouble enough already. Her only crimes, really, have been love for me, and a certain liking for the comforts money can buy. Can we not leave her out of this?"

"I do not see why she should escape, any more than you," but Mauleverer's voice was doubtful now.

Marianne was grateful for the shadows that hid her face: could it be that even after the discovery of how she had betrayed him, he loved Lady Heverdon still? She hurried into speech: "If he promises. . . . Must we really do anything? After all, nothing has really happened."

"Nothing happened?" Mauleverer's voice was dry. "Two houses burned down! Do you call that nothing? Not to speak of the attempts on you."

"Yes, but they failed. And, truly, I think it all my uncle's fault. Ralph is right about him——" How easily she had slip-ped back into using her cousin's first name. "It wasn't fair," she said again. "Could he not sign a paper, or something, and then go off and"—she paused—"well, why not? Would you like to be steward of Barsley, cousin?"

"He would do that well," she explained to Mauleverer. "It is true what he says; he does love the island, and the people there. It was only when Uncle sent him to England that he got into trouble."

"Cousin, you keep surprising me," but she could see that his eyes were suddenly bright.

"Hush!" Mauleverer held up a hand. "There is a carriage coming up the drive—or maybe two, by the sound of it. Who on earth can it be, at this time of night?"

Marianne felt herself colouring. "It might be the Duke." She was sure it was. If only she and Mauleverer had had time for some sort of explanation! What must he think of her for believing Urban's lies? It did not bear thinking of.

"The Duke?"

"I left a note, saying I had come down here. I did not say why."

"No? And you think he will have followed you so soon?"

"I don't know." Passionately, she wished now that she had said nothing.

"Well, we shall soon see." The first carriage had stopped at the door and he turned, after a swift look to make sure that Urban was still securely tied, to swing it open.

There was a little bustle outside and then four people entered the hall. First came the Duchess, warmly wrapped in her old army greatcoat, and then, behind her, the Duke and a squat, short stranger, one on either side of Lady Heverdon.

"Well," the Duchess took in the scene. "You seem to have managed well enough without us. He is safely tied up, I trust?" She looked, without interest, at Urban, then turned again to Marianne, "I am glad to see you, child. But, surely, a little more light would be an improvement?"

"Of course." Marianne hurried to fetch the two big silver candelabra from the dining-room and lit their candles with a shaking hand before she snuffed out the few that still guttered in their sockets.

"That's better." The Duchess looked about her. "Mr. Mauleverer, of course." And then, as he made his bow as formally as if they were at St. James's. "And I must present Mr. Barnaby, of Bow Street."

The squat man took a short step forward and made an awkward all-inclusive bow to the company, but all the time the sharp eyes under his shaggy brows were fixed on Marianne. "Miss Urban?" his voice was questioning.

"Yes." Marianne turned to the Duchess. "I have remembered—everything."

"Well, that's a comfort. I was wondering where to begin breaking it to you." The Duchess turned to John Barnaby. "Well, Mr. Barnaby, you have found your missing heiress." She yawned enormously. "And the hour is late. I am sure that Mr. Mauleverer's servants will find you accommodation for the night."

Marianne laughed and intervened. "The fact is, ma'am, that there are no servants. They have all been sent off to Exton."

"I see." It was clear that the Duchess saw a great deal. "Then we are like to have an uncomfortable night of it. But

240

I have no doubt an old campaigner like you, Mr. Barnaby, will be able to look out for yourself." A significant glance directed him to the green baize door at the far end of the hall.

He took another step forward. "But, your Grace," his face was red with the effort of making himself speak to her, "so far as I can see, there's been vilence done here, and vilence is Bow Street's business."

"Violence?" said the Duchess, looking about her. "Oh, you mean the swords? An odd time of night, I admit, for fencing practice, but as to violence?" her eyes, on Urban, in his chair, defied him to contradict her, "I see no signs of it. You may go, Mr. Barnaby; it will be time enough to talk law business in the morning."

He made a last stand. "That's all very well, ma'am—your Grace, I should say, but if you didn't expect vilence, why did you come down here in such a hurry? This gentleman here's bleeding too! Do you expect me to take no notice of that?"

"Yes," said the Duchess. "That is exactly what I expect, Mr. Barnaby. We have things to talk over. In the morning, perhaps——" Her tone made it clear that she promised nothing. Then, to her nephew, "John, Mr. Barnaby seems unable to find his way to the servants' quarters."

The Duke smiled and moved forward. "This way, Mr. Barnaby."

The little man looked round the company. The Duchess ignored his anxious glance; Lady Heverdon was speaking quickly, in a low voice, to Mauleverer. He gave it up. "Just the same," he moved away down the hall, "vilence is Bow Street's business."

"He may be right at that," said the Duchess thoughtfully, "but we had better talk things over first. What, for instance, has Lady Heverdon to say?"

Marianne had been straining her ears in a vain attempt to try and hear what Lady Heverdon had been saying to Mauleverer in her rapid, half-whispering, pleading voice. Now he turned to the Duchess, his voice dry. "She says, your Grace, that it is all a terrible mistake. She knew nothing of any plot; cares nothing for Mr. Urban there; cannot imagine why you and your nephew have thought fit to abduct her. I use her words, you understand."

"But it is true." Lady Heverdon moved forward into the

full glow of the candlelight. She was wrapped in a blue cloak that showed up the gold in her hair. Dark shadows under her eyes merely gave an unwonted distinction to her candy-floss beauty. Her face, as she turned great pleading eyes from Mauleverer to the Duchess, was that of a child misunderstood. "Mr. Urban and I are old friends, it is true, have often, jestingly, called each other cousin, but—you know who it is that I love." Her huge eyes pleaded with Mauleverer. "If Mr. Urban has deluded himself that I felt more for him than friendship, it is not my fault. Though I still cannot believe he is guilty of the things you have told me. Surely there must be some mistake."

"Mistake!" Ralph Urban spoke explosively from his chair. "There has indeed been a mistake—mine. So you would throw me over, so lightly, in defeat, would you, Miranda? Never loved me, did you? Never promised me——" he stopped. "Never mind. Because you show yourself worthless, I need not do the same. Cousin," to Marianne, "I owe you a greater apology than I thought. I would have sent you to the madhouse for That." His burning eyes, fixed on Lady Heverdon, underlined his words.

She pouted. "But I have been engaged to Mauleverer this age. Everyone who knows anything, knows that."

Silence. Everyone's eyes turned to Mauleverer, except the Duke's, which Marianne felt fixed on her own face. For a long moment, Mauleverer was silent, gazing down into the beautiful face so becomingly tilted up to his. One little white hand held the cloak loosely around her, the other crept out to touch the front of his coat in a gesture at once pleading and proprietorial. His own hand moved towards it and Marianne's teeth clenched hard together. Then, gently, ruthlessly, he brushed it off. "I am loth to give the lie to a lady, and so publicly, too, but you know, madam, that there has never been any question of an engagement between us. I am your stepson's guardian; that is all."

"Oh, monstrous." Her wild eyes appealed to them all. "How can you say such a thing! And if you betray me, who will stand my friend?" Tears flooded from the great blue eyes as she turned from the silent Duke to the Duchess and then at last, as if involuntarily to Urban, very still in his chair.

It was he who answered her. "Not I, for one, Miranda. I

hope he has betrayed you, though, frankly, I doubt it. You have taken your goods to too many markets at last, cousin." The last word was a mockery. "Do you see it all ahead of you? Widowhood—poverty—the long, solitary years? Last year's black's turned and turned again—tallow candles taking the place of wax—one man, if you are lucky, acting footman, butler, everything, in greasy outmoded livery. And then, the gossip, just think of the gossip, cousin. Lady Heverdon—she was the beautiful Lady Heverdon once—not considered fit to have charge of her own stepson." His mocking eyes swept from her to Mauleverer and back. "Am I not right?"

Mauleverer said nothing, but his face was confirmation enough. Lady Heverdon did the only thing left to her. She went into violent hysterics.

"How tedious," said the Duchess. "What shall we do with her?"

Inevitably, Marianne moved forward. "I will take her upstairs," she said.

"Good. *Sal volatile* and bed, I should think. As for me, I am absolutely perished with cold. Is there a fire anywhere in this freezing house?"

"In the kitchen," said Marianne, as she put her arm around Lady Heverdon's waist and prepared to help her upstairs.

"Then let us adjourn to the kitchen. With your good leave, Mr. Mauleverer?"

"Of course. I am only sorry you find my house so at sixes and sevens."

"Oh, well," she shrugged, "let us hope there is ham—and eggs. It occurs to me that I am starving. Don't look so shocked, John. Have you never eaten in a kitchen before?"

He laughed. "Do you know, I don't believe that I have. But what are we to do with Mr. Urban there?"

The Duchess looked at him reflectively and he returned look for look. "Personally," she said at last, "I am inclined to take him to the kitchen and feed him ham and eggs, but it must be entirely your decision, Mr. Mauleverer."

"Marianne!" Mauleverer's voice made her turn half-way up the stairs. "What do you think?"

"I think he is punished already," she said, and turned back to guide the sobbing, screaming Lady Heverdon round the curve of the stairs.

18

THE kitchen was full of light and bustle. All the lamps were burning, wood had been piled high on the open hearth and the Duchess was watching Ralph Urban build up the fire in the huge cooking range. Mauleverer was arranging champagne bottles on the scrubbed deal table while the Duke stood in the middle of the room finishing an impassioned speech of protest.

"Yes," said the Duchess as Marianne entered the room, "that is all very well, but Mr. Urban can light a kitchen fire, which is more than I can say for either of you two. Ah—Marianne—you are just in time. Eggs from the larder, please."

"Yes." Marianne looked around. "What did you do with Mr. Barnaby?"

"Sent him to bed, of course. And Lady Heverdon?"

"Martha gave her some of Mrs. Mauleverer's drops." Her eyes met Mauleverer's. "She will sleep now, I think."

"Good. John, if you will stop arguing and slice that ham, we are almost ready to eat. There will be time enough for argument, afterwards. But where is my champagne?"

"Here." As Mauleverer spoke, the cork flew out of the bottle and hit the ceiling while wine began to foam on to the table. Marianne hurried to his help with a couple of kitchen tumblers. "Thank you." His voice was formal and his eyes would not meet hers. They worked together silently, pouring and passing wine, their hands in unison, their minds poles apart.

The Duchess broke a silence that seemed to stretch out endlessly. "There!" Triumphantly, she brought the huge iron frying pan to the table and began to serve delicately fried eggs on to the slices of ham the Duke had cut. "Food at last. Mr. Urban, you may leave the fire now, and come and eat. John, I've had enough of your arguing. Mr. Mauleverer, perhaps you will cut the bread. Marianne, come and sit here by me, and you on the other side, Mr. Urban." She had thus separated him by the greatest possible distance from Mauleverer and the Duke.

Mauleverer was smiling now. "A truce, is it? Very well, ma'am, if you wish it." He began to cut great slices off the loaf and pass them around, while the Duke took his place on the far side of Marianne.

The Duchess raised her glass. "A toast," she said. "Marianne, and her memory." And then, "Come, Mr. Urban, you have nothing to lose by drinking, and making yourself pleasant."

"And not much to gain either." But he raised his glass with the others in the toast.

Blushing and thanking them, Marianne tried, once more, in vain to catch Mauleverer's eye. If only she knew whether it was himself he could not forgive, or her. But the Duchess, busy spreading her bread with half an inch of butter, was dauntlessly initiating a general conversation about, of all things, the Reform Bill. She soon had Mauleverer and the Duke at it hammer and tongs. The Duke maintained that the first election after what he admitted to be the bill's almost certain passing would mean the end of order in the country. Mauleverer, on the other hand, urged that the bill was the only hope of saving democracy; without it, there would be revolution, maybe as bloody as that in France.

Urban was silent at first, but Marianne could see that he was following the argument with close interest. Soon, he joined in, offering some shrewdly sensible suggestions—on Mauleverer's side. The Duchess smiled at Marianne, pushed aside her plate and rose to pass Mauleverer a second bottle of champagne and put on the huge kettle. "Coffee, I think," she said quietly to Marianne, and then: "There's nothing like politics." She and Marianne worked quietly together, clearing the table and putting out heavy Queen's Ware coffee cups, and still the argument raged. Pouring coffee, Marianne couldn't tell that Mauleverer and Urban had got the Duke cornered with historical analogies and were forcing him to admit that after all the bill might not, perhaps, be quite the dramatic disaster he expected. But he had the last word: "You may be right, but I still think it the end of all true order. In a hundred years' time anyone may get to be First Minister! Cobblers in the cabinet——"

"A hundred years' time!" His aunt interrupted him, with the effect of calling the meeting to order. "We have more immediate problems to consider. It will be dawn soon. Mr.

Barnaby and his conscience will be awake. We must decide what we are going to do with Mr. Urban."

"'Yes . . . yes, of course.' The Duke came back from a great distance. "So we must. What is your view, Mauleverer? After all, he was going to kill you."

Mauleverer, too, had been far away. Now he drained his glass and turned to look at his late companion in argument. "What do you suggest, Urban?"

He shrugged expressively. "Well, since you ask me, I should very much prefer not to be turned over to that Mr. Barnaby, who struck me as a singularly unimaginative character and not at all the kind of man with whom I should wish to associate. My cousin"—here a courtly bow across his coffee cup to Marianne—"was so good as to suggest, some time ago, that I have been punished enough. And," his face darkened, "I am not sure that she is not right. Lady Heverdon——" He stopped. "We will not talk of that. Though I might, perhaps, point out, in passing, that any scruples I might have had about exposing her part in the business have been most effectively laid to rest by her behaviour. Take me to court, Mr. Mauleverer, for what I have failed to do, and I shall have the greatest pleasure in dragging her down with me."

"Quite so," said the Duchess. "That is just what I thought you would say. It would make a nine days' wonder for Mr. Westmacott and *The Age*. There's been nothing like it since the Trial of Queen Caroline, or that uncomfortable business of the Duke of Cumberland and his page. Hard on the child, of course, being left to bear the name."

"Yes, I had thought of that," said Mauleverer. "Poor little creature, he starts life with heavy enough disadvantages as it is." He shrugged. "I confess it goes a little against the grain with me, but I believe we are going to have to let you go, Urban. With proper safeguards, of course. A signed confession, to begin with. Preferably one that does not involve Lady Heverdon."

Still harping on Lady Heverdon! Marianne scalded herself with a great draught of hot coffee and would almost have started a protest if she had not felt the Duchess's restraining hand on hers under the table. She choked, and was silent.

"I should find that difficult to do," said Ralph Urban.

Mauleverer's hands clenched on the table. "You have the

insolence, I believe, to think that we will bribe you into silence about her part in the affair. Bribe you!" His scar stood out livid on his angry face. "Consider yourself bribed enough if you escape imprisonment—transportation, perhaps."

Urban smiled. "What a trial scene it would be," he said thoughtfully. "I think I should act as my own lawyer. . . . When I had finished describing the spell Lady Heverdon cast over me, I should turn to cross examine my accusers." He looked from Mauleverer to Marianne and then back again. "How would you like answering my questions?" he asked mildly. Myself, I think I should enjoy showing in open court what a couple of gullible fools you were. You," he turned to Marianne, "believing me a Bow Street officer, Mr. Barnaby himself—Lord, how the court would laugh. And rushing down here to save Mr. Mauleverer from the consequences of his crime! I spun her a fine yarn, at that," he turned to Mauleverer now. "I told her Lord Grey had given special instructions for your protection—if possible—because it would be such an embarrassment to him for you to be arrested. I don't suppose," he said casually, "that he would like it overmuch to have you involved in such a case. And then, you, too, so easy to deceive. You really believed that my cousin here"—a mocking bow to Marianne—"that my dear cousin had carried off the child the first time in a moment of madness and would do so again to prevent her crime being discovered. It will indeed, as Her Grace remarked, make a notable scandal for *The Age*." He leaned back, both hands in pockets, and surveyed them all blandly.

Mauleverer pushed his own chair back and rose. "I'll stand no more of this!"

"Quite right," said the Duchess, "we need another bottle of champagne, and, when you have opened it, I have a suggestion to make in the meanwhile, Mr. Urban I recommend that you keep quiet, if you can contrive to. You have said, I think, quite enough. John, some more wood on the fire, if you please. It is perfectly obvious that we are none of us going to get to bed tonight; we may as well be comfortable while we sit up. More coffee, Marianne?"

'No thank you." Marianne watched with amused admiration as the two men obeyed the Duchess's commands, which had effectively eased the tension that had built up in the room.

It would not be her fault if reason did not prevail tonight. And, more and more, she was herself convinced that any attempt to prosecute Urban must bring nothing but disaster in its train. Besides—she did not want him prosecuted. The habit of affection dies hard, and they had spent their childhood together.

He turned his head and his eyes met hers with a flash of comprehension. He smiled, and leaned towards her across the table. Behind him, the Duke was still busy with the fire and Mauleverer concentrated on easing yet another cork out of its bottle. "I have been the greatest fool of all, have I not cousin?" Urban kept his voice low. "Imagine losing my heart to that pretty doll upstairs, when I knew you. I suppose the only explanation is that I knew you too well. Do you remember hide-and-seek along the cliffs? And the day the smuggler's ship was thrown ashore? And Uncle Urban acting the perfect Magistrate, as if everyone did not know where *his* brandy came from? And the time I ran away? And how you pleaded my case with him?"

"Yes, I remember." Marianne's eyes were far away, seeing the past.

"My God, what a fool." His hand struck his forehead. "Marianne, is it too late? You and I—home on the island together. You admit that my uncle has been unjust: there is the perfect solution. Is your heart large enough to forget and forgive? It is what the islanders have always wanted, as you must know." His intimate, pleading tone was for her alone. The Duchess, leaning back in her chair between them, might not have existed.

Marianne raised her eyes to meet his. 'God knows, you're a brave man, Ralph, but—no." She could not help smiling at the monstrous bravado of his proposition. "You have fooled me, as you boasted yourself, quite enough already. Enough is enough. I'll not add marrying you to my lunacies."

He smiled back at her amicably. "I was afraid you would not. A pity though; it would have solved so many problems."

"For you," she said.

"I must say," the Duchess leaned forward to join in the conversation, "one can but admire your spirit, Mr. Urban. What a pity that you should not have thought fit to use your capacities in a more profitable direction."

He bowed ironically. "I am still hoping that I may have the chance to do that very thing, ma'am. Ah, thank you." Mauleverer had just refilled his glass.

The Duke returned to his place, and now Mauleverer, too, sat down again at the table. From their behaviour, Marianne could only infer that the rattling of the fire-tongs had drowned out Urban's remarkable proposal. She leaned forward. They were calmer now. It was the moment for her own suggestion. "Cousin," she found she could speak to Urban with perfect calm. "My proposal is still open to you. Why should you not be Steward of Barsley. I truly do not wish to go back there." Impossible to explain her reasons for this, but then, why should she? "You would be the best possible substitute—indeed, better than I could ever be, since you love the island so dearly."

"You really mean it?" His eyes were very bright.

"Yes. The business details would have to be worked out, of course. And—I should ask that you sign a paper of the kind that Mr. Mauleverer was talking about earlier. One that would cause embarrassment neither to Lady Heverdon, nor, in the future, to little Thomas."

"Nor to you?"

She looked at him steadily. "Nor to me. Write out such a confession, cousin, at once, and I will ask Mr. Mauleverer and the Duke, since they know all about it, to act as my agents in making the arrangements with you. I promise you that, so far as I can, I will leave you a free agent on Barsley."

"You would have to come over once a year, for the islanders' homage-taking."

"Yes, so I would." She had forgotten this medieval ceremony which was much valued by the islanders.

"That is essential?" The Duchess looked very straight at Urban, who nodded. "And how does the island's succession lie?" she asked.

Urban looked at her with respect. "My uncle stipulated in his will that if my cousin died childless, I should inherit."

"Quite so." She gave him a friendly smile. "How wise you are, Mr. Urban, to admit what we could so easily find out for ourselves. In that case, Marianne, I do not recommend that you visit the island—under Mr. Urban's benevolent jurisdiction—until you have taken the precaution of equipping yourself with an heir. Aside from that, the suggestion seems to me an admirable one. Miss Urban says she does not wish to live on Barsley; Mr. Urban, it seems, loves the island almost too well. What do you say, Mr. Urban?"

"Give me pen and paper. I had best begin confessing."

"You do not propose to thank your cousin for her extraordinary generous offer."

He smiled his cynical smile. "What would be the use?" he said, "since you are all convinced I would murder her if I got the chance. Besides, she is right. I shall make a very much better governor of Barsley than she ever would."

"You are an honest villain, I must say," said the Duchess approvingly. "I think, perhaps, you had best give us an undertaking not to leave Barsley until we give you permission."

"You think I might try again?"

"I think you capable of anything. Mr. Mauleverer, do you think you could find paper and a pen for Mr. Urban?"

"Of course." He took a candle and disappeared through the green baize door to the front of the house. He had been very silent, Marianne thought, during this last interchange. If only she knew what he was thinking. Did he understand that she would gladly give away all title to Barsley, if only that would make him feel free to ask her to marry him? But very likely he no longer wanted to. She could not forget his anger on the night of the ball—and since then she had believed him capable of murder. How could he forgive her? How could she forgive herself? And yet—how skilfully Urban had played on their feelings. It was just because they loved each other that they had been so easily deceived. Did Mauleverer see this? Certainly Urban had been at pains to point it out. Was that why she had given him the stewardship of Barsley? She smiled to herself, recognizing her cousin's cleverness. Of course he had intended to rouse their gratitude in just this way. He might have played and lost, but there was no doubt about his skill.

Once again he seemed to read her thoughts: "Grateful to me, cousin?"

She was spared the need to answer by Mauleverer's return. He laid down pen, inkwell and paper on the far end of the big table. "Now, Mr. Urban?"

He rose. "It will take me a little while."

"I should think so," said the Duchess. "Lord knows, you have enough to confess. I do urge that you make a thorough job of it the first time and spare us the trouble of a repetition. John, I think it would be best if you were to sit with Mr. Urban in case he should be struck with another of his bright ideas. I am going to exert the privilege of age and fall asleep, here by the fire." She removed the cook's cat from the rocking chair and settled herself in its place. "Marianne, a stool for my feet, if you please? And then, perhaps, you and Mr. Mauleverer would feel like clearing up the kitchen a little. After all, so far as I can see, we are going to have to make breakfast ourselves. We can hardly do it among empty champagne glasses. Washing dishes should prove a novel experience to you, Mr. Mauleverer."

"This night has been full of them." He rose and picked up a couple of glasses. "I am ashamed to confess that I am not quite sure where it is done."

"Down the hall here." Marianne was already stacking plates on a big tray, silently blessing the Duchess for this ingenious device to give her a little while alone with Mauleverer. The Duke had drawn up a chair across the table from Urban, who had begun to write, slowly and with a good deal of scratching out. It looked like being a long business. She put the last glass on the tray and pushed it gently across the table to Mauleverer. "I will bring the kettle." He followed her down the long flagged hall that led to the sculleries. "Do you know, I am not sure that I have ever been out here before."

"Why should you?" She put the candlestick she was carrying on the shelf above the sink. "It is not exactly the purlieu of the master of the house."

"I suppose not." He looked around the shadowy room. "You would hardly call it luxurious, would you?"

"No—and absurdly far from the kitchen. I have often thought that if you ever were altering the Hall, the kitchen quarters could well be improved."

"But not by a Gothic front?"

She laughed. "No, indeed. I should like to see much more light in here, rather than less. You have no idea what a damp and dismal room this is in the daytime."

"I can imagine." And then, in a completely different tone, "Marianne!"

"Yes?" Her hand shook as she carried glasses over to the sink.

"What can I say to you? Or is it not too late to say anything? I said too much, I know—horribly too much, at the Duchess's ball. What is the use of saying that I had been grossly mislead about you! You cannot help but think me the world's greatest fool to have believed Lady Heverdon when she told me you were as good as engaged to the Duke. Nor can I expect you to forgive me for what I said. And, besides— you are an heiress now. Barsley is yours. It is plain that the Duke adores you. He will ask you again, I am sure of it. It is in every way a most suitable match, and God knows he will make you a better husband than I ever could. I have no fortune —and very likely no career if this night's doings get out. Your cousin is quite right there. It is not at all the kind of scandal Lord Grey would relish. I shall end up as a bad-tempered old failure, the terror of his servants, the recluse of Maulever Hall."

Marianne dried a glass and put it carefully down on the table. "Poor Thomas," she said.

"What do you mean?"

"You are his guardian, are you not? You surely cannot intend to let Lady Heverdon have him. Or—do you?"

"You mean, am I a complete, a hopeless fool? No, no, give me credit for that much sense. It was pride, Miss Lamb; mere, miserable pride that made me appear once more her slave this autumn—and a damned tedious business I found it, too. No, no, Thomas stays here—Martha can look after him. She seems to do that well enough."

Madness to have hoped anything from this conversation. Give it up. Give it all up. Let it be over with: quickly. But there was something she must say. "Do you know," she managed to keep her voice steady. "I am very much afraid that I have been mistaken about Martha. I begin to think that I made a fool of myself—and misled you about those drops she gives your mother."

"You a fool? Never." Was there resentment in his tone? "But I am glad to have your favourable opinion of Martha, for I do not see what else I can do with the boy."

"No?" If his pride was a fatal obstacle between them, so was hers. How could she say, "Marry me, my love, and I'll look after Thomas." She could not. It was all hopeless. Her fortune and his pride stood between them, insuperable barriers.

And yet—surely he loved her still. But an overture from her must be fatal for their future happiness. He would never forget that it was she who had made the first move. He was not the kind of man who could allow the initiative to be taken by a woman. And, more and more obviously, he would do nothing himself. She had quietly finished washing the dishes while they talked. Now, keeping her face carefully turned away from him, she began to put them away in their shelves. It was all over. Tears ran silently down her cheeks as she moved past him to the china cupboard that opened off the far corner of the scullery.

Something crunched under her foot. She looked down—and screamed. The floor was alive with cockroaches.

"Marianne!" As she dropped the glass she was holding and backed out of the pantry, he came towards her, arms outstretched.

She stumbled into them and felt herself enfolded in that firm embrace she had feared never to feel again. "Oh, my darling," his lips were on her hair, "is there really something you are afraid of?"

"Without you," she looked up at him, "everything."

For a long moment, their eyes met and held. Then, slowly, like the beginning of day, his smile transformed his face. "So much for pride." He bent towards her.

They were roused from a kiss that should have been endless by the Duchess's voice from behind them. "Very satisfactory," she said.

Marianne turned, still in the safe compass of his arms, to smile at her friend. "Would you say that I was sufficiently compromised so he must marry me?"

"Oh, amply. If he needs compulsion, which I doubt, Besides, Mr. Mauleverer, you should remember that my poor Marianne must get herself an heir, or go in daily fear of murder by that ingenious cousin of hers."

Mauleverer smiled down at Marianne. "My love fears nothing," he said, "except cockroaches, God bless her. But—I could do with an heir myself."

"Mauleverer of Maulever Hall?" Loving laughter trembled in her voice.

He shook her, just a little, gently. "And I thought you would never tease me again, my shrew."

HERE COMES A CANDLE

by Jane Aiken Hodge

Here is a fine novel of romance, betrayal and mystery.

When the Americans sacked the English capital of Canada at the outbreak of the war of 1812, Kate Croston, newly widowed and seemingly lost, was only too glad to flee her shadowed past and accept the offer of help given by an American civilian, Jonathan Penrose.

But as soon as she became the ward of Jonathan's daughter, little Sarah, Kate found herself caught in a web of intrigue and suspicion.

Was Jonathan wise to defy his arrogant wife, Arabella, and place Sarah in Kate's care?

And what was the role of the handsome Englishman, Captain Manningham, in this affair?

It was only when Arabella showed that she would stop at nothing – even kidnapping her own daughter – to get at her husband's fortune, and when the war suddenly became one that was intensely close to all their aspirations, that the mystery came into the open.

'Highly entertaining and diverting ... anyone who enjoys full-blooded historical novels will certainly enjoy this one'
The Scotsman

'Historical story served up with suspense and generously spiced with intrigue and romance' *Evening Standard*

CORONET BOOKS

STRANGERS IN COMPANY

by Jane Aiken Hodge

A HOLIDAY COACH TOUR – OR A GREEK NIGHTMARE?

Marian and Stella were strangers when they met at the airport, ready to depart for Athens and their Mercury bus tour of Greece. Marian, plagued by bitter memories from the past, was nominally in charge of her young companion.

But this was no ordinary bus tour and their fellow travellers no ordinary holidaymakers. Haunted by death and danger, the two of them see their travelling companions struck down one by one, until at last it becomes a mere struggle for survival. But as the tension mounts against the ever-changing background of classical Greece, Marian and Stella become strangers no longer, but unite to face the dangerous nightmare of the world around them.

'A cliff-hanging climax brings this sharply-observed and well-told story to a happy ending'   *Sunday Telegraph*

'Enjoyable thriller with a picturesque background ... the story builds up to a very exciting and unexpected climax'
Woman's Journal

'All the lightness of Georgette Heyer and with added substance besides'   *New Statesman*

CORONET BOOKS

MASTERFUL NOVELS FROM JANE AIKEN HODGE